W9-BOL-688

Praise for *Confessions of a High School Disaster*

"Chloe Snow's diary goes far beyond the expected awesomeness + angst of a freshman in high school, though it has both of those qualities in spades. But Chloe Snow, in all her hilarious brilliance, will also break your heart and make you bawl those 'happy to be alive' tears. Amazing."

—*Lauren Myracle*, *New York Times* bestselling author of *The Infinite Moment of Us*

"Chastain captures a spot-on teen voice that would feel at home in an updated version of the film *Mean Girls*."

—*School Library Journal*

"Recommended for fans of Louise Rennison or anyone who needs a good laugh."

—*VOYA*

"Chloe is refreshingly honest and unfiltered."

—*Booklist*

Praise for *The Year of Living Awkwardly*

"Remarkably relatable. . . . There are few protagonists . . . as believable and endearing as Chloe Snow."

—*Booklist*

"Spot-on teenage angst."

—*School Library Journal*

NOTES FROM A FORMER Virgin

JUNIOR YEAR

EMMA CHASTAIN

Simon Pulse

NEW YORK LONDON TORONTO SYDNEY NEW DELHI

Simon Pulse

An imprint of Simon & Schuster Children's Publishing Division
1230 Avenue of the Americas, New York, New York 10020
First Simon Pulse hardcover edition July 2019
Text copyright © 2019 by Emma Chastain
Jacket photographs copyright © 2019 by Jill Wachter (boy's body and girl),
Getty Images (boy, glasses, and curtain), and iStock.com/Pratchaya (back cover curtain)
Photo composite by Steve Gardner/PixelWorks Studios

SIMON PULSE and colophon are registered trademarks of Simon & Schuster, Inc.
For information about special discounts for bulk purchases, please contact
Simon & Schuster Special Sales at 1-866-506-1949 or business@simonandschuster.com.
The Simon & Schuster Speakers Bureau can bring authors to your live event.
For more information or to book an event contact the Simon & Schuster Speakers Bureau
at 1-866-248-3049 or visit our website at www.simonspeakers.com.
Series designed by Jessica Handelman
Jacket designed by Heather Palisi
Interior designed by Mike Rosamilia
The text of this book was set in Electra MT.
Manufactured in the United States of America
2 4 6 8 10 9 7 5 3 1
Library of Congress Cataloging-in-Publication Data
Names: Chastain, Emma, 1979- author.
Title: Notes from a former virgin : junior year / by Emma Chastain.
Description: First Simon Pulse hardcover edition. | New York : Simon Pulse,
2019. | Summary: "Lovably flawed high school student Chloe Snow chronicles
her junior year as she navigates the highs and lows of family, friendship,
school, and losing her virginity"—Provided by publisher.
Identifiers: LCCN 2018058343 (print) | LCCN 2018060320 (eBook) |
ISBN 9781534421127 (eBook) | ISBN 9781534421103 (hc)
Subjects: | CYAC: Friendship—Fiction. | Dating (Social customs)—Fiction. | Family life—Fiction. |
High schools—Fiction. | Schools—Fiction. | Diaries—Fiction.
Classification: LCC PZ7.1.C4955 (eBook) | LCC PZ7.1.C4955 No 2019 (print) |
DDC [Fic]—dc23
LC record available at https://lccn.loc.gov/2018058343

For my mother,
Patricia Anne Chastain,
who is nothing like Veronica

Thursday, August 10

I'm not going to have sex with Grady. I'm dying to. But I won't. I won't. I won't.

Maybe if I write it down in my diary enough times, I'll stick to my guns.

Friday, August 11

I can't believe I'm even in this situation. Last summer I considered Grady the annoying younger brother I never wanted. When Mrs. Franco scheduled us to work together, we'd spend the whole shift bickering in the concession stand. Whenever Grady bumped into me—which was constantly, since our work space was about the size of a large shoe box—I'd shriek in irritation. We used to push each other into the pool, and not in a flirty way. And now look at me! I'm obsessed with the kid. I can't understand why I ever thought he was annoying. He's a brilliant artist. He's funny. He's interesting. He's a lifeguard now, and he looks so freaking hot in his orange trunks. When we're together, I stare at his cheekbones. When we're apart, I scroll through pictures of him and reread our text messages, analyzing them for proof that he's into me (or, if I'm in a worried mood, looking for signs that he's not into me). We keep sneaking back into the pool after closing it down and messing around for four hours in a row. My chin is red and actually bleeding in some spots from rubbing against his stubble for so long. I like him so much it hurts (my heart, and also my face).

Saturday, August 12

Reasons I shouldn't have sex with Grady:

1. I'm only 16 (but isn't that old enough?).
2. He won't even be 16 until September 14.
3. TEEN MOM
4. SEXUALLY TRANSMITTED DISEASES AND INFECTIONS
5. We haven't said "I love you" yet . . .
6. . . . because we started going out on July 31. That's less than two weeks ago.

7. You can't lose your virginity after two weeks. You just can't.

8. Even though I haven't said it out loud, I'm desperately in love with him, and what if DOING IT makes me fall even more in love with him, and I get clingy and pathetic, and he's disgusted by this new post-sex version of me and dumps me?

9. And what if he doesn't even love me? Why WOULD he love me? See #6. Normal people don't love other people they've been dating for 13 days.

10. Reese would find out somehow, using her Popular Girl powers of intuition. It's bad enough that I'm going out with her ex-boyfriend. If she knew we were having sex, she'd . . . I don't even know what she'd do. Tie me to a cafeteria table and tattoo "SLUT" across my forehead while livestreaming the whole thing, probably.

11. Wait. Did Reese and Grady have sex????? Oh God.

Sunday, August 13

I forced Tristan and Hannah to come over first thing in the morning. My dad was out somewhere, probably having a romantic brunch with Miss Murphy.

"What's the big emergency?" Tris said. He still had a pillow mark on his cheek.

"It has to do with Grady," I said.

Hannah groaned and picked up her bike helmet. "I'm leaving. If I miss church now, I'll have to go to late Mass."

"Wait!" I said. "I'll make it quick. Do you think Grady and Reese had sex?"

"Hmm," Tris said. He looked thoughtful.

"What's 'hmm'?" I said in a panic. "If you know something, tell me fast. Put me out of my misery."

"I'm thinking!" Tris said. "That was a 'hmm' of contemplation."

Hannah cleared her throat. "Well, I really should get going. Bye."

I wheeled around to look at her. I could tell from her voice that she had the answer. She's been my best friend since kindergarten. She can't fool me.

"Hannah," I said.

"She told me in confidence!" she said. "I shouldn't talk to you about this."

"That was before she stole your boyfriend and stopped being friends with you!" I said.

Hannah fiddled with the clasp of her helmet. "Those things are unrelated to your question," she said.

"Blink twice if they had sex," Tris said.

"Both of you, stop it," Hannah said.

"I have to assume they did," I said. "Otherwise you wouldn't look so nervous."

"They didn't, OK?" she said. "He wanted to, but she wouldn't."

As soon as she'd spilled the beans, I felt terrible for forcing her to.

"I'm sorry, Hannah," I said.

"I shouldn't have said that. I don't even know if there's confession after church today," she said angrily.

After she left, Tris and I made wincing faces at each other.

"Was that really bad?" I asked him.

"Kind of," he said. "But are you relieved about Grady?"

I was relieved. And scared. So he wants to have sex . . . and I want to have sex. What's going to stop us from having sex?!

Monday, August 14

Grady wasn't lifeguarding today, but he came to work anyway, to keep me company. We can't make out when the pool's open, but we can lightly run our fingers across each other's thighs under the concession stand counter until we're both hallucinating. And we can talk.

Reese was there. Her strategy so far has been to

broadcast how happy she is for us and how much she adores Zach. He picks her up every single day, and she leaps into his arms like he's a combat veteran walking off a plane. I should be grateful she's not turning Grady against me, or trying to win him back, or making up rumors about us, and I am grateful. It's just that I don't trust her not to do any of those things if her whim changes.

Today she sat across the pool from us, periodically blowing us kisses. I smiled and waved at her. It's important to stay on her good side. You don't want to make an enemy of the class queen.

Tuesday, August 15

Grady was babysitting Bear, and I wasn't working, so I rode my bike over to Noelle's and sat in the bathroom with her while she dyed her roots.

"I have to cut it all off soon," she said. She was squeezing gel onto her head from an applicator bottle. "The bleach is making it brittle."

"Should you be smoking right now?" I said. "Won't the chemicals catch on fire and blow us up?"

"Calm down," she said. "The window's wide open."

"Doesn't your mom yell at you when she smells cigarettes?"

"Yes, she's always on my ass, just like someone else I could mention."

"Fine." I put my face next to the window screen, to get as close to the fresh air as I could.

"How's it going with Grady?" she said. Her eyes flicked over to me in the mirror, then went back to her scalp.

"Good."

"Still into him?"

"Yeah."

"You can tell me stuff. I won't go running back to Reese."

"I know."

But I don't. This is never going to work. I can't be friends with Reese's best friend. It's like swimming in piranha-infested waters and hoping you won't lose a toe.

Wednesday, August 16

Grady came over during adult swim to talk to me and have a snack.

"I was reading this article," he said, and bit into his Spider-Man ice cream bar. "It was about whether the world's getting better or worse."

"Isn't it obvious?" I said. "Our democracy is crumbling before our eyes."

"But worldwide, literacy rates are way up, fewer people are living in poverty, and basically health and happiness are on the rise year after year."

"It doesn't feel like that."

He ate Spider-Man's left eye. "Because it's more exciting for reporters to write about horrible events that are actually outliers."

"You'll be singing a different tune when we're doing nuclear war drills in the cafeteria in a few weeks."

"Our grandparents felt exactly like this in the '50s. Worse!"

"Our grandparents didn't have to do tick checks every half hour. Did you notice we basically didn't have a winter last year? Soon there won't be any cooling season and we'll all die of Lyme disease, if the droughts don't get us first."

We kept arguing about it. I believed what I was saying, but at the same time my own pessimism felt slightly ridiculous, because there I was, wearing a bikini, eating caramel M&M's, watching the sun throw light on the water, listening to "Three Little Birds" on a phone thanks to the Wi-Fi I take for granted to such an extent that I actually have the nerve to get irritated when it goes down, and most of all, hovering above myself, reveling in having an interesting discussion with my interesting boyfriend.

Thursday, August 17

Grady and I closed down the pool last night, texted our parents we were going to our friends' houses (me to Hannah's, Grady to Elliott's), and then let ourselves back in and messed around on the grass for hours. He makes noise sometimes, and it's not embarrassing. He sounds like he's eating a delicious ice cream sundae. I'm ice cream!

When we needed a break, we got in the pool and talked quietly. "Bear's freaking out about pre-K," he said. "Last night at dinner he was like, 'I can't do it. I'll be all alone,' and started crying. I feel so bad for the kid."

"Oh, Bear," I said. "God, school is the worst. It never gets better. Don't tell him that."

He raised his legs so his toes poked through the surface of the water. "You stop having a panic attack every time your mom drops you off at school, though."

"Yeah, but you start worrying about popularity and all that stuff."

"Not me," said Grady, flicking a dead bug onto the pool deck.

"Really!"

"Nope. I don't care about popularity. I just mind my own business and think about what will look good on my college applications."

"So you float above it all, like a cloud?"

"Basically."

"Well, aren't you special!"

"Really special," he said. "And really handsome."

"You forgot to mention well endowed."

He held his hands about a foot apart. "I mean, minimum." He moved them a foot farther apart. "That's more like it, right?"

Then we splashed each other for a while, and he dunked me, and I whacked him on the side of the head with my pool noodle. Then we whisper-screamed, "SHUT UP!" "NO, YOU SHUT UP!" "THE NEIGHBORS ARE GOING TO CALL MRS. FRANCO!" and then we started hooking up, of course.

Friday, August 18

I GAVE GRADY A BLOW JOB! AND IT WAS WONDERFUL!

It happened in the lifeguard shack two hours ago. We'd been fooling around forever, and all the grinding and pressing didn't feel like enough. I pushed him against the table and pulled down his suit and he put his hands in my hair and came in, like, two minutes!

I had recently read an article online about how to give a BJ. It's terrible to live in a world where you can do that, I guess, but at the same time, it was full of helpful tips that made me feel like I knew what I was doing.

Additional things I learned from real-world experience:

1. It doesn't seem like there's enough room in your mouth for a penis, and there kind of isn't.
2. Spit gets everywhere, but that's OK and even useful.
3. You feel powerful doing it, because you're making a boy you like (/love) moan and shake.
4. Cum tastes like salty soup!

After I finished, I stood up and smiled at Grady. We put our hands on each other's shoulders and grinned and grinned.

"Holy shit," he said.

"Holy shit!" I agreed.

Am I supposed to feel like a big slut now, according to society? Well, screw you, society! I don't! I feel so happy!

Saturday, August 19

Went to the beach with my dad and Miss Murphy and was in agony the whole time. All I wanted to do was drive home, find Grady, and take his pants off. I lay on the towel thinking fast. What if I pretended to be sick? They'd have to take me home. But no. Then they'd expect me to lie in bed, not go to the pool. Could

I somehow WALK back and explain later? No, absurd. Walking would take hours.

Finally Dad suggested heading home. In the car, Miss Murphy tried to talk to me about summer reading, her struggle to settle on a musical, etc. She might as well have been speaking French. Her words could not penetrate the dense mental atmosphere of Grady.

As soon as we got back, I raced over and caught him at the end of his shift. It turned out he'd agreed to babysit Bear in the evening, so we couldn't hook up. Instead we stood in the shallow end, chatting.

"How was your beach day with Murph?" he asked.

"Good. Weird. I don't know."

"Do she and your dad, like, snuggle in front of you?"

"No! Do your mom and stepdad?"

"Yes, constantly. It's disgusting."

"If you liked him, you'd think it was cute."

He snorted. "That's a big if."

I bent my knees and lowered myself until my chin touched the surface of the water. "My parents used to snuggle when they weren't yelling at each other."

"Did you think it was cute?"

"God, no!"

"There you go, then."

He ducked under the water and did a headstand, like he was putting an exclamation point on his logical victory. While he was submerged, I thought about my parents kissing in the kitchen after they'd had a huge fight. It used to enrage me, seeing them being lovey-dovey when I was still petrified and jangly from their screaming. Was my mom brawling with Javi somewhere? Had she broken up with him? What was she doing right this minute, while I stared at my boyfriend's upside-down shins?

"You have to admit my form is amazing," Grady said when he'd come up.

"Do you think my mom's dead?" I said.

He didn't bat an eyelash. "Seems unlikely."

"It's not like I care what she's doing, but it's weird not to know."

He nodded. He knows what it's like. I mean, he doesn't, because no one I've met can understand how it feels when your mother leaves you to move to Mexico. But he has a stepfather he can't stand and a father he never sees. Close enough.

Sunday, August 20

Holy cats. Grady went down on me. I was worried about it, because what if I was too noisy, or not noisy enough, or what if my bathing suit area smelled weird? And even though he was the one kneeling in front of me in the lifeguard shack this time, I felt less in control than when I was the one kneeling. But then a few minutes passed, and I forgot all that stuff and my mind emptied out, and then it filled back up again with the most vivid image of a black sky churning like an ocean. Grady makes me dream while I'm awake.

I don't think I had an orgasm. Or maybe I did. I'm not 100% clear on what an orgasm is, and searching online for clarification mostly yields Pornhub results.

Monday, August 21
I chip off my nail polish, or pull my hair into a ponytail, or watch the breeze ruffling the summer leaves, or clip Snickers's leash onto his collar, and it all makes me think about SEX SEX SEX. I feel like a maniac.

Tuesday, August 22
I need to calm down and approach this rationally. I'm only 16. I have plenty of time to lose my virginity. I don't want to do something I'll regret. And I want the first time to be special, not rushed and awkward.

Wednesday, August 23
WHEEEEEEE GRADY AND I HAD SEX AHHHH AHAHAHAHA

Thursday, August 24
I don't care about this diary! I don't care about anything!

I never want to go to college or get a job! All I want to do is have as much sex with Grady as I can between now and whenever I die!

Friday, August 25

What happened on Wednesday was, we snuck back into the pool, as usual. We swam for a while (quietly, without splashing, so no one passing by would hear us) and then sat on the deck with our feet in the water, whispering. It was getting dark by that time, and the crickets were chirping. I could smell the chlorine on us, and the sunscreen. Grady's hand was next to mine on the concrete. Long tanned fingers, big square palms. Beads of water on his wrist. I was wondering how long I could go without touching him when he put his arm around me and started kissing me.

After a while he pulled me to my feet and we walked over to his towel on the grass. It's striped in blue and white, and we've been making out on it all summer long. I want to put it under glass, or burn it and wear the ashes in a locket around my neck.

We'd been grinding against each other like we were actually trying to rip holes in our bathing suits when I pushed his hips up and said, "I don't think we should have sex yet."

"That's fine," he said. He was panting.

"I mean, I want to," I said.

"Me too." He smiled at me.

"No, but I really want to," I said.

"I have a condom," he said.

"Go get it!"

So he did, and he knew how to put it on, which should have looked like a sex-ed class come to life but which actually looked really hot, because he was kneeling above me, looking down with a serious, excited look on his face, and then we HAD SEX on his blue-and-white striped towel, and it DID NOT HURT, but instead felt REALLY AMAZING, which they never mention in sex ed! All you hear about is HPV and AIDS and genital warts, and all of those things are terrible and important, but what about the fact that sex is the most fun thing I've ever done in my entire life?!?! Grady's body was inside my body! I've never smelled him or tasted him or felt him that much, and I still wanted more, and I still do right now, and I think I always will. Grady, Grady, Grady Grady Grady Grady Grady Grady GRADY!

Saturday, August 26

Every magazine article and confessional blog post warns you that the first time you have sex, you might bleed, it'll probably hurt a ton, and at the very least it'll be awkward. None of that was true for me, which means either

(a) I'm a phenom, (b) Grady's a phenom, (c) we got lucky, or (d) all that dry humping we did (and, uhhh, I did with Mac) was actually good practice. Probably mostly (c) and a little dash of (d).

We kind of WERE bumbling around that first time, which I now understand because we've had sex every day since Wednesday, and we're getting better as we go. Last night we were lying on our backs on the towel looking up at the stars, and Grady said, "Does your dad think you're at Hannah's?"

"Yep. Same lie every night. He's never questioned it. Why, is your mom getting suspicious?"

"No. Elliott and I used to hang out all the time, so it's a good cover story."

"Is Elliott mad that you never see him anymore?" I asked.

"Probably."

We laughed, I think because we were being such dicks to our friends, and because there was no way we could stop ourselves from continuing to neglect them. Had I even seen Hannah since the day she came over and I interrogated her about Grady and Reese?

I reached for Grady's hand. "You didn't have sex with Reese, right?" I asked.

"No," he said. "Did you have sex with Mac?"

"No."

"Not that it would bother me if you had."

"Right, no, me neither."

"Really?" he said.

"Well, no," I said. "I think I would have felt jealous and insecure."

"OK, good," he said. "Me too."

"I don't think we're supposed to feel that way."

"According to what?"

"I don't know. The internet?"

He made a *psshh* sound. "We can feel however we want."

"Do you feel different," I said, "not being a virgin anymore?"

"Not really," he said. "I'm happier than usual. But I still feel like myself. Do you feel different?"

"No," I said. "I feel happier too, but otherwise I feel exactly the same."

I really do. I'm not suddenly more vulnerable, and I don't feel even a little bit guilty.

Sunday, August 27

I woke up this morning to Tris and Hannah standing above my bed, staring down at me. Even in my sleepy confusion, I knew why they were there.

"Hi," I said.

"Well, at least we know you're alive," Tris said.

I sat up and started picking at the sleep boogers in

my eyes. "Don't be melodramatic," I said. "I've been texting you."

"Random emojis!" Tris said. "I ask you if you can hang out and you text me the creepy moon. I thought something bad had happened."

I frowned up at him. "What bad thing could possibly happen that would lead to me texting you the creepy moon?"

"It could be code for something," Hannah said solemnly.

"Like, 'can't talk, I've been kidnapped by an astronomer'?" I said.

Tris sat down on my bed. "You can't disappear every time you get a boyfriend," he said. "It's not OK." Hannah was nodding.

"I know," I said. "I know. I know. You're right."

"And Grady's doing the same thing to Elliott," Tris said. "Elliott is very hurt."

"How are you and Elliott, anyway?" I asked Tris.

"Don't try to distract me," he said.

"Listen," I started, and then I said, "Wait," and ran to the bathroom. I couldn't tell them this momentous news without peeing and brushing my teeth. When I got back, they were both sitting on my bed. I stood in front of them in my underpants and FEMINIST AF T-shirt and said, "Grady and I are having sex."

Tris screamed and Hannah gasped. Tris said, "I knew

it!" and Hannah said, "Please tell me you're being safe." Then Tris asked for all the details and even though Hannah wanted to pretend like it was none of her business, she listened to everything I said, especially the gross parts. She's a great audience for X-rated stories, because she looks like she's about to faint. The best is when she shakes her head in shocked disapproval. In terms of messing around, she's done everything I have and probably way more, but she hates to talk about it. She's modest, I guess.

Monday, August 28

When Grady keeps me company in the concession stand, the afternoons feel so long. All those syrupy hours. Taking damp singles from the kids who run up soaking wet to buy ice cream. Chatting. Putting on and taking off baseball caps and sunglasses as the sun moves through the sky. Eating Tootsie Pop after Tootsie Pop. Singing along to the radio. It seems like the day will never end. But the pool's closing this Thursday, and summer will be over. I don't know how it raced by so fast. It feels like I'll always be 16, sitting on Grady's lap and feeling his hard-on against my butt. But I won't. It's an awful thought.

Tuesday, August 29

I fell asleep at the pool with Grady last night and totally got caught oh God oh God oh God

Wednesday, August 30

Miss Murphy betrayed me. I can't believe it.

It was so hot on Monday night. Really, the weather's to blame. Grady and I messed around until we were too hungry to keep going, and then we ordered a pizza and ate it sitting on the steps in the shallow end while discussing one of the other lifeguards, Quentin, and whether he refuses to smile or make facial expressions of any kind because he's odd (Grady's argument) or rude and jerky (my argument). After we finished eating, we lay down on the blue-and-white striped towel and kept talking and talking. I never run out of things to say to him. We spend all day together and then text each other most of the night from home, and in the morning I get ready as fast as I can so I can come back to the pool and keep talking to him. He has opinions, and he wants to hear my opinions. He doesn't make fun of any of my thoughts, even the odd ones. He's interested in people and in the world. God, I love him so much.

The point is, we passed out talking. I kept thinking I should get up, but we were holding hands, and the heat was making me so sleepy, and the next thing I knew, I was sitting up fast, heart pounding, looking at the dark sky above me and at Grady sleeping next to me and then at my phone and it was 3:04 a.m. and there were four texts from Miss Murphy!

MM: Chloe, are you OK?

*MM: Your dad fell asleep, but
I'm awake and concerned.*

*MM: Please call me as soon as
you can.*

MM: Chloe, this is not good.

I texted her back as fast as I could.

> *Chloe: Fell asleep at
> Hannah's so sorry please
> don't tell my dad it'll make
> him worry for no reason
> coming home now*

I woke Grady up, and when he saw me, he smiled and pulled me toward him to make out, even though he was still half asleep, and there's something wrong with me, because I did make out with him for kind of a long time even though I knew I was in huge trouble and he might be too, but finally I stopped and said, "We fell asleep. It's three o'clock in the morning." We both jumped up and started pulling our clothes on and cramming our stuff into our backpacks. After we'd hopped the fence, he gave me a big hug and said, "Good luck," and then we MADE OUT AGAIN for a long time and I'm not kidding, we almost had sex right there in the parking lot! I must have a death wish. By the time I got home, it was after four o'clock, and I thought Miss Murphy had probably gone to bed, since she knew I was OK and she didn't have to stay up worrying about me. I turned my key in the lock as quietly as I could, so that I wouldn't wake up her or my dad, and crept through the front door like a cat burglar, but then immediately I could tell that the kitchen light was on. My heart sank.

She was sitting at the island, wearing a T-shirt and a pair of Dad's boxers, frowning down at her phone. When I came in, she looked at me, then turned off her screen and stood up.

"I'm off to bed," she said.

"Are you mad?" I said.

"It's not really my place to be mad," she said.

For a second I felt relieved. Then she said, "But Chloe, I have to mention this to your dad."

"What? No, you don't!"

"I wish I could cover for you, but I'm not comfortable keeping this from him."

"But nothing bad happened! Please, I promise I'll never do it again."

"I'm sorry."

She did sound sorry, but what did that matter? I sat in the kitchen fuming for a while, and then went upstairs and got into bed without brushing my teeth. Grady texted me that he'd snuck into his house without anyone noticing. I texted back the thumbs-up emoji, because I didn't want to get into it, then put my phone down and fell asleep. After what felt like only a few minutes, I jerked awake to the sound of Dad standing in my doorway, saying my name sternly. He asked me to please get up and join him in the kitchen.

I threw on my bathrobe. When I got downstairs, Dad was waiting for me. Just waiting, not even loading the dishwasher or putting his laptop in his briefcase. "I'd like to know where you were last night," he said in a voice that was supposed to sound pleasant. He was wearing a gray suit and a navy-blue tie. He smelled like aftershave. I felt stunned from lack of sleep.

"Hannah's," I said.

"So if I call Mrs. Egan right now, she'll tell me you were there?" he said.

I nodded. My throat felt dry.

Dad looked at me like I might be a lobster or a bar of soap. A random object masquerading as his daughter. "If you were at Hannah's, why didn't you stay there instead of coming home in the middle of the night?"

I squeezed at the floor with my toes. "I wasn't think-ing straight. I was barely awake."

"I don't appreciate being lied to," Dad said. My heart seized up. I said nothing.

Dad picked up his briefcase. "In my family, teen-age rebellion was not allowed. It wasn't even a thought. You're not living in a movie, Chloe. I expect you to tell me the truth. I expect you to get good grades. I expect you to stay away from alcohol and drugs. Is that clear?"

I nodded, looking at the floor.

"Is that clear?" he said again.

"Yes," I said.

After he left, I got dressed, called to Snickers, and went out for a walk, crying behind my sunglasses. I DO get good grades. I DON'T drink or do drugs. I mean, I've gotten drunk a few times, but that hardly qualifies as "drinking." And, OK, I lie to Dad occasionally, but only to stop him from worrying about me, or to avoid a big pointless fight about something I know isn't a big deal, but that he would consider a huge deal. Such as acci-dentally falling asleep in the grass next to my boyfriend.

He talked to me like I'm a bad kid. Like he thinks I was out late popping painkillers and burning my PSAT prep books. Does he even realize how much worse he could have it? I'm a living angel compared to half of the cheaters and addicts at school. I mean, I'm using condoms, every single time! Not that I could ever tell him that.

I made Snickers stop so I could give him a hug, which he tolerated patiently. His cluelessness made me cry more. He doesn't understand what's wrong. He loves me no matter what I do.

And Miss Murphy! I thought she was my friend. She didn't have to tell him. She really didn't. I came home in one piece. What does she care? She's not my mother. She does all these nice things for me, like teaching me how to drive and asking my opinion about whatever book I'm reading, but when it comes down to it, she's not on my side.

Thursday, August 31

Last day of work. Hot and bright. Everyone was there—kids, nannies, moms, staff, even Mrs. Franco. We organized games of Sharks and Minnows and made blue and turquoise friendship bracelets with the kids. Grady couldn't talk much, because he was lifeguarding and the pool was swarmed, but he grinned at me from across the water. Reese hugged everyone. Nadia, who I work with sometimes and who is nervous about being a freshman, made me swear that I'll wave to her in the halls.

The pool closed late, so I avoided another awkward dinner with Dad and Miss Murphy. I know it's immature, but I can't help going silent and sullen when I'm mad, and the longer I do it, the more impossible it seems to stop doing it. Like, what, will I come downstairs one day and chirp, "Mmm, something smells delicious!" after a week of grunting non-responses at them? And I know that as soon as I thaw out, they'll give each other meaningful looks over their wine, and as they're sitting around after dinner while I do the dishes, they'll murmur, "It seems like she's doing better," or something equally infuriating.

Grady and I snuck back in after we closed down, obviously. We've gotten so good at hopping the fence. It takes us mere seconds and we never scrape our legs anymore.

We were lying on the towel facing each other, noses millimeters apart.

"I can't stay too late," I said. "I keep catching my dad squinting at me. Like, studying me."

"For signs of lying?"

I nodded. "I told him I was going to a thing for pool staff tonight. Which is true."

He laughed.

"Can we keep sneaking back in here even though today's the last day of the season?" I said.

"Of course. We can sneak in here when there's two feet of snow on the ground if you want."

I brought his hand to my lips and kissed his fingers. "It's not going to change when we go back to school, is it?" I said.

"What, this? Us?" We were whispering, I don't know why. It felt like we were in church, lying under the big navy dome of stars, so close to each other. "It won't change," he said.

It probably will, a little. I can't think about it. Too scary.

Friday, September 1

Snickers threw up after eating a bunch of grass, and that broke the ice with my dad, because neither of us could stop ourselves from saying "Gah!" and "Not on the rug!" in our authentic voices, not the stiff, polite ones we've been using for days. Thank you, Snickers.

I do understand that Dad didn't say anything so terribly terrible to me. Of course he wants me to be a good kid, and he's right that I shouldn't lie to him.

But I'm still mad at Miss Murphy. She insisted on taking me out driving today. She was being her usual nonchalant self. Singing along to '90s R & B, looking out at the trees flashing by. She asked me if I have a boyfriend.

"No," I said immediately. It wasn't an intentional lie. It popped out.

"Oh," she said. "I thought maybe you were out late with a guy last week."

"Nope."

I got on the rotary a little too fast, and the tires squealed. She didn't mention it.

"If you're angry, I understand," she said. "I'm trying not to overstep my bounds here. Giving you a pass on staying out all night—that's something only your biological parent should do. I don't want you to think I'm trying to replace your mother."

"OK," I said. I could tell she was waiting for me to say more, but I couldn't. Replace my mother? It hadn't occurred to me that she'd try. I mean, I detest my mother. She's a deluded horror show who probably misses Snickers more than she misses me. But she's my mother. No one else could be. And Miss Murphy would only say something like that if she and Dad were serious. Which I know they are! I've been telling myself for months that they might get married if Mom ever crawls back from Mexico and agrees to get divorced. So why is the idea so upsetting to me now that it seems more real?

Saturday, September 2

Dear Mom,

Just wanted to say hello. How's Mexico? Hope all is well with you. Take care,

Chloe

Banged that out and fired it off without letting myself think twice. Instantly I regretted it. She never writes back, and now I'll have to spend weeks wondering if I offended her somehow, or if she thinks I've forgiven her for all of her parenting crimes, or if she actually is dead. Then, as I was staring at my inbox without seeing it, a bold black sender's name appeared: Veronica Snow.

> Dearest Chloe,
>
> So lovely to hear from you! I'm well and am currently on the move. Please pardon the mystery I'm creating, but I can't say too much. How I miss our former closeness, and how I adore you.

WTF. I thought she was supposed to be furious at me for refusing to move to Mexico and be a yoga studio greeter, or whatever she wanted me to do there. She's bananas. I should be sending her to spam, not emailing her just because Miss Murphy irritated me.

Sunday, September 3

Grady's away with his family for the long weekend, which meant that when I hung out with Tris and Hannah today, I wasn't distracted for a change, because I wasn't counting down the minutes until I could leave and have sex.

We talked about guys, of course. Hannah's still claiming she doesn't want to date anyone else until she gets to college. Tristan says everything's fine with Elliott.

"Fine?" I said.

"You know, fine, good, whatever," he said.

"You're not texting with Roy, are you?"

"God no," he said. "It's weird. When Roy dumped me, I thought I wanted my next boyfriend to be his opposite. Nice to me, into me, not playing games. Now I have that, and it's boring. Sometimes I try to make Elliott mad, because I think if he stopped loving me so much, I'd like him more. Is that sick?"

"How do you make him mad?" Hannah asked.

"Um, I just snap at him and criticize him," Tris said.

Poor Elliott, with his cute glasses and skinny arms and worried expression.

"Don't be mean to him," I said.

"I know I shouldn't be," Tris said.

It's hard to do the right thing. For example, I know I'm a bad friend, and also privileged, self-absorbed, etc., etc., but I can't seem to fix it.

Monday, September 4

Last day of summer vacation. I spent it organizing my backpack, trying on possible outfits for tomorrow, feeling nervous, and staring at my phone, hoping Grady would get back early. Instead he got back at 8 p.m., like he said he would. I told my dad and Miss Murphy I was going for a walk, and met him at the pool. He'd already hopped the fence, and he ran over to help me down. Oh, to see him after three days of not seeing him! There he was, smiling up at me, giving me his hand! He looked more vivid than life.

"God, I MISSED you," I said. He was already unbuttoning my shorts. We did it on the lifeguard chair, which was a first. Afterward we sat there next to each other, looking out at the water.

"Do you ever worry about the condom breaking?" he said.

"It hasn't so far," I said.

"I was Googling birth control," he said.

"What?? You don't want to have a baby with me?" I said.

"Don't even joke," he said, and knocked on the chair. It kind of hurt my feelings, which is ridiculous, because getting pregnant would be a tremendous disaster.

"I should go on the pill, I guess," I said. "But I don't know who could take me to the doctor. I guess I could ask my father." The thought made me want to barf.

"Miss Murphy?" he said.

I shook my head no. "We're not getting along right now."

Grady squeezed my hand.

Summer's over. We have to go back to our warped high school society. It'll get too cold to bone at the pool. I have to look up Planned Parenthood and bike there in secret, or something. Darkness is coming.

Tuesday, September 5

School was fine. By which I mean school was terrible, exactly as I predicted. As soon as I arrived in the morning, I saw Reese and her friends sitting on their throne: the top step of the wide stairs by the entrance, the step people feel weird even putting their feet on, because it's universally regarded as the squad's property. There they were, smiling down at their phones, shrieking at each other, making tiny adjustments to their hair and clothes, and pretending they didn't notice any non-squaddies' existence. Why do we all let them make us so miserable? Why do we sneak admiring, interested looks at them, instead of ignoring them the way they ignore us?

In other depressing news, it turns out the nearest Planned Parenthood is 2 hours and 20 minutes away by bike.

I have my road test scheduled for November 22. I have to pass. And I have to prevent myself from getting pregnant until then. Maybe Grady and I should stop having sex for a while.

Wednesday, September 6

I suggested the no-sex plan to Grady at the pool tonight, and he said he thought it was a good idea. To avoid actually doing it, I gave him head in the girls' bathroom, and then he went down on me, but unfortunately it wasn't enough and we wound up having sex once in the bathroom and then again on the grass. :(, but really :D :D :D

Thursday, September 7

Tris found me after school and said, "Something strange just happened."

"Go on," I said, and slammed my locker shut.

"So I'm talking to Elliott outside my math class, and this sophomore named Jay comes up and asks Elliott if he knows what the homework is for English. Elliott tells him, and then Jay's like, 'Have you ever noticed Mr. Isaac sniffs the dry-erase markers when he thinks no one's looking?' and Elliott's like, 'TOTALLY!' and they start freaking out together."

"Is huffing dry-erase markers a thing?" I said.

"The point is, Jay never once made eye contact with me, and Elliott didn't introduce him. Don't you think that's weird?"

"It's definitely rude."

"You don't think something's going on with them, do you?"

"With Elliott and—what did you say, Jay? No!"

Tris stared into space, probably imagining Elliott and Jay making out. He's been scarred for life by stupid cheating Roy.

Friday, September 8

Tris was right! Jay asked Elliott out. Full-on invited him to a movie. Elliott told him he has a boyfriend, and Jay claimed he'd had no idea, but come on. You can't help knowing everyone's precise relationship status around here. This school is a freaking panopticon.

Saturday, September 9

I'm sorry Tris had to suffer through 48 hours of stress, but not THAT sorry, because I've never seen him and Elliott so happy. They came over to my house with Hannah tonight, and Tris was all over Elliott. Holding his hand, stroking his hair, jumping up to get him a drink, laughing at his jokes. Elliott was basking in the attention. I feel like writing Jay a thank-you note.

Sunday, September 10

Dad and Miss Murphy went apple picking. They kept

asking me to come, but I insisted I had way too much homework to leave the house. Meanwhile, I was texting Grady. As soon as they left, I threw on my helmet and biked as hard as I could to the bagel place halfway between Grady's house and mine. He showed up five minutes after I arrived.

"When do you get your license again?" he asked.

"November 22," I said.

"That's a long way away." He was panting and the hair by his temples was damp with sweat. His skin flushes red when he exercises. It's so cute, I want to drop out of school and have a baby with him.

"Ask your mom if you can move closer to civilization," I said.

"But then my stepdad would have to relocate his precious archery range," he said.

"What, like bows and arrows?" I asked.

"He keeps talking about going big-game hunting. He's an ass," Grady said.

We both got raisin bagels with cream cheese.

"I think I could make it to your house in an hour if I rode really fast," I said. "But then it would take an hour to get back, and when are our parents ever gone for three hours at a time?"

"So you're calculating we need an hour alone?" Grady said. "How many times did you want to—"

"SHHHH," I said, and put my hand over his mouth. He licked my fingers and got cream cheese all over them.

"Grady, gross!" I said.

"You started it!"

I noticed the woman behind the counter looking at us fondly, which made me feel simultaneously proud to be young and in love and embarrassed to be young and in love.

Monday, September 11

It wasn't really hot enough to go swimming, but we did anyway. We'd gone to all the trouble of sneaking in, and the pool was there, turning dark turquoise as the sun set. Grady bet me his last stick of gum he could swim underwater for longer than I could, so we slipped in (diving is too noisy). After he'd beaten me, he gave me his gum anyway, and we floated around the deep end draped over two pool noodles, whispering to each other.

Tuesday, September 12

Grady's birthday is on Thursday, and instead of doing homework, I've been Googling "cute presents for boyfriends" and "birthday presents guys unique fun thoughtful." The internet is suggesting things like a sweet and salty food basket or a personalized Rubik's Cube. Thanks for nothing, internet.

Would it be lame to decorate his locker? I don't want to embarrass him, but I want him to feel special.

Wednesday, September 13

Hannah and Tris and Elliott are being very patient, but really, you can only text so many questions about turquoise streamers versus blue streamers before even the saintliest friends get irritated.

Thursday, September 14

I went with the blue streamers for the outside of his locker and filled the inside (I know the combination) with turquoise balloons. After school, sitting in the courtyard, I gave him his present: a print of a painting showing a girl in a red bikini floating underwater in a pool. It reminded me of his art, and of the summer, and of myself, I guess. I also gave him a homemade card, which I'd covered in puffy stickers, and a 16-paragraph love letter written in tiny print that I'd worried he might consider deranged (16 paragraphs?) but that he seemed to love. Inside the card I'd stuck a gift certificate entitling the bearer to 10 free blow jobs. We're going to meet at the pool tomorrow night so he can start redeeming it.

Friday, September 15

Well, we've been cast out of Eden.

Grady and I met up as soon as it got dark enough. We were sitting on the chair fully dressed, talking, when we heard a key in the gate lock and then saw the big wooden door opening. It didn't happen very fast. We probably had time to jump up and hide in the lifeguard shack. But we didn't do anything. We didn't even speak. We both sat motionless, staring at the opening door as if it were a portal to another dimension appearing before our eyes.

Mrs. Franco walked in, looking down at her phone. Then she turned on the floodlight, saw us, and shrieked.

"Jesus!" She had her hand over her heart.

"We weren't doing anything," Grady said. He'd gotten up and was walking toward her slowly, like he didn't want to scare her.

"I thought I could trust you two. Do you realize what kind of legal jeopardy you're putting us in here? God forbid either of you drowned. Chloe, tell me that's not what I think it is."

"It's a fancy lemonade," I said, lifting the bottle so she could see.

"Please don't call my mom," Grady said. "My stepdad will lose his mind."

She stood looking at us. She was wearing leggings with cutouts, sneakers, and a stretchy long-sleeved shirt. "Were you two planning on working here next summer?"

"Yes," we both said. My heart clenched. I imagined

having to get a job serving pizza or making coffee. Trapped inside on the hot days I love so much. Kept away from Grady. Coming home smelling like grease instead of sunscreen.

"Then don't let me catch you here again," she said.

"Thankyouthankyouthankyou," we said.

We grabbed our stuff and scuttled away. I didn't make eye contact with Mrs. Franco, although I smiled meekly in her general direction as I walked to the door.

We didn't speak until we were on our bikes, pedaling slowly, going nowhere in particular.

"Do you think she'll tell?" I said.

"Nah."

I braked for a squirrel. "It could have been way worse."

"If she'd walked in 20 minutes later . . ."

"I know."

We looked down the road, imagining what she could have seen.

"Why was she even there?" I said. "Do you think she was trying to catch us?"

"I doubt it," Grady said. "She was probably doing some pool-closing prep thing."

"Isn't the pool already closed?"

"They have to get it ready for the cold weather. Balance the water, add algae-killer, put the winter cover on, all that stuff."

I glanced over at him and raised my eyebrows. "I like your sexy lifeguard expertise," I said.

He was smiling at me when some middle-aged guy wearing '80s wraparound sunglasses and a sleeveless T-shirt raced past us in his Nissan Pathfinder, blaring hip-hop and looking at his phone. We had to ride into the grass to avoid getting smashed.

"GET OFF FACEBOOK, DAD!" I screamed. He didn't slow down, but he did jerk his head over to me, so at least I know he heard me taunting him.

Grady climbed off his bike and put his arms around me.

"Where can we go?" I said into his shoulder.

We considered and rejected the quarry (too sharp), the framed-out house being built two streets away (too dangerous), and the arboretum (too popular—that place is teeming with kids from our school who sneak in to get drunk under some crab apple trees).

In the end we rode our bikes around for an hour, chatting. It was great, but we didn't get to do it, and I feel like I was about to eat a big chocolate bar and someone snatched it out of my hands.

Saturday, September 16

What are we going to do? We need to have sex, but where? We can't go to Grady's place, because his stepfather is a contractor and stops at home at unpredictable times. Plus,

Bear's usually there with his babysitter. My house might work, though. We live an hour apart from each other by bike, but it only takes me 10 minutes to ride home from school. If Grady came over right after classes ended, he could stay until five and make it home for dinner. There's a chance we'd get caught, because Miss Murphy comes home early from work occasionally, but usually she's out until six, so we'd probably be OK. If she dropped in unexpectedly, I could . . . I don't know. I could stuff Grady in my closet or push him underneath my bed.

I just read over that last paragraph and it sounds unhinged. I feel like a scarily intense FBI agent running all over my living room, connecting index cards with color-coded string.

Sunday, September 17

Proposed my plan to Grady over text. He gave it a thumbs-up. We're going to try it tomorrow. I'm probably nervous, but I can't even tell, because my overwhelming excitement about getting laid is drowning out all other sensations, including hunger, thirst, and fear of the fact that I haven't even started my homework and it's already 11 p.m.

Monday, September 18

It worked!!! Why was I so scared to bring him over? Aside from the terror of getting caught, I think I was worried that if I brought him into my regular old house, it would drain the magic out of him. Like even he would turn ordinary if he had to stand near the blue Dawn and the ice dispenser. But I hardly even knew where we were. All I could see was Grady's face, Grady's hands, Grady's T-shirt. We dropped our backpacks on the front hall floor and ran up the stairs. As soon as we got to my room, I reached for his jeans and unbuttoned them, so he pulled my T-shirt over my head, so I pushed down his boxer briefs, and at first we were laughing, but then it got very serious and quiet.

When we were done, we lay there panting and staring at the ceiling for a while. Then he got up and wandered around my room, examining my knickknacks and books. "Harry Styles, huh?" he said, picking up a framed picture.

"Hannah got me that as a joke," I said.

"Sure. What are these dolls that look like sex workers?"

"Excuse me, those were my favorite toys when I was five years old! They're fashion-forward, not slutty. Not that being slutty's even a thing."

"I wasn't judging them. Five years old? Jesus." He held up Jade and gave her a squeaky voice. "I'm cold! I need pants!"

After we got dressed, we went downstairs and ate

PB&Js, and then he biked home. By the time Miss Murphy got back from work, I'd finished my homework and was getting dinner ready while singing "I Don't Need Anything but You."

"This is a pleasant scene," she said, thumping her bag onto a chair. "What are you making?"

"Smoky white bean shakshuka," I said.

"Well, fantastic," she said. She looked like she was about to ask me something, but then she poured herself a glass of white wine instead.

I'm so happy!

Tuesday, September 19

I jinxed myself. "I'm so happy"—I tempted the gods is what I did.

Mom's back.

She came to the house. THE HOUSE. Just showed up without calling ahead. I'm surprised she didn't let herself in with her old key. Probably she lost it. If she'd had it, she would have used it. I can't imagine her realizing it would be intrusive to burst in like she still owns the place.

Dad was making dinner, and Miss Murphy was grading papers and reading grammatical errors out loud to make us laugh. A normal Tuesday night. Nothing sinister in the air. It should have been storming violently.

Hailing and thundering. There should have been a stiff breeze at least. A little foreshadowing! But no, the doorbell rang and I jumped up and said, "I'll get it!" I sang it out, actually. That's how happy I was.

I opened the door and there was my mother, standing at the top of the stoop.

"Mom," I said stupidly. It had been over a year since I'd seen her, and she looked older. Skinnier in the face, maybe a little wrinklier. She was wearing black jeans and a peasant blouse with a square-cut neck. Also open-toed wedges, which was unlike her. How many times has she lectured me on the spectrum of patriarchal physical oppression running from high heels to foot binding?

Anyone halfway normal would look nervous, showing up out of the blue like that after ditching her family. But Mom stood there beaming at me, already opening her arms for a hug, like she'd forgotten that I hate her now. "Sweetheart," she said.

To get out of hugging her, I said, "Do you want to come in?" and stepped aside.

"If it's a good time," she said, and didn't wait for an answer before striding in and heading to the kitchen.

I followed her, watching her familiar walk. I thought of that vampire movie. They can't come in uninvited. You have to want to ruin your life. I could have slammed the door in her face. Instead I'd ushered her inside. My heart jumped around as we got closer to the kitchen. Should I call out and warn my dad and Miss Murphy?

My mouth felt frozen, and I couldn't speak, but it didn't matter: when we walked in, it was obvious they'd already heard her voice and knew she was coming. They were standing shoulder to shoulder behind the island, like it was a barricade they were prepared to defend. Dad was white around the lips.

"Veronica," he said, and that was all.

"Hello, Charlie," she said. "I'm sorry to spring myself on you like this, but I couldn't wait to see this little dumpling." She turned to me and cupped my cheek tenderly. I wanted to slap her hand away, but I only leaned slowly out of her reach.

Dad took a breath. I thought he might be gearing up to tell her she was out of line, surprising us like this. Before he could speak, Mom looked at Miss Murphy and said, "This must be your adorable girlfriend." She said "girlfriend" the way you'd say "half-witted teacup terrier puppy."

"Hello," said Miss Murphy. Her voice was low and even. One word and you could tell she wasn't someone to mess with.

"Well," Mom said. "It's surreal to be here." She laughed. No one else did. She looked down at her own exposed toes with admiration. They were painted bright orange. "I forgot how chilly it can be in New England, even at this time of year."

"Are you back for a visit?" I said.

"I'm back for the foreseeable future," she said, smiling at me. "I couldn't bear to be apart from you any longer."

My entire body started sweating. I looked at Dad in a panic. He caught my eye and said, "Veronica, there are custody concerns to address. You can't—"

"I'm not going to kidnap anyone, Charlie," she said, rolling her eyes at me like it was the old days and I was still a member of her two-person anti-Dad club.

"I thought you were living in Mexico City," I said. I couldn't make myself understand what she was saying. She'd moved back? To our town? The one where I lived?

"That was true for a time," she said.

"You said Dad and I would never find you," I said.

She looked at me with an *oh, come on* expression, like I was being a melodramatic teenager. "I would never say that, Chloe."

I wanted to pull out my phone and show her the email evidence, but if I'd done it, she would have said she'd clearly been joking around and I needed to lighten up.

"What's your plan?" my dad asked her.

She opened her arms wide. "To seek my own truth and follow my muse wherever it leads me."

I snuck a glance at Miss Murphy. Her face was expressionless, except for maybe a flicker around the eyebrows. What must she think of me and Dad? He'd married this person on purpose. I shared half my DNA with her. It was humiliating.

"Where are you staying?" I asked, trying to bring her out of fake-artist cotton-candy-sparkle land and into the physical world.

"For now, a dreary little Airbnb, but I have a lead on a condo unit for rent not far away."

She was here. She'd found a condo. She wanted to be my mother again.

Dad took a look at me and said, "Well, Veronica, we should really get started on dinner, so . . ."

She inhaled theatrically. "It smells delicious. Your cranberry chicken, am I right?"

She looked at us expectantly. She really thought Dad was going to invite her to stay.

Finally he said, "Let me walk you out."

Mom came at me, trying for a hug again. I didn't see a way to escape, so I got it over with as fast as I could.

While my parents were outside, I set the table and Miss Murphy poured the drinks.

"You OK?" she said after a few minutes.

"Yeah. You?"

"I'm fine."

I don't know what Dad told her about Mom, but she must have been surprised to see the full extent of her. Well, not the full extent. She hasn't seen Mom lose her temper yet. She probably never will. Mom keeps it together around acquaintances and friends (which proves she is capable of keeping it together when she chooses to). She only pops off with blood relatives and with her husband. And with strangers who have disrespected her or done something she considers unforgivable, like driving too fast on a residential street.

When Dad came back inside, Miss Murphy offered to leave. "I'm sure you and Chloe want to talk," she said. She was right. I wanted to ask Dad about what would happen next. But Dad insisted that she stay. We did discuss Mom while we ate, of course, but we were all being polite. I said things like "I wonder why she came back," instead of "I hate her." I wanted to pretend to Miss Murphy that everything was OK and that the woman who gave birth to me isn't a malignant narcissist.

Wednesday, September 20

What's Mom going to do for work? Did Javi move back with her? How much does she expect me to see her— once a week? Once a month? Do I have to see her at all?

Is she going to show up at my school events? Is she plotting to get back together with Dad?

Of course she comes back now, right at the moment when everything was going so well, I felt like I was walking on a rainbow. I woke up this morning and thought *Grady!* as usual, and then I thought, *But Mom.* She's here, a few miles away, and it ruins everything.

Thursday, September 21

Miss Murphy slept at her own house tonight. She said her mother needed company, but I bet she wanted to give me and Dad time alone. I asked him all my questions about Mom, but he couldn't answer them. I knew he wouldn't be able to. It still helped to talk about it.

She's been calling me once a day. I decline the calls instantly and hope she thinks my phone is turned off. She calls Dad, too, which I know because I've overheard him talking in a low, strained voice. Once he said, "Just try that and see what happens," which was thrilling (he was threatening her!) but scary (he was threatening her). He doesn't exactly hide his feelings about Mom from me—he lets me see him grimace; he doesn't contradict me when I say she's awful—but he never outright complains about her. Sometimes I wish he would. We're on the same side, but not openly.

Friday, September 22

Having sex with Grady is the only thing that helps. It's like a miracle cleaner that wipes all the grease and dirt and dead bugs out of your mind. And we're so lucky. We love each other (although we still haven't said it, which I'm trying not to stress about). Miss Murphy doesn't come home early. The condoms don't break. I've stopped worrying. Nothing bad's going to happen. I mean, bad things are going to happen all the time, but not with me and Grady and sex.

Saturday, September 23

Mom left a voicemail for the first time. "Chloe, hi! I have some good news: I got the condo! I'm moving in tomorrow, and I'd love for you to see it. Maybe sometime next week? It's a two-bedroom unit. I've ordered a bed from IKEA for you, in case you ever feel like sleeping over. A double bed, I might add! Let's see if I manage to get it assembled. Anyway, call me when you can."

"In case you ever feel like sleeping over"—at least I know she doesn't expect me to spend half my time with her. But now I have to call her back, or not call her back and feel guilty. I have to think about her, and I don't want to.

Sunday, September 24

Grady and I rode our bikes to the football field. It was

warm out, almost 80 degrees. We sat on the bleachers looking down at the empty grass. I told Grady about my mom and the invitation.

"Oh, man," he said. "Are you gonna go?"

"I haven't decided," I said. "But what's the other option—refuse to see her for the rest of time?"

He shrugged. "You could."

"I'd feel so guilty. Even though I hate her."

He looked up at a plane sailing through the blue sky. "We're like robots," he said. "Everyone, I mean, not just kids. It's like we're programmed to be loyal to our parents forever, even when they abandon us or whatever."

I wanted to tell him he shouldn't worry about his father, or even think about him. Anyone who could abandon Grady doesn't deserve a second of thought, much less a lifetime of loyalty.

"Grady," I said.

He turned to look at me. "Yeah?"

My face was so close to his, I could see where one of his dark eyelashes had gotten misaligned. "Close your eyes," I said, and smoothed the lash back into place. "OK, open them," I said. He did. There he was again: attentive, smart, wry, looking right at me. Oh, I love him. I love him. I can't wait to tell him. But I don't want to do it now, when my stupid mother is looming over me like a storm cloud.

Monday, September 25

Tris thinks I should block my mom on my phone and on social media and in life. Hannah thinks I should try to forgive her. I think they're both right.

Tuesday, September 26

I texted Mom to tell her I'll stop by after school on Thursday. Whatever—I'll stay for 20 minutes, I'll get out of there, and then I won't have to feel like a terrible daughter. This approach is easier on me. Also, I'm kind of curious to see what her new place looks like.

Wednesday, September 27

Kept Noelle company in the clearing while she smoked a cigarette after lunch. I asked her for advice on dealing with my mother.

"If you're upset, don't let her see it," she said. "Pretend you're a statue."

"Is that what you do with your dad?"

She picked a dot of tobacco off her tongue and flicked it onto the dirt. "I try."

We were alone in the clearing aside from two goth kids with their heads together, watching a video on one of their phones. I wondered if their parents are nice.

"Here's a tip," Noelle said. "If you need to stop

yourself from crying, pick a spot on your palm and pinch the skin as hard as you can between your nails."

"What's wrong with crying, though?" I said.

She raised an eyebrow at me. "It's undignified, dude," she said.

I guess it is.

It's hard to explain to my friends what my mother is like and what my parents' relationship is like. And I can't really understand Noelle's dad or Grady's stepfather. Every divorce is unique, like a snowflake. A snowflake made of poop.

Thursday, September 28

I never should have gone. I don't want to feel sorry for Mom. I want to keep hating her.

Her new place is in the same complex where Mac's mother lives, which makes sense, since divorced people flock there. Mac! I used to love that guy so freaking much, and now I bike past his mom's place and think, *Hey, I wonder how Mac's doing. I should text him some-time.* It doesn't even rise to the level of nostalgia—it's not that strong of a feeling. I never would have believed my obsession with him would fade. I thought it was tattooed on my heart.

"You're HERE!" Mom said when she opened the door. She was wearing billowy pants with metallic stripes, a gauzy top, and a teal scarf wound around her neck in a complicated way. Also tons of clattery silver bangles. Her posture has really improved since she left, I guess from all that yoga. Also, her arms have gotten muscular. She looks like my mother, but not.

"Hello," I said.

"Come in, come in! Let me give you the tour!"

She's on the second floor. On the side, she has a view of trees and grass, but the front of the condo looks out on the parking lot. It's all on one level: kitchen (brown cabinets, plasticky countertops), living room (dark), master bedroom (empty aside from Mom's bed), hall bathroom (small, pink). The ceilings are low and the wall-to-wall carpet is the color of Band-Aids. The worst part is the guest bedroom. Mom opened the door with a flourish, and I saw that she'd managed to assemble the IKEA bed. It was all set up with sheets and a pillow and a bedspread and everything.

"I found a tutorial on YouTube," she said proudly. I couldn't believe it. The mother I knew couldn't even change a battery. She'd bring her electric toothbrush to Dad like she'd just crawled out of the woods and didn't know + from -.

"Wow," I said. "I'm impressed."

Her place is fine. It's luxurious compared to the way plenty of people live. I know that. But it's not our creaky, comfortable old house with the well-proportioned rooms and the afternoon sun. She can never come back home, which is her own fault, but still, how can she stand to live there when she used to live here? If she'd complained about how dumpy the condo was, it would have been easier. But she was trying so hard to be enthusiastic, showing me the decent counter space in the kitchen and the en suite bathroom in her room, pointing out the spot where she planned to write. My throat got sore with pity for her.

She made green tea, and we sat at her kitchen table and talked.

"I guess Javi didn't come with you," I said.

"He didn't," she said. "We parted ways."

"What happened?"

She put both hands around her mug. "There was another woman involved. A younger woman, I might add."

"I'm sorry, Mom."

She shook her head fast and smiled at me. "*Que será, será*. And it's all for the best: now I'm reunited with my darling one."

Jesus! It was like she'd dropped a pillow over my face. I felt smothered with love and pressure. I drank my tea as fast as I could.

"See you soon?" she called from the doorway.

"Bye!" I yelled back, and then ran to my bike like it was a lifeboat.

Friday, September 29

If she wants to move back here and sit in a tiny apartment by herself, that's her business. I didn't force her to do anything. I don't even want her here. She doesn't want to be here either! I'm sure if she could, she'd choose to be back in Mexico, living with her hot boyfriend. She's only here because she got dumped. It has nothing to do with me.

Saturday, September 30

It's ridiculous to worry about her like this. We're talking about the person who told me she was leaving for four months and then stayed away for two years, working on her tan and sending me nastygrams about how selfish I am. I'm allowed to hate her! I want to hate her.

Sunday, October 1

Miss Murphy slept over last night. I woke up early and was heading to the bathroom when I heard my name. Dad and Miss Murphy were talking in his bedroom. I froze in place to listen.

"Not to me," Dad said. "Has she to you?"

"No," Miss Murphy said. "But I haven't asked. I don't want to pry."

I could hear them bustling around in there, probably straightening up. They're both tidy, in contrast to Mom, who leaves a trail of receipts, Luna Bar wrappers, and empty coffee cups wherever she goes.

"Do you think I should intervene?" Dad said.

"In what way?"

"I don't know. Set a maximum number of visits per month. Insist on going over there with her. Remind her that her mother's batshit." I heard him sigh and thump down onto the bed.

"I doubt she needs reminding," Miss Murphy said.

Dad must have looked some way—sad, skeptical?—because she added, "Chloe's a smart kid. She can handle herself."

I walked to the bathroom, shut the door carefully, and sat on the closed lid of the toilet.

They treat me like a toddler. To my face they pretend everything's fine. Behind my back they tell each other the truth. And they know I know the truth! So why can't we discuss it honestly, like adults?

I doubt she needs reminding. So mean. So scornful. Laughing with my father about my mother.

She's right, that's the thing. Of course I don't need reminding that my mom's a mess. It's all I can think about as it is. But I don't want Miss Murphy to be right; I want her to be nice.

Monday, October 2

At lunch with Grady and Tris and Elliott, I threw myself into gossiping with the passion of a French courtier. I proposed conspiracy theories (what if Harper and Lianna are collaborating to take down Reese?) and dredged up ancient rumors dating back to freshman year (is it possible that Mrs. deWitt and Coach Patel are having an affair?). Elliott looked like he'd rather be reading. Tris and Grady are great gossips, but after a while even they seemed overwhelmed. It worked, though: I distracted myself for 23 minutes.

Tuesday, October 3

"My mom thinks I'm sneaking around getting high," Grady said. We were lying backward on my bed with our feet propped up on the wall above the headboard. I was wearing a shirt and nothing else, Winnie-the-Pooh style. He was naked.

"What?? Why?" I said.

"Because Bear's babysitter tattled on me and told her I'm never home after school anymore."

"What did you tell your mom?"

"That I've been hanging out with my girlfriend."

He turned his head to look into my eyes and smile. I'm Grady's GIRLFRIEND! I mean, obviously. But it was still exciting to hear him say it.

He took my hand. "I don't know if she believes me,

though. She was like, 'I want to meet her.' All suspicious."

"Are you trying to tell me you want me to meet your mother?" Without sitting up, I lifted my butt in the air and pulled on my underwear. It seemed rude to mention his mom with my vagina hanging out.

"Yeah, ASAP. I think she's been going through my drawers looking for bongs."

"You should probably meet my parents too. My dad. And my . . . Miss Murphy. That way if they catch us, we won't be in such big trouble."

We shook hands to seal the deal, which was awkward, since we were lying on our backs.

"Are you nervous?" I said. "To meet my dad?"

"I feel like I'm going to throw up just talking about it. So yeah."

"OK, good. Because I'm terrified to meet your mom."

"She'll love you," Grady said.

"My dad will love you too," I said.

"Love." We'd both said "love"! Not to each other, but *about* each other, which is almost the same thing. It made me so nervous I couldn't speak. Grady got quiet too, which was probably a coincidence. Maybe it hasn't even crossed his mind to tell me he loves me.

Wednesday, October 4

Here's our plan: I'll tell my dad and Miss Murphy that

Grady exists tonight. He will skip this step, since his parents already know about me. I'll go to his house for dinner on Saturday night. He'll come to my house on Sunday afternoon.

I'm with Grady: even writing this down makes me feel like I'm going to throw up.

Thursday, October 5

Between classes I ran to Grady's locker and quizzed him about his mom.

"What does she like?"

"Uh, ordering new clothes for Bear from Old Navy."

I shook his arm a little. "But what does she watch? What does she read?"

"Netflix? Stuff on her phone?"

"Argh. Never mind. What about your stepdad?"

"He likes shooting things and telling me I'm a hypocrite because I eat meat but won't kill it myself."

"He sounds great."

"Yeah, he's the best."

At least I have a basic sense of Grady's horrible step-father. His mother is a Netflix-watching mystery.

At dinner, I delivered the lines I'd written out for myself in my math notebook and memorized during my bike ride home. "I wanted to tell you guys I've been dating someone. Grady Lawrence. He's really nice. I was wondering if he could come over to meet you on Sunday."

Miss Murphy and my dad glanced at each other. I couldn't read their look. "That's great, Chloe," Dad said.

"We'd love to meet him!" Miss Murphy said. "I mean, I would. I shouldn't refer to myself and your father like we're one unit."

God. I know they're one unit. Who does she think she's kidding?

"Of course I'd love to meet him too," Dad said. "Sunday. Great. For dinner?"

"I'm having dinner with his parents the night before," I said. "If that's OK."

Another meaningful glance between my dad and Miss Murphy. They're so annoying. It's like they think I can't see them.

"Maybe we could do an afternoon thing instead," I said.

"Sure," Dad said. "I'll make cookies."

Dinner. Cookies. It's the food planning that makes this seem like it's really going to happen.

Friday, October 6

Tris and I went to the movies tonight. We were in the lobby afterward, waiting for his mom to pick us up, when he asked me if I felt sick.

"No," I said. "How come?"

"This is the first time ever you haven't stolen half my popcorn," he said. "It was so relaxing not bumping into your hand every two seconds."

"I'm too nervous to eat right now," I said.

"Really? Why?"

"I'm meeting Grady's parents tomorrow," I said.

"Whoa!"

"What do I do?" I said. "How do I make them like me?"

"Be yourself?" Tris said. He didn't sound too sure.

"I'm serious. How did you do it with Roy's parents?"

"Unless I'd actually flipped over their dining room table, they would have loved me. Roy's first boyfriend— they'd been waiting to show me how cool they were with me since Roy was six years old."

"Grady's mother doesn't even believe I exist," I said.

Tris looked out the glass doors to the parking lot, thinking. "Be polite," he said. "Call her Mrs. Lawrence."

"Mrs. Trevor. She changed her name when she got remarried."

"Mrs. Trevor, then. Bring something nice. A hostess present. Offer to help with the dishes."

I'd thought of the dishes but not of the present. "What else?" I said.

"If you disagree with something they say, just look

pleasant and be like, 'Oh, I've never thought of it that way.' Don't put your hands on Grady in front of them."

I got out my phone to take notes. What would I do without Tris?

Saturday, October 7

Dad agreed to stop at the garden center on his way to drop me off at the Trevors'. I bought a small plant in a white pot.

Grady met me at the door, and I could tell he was terrified, which didn't exactly make me feel better. "Hey! Come on in!" he said in a chipper tone of voice I've never heard him use before. I was so full of adrenaline that I sucked in every detail of my surroundings as he led me back through the house. Framed drawings by Bear in the foyer. Through a doorway, a living room. Braided rug, boxy TV, overstuffed couch. Through another doorway, the dining room. Upholstered chairs and an old-fashioned chandelier. In the kitchen, Bear was scribbling on a school handout with a green crayon, and Mrs. Trevor was flipping through a cookbook. She looked up when I came in and rushed over to give me a hug. "You're Chloe! Oh my God. You're real. You're adorable!" She was laughing over my shoulder and kind of jiggling me up and down.

"MOM," Grady said.

"Grady's going to lecture me later," she said. "I promised I wouldn't be too enthusiastic."

I couldn't speak from the shock. This was Grady's mom? She was SO YOUNG. She looked like him—or vice versa, I guess. Fine features, deep-set eyes. Her hair was pulled into a ponytail, and she was wearing a red-and-white striped shirt, socks with a pink star pattern, and boyfriend jeans. And she was what, 30? Maybe 35? I'm terrible at guessing adults' ages, but definitely under 40. She made my mother look like a crone.

"Is this for me?" she said, grabbing the pot. "Oh-em-gee! I love succulents!"

Grady cringed dramatically behind her back, to apologize for her. Was he really embarrassed by his cute, nice mother? Did he realize what I'd give to have a mom like this?

She was in the middle of asking me questions about myself (do I have siblings? What extracurriculars do I do? What do high school kids call it now, "going out" or "dating" or "hooking up" or what? [Grady threw his head back in pain when she said "hooking up."] What music do I listen to? How old was I when my parents let me get a phone?) when Mr. Trevor came into the kitchen. He said "hey" to me and grabbed a beer from the fridge. I thought he'd be some swaggering dad-bro in cargo pants, but he looked more like an ex-UFC fighter.

He had short hair, almost buzzed, a tattoo of an eagle on his forearm, and a crooked nose.

Grady could have given me a heads-up. *By the way, just so you're not surprised when you meet them, I should mention that my mom's really young and my stepdad is sexy in a glowering way.* Instead I was caught unaware, and my face probably looked like a surprised emoji.

At dinner, I ate every bite of my chicken and rice and tried not to say anything controversial. Mrs. Trevor said "Totally!" a lot and laughed whenever I tried to make a joke. She helped Bear spear his food and told him not to worry about it when he spilled some milk on his napkin. When she wasn't busy with him, she was rubbing Mr. Trevor's shoulder, scratching the back of his head, or asking him to tell us about the clients on Willow who wanted him to install a toilet right in the middle of the master bedroom. "Freaks," said Mr. Trevor, shrugging. He didn't say much more than that. Once Grady mentioned that the people next door got a new dog, and Mr. Trevor said, "Nah. The wife has allergies." There was silence for a while after that. I was confused. It wasn't like Grady was expressing an opinion; either they got a dog or they didn't. I tried to think of a way to say Grady must be right and finally came up with "What color?"

"Brown with a white diamond on its chest," said

Grady, staring at his stepdad, who didn't respond. I looked at Mrs. Trevor, who was pressing her lips together and pinching the end of her ponytail.

"How was it?" Dad asked when he picked me up.

"Good," I said.

He waited. "What are they like?" he asked, after it became obvious I wasn't going to elaborate.

"Pretty nice." I wasn't trying to be difficult. It seemed impossible to describe the evening or the Trevors beyond that.

I called Grady as soon as I got to my room.

"I'm sorry," he said, instead of "hi."

"What are you talking about? Your mom's amazing!"

"She's so . . . ugh, I don't know. She's so bubbly."

"That's a good thing, you weirdo."

"OK," he said, sounding relieved.

"She's pretty young, right?"

"She's 37," he said. "So's my dad. They had me when they were seniors in college." He sounded embarrassed and defensive.

"It's nice," I said. "Probably she can still remember what it was like to be in high school."

"She thinks she can, that's for sure," he said in a more normal voice.

"Is your stepdad always like that?" I said.

"What, silent and grouchy? Pretty much."

"Does your mom care?"

"I think she likes it. The moodier he gets, the more cheerful she gets. It's like she has to balance him out. And sometimes he'll goof around with her, and she loves that. It only happens once in a while, but she lives for it. Intermittent positive reinforcement, you know?" He's taking AP Psych. I've been hearing a lot about B. F. Skinner.

"He was mean to you," I said.

"Was he?" He sounded surprised.

"The dog thing."

"Oh." He laughed a little. "Yeah."

"Your mom looked upset."

He sighed. "It bugs her when he's a dick to me. But it's not like she's going to leave him."

It's so hard being a kid. If adults are trapped in a bad relationship, they can get out. What's Grady supposed to do? Live in L.A. with his dad who's not interested in him? Run away?

Sunday, October 8

Dad and Miss Murphy loved Grady and the visit went perfectly, which I don't even care about right now.

After Grady left, we ate dinner. I was about to start clearing the table when my dad and Miss Murphy exchanged a look. Right away I knew something was up.

Dad cleared his throat. "Marian and I want to talk to you."

I waited.

He glanced at her, and she said, "We've been discussing the possibility of me moving in here."

Dad said, "Obviously the divorce has been delayed longer than—"

"Where? Here?" I said. I looked around the dining room. The blue runner on the buffet; the green vase holding dusty paper flowers I made in fourth grade; the plaid L.L. Bean cushion Snickers likes to plop down on so he can be close to us while we're eating—she was going to sit here, in this dining room, every night?

"OK," I said, and pushed my chair back.

"Chloe, please take a seat," Dad said.

"We want to know how you feel about the idea," Miss Murphy said. "If it's too early or just too strange, I want you to tell us."

"It's fine," I said. "I don't care. May I be excused?"

I could see Dad struggling to figure out whether he could force me to sit back down.

"We can discuss this later, if you want," he said.

"Sounds good."

Twenty minutes later, I was staring at my math homework without seeing it when Dad knocked and came into my room.

"Sorry if you felt ambushed there, kiddo," he said. "Maybe it was a bad idea to talk to you together like that."

If he'd come in guns blazing, I probably would have been a meek little mouse, but his apology made me brave enough to get mad.

"When's she moving in?"

"We'd discussed early November. How does that sound?"

I laughed. "I can tell you really care about what I think."

"I do care."

"Right, that's why you already have the move-in date."

He didn't say anything.

"Where's her mom going?" I said. "What, she's dumping her in a nursing home to die of cancer alone?"

His face turned angry, and I regretted what I'd said. I didn't feel bad about it yet—I was too furious—but I wished I hadn't made a tactical error.

"I know you're not really that callow," he said.

I didn't respond. I can be callow if I want to be. It's my God-given right as an American teenager.

"Mrs. Murphy needs more help than Marian can give her," he said. "She's moving to Woodcrest next weekend. She'll be in assisted living for the time being,

but they have nursing care and an excellent hospice program, so when the time comes, she can transition there
easily. Marian's devastated by the whole situation, as you
can imagine."

I looked out the window behind Dad. The wind was
whipping red and orange leaves off the trees like a mean
kid ruining something beautiful for kicks.

I had no comeback. I was upset that my dad's girlfriend is moving in? Well, my dad's girlfriend was upset
because her mother is sick. I couldn't compete.

"Sorry," I muttered.

Dad shook his head slightly, like he couldn't believe
this ingrate was the same girl who used to ride on his
shoulders and pick dandelion bouquets for him.

Monday, October 9

On top of everything else, Mom texts me at least once a
day. Nice stuff. "Just wanted to say hi. Hi!" "Saw something about Webkinz online and thought of you. Do
you still have your collection?" "Hope you're having a
great day off from school!" I hate it. I hate it so much.
She thinks she can use a few happy texts to cancel out
years of hissing at me over nothing, calling me names,
and leaving me. And it WORKS. I can't be mean to
her in response. I feel too guilty. I send her smiley faces
or answers ending in exclamation points ("Hi!" "LOL

nope!" "Thanks!"). Don't worry, Mom! I'll pretend you're a great parent and always have been! Anything to avoid being mean or making you feel bad!

Tuesday, October 10

I was doing my homework in the kitchen, and Dad and Miss Murphy were talking in the living room. I wasn't eavesdropping. In fact, I was intentionally trying not to listen, because I'd heard Dad say the word "constipation," and I really didn't want to overhear any details. Then Miss Murphy started talking in a voice I'd never heard her use before.

"She's always been the most dignified person I know," she said. I realized—she was crying. That's why she sounded so strange.

"This is the right thing," Dad said. "She doesn't want you to be the one giving her suppositories."

"It's better if some stranger does it?" Miss Murphy said.

"Yes," Dad said firmly.

I want to think I'll never be like Miss Murphy, sobbing over suppositories, spending hours at my mother's sorting through her old books and broken tennis rackets. But of course I will. I will get older, and so will my parents, and someday I will have to help them like she's helping her mother.

Wednesday, October 11

Took the PSATs. Not to jinx anything, but I think I might have done OK. It was a relief to sit in a quiet room focusing on linear equations instead of pacing around my house thinking about death and divorce.

Thursday, October 12

I offered to help out with the Woodcrest move this Saturday, but Miss Murphy said there wasn't much stuff to carry in. She looked so miserable, I changed the subject.

Friday, October 13

It's not that I'm not having sex with Grady constantly, because I am. It's that I feel guilty writing about it in my diary when people's mothers are sick.

Saturday, October 14

I thought Miss Murphy would be a mess tonight after the move, but she seemed OK. Quiet, but not crying or pale. Maybe she was relieved that this day she'd been dreading was almost over. Dad ordered Indian food for dinner, but no one ate much. I thought maybe one of the adults would bring up our own living situation, but neither did. When they'd almost finished a bottle of wine, I said, "Miss Murphy, are you going to sell your mom's house now?"

"Chloe," Dad said. "Let's discuss that some other night."

She ignored him. "I'm hoping to, although we'll see if I can unload it this close to the holidays."

"And then . . . ," I said, and paused.

She shrugged. "Find an apartment. We'll see." She cleared her throat and moved a forkful of tandoori chicken toward her mouth, then changed her mind and set the fork down again.

I heard myself say, "Don't rent an apartment. You should come here. It doesn't bother me."

"Really?" she said, and when I said, "Yes, really," the look of relief that came over her made me happy I'd lied.

Sunday, October 15

I don't know what made me ride my bike over to Mom's. I hadn't texted her to tell her I was coming. She opened the door wearing loose pants and a T-shirt with no bra. I could feel her floppy boobs pressing against me when she hugged me hello. I felt revolted, and then guilty for being horrified by my own mother's body. Probably her boobs were so limp because I'd breastfed all the life out of them. God, GROSS.

"You've caught me job-hunting!" she said, gesturing back at her open laptop. "There's an assistant professorship in creative writing that looks *very* interesting."

"That's great, Mom," I said. I followed her to the living room. "What's going on with your novel, anyway?" I tried to make my voice sound neutral. She took her novel seriously, even if no one else did.

"I'm struggling to find an agent who understands my vision," she said. "Self-publishing may be the way to go. You know that's how E. L. James got her start? Not that I'm writing erotica. Far from it."

Most parents know not to discuss erotica with their teenagers, but not my mother.

She dashed around cracking ice cubes into glasses and putting macadamia nuts in a bowl. "I wish you'd texted me, darling. Of course, you should feel free to drop by whenever you like. This house is your home. It's just that I'm woefully short on food."

She asked how Dad was doing in this exaggeratedly friendly, I'm-totally-fine/I-think-of-your-father-as-a-dear-friend voice that I didn't buy for a second. I think I'd gone over there planning to tell her everything, because it seems wrong that she doesn't know, but then I couldn't. To mention Miss Murphy or the move or Miss Murphy's mother's suppository—I couldn't do it. Mom's face would have done something terrible. Maybe she would have cried. And it would have been disloyal to Dad.

"He's fine," I said. "Busy with work."

"And his friend?"

Assuming she meant Miss Murphy, I said, "Also fine."

"I suppose I can't fault him for finding love despite being legally married to me. After all, I did, with darling Javi. But there is something strange about it."

"What's happening with the divorce?" I said.

"Your father hasn't told you?" She looked excited that I was asking her, not him. "I unilaterally fired that hideous mediator. She was so brainwashed by the patriarchy, she was incapable of identifying objective truths. She took your father's side on every single point."

What a shocker. "So do you have to find a new one?"

She patted my hand. "I'm in no rush. It'll happen when it happens."

Even she can't really think a divorce lawyer is going to fall out of the sky when the time is right. She's so obviously stalling to irritate Dad and torture Miss Murphy. Or maybe she wants to stay married to Dad, which is deluded, sad, and understandable.

Monday, October 16

Miss Murphy was at Woodcrest, and Dad was getting dinner together while I sort of did homework, sort of concentrated on eating rainbow Goldfish. I mentioned I'd gone over to Mom's yesterday, and at first all he said was, "Huh. How was that?" which was fine. I shrugged and said, "OK. Pretty good." I could tell he was waiting for more, so I added, "She's looking for a job." He grunt-laughed and said, "That's a first."

I know I said I wish he'd be more open with me, but I was wrong. I don't want to hear his snide little remarks. And I don't want to hear Mom's, either. I don't want to hear about the mediator, I don't want to hear about Javi, I don't want to hear about any of it. Don't they know that? Haven't they Googled it? Read ONE blog post about how to help your kids handle divorce; I promise you it'll say, "Don't criticize your ex to your children." I know, because I've Googled! But they haven't, or they have but they thought, *Oh, but Chloe's different. She'll understand.* No, I won't! I'm not different! I'm exactly like every other kid whose parents are splitting up, and I wish they'd pull their heads out of their butts and notice that.

Tuesday, October 17

Grady and I rode our bikes to the cemetery after school. It was my idea. I wanted to be somewhere quiet. The air was chilly. We held hands as we walked.

"My mom got rid of the mediator," I said.

"Really? What does that mean? Will the divorce take longer?"

"I guess. It's not like I'm in a rush for them to do it,

but I kind of am. I want to get it over with, and I want to stop talking about it with them."

Grady laughed. "Chlo, it doesn't stop. I mean, not to burst your bubble."

"Your parents still say mean stuff about each other?"

"If anything, it's gotten worse."

"Well, that's just wonderful."

The wind picked up, and Grady let go of my hand to put his arm around me.

I said, "Two years isn't that long of a time."

"Compared to what?"

"I mean, it's not that far away. College. I can wait for two years."

He dropped his arm. "Man, you are *cold*! Are you that excited to get away from me?"

He was trying to sound jokey, but I could tell I'd hurt his feelings. "No! That's not what I meant. My parents— they're the reason—it's all their drama, and the fighting."

We'd stopped and were looking at each other in the middle of a smooth paved pathway, underneath a beech tree rustling its yellow leaves. Grady was wearing a black crewneck sweater and half smiling at me. *I love you*, I thought. The words were right behind my lips. I wanted to say them out loud. But it seemed dangerous to do it spontaneously, without thinking it through and having a plan and building up to it. To blurt out "I love you" in the middle of a cemetery? I couldn't, so instead I said, "I don't want to leave you."

I put my arms around his neck. Over his shoulder I could see all the hundreds and hundreds of gravestones stretching away toward the trees on one side and the road on the other.

"These poor people," I said. "It's not fair, that they're dead and we're alive."

He hugged me tighter. "They had their turn," he said. "Don't feel guilty."

His head was pressed against mine, and his voice made my skull vibrate. My skull, which would one day decompose in the ground.

"I hope they had fun when they were kids," I said. "And I hope their parents weren't jerks."

I could feel him smiling even though I couldn't see his face. "Their parents probably *were* jerks, but maybe they had nice lives anyway."

I touched his hair. "Let's get out of here."

He lifted me up a few inches and set me back down on the ground gently. "Let's."

I held on to him for one more second and thought, *I love you. I love you. I love you.*

Wednesday, October 18

Should I wait for him to tell me he loves me first, or

is that outdated self-hating misogynist nonsense that would disappoint Gloria Steinem? I don't want to say it first, but as a proud feminist, I don't think I'm supposed to feel that way.

Was it a mistake to have sex with him before we even said it? Is he not taking me seriously because he's getting the milk in the barn, or whatever that stupid expression is? But no, this is nuts—I met his parents! He's into me.

Maybe he hasn't said it yet because he's worried I won't say it back. Except that doesn't make sense. He must know I love him. I think he might have even known I was about to say it yesterday. So, what, is he messing with me? He wouldn't. This is Grady we're talking about, not some mean bro. Maybe he's waiting for a special event! Yes, that's probably it. He's going to tell me on our three-month anniversary, or under a full moon, or something like that. I need to calm down.

Thursday, October 19

I'm not going to wait for Grady. If the perfect moment presents itself, or if I just can't help it and "I love you" comes flying out of my mouth, I'll let it happen.

Friday, October 20

Grady and I went to the movies with Tris and Elliott. Everyone held hands with his or her BF or GF, and eventually Grady put his arm around me. It was exactly like I thought high school might be when I was nine years old. Also, Grady and I shared a large popcorn, and he didn't mind when my fingers bumped into his, and the movie was funny. The only minor distraction was the voice in my head saying, *What if you leaned over right now and whispered "I love you"?* But I ignored the voice. After the lights came up, we walked a mile down a four-lane highway to get to the pizza place with the good fountain soda.

Once we were sitting down, Tris said, "So what's everyone thinking for the Halloween dance? Any costume ideas?"

The Halloween dance! I'd forgotten all about it. And how could that be, when last year I thought about nothing else for the first two months of school?

"I've got nothing," I said.

"We're going as Darth Vader and Luke Skywalker," Elliott said.

"No, we're not," said Tris. Making eye contact with me, he said, "Elliott is *really* into Star Wars."

"Like every other normal American dude," Grady said.

"Grady and I used to watch *A New Hope* after school, like, four times a week," Elliott explained to me.

"What's *A New Hope*?" I said.

Grady and Elliott looked shocked.

"It's—" Elliott said, but Tris interrupted him. "No! If you start, we won't get to talk about anything else before curfew."

"Oh, man," Grady said to Elliott, "I keep meaning to text you all these old pics my mom found of us. Remember that Darth Vader costume?"

Elliott snorted. "You mean *my* Darth Vader costume."

"Jesus, you're still giving me shit for borrowing it! We were in kindergarten!"

"It's not the borrowing so much as the breaking."

"It was broken when you gave it to me."

As they kept bickering, Tris leaned across the table toward me and whispered, "I honestly hate this. It makes me feel itchy all over. Has Grady made you watch the movies? Those ones from the '70s that are supposed to be amazing? They're so slow. And so beige."

"I have to tell you something," I whispered. "Miss Murphy is moving in."

"Moving in where?" he said.

"My house!"

His mouth fell open. "God! When?"

"I don't know, actually. I think soon."

"So, what, you'll come home one day and her stuff will be sprinkled all over the place?"

"They'll probably give me a heads-up."

Tris pushed his milkshake across the table to me. "I've been meaning to tell you, Elliott's over at my house all the time now."

"That's great! Do you sneak him in when your parents are out?"

"Sometimes, but he comes when they're home, too."

"And your dad hasn't had a meltdown?"

"He hasn't said one word. Sometimes he even asks me how my friend Elliott is doing."

"Does he know?"

"He must."

"Wow."

"I know."

We smiled at each other, and he said, "I wish we had more time to hang out, just the two of us."

"I know," I said. We were still whispering. My throat was getting hoarse. "Sometimes I think . . ."

"What?"

"I don't know. Nothing. I miss you."

Most of the time I'm sure I'll be with Grady forever. It's not that I imagine us being middle-aged with two kids. It's that I can't imagine breaking up with him. But sometimes, for a second, I think we probably will break up, because most high school couples do. And I *know* Tris and I will still be friends when we're 20, and 40, and forever. And if we're not still with Elliott and Grady, we'll regret all the time we spent with them and not each other in high school. We'll wish we'd taken more selfies together, and written exclusively about each other in our diaries (does Tris keep a diary?), and spent every afternoon at each other's houses, because we'll want as many shared memories as possible. I think Tris thinks the same thing. But we can't not want to be with our boyfriends all the time. We're trapped in an invisible jail built by our own hormones.

Saturday, October 21

Maybe I'm kidding myself, but I swear Grady almost told me he loves me. We weren't doing anything special, just sitting on the bench outside Strawberry Hills, chatting. Somehow we got to talking about our hidden talents, and I was showing him how I can wiggle my ears.

"Wait, let me pull my hair back so you can really see," I said. I held my hair in a ponytail and rearranged myself so he could see me in profile. When I'd finished, I turned back and said, "Pretty impressive, right?" He was smiling at me, and his face was full of affection.

"Chloe . . . ," he said, and my heart started racing. But then he chickened out, or maybe I'm wrong and he wasn't about to say it in the first place. He paused, and then all he said was, "I bet if I practiced, I could do that too," and we moved on to arguing about whether ear wiggling is innate or learned.

Sunday, October 22

Mr. and Mrs. Trevor took Bear to a monster truck rally, so I told Dad I was going to Hannah's and rode my bike over to Grady's through the cold fall day, my heart pounding with excitement. Grady opened the door, and I rushed in like someone was spying on us from the street (which someone may have been; in the suburbs, everyone's an informant).

"Hey," he said.

"Hey." We were both whispering.

Inside, the furniture, the walls, the air, it all seemed to be watching us. The silence pressed into my ears.

"Are you sure they're not coming back?" I said.

"They'll be gone until at least eight. My mom was all stressed out about Bear going to bed so late."

We didn't have sex right away. I was nervous, and Grady must have known. I felt better once we were in his bedroom with the door closed. His room is plain and boyish. Navy-blue duvet on the bed. White Christmas lights bordering the walls. A corkboard above his desk decorated with reproduced paintings on postcards: A man in a suit sitting sideways on a red velvet chair. A woman wearing angular sunglasses, a brown fur, and a wry expression. A young pregnant woman (a teen-ager?) eating a small piece of black fruit, I think a plum. I wanted to look at the postcards for a long time, and ask about them, but I didn't. This was maybe the art he loved best, and I didn't want to be intrusive. I wouldn't want him rifling through my bookshelf, questioning me.

We got under the covers, fully dressed, and chatted with our faces almost touching.

"Was it weird when your stepdad moved in?" I said.

"It's still weird. Sometimes he walks into a room and I'm like, 'What are *you* doing in my house?' and then I remember."

"I wish we could move in together," I said.

"You and me? Let's do it," he said.

"I'm sure our parents won't mind," I said.

Pause. *I love you,* I thought at him. *I love you,* he thought back at me, maybe.

Then I took my shirt off, and one thing led to another, just like they tell you it will in sex-ed class. He was on top, and my legs were up on his shoulders, and we were looking right at each other and grinning, and then he started moving faster, and he closed his eyes and looked tortured, which turns me on so much, and we were really going hard, and then the condom broke.

I'm the one who started laughing. I don't know why; it wasn't funny! But his eyes—they went perfectly round, like a fish's. And he pulled out so fast I heard a pop like a cork coming out of a bottle. I must have been in shock, because I got hysterical. At first Grady was just staring at me, and then I said, "Did you hear . . . ?" I couldn't speak, I was laughing so hard, and he started laughing too. "Did you hear . . . that pop?" Soon we were clutching each other's arms and there were tears running down my cheeks.

"What do we do?" I said, trying to calm down. "Is there something about Coke?"

"COKE?" he said.

"Like, putting Coke up your cooch? Doesn't it kill sperm?"

"That's got to be a myth," he said. "Anyway, I pulled out in time." But he was reaching for his phone, and I got mine out too. I was concentrating on typing, but I was also thanking my lucky stars that I can say "cooch" to my boyfriend. I couldn't say anything to Mac. I would have been horrified if he'd heard me peeing. I wanted to be like a plastic doll for him: odorless and dischargeless and bodily functionless.

After a few minutes of looking I said, "Coke doesn't work at all. Krest Bitter Lemon kind of does, but I think it might only be available in Nigeria."

Grady said, "Get your pants on. We're going to CVS."

"Why?"

"To get Plan B. You don't need a prescription."

"Don't I have to be 18?"

"Nope."

He's a much better Googler than I am.

It was exciting, riding our bikes fast, on a mission, speeding along past the colonial houses and the jogging moms who probably can't remember what it's like to need Plan B. When Grady was in front of me, I checked out his cute butt, and then I thought, *Is it wrong to be looking at my boyfriend's butt when the condom just broke? Shouldn't I be feeling worried?* I didn't feel worried, not at all. I felt glad I live in the modern age and can buy a pill at the same store that sells light-up toothbrushes and lotion with avocado oil.

We found the box on the shelf and brought it to the register. "I'll buy it," Grady said in a low voice.

"Thanks," I said.

"Wait, one sec," he said, and left me standing at the counter. The clerk was a bored-looking kid, maybe in his 20s, with thin black hair pulled into a ponytail. STUART, his name tag said. Stuart was busy texting with his phone half hidden under the register. I don't think he noticed me.

Grady came back with two pamplemousse LaCroix, a jumbo box of Junior Mints, and a giant package of new condoms. He had to say "excuse me" to get Stuart's attention.

Did Stuart smirk a tiny bit as he rang us up? Maybe, but I'm telling myself he didn't. And at least it was marginal enough that I wasn't sure either way.

In the parking lot, we got on our bikes and put on our helmets. Grady ripped open the box, handed me a white pill, then opened one of the LaCroix cans and gave it to me.

"Right here?" I said.

"As soon as possible, the directions said. And the second one 12 hours from now."

"Take a picture," I said.

He got out his phone. I held the pill between my thumb and index finger and did a "cheers" motion with the can.

"You look so cute," he said.

Plan B is not a big whoop. It stops your ovaries from releasing an egg, that's all. But is it OK that I don't feel anything about it? Not sad or wistful or upset or whatever? I feel like I took an Advil.

Monday, October 23

I woke up at 5 a.m. in a sweat. Going to sleep restarted my mind, and now I'm seeing clearly. THE CONDOM BROKE. Why was I so calm?

> *Chloe: Did you come inside*
> *me AT ALL on Sunday?*

Grady: Not really

            Chloe: ?????

Grady: Like a tiny bit before
the condom broke

I'd just started

            Chloe: Oh god

Grady: You took the pill!
You remembered to take the
second one right?

            Chloe: Yeah

Grady: So don't worry

I went to chemistry and didn't hear a single word Ms. Ronaldo said. When I looked at my phone after class was over, a text was waiting for me.

Grady: When are you supposed
to get your period?

Chloe: Are you worried
now????

Grady: No

Just wondering

Chloe: In a week I think

Give or take

Say something!

Grady: Sorry was googling

I don't think you could
have gotten pregnant
anyway

Unless you ovulated really
late

Chloe: omg ovulated

Grady: ?

Chloe: That word makes
me think of a chicken
pooping out an egg

Grady: That's basically
what it means

Chloe: What are we
gonna do

Grady: Don't worry
sweetie pie

Everything will be fine

Tuesday, October 24

The symptoms of pregnancy are nausea, food aversions, tender breasts, cramping, fatigue, backaches, headaches, and mood swings. (Do they have to say "tender breasts"? It makes it sound like someone's going to salt and pepper them and eat them with a fork.) I think I have each and every one of those symptoms. But did I have them before I started reading about them?

Wednesday, October 25

Grady came over after school. Without talking about it,

we stayed in the living room the whole time. For a while we played Bananagrams, and then we even did some homework! I almost wanted my dad to come home and catch us being wholesome.

While Grady was here, I felt calm. I was thinking, *Look, I took the first pill minutes after we had sex and the second one 12 hours later, on the dot. Anyway, it wasn't the right time in my cycle to get pregnant. Everything's fine.*

As soon as he left, I started freaking out. Yes, I took the pill, but it's only effective in eight out of nine cases—it says so right there in the instructions. And yes, I keep telling myself it wasn't the right time of the month, but am I sure about that? I don't even know when I'm actually supposed to get my period.

Then I went online, which made me freak out more. If I don't want to hear stories about teen moms who got pregnant after taking the morning-after pill, I shouldn't Google "teen moms who got pregnant after taking the morning-after pill."

Thursday, October 26

I came out of a kind of trance today to find Mr. Huang standing in front of me, snapping his fingers in my face to get my attention. I can't concentrate on anything but my symptoms, or phantom symptoms.

Friday, October 27

No one at our school has babies. But that doesn't mean no one gets pregnant. I can't believe I've never put this together before.

If I'm pregnant, there's nothing I can do. I can't have the baby. I can't get an abortion. I can't put the baby up for adoption. I mean, I *could* do any of those three things, but it's like being forced to walk through one of three doors and behind each door is a wall of fire.

Saturday, October 28

Grady: How's it going?

Chloe: I don't have my period if that's what you're asking

Grady: You'll get it

You were supposed to today?

Chloe: I'm not completely sure

I don't really write it down

Grady:
[link to a period tracking app]

Sunday, October 29

I'm not kidding, I'm cramping and my lower back hurts and my boobs feel bigger. Of course, that's what happens before I get my period, too. What kind of evolutionary boner led to pregnancy symptoms being exactly the same as period symptoms?

Monday, October 30

Still nothing. I hate the moron who was laughing hysterically when the condom broke. There's nothing funny about cells multiplying in my body at a miraculous and terrifying rate. I don't even want to look up what might be happening in there at this stage of a you-know-what. I really do feel sick, but maybe that's because I'm so upset and worried.

Tuesday, October 31

Tris: I talked Elliott out of the
Star Wars costumes, yessss

Want to meet outside at 7?

Chloe: See you there!

Chloe: We forgot about the Halloween dance

Grady: Whoops

Chloe: I told Tris we'd go

Grady: We should

It'll be a good distraction

But costumes???

We agreed to wear black hoodies and black jeans, and Grady said he'd stop by CVS on the way to school. We met in the parking lot at 6:30. Grady showed me his purchases: white and red face paint and two sets of vampire teeth. We pulled up a tutorial on YouTube and I did his face, scanning back through the video every few seconds to review the steps. Then he held up my pocket mirror so I could see, and I did my own face. I think my period/pregnancy panic was good for my makeup artistry: if I do say so myself, we looked terrifying when I was done. After we pulled up our hoods and walked toward the school, we kept scaring kids. Our regular clothes helped. If you saw us from the back or the side, we looked normal. Then we turned our faces and: VAMPIRES. Maybe our grim expressions helped too.

Tris and Elliott were waiting for us at the entrance, dressed as Mario (Tris) and Luigi (Elliott). They looked taken aback when they saw me and Grady.

"You didn't go the sexy nurse and doctor route, I see," Tris said.

"You guys look great," I said. "Where did you find those mustaches?"

"I lifted them from the costume department," Tris said. "The spirit gum I already had, obviously."

Elliott looked grumpy. "I feel ridiculous."

Tris patted his arm. "You look adorable."

"I don't want to look adorable," Elliott said. "I want to look menacing."

We all cheered up once we got inside and started eating mini candy bars.

"Do you want to dance?" Grady said when the first slow song came on.

Most people were still swaying back and forth at arm's length—it was only a few minutes into the event— but Grady and I clung to each other like we had seconds left to live.

"I'm scared," I said.

"I know," he said.

"Are you?"

"No," he said right away. "I know it'll be fine."

I squeezed him like I was trying to crush his vertebrae.

I hardly even noticed when Zach and Reese made their big entrance as Batman and Poison Ivy. They looked like chiseled celebrities, and I didn't care. I had bigger problems.

It happened when Tris and Elliott were enthusiastically busting a move to "Despacito" and Grady and I were gamely trying to look happy dancing next to them.

"What?" Grady said when he saw my face.

"Hang on," I said, and hurried to the bathroom. I found a free stall, yanked my jeans down, and there it was: BLOOD! Beautiful, gorgeous period blood!!!!! I felt like hugging my underpants.

I pulled my jeans back up and stuck my head around the stall door. "Does anyone have a tampon?" I called out. I was too happy to feel embarrassed. Jacqueline Foster said, "I do," and handed me a regular in a bright yellow wrapper.

When I was done, I speed-walked back to the cafeteria. I spotted Grady immediately, but he didn't see me yet. He was listening to Elliott say something, but from the far-off look in his eyes, I could tell he wasn't actually hearing him. I couldn't stand it, the sight of his innocent, still-worried face. I knew we were fine, but he didn't yet, and he wouldn't until I got to him. It felt like it took hours, pushing through the crowd of twerking kids. "Sorry to interrupt, Elliott," I said, and pulled Grady off to the side.

I cupped my hands around my mouth and whispered in his ear, "I got my period."

He grabbed my shoulders and pushed me back so he could see my face. "Really? Really??"

"Really!"

He kind of collapsed into a crouch, with his head resting in his hands. I crouched down next to him.

"Thank God," he said, looking at me.

"Thank God," I said.

"I was so scared," he said.

"You were? Why didn't you tell me?"

"We couldn't both be scared at the same time."

"But we were!"

"Well, I didn't want to make you more upset."

He put his hands on my face. I put my hands on his face. He looked so beautiful and sweet, even made up like a half-dead person with blood dripping from his bottom lip. Blood! Glorious blood!

"I love you," I said.

He started laughing and fell forward, taking me down with him. We were both lying on the floor when he said, "I love you too! I love you so much!"

If you want to have the best night of your life, just

have a pregnancy scare that ends during a school dance, tell your boyfriend you love him, and then spend the next two hours dancing wildly to express your inexpressible joy and relief.

Wednesday, November 1

The second day of my period is always the worst. I bleed like someone knifed me, and it feels like there's a bowling ball bearing down on my vagina. I couldn't get enough of it today. The more it hurt, the more I remembered I'm not pregnant.

Grady came over after school and we lay around staring at each other and saying "I love you" every few minutes.

"Was it mean that I was so excited not to be pregnant?" I said.

"Mean to who?"

"Our imaginary baby!"

"Our imaginary baby wants you to go to college," he said.

Nothing makes me happier than when he talks about the future like we'll still be together when it gets here.

Thursday, November 2

We agreed: no more sex until I'm on the pill. It'll be easy: I will never forget the terror of the past week, and therefore I will never again be tempted to have sex using only one form of protection.

Friday, November 3

I forgot how I lose control and turn into a feral animal whenever Grady breathes into my ear. It was close today, but we didn't Do It. We've added ear-breathing to the list of banned activities.

Saturday, November 4

Dad woke me up this morning banging around. I threw on clothes and ran downstairs.

"I'm trying to *sleep*," I said when I found him in the kitchen. He was standing on a stepstool, pulling a blender out of a high cabinet.

"Sorry, Your Majesty," he said. OK, maybe I sounded spoiled, but could he show a little sympathy? I'm a teenager. Nature wants me to fall asleep at midnight and wake up at 10 a.m. Every weekday, I spend the first four hours of school dying to go back to bed—we all do! We have two shots per week at catching up and feeling normal, and Dad was ruining one of them with his random blender banging.

"I thought you could start with the front hall closet," he said. "Maybe cull your outgrown coats. I think there are some old ones of your mother's, too. You might want to bring them over to her. I picked up some heavy-duty trash bags." He jerked his head toward a box on the island.

"Wait," I said. Light was dawning. "Is Miss Murphy moving in tomorrow?"

"We talked about this."

"You said the beginning of November. You didn't give me a date."

"I'm sure I did," he said. Oh, OK! As long as he was sure. Grown-ups are always so convinced that *you're* the scatterbrained one who's too absorbed in your phone to pay attention to the important things people are saying. They should take a look in the mirror!

"You didn't," I said, but he was rooting through the utensil drawer and failed to notice the fury in my voice.

"Well, we agree I said the beginning of November, and this is the beginning of November. Why do we have four ice cream scoops?"

It was actually easy to declutter in the beginning, because I was so angry. I yanked things off of hangers and threw them in the donation pile without a qualm. I got through the coats, winter accessories, umbrella pile, and shoe rack without even having coffee. Eating breakfast calmed me down, and after that I worked more slowly. It was even kind of fun, pulling out all our junk and organizing the stuff that remained. I got so into it that after a few hours I lost track of the purpose of all this tidying: to make room for my married dad's girlfriend to move into our house and stay forever.

Sunday, November 5

She's here. She didn't bring much stuff. Four giant suitcases. Five boxes. A few vases. Lots of books. A Keurig, a coral-colored blanket, two throw pillows with a palm leaf design. No furniture, though. When she watched Dad pull her stand mixer out of a box, she said, "That thing takes up a ton of counter space. We can junk it if you want." Of course he said no, no, he would get lots of use out of it, he was so sick of using his hand mixer, etc. She unpacked quickly and then left to visit her mother. Now she's back, we've had dinner, and I'm hiding in my room. I guess that's my plan: hide in my room until it's time to leave for college.

Monday, November 6

Woke up in the morning to the sound of Dad and Miss Murphy giggling in their bedroom. After I showered and got dressed, I went downstairs and caught him squeezing her butt in the kitchen as she poured oatmeal into a bowl. We all pretended I hadn't seen anything. Then at dinner, they got drunk on wine, held hands, and told stories about their college exploits. I'm the third wheel in my own house. It would be one thing if Miss Murphy were giving me inside information about which musical she's picked, but she won't even do that (I've already asked twice).

I think about what Noelle told me and try to be dignified. I don't want to be the sulky teenager who's jealous of her dad's girlfriend. So I act cheerful. I walk around smiling all the time. I answer politely whenever they speak to me, but I don't speak first. I can't tell if they're noticing any of this.

Tuesday, November 7

The house is still empty after school, thank God. Between 3 and 6, it's like Miss Murphy never moved in at all.

Wednesday, November 8

Grady came over and we hooked up for about four hours. It was like the good/bad old days: grinding with our pants on until I was ready to punch him, and then myself, from frustration. He wanted to go down on me. I was worried it would make me crave sex too much, but of course I was dying for him to do it, and then when I finally said yes, I made it about 30 seconds before I was like, "Let's just do it!" and he said, "We can't, we can't," and I said, "PLEASE," and it went on like that for a while until he said, "We have to stop," and *I actually cried a little.*

Thursday, November 9

Grady suggested hanging out but not hooking up, which sounded brilliant to me, but if anything, it was worse than yesterday. We sat in the kitchen eating Toll House cookies. So far, so good. Then he got some strawberry jelly on his thumb. He licked it off in a brisk, boyish way—he wasn't goofing around and pretending to be sexy about it or anything—and still, I swear to God, I almost had an orgasm. (I think. I'm still not entirely sure what they are or how you know you've had one.)

Friday, November 10

Chloe: What if I can't wait until the 22nd?

Or later actually because my test isn't until the afternoon, and I probably can't drive to planned parenthood right after

Grady: And then it's thanksgiving

Chloe: OH GOD I forgot

*Grady: We can make it
another few weeks*

*Chloe: I seriously don't think
we can*

Grady: I know

*Do Tris or Hannah
have their licenses?*

*Chloe: They haven't even
taken driver's ed yet*

Grady: Noelle?

Chloe: She does

But I can't ask her

*She's friends with Reese
again*

She'd tell her

*Anyone I asked might tell
anyone*

*And then everyone would
know we're DOING IT*

Grady: So?

*Chloe: So it might be fine or
people might freak out*

Grady: Really?

Even Grady doesn't get it. No guy possibly could. I'm already on thin ice because people think I was boning Mac when I was only a freshman. If it got out that I'm having sex with Reese's ex-boyfriend . . . it could be fine. You can't predict these things. But it could be bad. Like transfer-to-another-school bad. It would all depend on how Reese decided to react and whether someone was in the mood to make up a rumor about me ("Did you hear they were 69ing on the floor during the Halloween dance?"), and how many other girls had gotten caught messing around that month, and how scandalous their behavior was (the more scandalous the better; that way people wouldn't be starving for even vanilla stories like "girl and boy do it in girl's bedroom"). I'm not about to risk it.

Saturday, November 11

I haven't been practicing driving enough. That's all I need, to fail my test. Not that I will. I don't even know anyone who hasn't passed on the first try. But I might as well overprepare. Part of the problem is Miss Murphy. She's the one who used to take me out, since driving with Dad makes me too nervous, but I've been avoiding her recently. That has to stop. For the sake of having sex with my boyfriend, I'll deal with the awkwardness and ask her if she'll help me.

Sunday, November 12

Miss Murphy was so excited when I suggested going out in her Jeep. I said, "Whenever you have time," but she dropped her book and went to get her jacket that instant.

"When's your road test?" she said, once I'd backed out of the driveway.

"The twenty-second."

"That's coming right up."

"Yeah, it's soon."

"Whoa," she said. I'd accelerated like I was drag racing.

"Sorry," I said. "I'm kind of rusty."

"We haven't done this in a while," she said.

A silence fell. I was thinking about how strained things were between us and wondering how that had happened, when a few months ago I almost loved her. Maybe she was thinking something similar, because she said, "How is it, having me underfoot all the time?"

"It's fine," I said. I couldn't exactly say, *I feel like I'm in the way. You and Dad are still in the honeymoon phase, and no one wants a teenager on her honeymoon. Also, I keep thinking you'll leave sometime and things will go back to normal and then remembering that no, you're never going to leave again.*

Monday, November 13

I was heading through the living room to go to bed when Dad looked up from his laptop and said, "Hey, Chloe, I wanted to talk to you about Thanksgiving."

I paused behind the armchair. "What about it?"

"Marian's mother isn't up for going anywhere, so Marian was thinking of bringing food over to Woodcrest and eating with her there."

"Can her mom eat a big Thanksgiving dinner?" I was picturing Mrs. Murphy connected to IVs, spending most of the day asleep.

He looked impatient. "She'll probably be able to

manage a few bites. It's less about the food and more about being with her on a major holiday."

I squeezed the chair. I'd lied to him *once*. (Once that he knows about.) I'd said *one* mean thing about Miss Murphy's mom. I didn't run around tossing confetti in the air when he told me Miss Murphy was moving in. And because of these three crimes he's decided I'm a monster who hates cancer patients?

He was looking at me like I was supposed to say something. When I didn't, he said, "Would you like to go to Woodcrest as a family?"

"What, like you and me? And Miss Murphy? And miss Thanksgiving?"

"We wouldn't miss it," he said. "I'll make everything I usually do. It would be a venue change."

A great and terrible rage filled my heart. "No, thank you," I said politely.

He closed his laptop carefully. "That's disappointing."

"It is," I said.

"I understand how important traditions are—"

"You should go, though," I said. "Really. You go and be with Miss Murphy and her mother." He looked at me like he wasn't sure if I was being sincere or flip. (It was flip, but through such an amazing performance of sincerity that he'd never be able to call me on it.) "I'll go over to Mom's," I said. "I'd rather do that anyway."

I regretted saying it immediately, but I couldn't take it back, even when I saw pain wash over his face. I was still too mad.

Tuesday, November 14

Parents don't understand how annoying it is when they freak out with joy or anger or worry. They should be like living portraits that can hardly move their mouths or change expressions. Mom almost sang an aria when I called her to ask if I could come over for Thanksgiving. "Of *course*, sweetheart. I'm so delighted! I can't—to what do I owe this honor? No, don't tell me. I'd never ask you to impugn your father or his—well, I need to start digging up recipes! A meat thermometer, a roasting pan—let me get a pen."

"You don't have to make a big thing of it," I said. "Let's just order something." I was rigid with regret. Why had I even called her? I could have told Dad and Miss Murphy I was going to her house, and then, once they left for Woodcrest, sat at home alone eating cheese and crackers for dinner.

Wednesday, November 15

Grady, Tris, Elliott, Hannah, and I walked to McDonald's after school and had fries and milkshakes. We talked about what we're doing for Thanksgiving, whether Señora

Friedman has ever visited a Spanish-speaking country, if Luke Powers really beat someone up for touching his hockey bag, true-crime podcasts and whether listening to them is immoral because they repackage violent deaths as entertainment (guess what Hannah thought?), and those kids who tried to kill their friend for Slender Man and whether teenagers have always been this insane or the internet makes them worse. Now that I write it down, I see that it was kind of a grim conversation, but during it I felt so happy. There's nothing better than being with a bunch of kids your own age, as long as you like those kids.

Thursday, November 16

Miss Murphy took me out driving after dinner. It was the first time I'd gone at night, and it was terrifying. How do people do it? You can't see past your headlights! I don't think I got above 15 miles an hour the whole time.

Miss Murphy brought up Thanksgiving. I knew she would.

"I'm concerned," she said. "It was never my intention to mess up the day."

But that's what you're doing, I thought. "Don't worry," I said. "I like this plan better anyway."

"So you're truly happy going over to your mother's?"

"Yeah," I said. Like I was going to sell out my own

mother! My mom could be a war criminal and I still wouldn't do that.

Friday, November 17

Another driving session. I tried parallel parking for the first time and wound up about five feet from the curb.

Saturday, November 18

My mother has her teeth into Thanksgiving like a cat shaking a bird to death. She texts me at least five times every day with supposedly important questions. (What time do I want to come over? Will I spend the night? Do I have any new food restrictions she should know about?) She's trying so hard that I can't be mad, and it's uncomfortable. I wish she'd disappear again or get in my face like she did so many millions of times before she left, so that I could hate her again with a pure and righteous hatred.

Sunday, November 19

Dad and Miss Murphy asked if I wanted to play Scrabble tonight. I did want to, but I couldn't tell if they were truly in the mood to hang out with me or if they were inviting me out of a sense of obligation, so I said no, and they didn't press me. I brought Snickers up to my room and made him snuggle with me while I cried. I could have distracted myself with my phone, but instead

I chose to weep while looking at the moon and listening to the sound of affectionate laughter floating up from downstairs.

Monday, November 20

Met Noelle in the clearing during lunch. Now that it's cold out, she wears a floppy gray beanie and an oversized black wool coat. She always looks cool, always. How does she do it? I could ask her which fashion blogs she reads and where she gets her clothes, but she'd make fun of me, I'm pretty sure, and then give me some jokey answer as a way of avoiding the question. She never wants to admit to making an effort.

"I'm going to my mom's for Thanksgiving," I said.

"Jesus. Why?"

I told her about my dad and the Woodcrest thing.

She shook her head. "You're playing right into her hands."

"Whose?"

"Murphy's!"

"She didn't plan this."

"That's what you think."

The trees stood around us patiently, thinking their tree thoughts, not concerned with the sniping of two unhappy teenagers.

Was it possible that Miss Murphy was intentionally

trying to come between me and my father? I really didn't think so, but Noelle understands these things better than I do.

"When are you leaving for your dad's?" I said.

"After school on Wednesday."

"Dreading it?"

She looked up at the sky. "I have a feeling he might propose to his girlfriend. Maybe this weekend, maybe over Christmas."

"Oh my God," I said. "What makes you think that?"

"Lots of hints about having great news to share soon." She rolled her eyes. "Yeah, it's really great news that some 30-year-old gold digger is going to make him rewrite his will."

"Noelle!"

"Yes?" she said patiently.

She makes me feel so naive. I know it happens in movies, but I don't want to think the real world is like this, full of women who marry for money and kids who think about how big their inheritance will be when their parents die.

Tuesday, November 21

I HAD AN ORGASM! AND IT WAS GLORIOUS!!!!!!!

Here's what happened. Grady came over to say goodbye. He's going away until Monday, so we won't see each other for five whole days—so basically, an eternity. We lay in my bed staring into each other's eyes like he was about to move across the country. (He's actually going to an Airbnb in Vermont with his family and his mom's sister and her kids.)

Then we started talking about how impressive it is that we're not having sex. We were lying on my bed, which was risky, but we had all our clothes on, and we'd started to trust ourselves.

"I never thought we could do it," I said.

"I know." He patted his own back, then reached over and patted mine.

"Whenever I'm alone with you, I feel like I have to get naked or I'll die," I said. "Like, it feels like my clothes are cutting off my circulation and I can't breathe. And STILL, we haven't had sex!"

"Really, you feel like you're going to die?" He lifted himself up on one elbow and looked down at me. His eyes are deep-set, and when he's about to make a move on me, he narrows them until they're glittery crescents.

"Don't do the eye thing," I said.

"Then don't do the mouth thing," he said. I didn't even know I did a mouth thing!

To make a long story short, I got the condoms out of their hiding place in the front pocket of my *Lilo & Stitch* backpack from third grade, and we had sex, and it was over in approximately 10 seconds. "Oh man," Grady said. "It's been too long!"

I was so disappointed I wanted to cry, but of course I tried to be nice about it. "It's not a big deal," I said.

He groaned and pulled the duvet over his head. I pulled it back down and said, "Can I ask you something?" His eyes were shut, but he nodded. "You lasted way longer the first time we did it. Did you secretly have sex with someone else the day before?"

He opened his eyes and turned pink. "Uh, no. It was good timing, because I'd just . . . you know."

"What?"

"You know!"

He could tell I wasn't getting it, because he mimed jerking off.

"OH!" I said. "Oh. OK."

We were quiet for a while. Then he said, "I have a question too."

"Go ahead." I knew what he was going to say, and then he said it: "You're not having orgasms, right?"

I pulled the duvet over *my* head. He pulled it down and said, "You can tell me."

I covered my eyes with my hands. "I'm not sure."

"If you're not sure, you're not. But I have an idea!"

His idea was eating me out for approximately one hour. I kept feeling guilty that he'd been going for so long, and trying to haul him up by his armpits, and he kept waving me off. Once I said, "Your tongue's going to fall off," and he said, "I'm fine. Stop joking around and relax." So finally I did relax, and then some time passed, and then my legs started shaking, and then I saw the black sky covered in ocean waves, and then stars appeared in the water/sky, and then I got scared, and then I told myself to stop being scared, and then I had an orgasm, and if nothing good ever happens to me again, I can't complain, because Grady transformed my vagina from a papier-mâché donkey into an explosion of candy.

After I was done, I started screaming and laughing, and Grady grinned at me and said, "Not bad, right?" and naturally we had sex again.

I know old people were young once and presumably they got laid, but not like THIS. No one in the course of human history has ever felt the way Grady makes me feel.

Wednesday, November 22

I woke up terrified that somehow I'm pregnant. But that makes no sense, right? The condom didn't break! I'm so nervous, I have to keep running to the bathroom. I've probably peed 16 times and it's only 3 p.m.

My driving test is in one hour. Miss Murphy took me out for parallel parking practice last night after dinner, and I understand why, after my horrible performance last week. But I've watched a bunch of videos explaining how to do it, and more importantly, I have to pass this test, because I have to drive myself to get a pill prescription. I can't be this scared all the time, and obviously I can't be trusted not to have sex. Necessity is the mother of perfect parallel parking. I'll be fine.

Thursday, November 23

I AM DELUSIONAL. Of course I flunked!!!!! I mean, of COURSE I did. And I was shocked! I really, truly thought that wanting to pass the test so badly would magically turn me into a skilled driver.

Miss Murphy sat in the back, and the examiner, Andre, sat in the front. He was a cheerful guy with a potbelly. Before we got in the car, he hiked up his pants to show me his socks: brown with a turkey pattern.

The on-the-road part was OK, except for one moment when I drifted a tiny bit too close to oncoming traffic and Andre sucked in his breath. But the parking lot section did not go well. First I ran over not one but two orange cones while I tried to parallel park. Then Andre asked me to turn on the headlights, which I really do know how to do, but I was so flustered after the parking mishap that I turned on the windshield wipers instead, and then I couldn't figure out how to turn them off. When I finally managed it, Andre said I could switch off the ignition, and we all sat in silence for a second.

"Well, Ms. Snow, I'm truly sorry to do this to you the day before Thanksgiving," Andre said. "But I'm afraid I can't pass you this time."

While he listed my mistakes (or "things to work on," as he put it), I started crying, not really because I was upset or embarrassed, but because he was being so nice. I looked down and caught a glimpse of his sock turkeys, and that made it worse.

"You can take another test as soon as you want," he said. "But why not practice a little more first?"

"I will," I said. He pretended not to notice my tears, which is the kindest thing he could have done.

I got a 100% on the written test, not that it matters.

On the way home Miss Murphy asked me if I could think of anything that would cheer me up, and I said, "Yes. Tell me what the musical is," but she just laughed and said, "I was thinking more along the lines of Sour Patch Kids."

Dad is currently downstairs frying bacon for the green beans. He set his alarm for 5 a.m. so he could get all his cooking done. He asked if I wanted to take food over to Mom's, which I don't think he meant in a mean way, but what is he thinking? How would Mom feel if I showed up with a premade dinner when she's probably been cooking since 5 a.m. too?

My hands are clammy and my heart is racing. I'm *nervous* to see my own mother. How sick is that?

Friday, November 24

Yesterday was . . . I'm not sure what it was.

When I showed up on my bike, the parking lot in front of Mom's condo was almost empty. I guess all the other divorced people who live in her complex have better places to be on Thanksgiving. It gave me a spooky feeling, walking up past the other units knowing they were most likely empty.

"Honey!" Mom said when she opened the door. "You *came!*" She was wearing a floor-length high-waisted skirt and a crop top that I had to admit looked great on her.

"Thanks for having me," I said, and handed her the bag of blue Lindt chocolates I picked up at CVS a few days ago. She blinked fast. Maybe she was thinking the same thing I was, that "thanks for having me" sounded like something you'd say to your friend's mom.

"It looks nice in here," I said, once we were inside. She'd hung up some canvas prints. One said BE A WARRIOR / NOT A WORRIER, but that was the only annoying one. The others were abstract prints. In the living room, she'd added a small dining room table, which was set for dinner with magenta place mats and striped nap-kins. There were dark purple and red flowers in a vase and a pillar candle on a green dish. Something seemed strange, but I couldn't figure out what. Maybe it was just the fact that I was in my mom's weird new apartment, surrounded by her weird new stuff. I watched her mak-ing drinks: seltzer with a splash of cranberry juice and a lime garnish. She looked excited and nervous. I didn't forgive her for anything, but it was hard not to respond to all this trying.

Then she said, "The food arrived a minute ago. Let me get it on plates before it cools off," and I knew what was strange: I was smelling Thai takeout.

I got a lump in my throat. I like Thai. I love Thai! But not on Thanksgiving. On Thanksgiving I want tur-key and cranberry sauce and potatoes with four sticks of butter mashed into them, and I don't care if that's babyish or spoiled. I don't think it is! I don't think it's too much to expect Thanksgiving dinner if your mother invites you over for Thanksgiving dinner! God, MY MOTHER. How I loathed her as she pulled to-go con-tainers out of a brown paper bag with a happy smile on her stupid face. "Fried spring rolls, green papaya salad, panang curry, pad thai with shrimp, and kee mao with chicken. All your favorites!"

She glanced over at me, and the smile faded from

her face. "What's wrong," she said. She wasn't asking a question. My heart beat faster. Her chilly voice, her face like a mask: she was angry. It was only a matter of time before she lost it. I'd already almost forgotten this part, the worst part, but also the most exciting: the space between the moment you realize it's coming and the moment it comes. Every time, you think maybe you can tiptoe over the eggshells skillfully enough that none of them will break, but every time, you're wrong.

"You said you wanted to order something," she said. "Remember? You explicitly asked me not to cook, in fact."

This is another thing she does. She quotes you back to yourself, and you think, No, *that's wrong; she's twisting my words.* But it's not like you have a transcript of what you said, and you think, *DID I say that?* You start wondering if you really are to blame.

She was holding a black container with a translucent top, squeezing it a little. Was she going to throw it against the wall?

"I should go," I said. I thought saying that would flip her switch and she'd come toward me with her eyes darting back and forth, spitting insults in her low, I'm-not-yelling-so-this-is-not-abusive voice, but instead the anger left her face.

"No!" she said. "Please don't leave."

Somehow I'd made it over the eggshells. She wasn't going to rage at me. I'd saved myself by threatening to leave. I really had meant to go, but seeing the desperation on her face, I thought maybe it would be cruel to take off. I was wondering what to do—bike home to an empty house, or stay and try to choke down some spring rolls?—when suddenly I had to rush to the bathroom. When I tried to pee, almost nothing came out, and it *hurt*. It burned.

I stayed on the toilet for a minute. Everything around me was pink: the tiles, the vanity, the walls. How had I wound up here, in a pig-colored half bath, hiding from my mother, peeing fire? I stared down at my own bare knees, which at least were a familiar sight. If only I hadn't left my phone in the living room. I was dying to text Noelle, or Grady, or Tris, or Hannah. "I hate my mother," I would write, and they'd respond with something sympathetic or funny.

I decided not to say anything about the burning, have dinner, and get home as quickly as I could. "Sorry about before," I said when I got back to the living room. "I'm hungry. Let's eat." But we'd only had a few bites when I had to run to the bathroom again, and this time I peed blood. I was too scared not to tell Mom.

"Oh, sweetie," she said. "Are you having sex?" She was sitting at the table, holding her fork, looking up at me with a sympathetic expression. I didn't respond right away; I was too shocked. How had she guessed?

"You know what, I rescind the question," she said. "I don't want to invade your privacy. You're a mature person. I'll just say this: sexually active women sometimes get UTIs. Urinary tract infections. They're very uncomfortable, but if they're treated promptly, they're not at all dangerous. Do you have an ob-gyn?"

"I don't think so," I said.

"Who's your doctor?"

"Dr. Shibutani."

"So your father still has you seeing your childhood pediatrician!" she said brightly.

"I haven't asked him to switch," I said. "Hang on." I ran back to the bathroom. It was hard not to grunt or shriek. I didn't want to pee, so I was clenching against it, but I felt an irrepressible urge to, and when finally I forced myself, curled over like a shrimp, clutching the toilet seat with both hands, a few measly drops of blood came out. I wanted to stay in the bathroom forever, and I also wanted to never pee again.

When I came out, Mom was on the phone. "If it weren't urgent, I wouldn't be calling." She held up one finger to me. "I appreciate that. Happy Thanksgiving."

She hung up and said, "We may have to wait a while. In the meantime, you need to drink water—" Her phone rang. "Dr. Zimmerman! I'm so sorry to bother you on the holiday. I'll make it brief; I have a UTI. Yes, absolutely positive. The frequent urination, the burning . . . Would you? Oh, that's fabulous. On Court Road? Exactly. Thanks a million. You too. I will! Take care."

She set her phone down with a flourish. "All set! I'll head over to pick up the prescription now. She said she'll call it in right away."

"But are you sure I have a UTI? What if it's something else?"

She waved her hand. "I'm sure. And if I'm wrong, which I'm not, the worst that'll happen is you'll have a teeny course of Cipro. Not great for your flora, but I'll buy some probiotics while I'm at the pharmacy."

As she leaned over to pull on her boots, she said, "If you don't object, I'd like to take you to a proper doctor next week. And I'm not assuming anything, but you might want to talk to her about birth control options." She flipped upright, making her hair fly over her head in an arc, and smiled at me. She looked flushed, probably with triumph at her own amazing parenting.

She shut the door and I heard her walk down the outside stairs. Then footsteps ascended and she reappeared. "Essential tip!" she said. "Pee right after you have sex. I'm not talking about 20 minutes. I'm talking about right away. Peeing beforehand doesn't hurt either."

After she'd left for real, I had to run to the bathroom again. I brought my phone this time, but I didn't know what to text anyone. "My mother scared me but then saved me"? "Sex can make you pee blood"? In the end I sent around some turkeys and hearts and left it at that.

Saturday, November 25

I know it's probably not responsible of my mother to lie to her doctor to get a prescription for me for an infection she's not even sure I have, but I'm so glad she did, because I'm cured! I never even knew I should feel grateful for not peeing bloody fire, but now I know, and I'll never forget.

Sunday, November 26

Noelle texted me that her dad hasn't proposed to his girlfriend.

> Noelle: And I don't think he will
> at Christmas either
>
> His "great news" is he got a
> promotion
>
> And his GF hasn't been over
> here much

Chloe: That's good right?

Noelle: Yeah it's good

What's going on with you?

It seemed like a lot to get into, so I said "same old, same old" and left it at that.

Monday, November 27

GRADY'S BACK! GRADY'S BACK! GRADY'S BAAAAAACK! Seeing his grinning face in the hall—ah! We didn't make out or anything—we just hugged each other—but still, people yelled, "Get a room!" and "PDA alert!" Reese happened to be passing by, and she said, "Awwwwww!" like we were a basket full of puppies. I'm sure she hates seeing us together—who would enjoy watching her ex-boyfriend with his new girlfriend?—but she'd never show it. Instead she's condescending in such a sweet way, you'd sound nuts if you commented on it.

But who cares about Reese? Everything's coming up roses: I can pee like a normal human, Grady's back, and I got my period in chemistry class!

My diary is like vagina vagina pregnancy scare bleeding peeing bloody bloody vagina blood. And WHAT OF

IT? I'm 16, I have a body, and I'm having sex. I refuse to feel embarrassed.

Tuesday, November 28

I did homework for hours and hours without looking at my phone once. I *love* doing homework this year. It's a relief, thinking about World War II and binomials instead of my parents, my reproductive system, even Grady. I open my textbook or start making flash cards, and after a few minutes my brain feels less like a bucket of screws someone's violently shaking and more like the calm-down jar Mr. Grayson keeps on the bench outside his office: a handful of purple glitter moving gently through liquid. My grades have never been better.

Wednesday, November 29

My mother made me an ob-gyn appointment for tomorrow. I thought I wanted to go, and I guess I still do, but I'm so nervous. Will the doctor ask me about my sex life? Will she want to know, like, how many times a week I do it? Will she need to stick her fingers or some scary device inside my cooch? Will she act like I should be ashamed of myself? Will she tell my mother I'm going on birth control? Will she warn me how hard it is to be a teen mom?

Thursday, November 30

Oh my stars and garters, I'm getting an IUD! As soon as Dr. Stauffer walked in, I relaxed. She had a tan, a short haircut, and a brisk vibe. She couldn't have been less interested in my sex life. I mean, she did ask if I'm sexually active, how many partners I have, whether we use condoms, etc., but she said it like she was asking if I eat cereal for breakfast, what kind I prefer, and whether I put skim, 2%, or full-fat milk on it. Friendly but not fascinated. The internal exam was fine. It took about 30 seconds and didn't hurt. She said condoms can fail and she would suggest a second form of birth control—was that something I'd consider? I nodded and said, "Like the pill?"

She said, "The pill is an option, but you have to take it faithfully at the same time every day. If that might be a challenge for you, I'd suggest an IUD. It's a small T-shaped device that's inserted into your uterus. Depending on the kind we go with, it will protect you from pregnancy for between three and ten years."

Three and ten YEARS? What was the catch? Would it hurt? She said some women experience pretty bad cramping and some spotting, but for others it feels like nothing more than a quick pinch.

I chose the copper one, because she asked if it would worry me to stop getting my period entirely, and I said yes. I had to leave a urine sample and get blood drawn so they could run some tests, and I'll go back on Monday to get the IUD inserted if everything looks good.

I walked out of there throwing off sparks of sunshine. I even agreed to go to a vegan restaurant with Mom after the appointment. I ate a whole plate of seitan and my joy turned it into steak. GOD BLESS MODERN MEDICINE!

Friday, December 1

Chloe: I'm getting an IUD!

Grady: Please hold, Googling

Wow awesome!

Wait but how?

Chloe: My mom took me

Grady: !!!!!!!!!!

Chloe: I know

We have to keep using condoms

Dr. Stauffer said so

Grady: I would never go
against Dr. Stauffer's advice

Also the internet says the
same thing

Chloe: No more stressing
until I'm 26

It's like a miracle

Grady: That's so good

You're lucky your mom
was cool about it

Chloe: So lucky

Saturday, December 2

This morning I went online, filled out a volunteer application form, and emailed it to Planned Parenthood. I won the lottery of life: My dad has health insurance, and it covers me. My mom isn't judgmental about sex. She offered to take me to an understanding doctor and drove me to the appointment in her leased Jetta, which she and my dad are rich enough to pay for. It's not fair that I have all these things and most girls don't. Most grown women don't! And insurance and Jettas are the least of it: I'm white, I'm straight, I'm vaguely Protestant—my parents don't care that actually I'm an atheist. The only way I could be more privileged is if I were a dude. I realize doing a few hours of volunteer work here and there won't exactly pay off my debt. But it's better than sitting on my butt doing nothing but tweeting in support of protesters and resisters and all the other good guys. I have to do something real, even if it's a tiny something.

Sunday, December 3

Mom asked if I wanted to drive to the city and walk past the holiday windows, and I had to say yes, given recent developments. It was about 60 degrees out, so it was hard to get in the spirit, but we didn't have a terrible time. It was good to be in a crowd of people and to have something to look at—it took the pressure off. In front of a window showing mannequins dressed entirely in red and green costume jewelry, Mom said, "'Crass' is too mild a word to describe this orgy of commercialism," which was such a classic Veronica thing to say I wished my dad were there to hear it. Whenever she annoyed me, I silently chanted, *The IUD, the IUD, the IUD*, and that gave me patience.

Monday, December 4

The eagle has landed in my uterus! The days of pregnancy scares are over! I'm writing this diary entry in the throes of horrible cramps, but who cares! I HAVE AN IUD!

Tuesday, December 5

Grady and I had sex after school and then split almost a whole huge carton of lemonade and ate Double Stuf Oreos in bed. Then we fell asleep for an hour by accident and had to rush through saying goodbye so we wouldn't get caught. I changed clothes, washed my face, and brushed my hair after Grady left, but still, my lips were all swollen. If Miss Murphy and Dad weren't so busy sparkling at each other over their wine at dinner every night, they might notice that I'm shagging my boyfriend. So, actually, I guess it's good for me that they're so in love.

Wednesday, December 6

I got an email from Planned Parenthood—I'm going to phonebank! Apparently that means calling people, telling them about whatever that week's biggest political threats are, and asking them to call their representatives. I can do it from home, and I'm going to aim for four hours a week. I'm scared. I'll have a script, and I'll be reaching out to Planned Parenthood supporters, so it's not like anyone will yell at me (unless I get connected with someone who's anti-PP, which the guide I got said might happen very occasionally). The problem is, I'm not used to talking on the phone. If I could text these people, that would be one thing. But transmitting my voice to them and hearing their voices in my ear, saying things to me that I then have to respond to?! Terrifying.

Thursday, December 7

I DID IT. Two hours of it! I sat in my room with Snickers and a big tumbler of water, and I phonebanked. It probably took five years off my life, because my heart was pounding uncontrollably the entire time. Almost no one picked up. I made 38 calls and talked to a grand total of three humans. Two people answered and then rushed me off the phone, and one woman was extremely nice and said she would call her senator. That's something, but it's not too much.

Friday, December 8

I stayed in tonight to finish my four hours. This time zero people said they'd call. I accomplished nothing.

Did I pick the wrong cause? Could I do more for a group that's trying to raise carbon taxes, or protest police brutality, or protect the freedom of the press, or outlaw assault weapons? There's so much that's wrong with the world. I want use my measly four hours a week to do the most good I can.

Saturday, December 9

Noelle stopped by my house, which she rarely does. As soon as we were alone in my bedroom, she said, "Don't tell anyone, but Reese and Zach broke up last night."

"WHAT? Are you sure?" I didn't mention it, because I didn't want to sound like a stalker, but they'd posted a selfie only a few days ago—a black-and-white shot of them in profile with their foreheads pressed together, captioned "Show me your scars and I won't walk away #beyonce #wisdom."

She shrugged.

"What happened?" I asked.

"They never see each other. He's always with the band, and she has student council."

I snorted. The old conflicting schedules excuse! "Noelle. Come on. That's not the real reason."

She looked mysterious.

"Who got dumped?"

She said nothing.

"Is she supposed to be the good guy? So far you're not making me think she's the good guy."

Noelle narrowed her eyes at me. What did narrowed eyes mean in this context?

"Message received," I said. "The official story is they mutually decided to break up. And, what, is this like the soft launch? Are you supposed to tell a few people and swear them to secrecy, knowing they'll tell everyone?"

"I gotta go," she said. "Later, tater."

She gave me a hug and ran down the stairs. I love Noelle, but I'll never understand why she's happy to be Reese's minion.

Sunday, December 10

Tris and I got together to do homework, but within 10 minutes we were discussing Reese and Zach, and somehow from there we segued into speculating about which musical Miss Murphy will choose, Googling "most popular high school musicals" and watching clips of old movies on YouTube.

"Are those bangs, or is the front section of her hair curled into, like, a tube?" I said, watching Judy Garland sing on a trolley.

"There's no way Murphy would pick this show," Tris said. "The chorus disappears for hours at a time."

"Maybe she'll blow our minds and go with something really modern."

"No way. It'll probably be *Guys and Dolls* or *On the Town*. Can't you take a quick peek at her email and see if you can find anything?"

"'A quick peek at her email'?" I said. "Are you serious?"

"If her phone's lying on the counter or something. I'm not saying you should go through her bag."

"I wish Hannah were here," I said. "She would love to hear this suggestion. Anyway, you have nothing to worry about. You'd be the lead even if you sang the ABCs for your audition song. I'm the one who should be sweating it."

"This year will be different," Tris said. "I'm not worried for you."

"I don't even care," I said. "If I'm in the chorus, I'll get to spend more time hanging out with Grady." But of course that's not true. I care a ton.

Monday, December 11

Reese came up to me and Grady in the hall and gave us both long hugs.

"You guys heard what happened, right?" she said.

We nodded.

"With me and Zach?" she added, which, since we'd

just nodded, made us seem like Reese obsessives who assume every question has to do with her, and not, say, national politics or world events.

"Are you OK?" I said.

"I'm devastated, but it was the right decision," she said. "We weren't meant to be." She formed a heart with her thumbs and index fingers and then broke it apart while pouting. She didn't seem that devastated to me. Truly crushed people don't pout cutely.

"Can I just tell you something?" she said, and grabbed one of my arms and one of Grady's. "You guys are fully my couple inspiration. You seem so in love and happy. Are you?"

"Uh, yeah," I said. If I sounded unsure, it was because (a) I was not prepared for Grady's ex-girlfriend to ask a question like that and (b) Reese is constantly working an angle, and I didn't know what this one was. Would I fall into her trap if I said yes, or no?

Grady leaned sideways and tapped my head with his. "Chloe's not bad," he said. "I think it's going OK."

Reese said, "You're adorable together. Seriously, adorable," and walked away while blowing us a kiss.

I turned to Grady. "'Not bad'? 'Going OK'?"

"What?"

"Why would you say that??"

"I was joking!"

I gave him an outraged look.

He said, "It's funny because it's obviously an understatement! You were just telling me a fancy word for that, like, a week ago!"

"Litotes."

"Yeah!"

"Litotes would be the 'not bad' part," I said. "Because it's a negative expressing . . . Forget it! Don't you see that Reese is going to think you're not actually into me?"

"Chloe, come on."

I didn't say anything.

"Chloe," he said.

"It's fine," I said. "It's not a big deal."

And it's probably not. I'm being paranoid.

Tuesday, December 12

I went to find Grady at his locker, and who should be there but Reese, kneeling at his feet, looking through his backpack. "Hey!" she said when she saw me. "I'm stealing gum." She found his Eclipse and popped out a rectangle. "Thanks, buddy," she said, and gave him a high five. On her way down the hall, she called, "See you guys!"

My heart was racing, but I tried to sound calm. "That was weird," I said.

Grady was checking his phone. "Mmm."

"Asking for gum? Pretty flirty."

He slipped his phone into his back pocket and shrugged. "She probably has built-up flirting power now that she's not with Zach, and she's discharging it randomly."

"Uh-huh."

He put his arm around me. "You're not worried, are you?"

I didn't want to sound pathetic. "Nah," I said.

He kept looking into my face, like he was giving me time to tell him the truth, but I didn't.

Wednesday, December 13

Miss Murphy drove me to the mall so I could do my Christmas shopping. It was quiet in the car, and for once it wasn't because I was feeling awkward around her. This time I was silently ruminating about Reese.

I really doubt she'd want to get back together with Grady. It wouldn't be on-brand. If only for the sake of her Instagram flow, she has to move ever upward in her dude selection. First a cute underclassman (Grady), then a hot upperclassman (Zach), now what? A college kid, probably.

Besides, even if she did want him back . . . he'd say no, right?

I think he would.

I'm almost positive he would.

Anyway, why am I freaking out? She took a piece of gum out of his backpack. It's not like she's giving him slow up-and-down looks while biting her lip or, like, sexting him.

Thursday, December 14

In the library there's a poster of a dog looking scared. Along the bottom it reads, JUST BECAUSE YOU'RE PARANOID DOESN'T MEAN THEY AREN'T AFTER YOU—Joseph Heller, *Catch-22*. I've always thought it's an odd and depressing choice for a school library, but today I realized I should have been soaking in its wisdom all along.

Reese sat with me and Grady at lunch. Plopped down onto the seat next to him like it was no big deal, even though her squad members were at their usual table in the back, waiting for her, keeping her central spot open. I saw them looking over at us with interest.

"Mind if I join you lovebirds?" she said, smiling.

"Not at all," I said. I'm so scared of her, that's the thing. She's a poisonous snake. She could sink her fangs into me at any moment. I want her to like me, even though I can't stand her.

"How's it going?" Grady said, and took a big bite of his turkey sandwich.

"It's hard," she said. "I'd already gotten Zach a

Christmas present. I saw it in my closet yesterday and, like, burst into tears." She bit into a baby carrot and smiled at Grady. "Remember what I gave *you* last Christmas?" She elbowed him in the ribs, then looked across the table at me. "Sorry, Chloe. I forgot you were sitting there!"

I'm not imagining things. She wants him back.

Friday, December 15

> Chloe: *Tell me what she gave you for Christmas*

Grady: No

> Chloe: *GRADY*

Grady: NO

It's nothing bad

But it's one of those things you don't want to picture

Like I don't want to picture certain things you did with Mac

You know?

Chloe: Don't drag Mac into this

Grady: Ugh sorry didn't mean to pick on your precious Mac

Chloe: He's not my precious anything! Don't turn this around

Grady: Sorry I'm just frustrated

Chloe: The longer we talk about this the worse it gets

Grady: I agree so let's stop

Chloe: We can as soon as you tell me

Grady: Lingerie

Chloe: ?

Grady: She came over in

Wait no

It's such a bad idea to tell
you this

          Chloe: You can't stop now

Grady: She came over in
her winter coat and she was
naked underneath except for
her bra and panties

          Chloe: What did they
          look like?

Grady: UGHHHHH

Red with white fur

Like Santa I guess

Honestly it was cheesy and I
was embarrassed

Chloe: I'm sure

Grady: Whatever it's the
truth Chloe

I shouldn't have made him tell me. I knew that even before I did it. He's right: now I can't stop picturing Reese unzipping her coat, sliding it off, and smiling at him with her hands on her hips, watching him watch her. I wonder if he looked shocked, or excited, or overwhelmed. I wonder if he said, "Oh my God," or "You're so beautiful," or "C'mere." I know they didn't have sex, but I bet they did everything else.

Googling "Victoria's Secret christmas lingerie santa" was another stupid idea.

Saturday, December 16

Chloe: Am I still coming
over to help decorate the
tree?

Grady: Do you want to?

Chloe: Yeah I guess

Grady: Then come I guess

We barely looked at each other when I got to his house. Mrs. Trevor noticed something was up, and she tried to lighten the mood by passing out green hats with felt elf ears sewn onto the sides. Grady and I put them on, but nothing changed. We were still two kids in a fight, not smiling, refusing to make eye contact. The only difference was that now we looked like angry elves. Bear sang, "Jingle bells, Batman smells, Robin laid an egg," and then glanced at me with a shy, proud smile. Mr. Trevor sat on the couch looking at his phone, ignoring all of us.

Mrs. Trevor didn't even comment when we marched upstairs to Grady's bedroom. She must have known we were going to fight, not mess around.

I sat on his desk chair. He leaned against the bureau and crossed his arms.

"Are you this mad about the Santa thing?" he said.

"The lingerie thing," I said. "And no."

"We've both dated other people," he said. "What do you want me to do, build a time machine?"

"I *want* you to admit that Reese likes you again."

"I really don't—"

"Admit it!"

"Fine! She likes me again!"

Silence. Grady pulled a tissue from the box on his bureau and started ripping it into tiny pieces. I thought

I'd feel better as soon as I got him to acknowledge the obvious truth, but I felt worse.

Grady stopped destroying the tissue and looked at me. "She can't magically . . . do anything."

"She can, though."

"Like what, hypnotize me?"

"Yes!"

He rolled his eyes. "Give me some credit, dude."

"Don't call me 'dude,' dude."

Immediately I regretted snapping at him. He's right: she can't use mind control to make him dump me. And I can't start fighting with him because I'm stressed about this. That's exactly what she wants to make me do.

I stood up, walked over to him, and leaned my forehead against his collarbone. "I'm sorry I was texting you mean things yesterday."

"It's OK." He sighed and rubbed my back. "Nothing bad is happening."

"I know. I know."

We stood there without talking for a while. Downstairs, Bear screamed, "Santa IS a snowman, I promise you!" Neither of us laughed—that's how somber the mood was.

Sunday, December 17

No. No no no no no no no. This isn't what I think it is.

Miss Murphy isn't pregnant.

Monday, December 18

I'm imagining things.

Yesterday she made oatmeal for breakfast. Nothing unusual about that; it's what she always has. But when it was ready, she looked down at it, took a sharp breath in through her nostrils, and scraped it into the organics bin.

That's all my evidence. It doesn't mean anything. Maybe she was upset about her mom or something that happened at school and she lost her appetite.

Tuesday, December 19

She threw up this morning.

Wednesday, December 20

"Do you think I'm overreacting?" I asked Grady.

We were in my bed with the duvet pulled all the way over our heads. It was stifling, but I didn't want to see the world.

"No. It's a big deal. I hated the idea of Bear at first. But that's before I knew he was Bear. Once you see the baby and get to know him, it'll be different."

"Or her," I said.

"Right," he said. "Or her."

"Maybe she's not even pregnant," I said.

"Yeah, totally," he said. He sounded kind, which meant he thought there was no way she wasn't pregnant.

I kissed him. Silver lining: obsessing about Miss Murphy's reproductive status has blotted out my fixation on Reese and made things normal between me and Grady.

"Should I ask them about it?" I said.

"I'd say no. They probably want to wait to be sure it sticks before they tell you."

"Oh. Right."

I didn't think about the chance that Miss Murphy could have a miscarriage. Of course I don't wish for that. It would be terrible for her, and anyway, it would only delay the inevitable. If she and my dad want to have a baby, they'll have one.

But I don't want them to have one. My dad doesn't even like me anymore. If he's comparing me to a baby who's too young to sass him or stomp up the stairs when she's mad, he'll really start to hate me.

"Hey, I heard some news you'll like," Grady said.

"Go on."

"Elliott got it from Lianna, so you know it's real."

"Tell me!"

"Reese is going to Europe with her parents for two weeks."

"WHAT?"

"Yep. All of winter break plus the next week. She won't be back until the eighth or something."

I flung the duvet off of us and bounced up and down on the bed on my knees.

"It's a Christmas miracle!" I said.

"Told you you'd like it!"

What a relief, knowing I can relax and let my guard down for HALF A MONTH!

Thursday, December 21

Miss Murphy's started eating dry cereal for breakfast. Not even something grown-ups pretend to like, such as Kashi. FROOT LOOPS. Case closed. If you're in your mid-30s, you don't eat half a box of Froot Loops in the morning unless you're knocked up.

When we were all at the beach last summer, I thought I'd kind of like it if Miss Murphy moved in. More company for me. More noise around the house. It was abstract then. Now she's here, and it's too concrete. The smells! I didn't think of the smells. I'm used to my parents' gross smells, but I can't handle a stranger's. It's not that she's a stinky person. She's normal. But normal people have coffee breath. They fart when they think no one's about to walk into the room, and then someone does. ME. If they have morning sickness, they barf in the closest bathroom they can find, and a few minutes later an innocent teenager walks in to get a Kleenex, smells vomit, and almost throws up herself. And what's a baby going to smell like??

Friday, December 22

I went to Grady's to see Bear, because I love Bear, and I wanted to remind myself that having a much younger sibling could be fun. Unfortunately, he was in a terrible mood (Mrs. Trevor said he hadn't napped, which I guess is a big problem) and he had a meltdown when Grady asked him if he wanted Pirate's Booty or Goldfish for his snack. "I CAN'T CHOOSE!" he screamed, and lay facedown on the floor, weeping until he'd made a little puddle under his eyes. When Grady tried to pick him up, he reared back violently and smashed Grady's chin with the back of his head, which made him cry harder. Poor little guy. I know this was one bad hour, not a harbinger of my future. I've read too many books, that's the problem. I'm seeing portents where there are none.

Maybe it'll be a girl and I can teach her how to . . . What girly stuff do I know how to do? I'm terrible at braiding my hair and doing my makeup. I'm good at reading. OK, I can read to her. Or him. I could also read to a boy. What do boys like? Trucks?

It's a moot point. By the time this kid is one, I'll be leaving for college.

So I'll leave for school and Dad will start all over again and redo his whole life, but correctly this time? He'll have a wife who doesn't seethe at him and a son or daughter who will probably grow up to be fascinated by the law and math? God, the thought makes me want to kick him in the nuts. I should be enough for him.

Saturday, December 23

According to her Instagram, Reese is currently boarding a plane bound for Rome! She'll be away for 14 glorious days! For two whole weeks, she can't take Grady's gum, remind him of past sexytimes, give him coy little looks, or hit on him in any way. I feel so free!

Sunday, December 24

Went to Mom's to exchange presents. There was a sad little tree in the corner, and she was playing Bing Crosby from her phone—she doesn't have real speakers. She got me some clothes that look like things she'd wear. I got her a memoir by some lady who loves yoga. We talked about current events. It was horrible from beginning to end, in other words.

Monday, December 25

Seriously, I'm the most self-absorbed, clueless, whiny person on planet Earth.

We went to Woodcrest in the morning after opening presents. I wasn't going to go, but when I said I was kind of tired and wanted to stay home, Dad looked so angry and disappointed that I felt ashamed and went to change out of my pajamas.

When we got there, Mrs. Murphy was sitting in an armchair under a heavy blanket, reading a book. She looked strange, which at first I thought was because she was so thin, or because she was wearing a fleece hat, but which I eventually realized was because she had no eyebrows or eyelashes. The chemo, of course. I'm embarrassed to say it, but I didn't want to get close to her. I couldn't believe it when Dad and Miss Murphy went right up to her and kissed her cheek like it was no big deal.

"Merry Christmas, Mom," Miss Murphy said. "This is Chloe, Charlie's daughter."

"Nice to meet you, Mrs. Murphy," I said.

"Miss Snow, hello," she said in a husky voice, and smiled.

We stayed for two hours. I never stopped feeling afraid, and also ashamed of myself for feeling afraid.

In the car on the way back, I texted my mother: "Love you Mom." She instantly texted back, "And I adore you, darling," which kind of ruined it, but I didn't care.

Tuesday, December 26

I don't know how Miss Murphy even brushes her teeth in the morning. She must be so sad—how can she find the energy to do the littlest things? Wash her hair, pick up groceries, figure out where she left her other glove? But she does all of that, and she also teaches class and talks to my dad about his job and prepares for the musical (what IS the musical? I can't wait to find out) and probably reads about pregnancy online and figures out what vitamins to buy, or whatever you do when you're knocked up.

If she doesn't want to tell me she's pregnant, fine. It's her business. She'll tell me when she's ready.

Wednesday, December 27

Grady came over for lunch. He brought a set of pine-scented hand soaps for my dad and Miss Murphy, which I assume his mom picked out, although maybe that's unfair. We had grilled cheese, and I made hot chocolate with whipped cream for everyone after we'd finished eating. The conversation was very awkward, but everyone was trying hard. The grown-ups asked Grady lots of questions about his artwork and his family, and he gave them nice long answers. It's not like I was relieved when he left, but I was relieved when the afternoon ended and I could go hide in my room and phonebank. As long as I was dialing, I wasn't thinking about my dad or Miss Murphy or their baby. Is it OK to volunteer as a way of escaping your real life? Maybe I'm doing it wrong.

Thursday, December 28

Miss Murphy asked me if I wanted to practice parallel parking, and I pretended I couldn't because I wanted to get a head start on my American history project. I should have said yes. I admire Miss Murphy. I like her. I feel sorry for her because of her mother. It's not her fault I want nothing to do with her now that she's living in my house and carrying my father's child.

Friday, December 29

The entire junior class is stressing out about New Year's Eve. Social media has turned into a furious series of rumors about whose parents will be out of town and whether the GoFundMe created to rent a heated tent and set it up at the quarry is an actual fundraiser or a practical joke. Grady invited me, Tris, Elliott, and Hannah to his house on New Year's Eve to eat chicken nuggets with Bear and watch movies after he goes to bed, so that's what we're going to do. Even though I'd rather be with those guys than with anyone else, I feel lame that we're not attending some rager. Being 16 sucks. Even when you know you're acting like an insecure idiot, you can't change yourself.

Saturday, December 30

Dad called Grady's mother to confirm that she'll be home tomorrow night. I'm mortified. He does realize that in two years he won't know where I am at any given time, doesn't he? That college is a parent-free zone? God!!

Sunday, December 31

This was the year I lost my virginity to my cute boyfriend—what a great one! I'm sad it's almost over.

I'm trying to feel optimistic about the new year too. Yes, I'm having some trouble with my dad and Miss Murphy, but I'm sure it'll smooth over. As far as I know (he'd tell me, wouldn't he?), Reese hasn't been texting Grady from Europe. Maybe she's moved on. I'm spending the night at a wholesome party with my honeybunch and my best friends, and because I don't need to impress anyone, I'm wearing my biggest, coziest sweater. Everything's good.

Monday, January 1

I'm never drinking again
   In big trouble with my dad
   Too hungover to write any more

Tuesday, January 2

I swear, I didn't mean to get so drunk on New Year's Eve. It was a terrible mistake. The first problem was, Grady's mom and stepdad got invited over to their neighbors' house at the last minute. After Bear went to bed, Mrs. Trevor set up the baby monitor in the living room, where we were, and asked us to keep our voices down so we wouldn't disturb him.

The second problem was Mr. Trevor.

"We'll be back sooner than you think," he said, staring at Grady.

Mrs. Trevor looked up at him. "You don't want to stay until midnight?" she said.

"No drinking," Mr. Trevor said, ignoring her and continuing to bore his eyes into Grady.

"Yup," Grady said. Then, when he saw Mr. Trevor's face, he tried again. "I understand."

"So you think you can behave responsibly for a few hours of your life?"

"Carsten," said Mrs. Trevor to Mr. Trevor.

"I sure can," said Grady. He does the same thing I do: talks in a voice so polite no adult could criticize it, even though both you and the adult know you're being sarcastic, not actually polite.

"That'll be a first," Mr. Trevor said.

Tris and Elliott and Hannah and I tried to vanish into the couch. It's one of the worst parts of being a kid—seeing your friends' parents being dicks to them and not knowing what to do. You're too scared to defend them, and anyway, doing that might be more humiliating than helpful. You're mad for your own reasons, because the parent is essentially treating you like an animal, some lesser being that doesn't understand what it's observing and wouldn't be able to take action even if it did. And you *are* a lesser being, because legally you're a child. You can't protect anyone. What are you going to do, call the cops and tell them your boyfriend's stepdad embarrassed him in front of his friends?

As soon as Mr. and Mrs. Trevor left, Grady got a bottle of Jack Daniel's out of the liquor cabinet. Even Hannah didn't protest. She understood, like we all did, that Mr. Trevor had basically forced him to do it.

It was 8:30 p.m. The plan was for my dad to pick up me and my friends at 12:15 and drive everyone home. I figured I could have one drink and sober up for the next three and a half hours. But as soon as I had a Jack and ginger (and four maraschino cherries), my caution seemed ridiculous. It was New Year's Eve! I was 16— almost an adult! In plenty of other countries, I'd be getting drunk *with my parents* at this moment! Not that I was going to get drunk. I was going to cautiously and responsibly SIP another drink or two, which would still leave me hours to chug water, eat something, and find some cinnamon gum, which Noelle says hides everything, including cigarette breath.

I did sip, but I sipped and sipped and sipped.

Another problem was, we were whispering, because we didn't want to wake up Bear, and eventually we all sat on the floor, around the coffee table, so our faces would be close and we could hear each other better. At first we were giggly, but then we got serious. We whispered about school, and the worst and best things to happen to us last year, and the things we hope will happen this year. Someone turned off most of the lights. Grady found a candle, lit it, and put it on the table in front of us. The whispering and the dimness and the candle-light and the whiskey made it feel like we were carrying out an important secret ritual. We started talking about the country, our democracy, and the world, and how scared we are. We talked about all the horrifying things that happened to kids our age this year. Then we talked about what it must be like to sit in a closet with your classmates, hiding from an active shooter while your teacher tells you she loves you and she's proud of you. Time passed. Before I knew it, we were all wasted. More time passed—I couldn't tell how much. Hannah was saying, "I was meant to live in the 1950s," and crying. Elliott jumped up and ran to the bathroom, I think to throw up. Grady and I made out right there in the living room and only stopped because we heard Tris say, "Oh my God, it's 10 past 12."

We all started running around. Tris and I actually

crashed into each other as he lunged toward the bathroom to find Elliott while I made a beeline for my coat. "What do we do? What do we do?" everyone said as they raced past each other, trying to put on shoes and find phones and will themselves into sobriety, but there was nothing *to* do but say good luck to Grady, go outside, and pray that we wouldn't bump into Mr. and Mrs. Trevor (we didn't), and that somehow we wouldn't make the car reek of whiskey just by exhaling (we did).

"Good night, Mr. Snow," Elliott said as we all slid in. "I mean, good evening."

My dad turned around to look at my friends in the backseat and then me in the front seat. "You're kidding me," he said flatly.

Hannah let out a hysterical giggle and then hiccupped and lapsed into silence.

Dad sat with his hands on the steering wheel, looking into the dark night, thinking. Then he started the car and backed out of Grady's driveway. He didn't speak, so neither did we. Hannah was first to get dropped off. Dad parked, walked her to her door, and rang the bell.

"Oh God, oh God, oh God," said Tris. I looked back and saw him and Elliott holding hands tightly. Grady! I wanted Grady. What was happening to him right now?

Hannah's mom appeared, wearing a pink hoodie

and jeans and looking worried. As she listened to my dad, her eyes darted to Hannah and her lips tightened.

"Should we make a run for it?" Elliott asked Tris.

"My dad will just call your parents," I said.

We sat in silence and watched Mrs. Egan order Hannah into the house like a dog.

We had to wait and wait at Elliott's house; when his father finally came to the door, it was obvious he'd been asleep.

"Please, Mr. Snow," Tris said as we drove to his house. "I know I messed up."

"Concealing this from your parents would be irresponsible," my dad said. Tris was quiet for the rest of the ride. Before he got out of the car, he squeezed my shoulder, so at least I knew he didn't blame me for this debacle. His mom came to the door wearing a baggy sweatshirt and pajama bottoms. She pulled him into the doorway next to her and put her arm around him. She kept it there even as my dad talked. As he turned and walked down the path, I saw her looking at Tris with a sympathetic, worried expression.

"We'll discuss this tomorrow," Dad said to me when he was back in the driver's seat. He didn't speak again, not even at home. He went upstairs without saying good night, turning the lights off behind him like I wasn't there at all.

Wednesday, January 3

Grady didn't get caught. His parents stayed out until three, by which time he'd cleaned up every trace of our hangout and gone to bed. Anyway, they were so drunk themselves that they woke him up crashing into things and laughing, so it's not like they would have noticed even if he'd left evidence everywhere. I'm not sure why my dad didn't rat him out—maybe because he didn't want to have an awkward conversation with Mrs. Trevor about why she'd left us alone when she'd said she wouldn't.

Elliott's grounded for a week. Hannah's grounded for two weeks. Tris's parents don't believe in grounding, but he had to have a long conversation with his mother about the family history of alcoholism and what it was like for her to watch her father die of liver disease. They both cried, and Tris promised her he'd never drink again.

I'm grounded for A MONTH. Dad used to be like Mrs. Flynn—he thought grounding was tyrannical and counterproductive. But that was when he liked me. Now he's decided I'm a bratty jerk, and he's fine with being a tyrant. He sat me down at the dining room table on Monday night to explain my punishment, which he called a consequence, exactly the way he used to call my time-outs consequences when I was five years old. I didn't know the word "euphemism" back then, but I do now.

"I'm disappointed, Chloe," he said. "I know some

parents turn a blind eye to underage drinking. I don't. Your brain isn't done growing. Alcohol really does damage it. And you're not able to protect yourself adequately when you're drunk. From assault, from bad decisions."

It was nothing I hadn't heard a thousand times in health class. What I wanted to know was how I was going to survive a month without Grady. "Can I still see my friends?" I said.

His mouth flattened out. Once again I'd disappointed him. I was supposed to be listening to his heartfelt lecture, and instead I was focused on me, me, me. "In school," he said. "And you can talk on the phone. But no meeting up with anyone. No guests at our house. I need to show you I'm serious, Chloe."

"This sucks," I muttered.

He leaned forward and tried to catch my eye. "You know what sucks? The fact that you were too hungover to go to Marian's brunch today."

I did feel bad about that, but did he have to rub it in? Obviously I would have enjoyed eating a waffle the size of my torso and belting out "Happy Birthday" more than staying home to throw up. I didn't need him to point out that I should be ashamed of myself.

"I'm sorry I ruined Miss Murphy's birthday," I said. I tried to sound genuine, but I could hear the rudeness in my voice.

He sat back in his chair. "I am too," he said coldly. "She deserves better from you." After that he went to change his clothes. He was taking Miss Murphy to a steakhouse for dinner. I'd been invited weeks ago, and I thought maybe I could still go, but they left without even saying anything to me. They treat Snickers with more respect. At least *he* still loves me. He licks away my tears, and even my vomit breath doesn't seem to bother him.

Thursday, January 4

A few weeks ago I was so excited about the musical, and now Miss Murphy's almost certainly pregnant, I was barfing during her birthday brunch, and in general everything is so monumentally uncomfortable between us that I didn't even feel a flicker of emotion today when she announced at school that the musical is *The Addams Family*. Whatever. I guess I'll figure out what the parts are and try out. And then spend ALL of my time with Miss Murphy. Because it's not awkward enough seeing her in my kitchen constantly; I might as well stare at her in rehearsals for four hours a day too.

Friday, January 5

We've never discussed it, but until now Grady and I have had an unspoken rule against going at it in school. But that was before I got grounded. Now school is the only place we can put our hands on each other for a few minutes. We try to find deserted places to do it, at least. Today we were making out hard-core by the gym, which is usually quiet during lunch, but of course a bunch of senior guys came by for some reason and heckled us as they walked past. I'm *pretty* sure they didn't see Grady's hand up my shirt—he snatched it out as soon as he heard the doors open—but I'm not positive.

If I turn into the school laughingstock, it'll be my father's fault.

Saturday, January 6

Miss Murphy insisted on taking me out for driving practice. We didn't talk much after I got on the highway, which I still hate doing. I can't believe you have to accelerate that fast to get off the on-ramp. Who designed it like that?? It makes me feel like the world's worst, most terrified race-car driver. And whenever I look over my left shoulder to see if it's safe to merge, I accidentally steer left too, and I'm constantly getting honked at and nearly sideswiped.

I'm never going to pass my test.

Once I'd made it to the middle lane and my heart rate was more normal, I said, "I'm so sorry about your birthday."

"Don't worry about it," she said. "Really. I'd rather skip the whole thing entirely."

She told me this story about the day she turned 30 and for the first time in her life, a shop clerk called her "ma'am," and then when she went for a blowout, the stylist said the haircut she'd requested would be "a little on the youthful side" for her. She was being funny and interesting, but I couldn't pay attention. I kept thinking, *You're pregnant. You're pregnant. You're pregnant.*

Are they ever going to tell me?

Sunday, January 7

I hate being trapped in my house, but at the same time, it's a good conversation piece. When I tell people about it, they're like, "A MONTH??" and "You're joking me" and "Your dad's insane!" and "How drunk *were* you?" It almost makes me proud. Today Noelle texted to invite me over, so I texted her the whole the saga of New Year's Eve, and she responded with dozens of exclamation points. Then she called me to hear more, and I got to enjoy the shock in her voice.

She said, "The longest I've ever been grounded for was a week, and that was after my mom caught me and Maisie smoking weed in my bedroom. She forgot about it after three days anyway." Her voice was full of respect for me, or maybe for Dad. I couldn't tell.

"You were smoking in your bedroom??"

"I thought my mother was working late."

I asked her about her visit with her dad. "What's going on with him and his girlfriend?"

"Ex-girlfriend. She called me on New Year's Day."

"She called *you*?"

"She thought I could talk my dad into taking her back. I feel kind of bad for her."

"You hate her!"

"I know, but she was crying so hard she was almost choking. She spent all that money on fake boobs and fake teeth and fake hair and what did she get? Dumped by some dad on New Year's Eve. He told her he needs more intellectual stimulation."

"She told you all this?"

"She told me they had anal sex because he insisted and then he broke up with her two weeks later."

"Oh my God, Noelle."

"I hate him way more than I hate her. I told her she can do better. Why would you want to go out with someone who's addicted to his phone and thinks no one knows he dyes his hair? He's rude to waitresses. He acts like he's an expert on everything. He doesn't listen. He leaves water all over the counter after he uses the bathroom. He's 20 years older than her! He pressures people into having butt sex, apparently! Who cares if he's rich?"

Snickers was lying on my stomach. I rubbed one of his ears between my fingers. It felt like a firm piece of silk. "I can't believe she made you listen to the . . . butt part."

Noelle sighed. "Grown-ups spend so much time yelling at us about porn and privacy and whatever, but the stuff that's messed me up the most is the stuff they've told me themselves. And it's not just Tara. So many of them do it."

"Who's Tara?"

"My dad's girlfriend!"

"You've never told me her name before."

Noelle was quiet. Then she said, "I don't want to be friends with my parents."

"God, me neither," I said fervently. "Why don't they understand that?"

But my dad does understand that, actually. He wouldn't ground me if he didn't.

Monday, January 8

Reese is back. I'd gotten so used to her absence, I'd forgotten to feel grateful that she wasn't around, flirting with Grady right in front of me. Then this morning there she was, flipping her hair and showing people pictures on her phone. *Maybe she's forgotten about Grady,* I told myself. *Maybe she met some interesting guy in Europe.*

And then, not 15 minutes later, she marched right

into my English class, which I was enjoying, thank you very much—we were discussing *A Raisin in the Sun,* and I had my hand up, waiting to contradict Griffin, who had just given a ridiculous analysis of Beneatha—and said, "So sorry to interrupt, Mr. Huang. Can I grab Chloe for a second? We're having a student council emergency." He nodded. Reese hurried me down the hall and out to the picnic tables. It was freezing outside, but Reese pretended not to notice, so I did too.

I'm so gullible that the first thing I said was, "What's the emergency?"

She put her hand on my arm and laughed. "You're so sweet! Nothing's wrong. I just felt like chatting for a minute."

My heart sank. "Oh!" I said. "OK. How was your trip?"

"Amazing," she said. "I got SO fat eating all the incredible food." She patted her concave stomach. "Seeing the art and the history there inspired me. It made me reflect on my priorities and on what really matters in this life, you know?"

"Definitely," I said.

"So, how are *you?*" she said, looking deeply into my eyes.

"Uh, good."

"And everything's going well with Grady?"

"Yeah."

"I'm so glad. You believe me, right? That I'm glad?"

"Sure."

She patted her own knee fondly. "I truly want him to be happy."

We were sitting backward on the bench, facing the gray brick side of our school. She scooted closer to me and leaned in to murmur in my ear.

"He's fun to hook up with, right?"

"Yeah. Um, yeah."

She laughed. "Chloe! Don't get shy on me. We should be friends!"

"We're friends," I said. Of course we're not friends, but what was I supposed to say?

"So let's tell each other everything," she said. She lowered her head and looked up at me with a little smile, like we were plotting a caper together. "Are you still a virgin?"

Reese deserves to be popular. She really does. She's a genius at manipulating people. Every remark she makes could be read as either innocent or offensive, and you're so busy trying to interpret what she means and figure out what you can possibly say that won't give her more leverage over you that you wind up blurting out exactly the information she needs. I wasn't going to do it, though.

"I don't know," I said, to stall.

"What do you mean you don't know? I'm not counting blow jobs, if that's what you're confused about. I heard you got grounded. Is that why? Did your dad catch you with Grady?"

I couldn't stand it, sitting outside being interrogated while Griffin was inside probably claiming that Asagai is right about everything and Beneatha should listen to his wisdom.

"I have to go," I said.

"Chloe," she said. Her voice still sounded smooth, but there was a vein of anger running through it.

"Sorry," I said, backing toward the door. "Talk to you later, OK?"

Is that the big revelation she had while touring the Louvre, or whatever? That what's really important is to come back to our poky little town and torment me about my sex life?

Tuesday, January 9

Tris had me act out the entire conversation, doing both parts. In the middle he made me start over, because he said my performance of Reese was too broad. He's going to be a great and annoying theater professor one day. After I finished, he said I handled myself well, and she definitely doesn't know whether or not I'm a virgin.

"What if she asks me again?" I said.

"Act outraged that she'd be so nosy."

Sure. Easy for him to say. I'd like to see him act outraged when Reese comes up and oozes poisonous syrup all over him.

Wednesday, January 10

Code red. No, what's more urgent than code red? Code maroon. Code blood.

Grady and I were standing at my locker when Reese came up to us and said, "My favorites!"

We smiled and said hi. "Listen," she said, "I'm organizing a ski trip for this weekend. I've been so depressed since we got back from Europe, I have to cheer myself up somehow. Totally last minute, but a bunch of kids are going up to Dylan's house in Vermont—it's right on the mountain. Grady, are you in?"

He glanced at me and then back at her. "I have to watch Bear, actually. Thanks for the invite, though."

"Are you serious?" she said. "Tell your mom you're not a free babysitter!"

"Sorry," he said.

"I'm not taking no for an answer," she said. "I'll ask you again tomorrow. It'll be so fun! Chloe, I'd obviously invite you, too, if you weren't grounded." She pointed a sympathetic expression at me.

"Thanks," I said. *Thanks!* Thank you, Reese, for

trying to steal my boyfriend right in front of my face! Thank you so very much!

As soon as she left, I covered my face with my hands. I wanted to cover my ears, too. I wanted to get in a sensory-deprivation tank and also turn off my mind. I can't stand the thought of the next few weeks and months. Waiting to see if she'll win. Feeling sick at the thought of what she's texting Grady and what she's saying to Grady when she catches him alone. Trying not to ask him about her, but then asking anyway and getting in a big fight. I want to skip ahead and find out what happens.

Grady pulled my hands away from my face.

"If you're going to dump me, go ahead and dump me," I said.

"Chloe, come on," he said. He was laughing, which made me furious.

"She invited you SKIING!" I said. I kind of yelled it. Most kids were in their next classes already, but the few who were around looked at us with interest.

"Shhh. I realize that."

"Don't *shhh* me!"

"Sorry. Jesus. What do you want me to do? I told her I can't go!"

"I want you to make her stop."

"How?"

"I don't know! Say something to her! Tell her we're engaged! Do anything!"

If only we could go to my house and have sex, like we usually do. Sex erases arguments. Without it, I have to sit here fuming into my diary pointlessly.

Thursday, January 11

Chloe: Did she ask you
again today?

Grady: Once in the hall and
once by text

Are you sure you want to
know this stuff?

Chloe: Yes

Grady: It just seems
annoying to hear

Chloe: IT IS

Grady: Are you mad at ME?

Chloe: No

I don't know

Grady: I swear to god there's
nothing to worry about

I want to believe that.

Friday, January 12

I cannot wait to grow up. If Grady and I were adults, I'd probably never meet his ex-girlfriend. I certainly wouldn't have to see her every single day. I wouldn't have a vivid mental image of what she looks like when she's eating a sandwich, the way she flares her nostrils when she's irritated, and every haircut she's had since kindergarten. It's like some evil science experiment, being forced to spend almost two decades with the same couple hundred people.

At least the weekend is almost here. Soon Reese will be posting selfies from atop a snowy mountain, and I won't have to worry that Grady's making out with her while I rot at home, grounded.

Saturday, January 13

For the first time I looked up some YouTube videos of *The Addams Family* musical. I've never even seen the movie. I know there's a sexy mom and a cranky daughter who never smiles. And an Uncle Lester or something. I need to get up to speed fast if I want to have any shot at a lead.

Sunday, January 14

Dad said I'm allowed to visit Mom, as long as he drops me off and picks me up, so I went over there for a change of scenery. She was outraged when I told her I've been grounded for a month.

"But that's draconian! What is he thinking?"

"I mean, I did get really drunk on New Year's Eve."

"You're 16! What on earth does he expect?"

It makes no sense, but as soon as Mom starts criticizing Dad, I want to stand up for him.

Monday, January 15

For Martin Luther King Jr. Day, I did four straight hours of phonebanking. Mostly I got people's voicemails, plus a few supporters who wanted to chat, both of which I'm used to now, but about two hours in, a man picked up and flew into a rage as soon as I said the words "Planned Parenthood."

"Oh, the baby killers! You people make me sick."

I remembered that the guide had a section about how to handle this situation, but I couldn't remember what it said.

"Planned Parenthood offers a lot of services," I said, in a voice that made ME sick: I sounded quavering and tiny. "Pap smears and cancer screenings—"

"And abortions. How old are you? Do you even know—"

The advice in the guide finally came back to me. "Thank you for your time!" I said, and hung up. My hands were shaking and my heart was racing, but I kept making calls. I can still hear the man's voice now, the sneering in it.

Tuesday, January 16

I guess I thought if I could make it through the ski weekend without losing Grady, everything would be OK. But Reese went skiing, and now she's back, and when I rounded the corner after second period, there she was at Grady's locker, smiling up at him and fixing his hair.

Yes! Smiling up at him! Fixing his hair! This is what it's come to!

He didn't look like he was enjoying it exactly, but he wasn't leaping back so she couldn't touch him, which is what I would have preferred. When she saw me, Reese waved, then turned back and gave Grady's head another pat, I guess to demonstrate that she had nothing to feel guilty about.

I turned and walked away without talking to either of them.

"Hey," Grady said when he found me after school.

"Hey," I said.

We walked out to the bike rack in silence. He gave me a long hug goodbye while I stood there with my arms dangling by my sides. He looked at me like *are you mad?* but I rode away without saying anything. Now I loathe myself. I'm wasting my precious time with him acting like an angry, jealous loser. Which I am! But I should hide it. I need to be chipper, unconcerned, and fun. What if he starts wondering why he's making this big effort to be with moody me when he could be with sparkly Reese?

Wednesday, January 17

After dinner I explained to Dad that Grady's ex-girlfriend is trying to get him back, and I have to see him more.

"Could I postpone being grounded for now and serve the rest of my time later in the year?" I said.

"It's not a prison sentence," Dad said.

"I don't want to leave him alone right now," I said.

"Do you trust this guy so little that you need to be in his physical presence to know he's not cheating on you?"

"DAD!"

"What?? Isn't that what you're saying?"

I started crying. "He's not going to cheat on me!"

Miss Murphy had been hovering in the kitchen. She came in and said, "I'm sure he's not. Charlie, can't you understand what Chloe's saying?"

"I don't need your help, Miss Murphy, but thanks anyway," I said, and got up so fast I knocked over my chair, which I then set upright again, still weeping.

Thursday, January 18

Grady and I talked on the phone for three hours tonight.

He called me and we chatted about nothing for a while. Dumb stuff. Then he said, "Is everything OK with us?"

My stomach fell into my feet. "What do you mean?"

"You seem so quiet and upset all the time."

"I guess I kind of am."

"I know the Reese thing is annoying, but can't we ignore it?"

"I can try." I was tearing up. All I do is cry. It's revolting. "Are you getting sick of me?" I said. PATHETIC.

"No. That's not what I'm saying."

I held the phone away from my face for a second so he wouldn't hear me gasping and sniffing. Snickers was asleep on my bed with most of his head under my pillow. If Grady dumps me, at least I'll still be able to snuggle with my dog.

"Are you there?" Grady said.

"Imagine if this were happening with Mac," I said. "If he were inviting me skiing a million times and flirting with me at my locker. How would you feel?"

Grady was quiet.

"Grady?"

"I see what you mean," he said. I couldn't read his tone. He sounded . . . something.

Friday, January 19

Grady was grinning when we sat down for lunch.

"I brought you a cookie," he said.

"Thanks," I said.

He slid the cookie and his phone across the table to me. My heart sped up.

"Read it," he said.

It was a text conversation between him and Reese.

Grady: Listen I need to talk
to you

Reese: Oooo sounds exciting

Grady: I'm not mad or anything
but I want you to know I'm not
breaking up with Chloe

Reese: OKKKKK

Grady: Not assuming you want
me to but it seems like you've
been kinda flirty recently?

Reese: Are you saying you never
think about me?

Grady: I think you're nice but
Chloe's my girlfriend

Reese: I was your GF too

Finders keepers LOL

Grady: Dude you cheated on me

Reese: What if I realized I made
a mistake?

Grady: I'm not interested

Not to sound harsh

Reese: You're just mad about Zach

Grady: Not mad

It's in the past

Just over it

Reese: Over ME

Grady: I mean yeah

Reese: Is Chloe with you right now? Is she telling you what to say?

Grady: No

She didn't ask me to text you

Reese: Yeah right

Grady: She didn't

Reese: So what you're gonna walk away from me if I talk to you?

Grady: I just don't think we should talk

So I guess so yeah

Reese: Are you joking?

Grady: No

Reese: You're an asshole

Grady: Don't be like that

Reese: I'll be how I want

Is this because I didn't want to you-know-what

Grady: It's not related

Reese: Because I've changed

Are you having sex with Chloe?

Grady: Not talking about this

Reese: So you are

Grady: It's private

*Reese: Yeah like when I was
giving you head in the guys'
dressing room, private like that?*

I put the phone facedown on the table. My God, she was *right there,* across the room, laughing with her friends.

Grady was looking at me proudly. "I think she blocked me after she sent that last one," he said. "Sorry you had to read about the dressing room, but I thought the rest would cancel it out. Chloe?"

"Yeah."

"What do you think?"

I laughed. I was terrified. Also relieved and excited, but mostly terrified. There was no way she was going to let me live after this. But Grady had done it! He'd told her to eff off, exactly like I'd wanted him to. He'd been brave.

"I think I want to take your pants off right now," I said.

We grinned and squeezed each other's hands.

"She's going to destroy us both," I said.

"Eh, who cares," Grady said.

Saturday, January 20

I waited as long as I could, because I didn't want to bother Noelle if she was sleeping in, but at 10 a.m. I couldn't take it anymore and texted her to ask if Reese is furious. She wrote back, "too much to type FT?" so I FaceTimed her instantly. She answered looking half-asleep, with tangled hair.

"Did I wake you up?" I said.

She yawned. "No. I was just lying around looking at the internet."

"You're still in bed, though?"

She flipped the phone around so I could see her view: her bare feet sticking out from under the duvet, and her bedroom in the background. I caught a glimpse of her bare walls (she's too cool to put up posters or photos or glow-in-the-dark stars), the hideous brown lamp that looks like it cost $1 at a yard sale, and the tan chair like a doughnut on legs that Noelle's mom moved upstairs when she redecorated the living room. Overall, the vibe is, *Only basic people spend time worrying about decor, and as you can see, I am not basic.*

Noelle flipped the phone back to her face and said, "What the hell did you do to Reese?"

"She didn't tell you?"

"She's furious. She said you're psychotic and Grady's delusional, but she wouldn't elaborate."

I'd known this was coming, but still, it was a kick in the shins to hear it out loud.

"Grady texted her," I said, "and told her to back off."

Noelle widened her eyes. "Go on."

"He told her he doesn't think they should talk anymore, he's over her, and he's not going to break up with me."

She laughed in an amazed way. "Wow. He has balls, I'll give him that."

"He had to say something. You saw her hitting on him!"

"She wouldn't shut up about him the whole time we were skiing. It was so annoying."

"So how can she say he's delusional?"

"You know what she's like."

I do. She's like a dictator who cares nothing for the truth. She *makes* the truth. In fact, the more obvious her lies, the better. Every time she forces the rest of the class to accept her obviously fake version of reality, the more they have invested in her reign of terror. Once you've decided an individual is more important than the truth, you have to support the individual even if it's snowing and she tells you it's a hot summer day and makes you walk outside wearing a bikini.

I felt sick. "What's she gonna do?"

Noelle rubbed her eyes. They were all smudged with yesterday's mascara and eyeliner. It looked great. "I'm not sure."

"Just tell me."

"Like I said, she's not talking to me about it yet. She's still at the quiet planning stage."

"So what *could* happen?"

"You know already. She could get the squad to turn on you. That would take two seconds. She could try to get a big chunk of the class to hate you, ignore you, make fun of you in the halls, all that stuff. Creating a villain out of thin air—she does that twice a year. It's a way of keeping everyone else in line. The more randomly she turns on someone, the better, because it makes people realize they could be next. That actually protects you, because you have history with her. Some kids would wonder if she was trying to get back at you for going out with her ex-boyfriend, so they'd be suspicious of whatever she says about you. She'd have to get around that." Noelle was terrifying me and impressing me. She was good at this! She was like some genius lady-in-waiting who looked innocent enough but secretly understood more than the royalty she was supposedly serving.

Noelle stared off into space. "She could spread a rumor about you." She looked back at me. It was obvious we were both thinking about the time Reese told everyone that Noelle had a threesome in France.

"What else?" I said.

"She might do nothing. Going after you—it's a risk. It could make her look jealous."

That was something. Maybe it would all go away. "Will you give me a heads-up? After she decides what to do?"

Noelle shook her head. "I can't. I shouldn't even be talking to you like this."

"I knew this would happen. I told you you couldn't be friends with both of us."

"Will you calm down? I just spent 15 minutes schooling you on Reese's operating tactics." She frowned into her phone, using it as a mirror as she tried to smooth out her hair. "Did I mention my mom's going away for work? I haven't told anyone yet, but I'm having a party on February 3. You won't be grounded then, will you?"

"That's the day after I'm done."

"Perfect."

"Do you think Reese will come?"

"Definitely. Oh, stop looking like that. You can't avoid her forever. Maybe you guys can talk." She grinned. "It'll be interesting!"

Yeah, interesting like putting Snickers into a closed room with a squirrel.

Sunday, January 21

Reese hasn't texted Grady (or so he says, and I believe him). She hasn't posted anything menacing online. No scary Snaps. One smoldering Instagram captioned with some Cardi B lyrics, but that could mean nothing. Everyone smolders and quotes Cardi. I need to stop stalking Reese and do my homework instead of cycling through every app in sequence like a gerbil stuck on a wheel.

Monday, January 22

She's ignoring me and Grady completely. It's like we're ghosts. She's also putting on a big show of giggling and shrieking in the halls like she's at an amazing cocktail party, tipsy on champagne. Not a care in the world. Grady who? That kind of thing. Her squad trails her everywhere, as usual, and they all sneak little glances at us, looking excited and mean while they do it. It should be a relief, sinking beneath her notice, but it feels terrible. To me, anyway. Grady seems fine with it. He wanted to talk about politics at lunch—US ones, not school ones.

Tuesday, January 23

Everything would be so much better if I could lie down with Grady in my bed with the door closed. It's not only the sex. I want to talk to him in private. I want to feel his breath on my nose.

I waited until right before bedtime, when Miss Murphy had gone upstairs to brush her teeth and Dad was turning off the lights in the living room, and said, "Dad, think I could get a few days off for good behavior?"

I was smiling, and he was too as he said, "I'm sorry, kiddo."

"I'm lonely," I said. "I miss my friends."

He paused by the couch. "You've been doing a great job, honey. It's almost over."

"You're being unreasonable!" I'd planned to stay calm, but I was shrieking a little.

"I see why you'd say that," he said. "I don't want to be unfair. But I said a month, so it's got to be a month."

"You're you! You're talking like past you is some federal judge you can't get around! You can change your own mind!"

"I figured out when you were a toddler that if I didn't stick to my word, it didn't go well the next time for either of us."

"I'm not a toddler anymore. I'm 16, and I have a boyfriend I haven't seen in a month."

"I'm not going to say yes, Chloe."

I was going to storm out, but he left the room before I could do it.

Wednesday, January 24

School was over for the day, and I was standing near my bike with Grady. "I miss you," I said.

"I miss you too," he said, instead of "but you see me constantly at school," because he knew what I was really talking about.

"I can't stand this," I said.

"Only a week left, right?" he said. He reached into my jacket and put his hand on my side and then slid his fingers under my shirt.

He was right: we were almost there. But that made it less bearable. When I knew we had to get through a month, it was easier. Now that I was days away from feeling his strong Grady body on top of mine, I couldn't take it.

"Let's go to my house," I said.

"We can't," he said, but his hand was still under my shirt.

"Your house, then."

"Bear's there with the babysitter."

"OK, my house."

"What if we get caught?"

"We won't. Miss Murphy's the one who can leave early sometimes, and I know for a fact she's staying late tonight."

Grady was wrinkling his eyebrows skeptically, but he was smiling, too, and I knew I'd talked him into it.

"Hurry up," I said, and started unlocking my bike as fast as I could.

The bliss of having sex after not having sex! It makes me want to get grounded all over again! (Not really.) It's better than water when you're thirsty or a cheeseburger when you're starving. I can't say for sure, but I bet it's better than doing drugs or winning a marathon or visiting the moon. It's the WHOLE POINT OF BEING ALIVE!

Maybe if I keep rhapsodizing about sex forever, I won't have to write about the disaster.

Dad came home. It was about as bad as it could have been. We were on our third time already, so at least we weren't still at DEFCON 1 levels of horniness, but Grady's penis was actually inside me when we heard the door open downstairs. Thank the Lord we were in the midst of one of those staring-into-each-other's-eyes-and-breathing-heavily bones and not a yelping-and-biting-each-other one, because otherwise we never would have heard him come in. There was maybe one second where we looked at each other in shock, and then we were pulling on our clothes like firefighters when the alarm goes off. Grady was silent. I was swearing and stubbing my toes. Pants on. Bra on. Shirt on. Hair still wild, probably. Underwear on the floor. I kicked it under the dresser. Two used condoms clearly visible in the trash can! I grabbed an old copy of the *New Yorker* and threw it over the evidence. Dad started coming up the stairs.

Grady was looking around like maybe he could hide under the bed or climb out the window.

Dad knocked.

"It's too late," I said to Grady, not even whispering, and opened the door.

Dad was shocked to see Grady there, I could tell. He'd come home early, intending to catch me—why else would he leave work in the afternoon for the first time in years?—but he hadn't really thought he'd find anything.

"Hi, Mr. Snow," Grady said. It must have REEKED of sex in my room.

"Grady," my dad said, nodding at him. For a second I thought it might be OK. Then Dad said, "I'll ask you to leave now."

Grady looked at me like he wasn't sure what to do, but he didn't have a choice. He couldn't exactly stand his ground.

"See you tomorrow," I said.

On his way out, he kissed my hand.

"You're in big trouble," my dad said as soon as Grady was gone.

I was so scared my legs felt trembly, so I sat down on the bed, which was a mistake. Dad stayed standing, and he loomed over me like an interrogator.

"You disobey me like this? You have your boyfriend over when no one's home? You take him to your bedroom and lock the door? You're acting like . . ."

He didn't finish the sentence, but I could imagine what he'd almost said. *Like a slut. Like a skank. Like a whore.*

"This would be unacceptable behavior even if you weren't grounded," he said. "But you are."

"Until when?" I said. I wanted to know the worst right away. Was he going to extend the punishment?

"That's all you have to say?" he said. "No apology?" The look of disgust on his face made me furious, and I stood up.

"Yeah, I'm sorry," I said. "I'm sorry I'm a normal teenager."

He shook his head.

"I'm so sorry I can't be 12 years old forever, Dad," I said. "I'm sorry you can only love me when I'm a child."

He laughed, to show me how ridiculous I was being.

"I know Miss Murphy's pregnant," I said. He stopped laughing, which I guess was what I intended. I don't know what I intended.

"You think I don't notice anything," I said. "Well, I do."

I thought he might apologize, but he looked angrier than ever. "Marian's pregnancy is not a bargaining chip you can use against me."

My nose prickled. I was about to start crying.

He left abruptly. Then I did start crying. A few minutes later he came back in. I was embarrassed to be caught in tears, but I thought maybe he'd calm down when he saw how upset I was. I even thought he'd say he was sorry I'd found out about Miss Murphy on my own. But he just pointed his finger at me and said, "If you're taking risks and YOU get pregnant, you can't imagine the pain you'll feel."

In a cold voice I said, "I have an IUD." The look of shock on his face made the whole argument worth it.

Thursday, January 25

Dad and I have barely spoken. Miss Murphy hovered near my bedroom while I was in there doing my homework with the door open, but I didn't look up, and she didn't come in.

Auditions are on Monday. The closest I've gotten to preparing is watching *The Addams Family*, which I really loved. I wish I could be like Wednesday: stoic and steely. I don't want to be murderous, obviously, but it would be fun to be murderous onstage.

Friday, January 26

Miss Murphy hovered again, and again I didn't look up, but this time she came in anyway.

"Can I interrupt you for a second?"

"Sure," I said.

She perched on my desk chair. I was sitting on my bed with my history textbook open across my lap.

"I'm sorry everything's so strained around here," she said.

I shrugged and said nothing.

"And to add to the chaos . . . I'm pregnant! As you know." She was still wearing her work clothes: dark-green pants, a gray blazer, a silky navy-blue shirt.

"Congratulations," I said. "I kind of noticed."

"The morning sickness?"

I nodded.

"I'm sorry I kept it to myself for so long. To be honest, I was dreading the conversation a little. I was worried I'd upset you, and I put off telling you for that reason."

I didn't want to have a frank discussion with her about my feelings, so I said, "When's your due date?"

"July 10. My mother had me two weeks late, though, so late July is probably more realistic." She tried to catch my eye. "How does all this grab you?"

"Uh, it's OK."

"Because I can imagine it would feel like you were being supplanted."

"No, I know Dad still loves me or whatever."

"He does. I do too."

She'd been great up to this point, but now I was grossed out. At best, Miss Murphy feels affection for me. Love is what she'll feel for her baby.

"It might be fun to have a brother or a sister," she said.

"Half," I said. "Half brother or sister."

Her face fell. "Right." She stood up. "Well . . . it was good to talk."

"Congratulations again," I said.

Saturday, January 27

Dad and I still aren't really speaking to each other. I know he's waiting for me to apologize for sneaking Grady in, and probably for having sex, and possibly for getting an IUD without informing him, but I can't seem to do it. I did help him shovel the driveway without being asked, though. When we were done, I said, "Am I still grounded after Thursday?"

He plunged his shovel into a snowbank to get it to stand upright. "No. Marian's talked me out of it. But I am going to ask for more details before you go out."

"What, on Friday?"

"Anytime. I need to know you're safe and supervised."

"Like I can't go to the movies with my friends if a parent isn't there?"

"The movies are fine, as long as I know who will be there and what time you'll be home."

Noelle's party, I thought. *He'll never let me go.*

Sunday, January 28

Snickers and I got back from a walk before lunch, and he ran to the kitchen to stare meaningfully at his food bowl while I took off my coat. "Hey," I called to Dad and Miss Murphy.

"Hi," they called back.

I followed Snickers to feed him and found the adults sitting at the island looking at a book together.

"What about Camilla?" Miss Murphy said.

"Parker Bowles?" said Dad.

She rolled her eyes. "No one under 50 will make that association."

"Catherine?"

"Nice," she said in a polite tone.

"OK, not Catherine. Alex?"

"I like Alex for a boy. Or, wait, what about Axel for a boy?" Miss Murphy said.

"AXEL?"

They were giggling and leaning into each other.

"What do you think, Chloe?" Miss Murphy said.

"I like Wednesday for a girl," I said.

If she knew I was being rude, she didn't acknowledge

it. "Hey, speaking of Wednesday, are you set for auditions tomorrow?"

"Oh." I took Snickers's water bowl to the sink. "I actually decided not to audition this year."

When I turned around, I was happy to see dismayed expressions on their faces. I'd said what I'd said impulsively, but knowing I was getting to them made me want to stick with it.

"You're kidding," Miss Murphy said. "Are you sure?"

"Positive," I said.

Dad looked grim. "Don't try to prove a point at the expense of doing something you love," he said.

"I don't know what that means," I said, which was a lie.

"Fine." He looked back down at the baby names book.

"If you change your mind, please come tomorrow," Miss Murphy said as I headed upstairs.

I called Tris right away, and for half an hour he tried to talk me into auditioning. He said he'll miss me, it'll be boring without me, my college applications won't be as strong if I skip a year, etc., etc. It was flattering, and he's right about the college applications. But then again, the baby name book and my new and searing hatred for my dad and Miss Murphy.

Monday, January 29
When I passed by the auditorium after school, all the

theater kids were outside, waiting for Miss Murphy to unlock the doors, hugging each other and talking in loud, excited voices. "Chloe!" Olivia called. "Where are you going?"

I stopped. Maybe I should audition after all. I was completely unprepared, but could I fake it through a scene and a song well enough to squeak past today, after which I could prepare hard for callbacks?

The doors opened and Miss Murphy appeared, smiling and holding a clipboard.

"I'm not auditioning this year," I told Olivia.

She gasped. "Seriously?"

"I gotta go," I said. "Break a leg!"

Tuesday, January 30

I do feel sick, knowing it's all going ahead without me. I'm home alone. I can hear Snickers's toenails clicking around in the kitchen and the heat thunking on. Meanwhile, the second batch of kids are auditioning now. Everyone's singing, warming up, and listening to Mrs. Cordoza shout, "FIVE, six, seven, and—"

I probably made a huge mistake. What else is new?

Wednesday, January 31

Tris says his audition went really well. I asked him if he had any competition, and he said he didn't want to sound arrogant, but not really. He's so confident, he's more worried about whether he'll get peer-pressured into drinking at Noelle's party than he is about callbacks. Word is out about the party now, and no one can stop talking about it. Tris is going (obviously). Elliott's going. Hannah's going. Grady says he won't go unless I can, but of course I'm not going to let him martyr himself. It's common knowledge that Reese and the other popular kids are going. Noelle is such a star at school this week, I almost feel shy about texting her, like I might be bothering her.

I have to trick Dad into letting me go somehow. I can't miss this.

Thursday, February 1

As of tomorrow, I'm UNGROUNDED!

Friday, February 2

Dad poked his head into my room tonight and said, "Aren't you going out? I thought you'd want to celebrate."

I said, "Nah, I'm tired. Anyway, I want to get a head start on my homework."

My cunning knows no bounds! He'll assume his punishment changed me and I've become compliant. Why else would I choose to stay at home on the very day most kids would desperately want to go out: the Friday

at the end of a month of house arrest? He won't suspect a thing when I casually mention I'm sleeping over
at Hannah's tomorrow.

Saturday, February 3

DAMMIT. It's 8 p.m. and I'm screwed. This morning
I said, "Hey, Dad, Hannah invited me to sleep over
tonight. Can I?"

He said, "Sure. Let me text Mrs. Egan to confirm
she'll be there."

I tried to read his expression, but he was gazing into
the bowl of eggs he was whisking.

"Are you serious?" I said. "It's Hannah."

"Purportedly," he said. Then he looked up and
smiled at me pleasantly.

"You know what, don't even bother," I said. "If you
don't trust me to hang out with my best friend, I'll cancel on her."

"So I shouldn't text Hannah's mom?" he said.

"No. I'll just stay in my bedroom forever. Anyway, I
doubt Hannah even told her I was coming. Not everyone's parents act like the Stasi."

Dad was boring holes into my eyes with his eyes. He
knew exactly what I was up to. He's an attorney. I can't
trick him with my fake anger and illogical preemptive
hedges. Of course Hannah would never invite me over

without getting her mother's permission first. I know that. Dad knows that.

"Canceling your plans is probably a good idea," he said.

I feel like an animal in some rinky-dink city zoo with cages the size of dressing rooms. It's snowing again, and everyone important is at the party of the year, including my boyfriend and his ex-girlfriend, and I'm trapped inside listening to my father and Miss Murphy look at nursery decor on Pinterest and bicker flirtatiously about faux sheepskin rugs. I can't stay here. I'll lose my mind. I have to get out of this house.

Sunday, February 4

I jumped out the window to get to the party.

I had to! Or, OK, I wanted to. I wanted to go to the party so badly, it felt like a physical need. My dad was clearly going to stay up, blocking my path out the front door, until it was too late for me to leave. There was only one solution.

I went downstairs and announced I was going to bed. I acted sullen, like I was still furious at him for refusing to believe my lie but had resigned myself to another night in. Then I snuck my coat, keys, gloves, and hat out of the front hall closet, walked upstairs, and pretended to get ready for bed: brushed my teeth, flushed the toilet, went to my room, closed the door, and turned off all the lights. Twenty minutes later I left through my window. First I lowered myself onto the roof of the screen porch. That part was a snap. I've done it a million times. Yes, it was a little trickier than it is in the summer because of the snow, but I made it. I even managed to stretch onto my tiptoes and pull the window closed behind me. Then I had to drop down from the roof to the patio. Holding on to the gutter while letting the rest of my body dangle in the air was the scariest part. No, letting go was the scariest part. It wasn't a big distance—maybe eight or nine feet—but still, I had to work up the courage to do it. Counting down from 10 didn't work, and neither did silently screaming *Jump, you baby!* at myself. Finally my arms got too wobbly to keep holding on, and I had to let go. And it was fine! Mostly! I landed in a pile of snow, and I must have felt something, but the adrenaline zooming through my body masked it.

It was freezing outside. Riding my bike to Noelle's, I was concentrating on not getting run over by a drunk driver or skidding on the icy roads. When I finally made it, I paused for a second to look up at the stars and the lit-up windows of Noelle's house. Then I put all my weight on my right foot to get off my bike, and a knife of pain shot up my leg. I hopped through the garage to the kitchen door, and almost as soon as I got inside, I saw

Grady. I must have looked terrible: red nose from the cold, staticky hair from the hat, pale face from the pain. But Grady yelled "YEAAHHH!!!!!" when he saw me and came pushing through the crowd of kids to pick me up and spin me around.

I gasped when he set me down on my feet.

"What's wrong?" he said.

"I think I messed up my ankle." I told him about sneaking out and riding over. As I talked, he led me out of the kitchen and to the front hall stairs. I leaned on him and hopped to get there. When I was sitting down, he pushed up the right ankle of my jeans—which was not easy, since obviously I was wearing my tightest pair of skinnies—pulled off my shoe and sock, and said, "Oh my God."

It looked like there was a small pillow protruding from my pants, with five little toes sticking out of it like buttons.

"Holy cankle!" I said, and started laughing. It did hurt like hell, but it looked so funny, and I was so relieved to be sitting on a stair pressed against Grady in a warm house filled with people, none of whom had the power to lock me in my room or foist a sibling on me, that I hardly cared.

"I wonder if you broke it," Grady said. He was not laughing. He was Googling. Sometimes when he's frowning into his phone, efficiently finding useful information, I can see what he'll be like as a dad: calm, sensible, helpful.

"You can kind of walk on it," he muttered to himself. "Does it hurt more around the tissue, or over the ankle bone?"

"Is the ankle bone the knobby one on the side?" I said.

"I'm not sure. Obviously we're not doctors," he said.

"We're NOT?"

He ignored me. "If it doesn't feel better after two to four days of rest, ice, compression, and elevation, you need to get it checked out. Let's find Noelle and ask her if there's an ACE bandage anywhere. We also need an ice pack and some Advil."

"You're a sexy nurse," I said.

"Wait, I changed my mind. I am a doctor."

"Don't be such a bad feminist. Men can be excellent nurses."

"Since we're pretending anyway, I might as well be a neurosurgeon."

"Dr. Lawrence, are you attracted to girls with one foot shaped like an ottoman?" I gave him a flirty look.

"Seriously, let's find Noelle. Aren't you in pain?"

"Yes. I feel like I'm going to throw up, actually, it hurts so much. But let's sit here for one more minute."

I could tell he wanted to hurry up and wrap my ankle, but he humored me and we sat side by side, looking around the foyer, which is open to the second floor. Most of the lights were turned off, but the giant chandelier was on. Kids drifted past underneath it, some talking loudly, some chasing each other, some looking shy or unsure. There went a senior field hockey player in tears. Here came a clump of guys arguing about who had stolen whose beer. A few people waved to me and Grady. Most ignored us, or didn't notice us. Music boomed from the kitchen. It was nothing like the balls I'm always reading about in Jane Austen novels, but it was exactly like them too. I don't think Jane would be shocked if she could see what we were up to.

Noelle came out of the kitchen holding a Solo cup and saw us. "Here you are!" she said. "Have you found Tris and Elliott yet? Hannah's around too. They might be outside. I think snow pong is happening."

I never wanted to go outside again. I felt sleepy. The throbbing in my ankle was almost pleasant. It took my mind off the fact that I'd snuck out of my house and possibly broken my ankle and was probably going to get grounded for the rest of my life.

"Hey, do you have an ACE bandage, by any chance?" Grady said. He stood up to talk to Noelle. I was leaning against the stair rails, resting my head, when I saw Reese through the living room door. She didn't see me. She was looking down at her phone and smiling. The lights were low in there, and her bright screen turned her face pale blue. Then she looked up and we locked eyes.

"Noelle," I said, "do you mind if I lie down for a minute? I feel weird."

"I don't mind," she said. "Use my room. Sneak up there, though. My mom's relaxed about stuff, but she'll decapitate me if anyone has sex on her bed. And once the first couple goes up . . ." She didn't finish her sentence, but I got it. Luke Powers had a party last year that basically turned into an orgy, or so everyone says.

"We'll hurry," I said. Grady was standing on the step below me. I climbed onto his back without asking.

"I guess I'm giving her a ride," Grady said.

"No one's looking. Go! Go!" Noelle said. Grady went.

It was dark in Noelle's room. "She said the stuff is in her mom's bathroom," Grady said. "I'll be right back."

I lowered myself onto Noelle's bed. Had I ever been happier? Maybe the first time Grady and I kissed, but this was a close second. I was out of my house and my school for the first time in a month. My boyfriend was fussing over me. My best friends were downstairs in the snow—I thought maybe I could hear them laughing if I listened carefully. Neither of my parents knew where

I was. If only I could untether Noelle's house and yard from Earth and send them spinning through space, so that I never had to face my family again.

"Jackpot!" Grady said, and came into the room holding the gear.

I really didn't think we were going to have sex. In fact, I specifically decided we shouldn't, since (a) my injury was giving me bizarre space-thoughts and (b) we were on Noelle's bed. But Grady was so gentle, wrapping the bandage around my ankle and clipping it, then handing me two Advil and a Dixie cup full of water. And we'd only had sex once in the past month. And I don't know, he lay down next to me and brushed my hair out of my face and the next thing I knew I'd taken my shirt off and climbed on top of him.

"Doesn't it hurt your foot?" Grady said.

"Not if I lean over like this," I said.

It was a long one, and a quiet one. Toward the end my eyes were closed, I remember that, because I also remember that when Grady stopped moving, I opened them to see what was wrong and saw that he wasn't looking at me but was staring over my shoulder with a shocked expression on his face. I turned, and there, in the doorway, was Reese.

I couldn't really make out her face, because she was backlit. She didn't say anything. For a while (a minute?

It felt like forever) she stood there, not moving, looking at us. I grabbed my shirt and tried to cover my boobs, but I stayed on top of Grady. I didn't want to scramble away like a cockroach. She wanted to catch us? She'd caught us.

Finally she left. After we'd heard her run down the stairs, Grady got up and shut the door.

"Hoo boy," he said, collapsing next to me on the bed.

"I'm gonna have to transfer," I said.

I was hungry, and worried, and I could feel my pulse through my whole body, even in my scalp, but somehow I still fell asleep and didn't wake up until 5 a.m. Actually, that's not true: I woke up a few hours later and realized I was spending the whole night with Grady for the first time, and I was so happy, so, so happy, even though I knew trouble was coming from all directions, and I put my arms around his waist and went back to sleep.

Monday, February 5

On the plus side, Dad didn't catch me! Grady and I went downstairs as soon as we woke up. There were sleeping kids everywhere—on the couches, on the floors. Grady said he could leave his bike at Noelle's and give me a ride home on my own handlebars, but the crying field hockey player from the night before was heading out too, and when she saw me limping and wincing, she offered to throw both of our bikes in her Subaru and give us rides. Her name is Ashlynn and she just got dumped by this guy from Springfield she doesn't even like, which she told us all about on the way home. Ashlynn is an angel.

I snuck in, thinking that at any minute Dad would jump out from behind a doorway and tell me I'm never allowed to leave my room again, but the house was quiet, and I tiptoed upstairs and climbed into my own bed like I'd never left it. I was so excited to have gotten away with my caper, I thought I'd never be able to sleep, but of course I passed out instantly and didn't wake up until 11, when I went downstairs and told my father I'd slipped getting out of the shower and hurt my foot somehow, which he was so concerned about, I almost felt guilty.

Then I answered all the texts.

Tris: Everyone good?

*Elliott: Home safe Mom asked
me if I had fun at Grady's*

*Grady: My mom asked me the
same re Elliott's*

*Hannah: I feel so guilty but my
parents don't suspect anything*

They really believe I slept at
Chloe's

Tris: Don't feel guilty

It's a rite of passage

Hannah: But I had two
beers, too

Tris: Oh Hannah

Elliott: I had five vodka tonics
and threw up in Noelle's bushes,
so there

Hannah: I still feel guilty

Tris: Grady where's Chloe why is
she not texting

Grady: That girl Ashlynn drove
us home

Not sure if Chloe got caught,
fingers crossed she didn't

Elliott: Did you hear Ashlynn's
BF dumped her

She was a hot mess last night

Tris: I've seen pictures of him on
Insta he's a babe

Elliott: Grrrr

Tris: Not as hot as you obviously

Hannah: Poor Ashlynn

                Chloe: Sorry just woke up

                I'm fine. Glad everyone else
                is too. Elliott are you feeling
                OK?

Elliott: Fine but starving
and my voice is really growly.
I like it

* * *

Noelle: Where are you

Hello

Are you alive

Chloe: Sorry just seeing
these

Yes fine

So sorry I slept in your bed

Noelle: No prob I slept in
my moms

More space anyway

Chloe: I have to tell you
something

It's gross

Noelle: What that you and
Grady had sex in my bed?

*The sheets are already in
the laundry lol*

Don't worry about it

Worry about Reese

*I've never seen her like
this*

Chloe: She told you?

Is she freaking out?

Noelle: No worse

Super quiet and intense

Be careful

Chloe: Careful how??

Noelle: I don't know I'm
just warning you

Chloe: GREAT

Tuesday, February 6

It started as soon as I got to school yesterday. Freshman year all over again, that month after I'd gotten caught cheating with Mac and the whole school knew. People whispering while staring at me, people giggling and turning away as I passed by, people muttering, "Shhhh. Here she comes." Quick glances. Long, interested looks. Elbows to friends' ribs to alert them that I was coming down the hall. From Noelle's squad, narrowed eyes and disgusted expressions. From Noelle, serenity and calmness and unawareness of my existence, like she has nothing to do with what's happening to me. It's quiet on social media so far. We'll see how long that lasts.

Wednesday, February 7

If I can get through this part, I'll be OK. It feels like I have to drop out of school, but I don't. I just have to keep myself from crying until I get home or, if I can't wait that long, until I'm in the girls' bathroom.

Thursday, February 8

All this interest in me, all this furtive gossiping, just because I had sex at a party? It's possible, but it seems over the top. What if Reese is embellishing? What if she's claiming that we were doing something disgusting or weird? If my friends know what she's been saying about me, they won't tell me. Noelle says she's "staying out of it." I have to hear the worst, but even the people who like me won't help.

Friday, February 9

Someone posted a picture of my head photoshopped onto a porn star's naked torso. #chloeho is back as a hashtag. It still pulls up results from freshman year. I can't stand this. It's all I can think about. My ankle is basically healed— I don't care. Grady sent me a massive bouquet of flowers for Carnation Day—I couldn't enjoy it. Nothing cheers me up.

Saturday, February 10

Not that it matters, but Miss Murphy cast the show a week ago. Tris is Gomez Addams. Olivia is Wednesday. Izzy, the girl who stole the lead from me last year, is playing a mom—I forget the character's name. Not a big part, anyway. Some freshman is Morticia. That freshman is having the best month of her life. I was her two years ago, so I know. She probably thinks she's found her calling and she'll be a happy musical theater geek for the rest of her life. Little does she know she might turn into me: a bitter, jaded junior who doesn't even remember to write down casting updates, much less bother to audition for the show.

Sunday, February 11

Mom took me to an art museum in the city. It was strange to see paintings of girls around my age, some of them running away from fauns, some of them posing with books, some of them sitting there looking out at you. They must have had problems at their schools too. They probably spent entire years cringing in embarrassment. What did their enemies say about them? What is Reese saying about me?

Monday, February 12

I got it out of Jacqueline. I thought I might, because she's both incredibly gossipy and also clueless or rude enough not to worry about hurting people's feelings.

I pulled her aside first thing, right before homeroom, and said, "Can I ask you something embarrassing?" (No human can resist this question.)

"Yeah, sure," she said.

"I don't know what Reese is telling people about me. Is it really bad?"

"You don't *know*?" She looked like I'd just read out her winning lottery numbers. She was going to get to pass on juicy dirt to the source of the dirt itself!

She came closer and lowered her voice. "She's telling everyone that at Noelle's party, you texted her asking her to come upstairs, and when she went, you and Grady were having sex. And then you asked her if she wanted to have a threesome."

I laughed. It was half forced, half real. "No one believes that, right?" I said.

She lifted one shoulder. "People aren't sure. Is it true?"

I looked at her. "Obviously not." Didn't she see? None of it made sense! How would Grady and I have managed the timing so that we were sure Reese would walk in on us? Did anyone who wasn't filming porn ask someone to join in on sex that was already under way? If I wanted to have a threesome, isn't my boyfriend's ex-girlfriend the one person I'd never ask to be the third? Why do the Puritans at this school even care if someone has a threesome? What's the big whoop? And doesn't anyone notice that Reese made up ALMOST THE EXACT SAME LIE about Noelle last year?! It's like she's a burglar with a signature and her signature is threesomes! It's not only obvious, it's lazy!

I tried to explain all of this, but I could tell Jacqueline didn't believe me. It didn't matter what I said or how stupid Reese's claim was. I could go around denying it to every single junior individually and they'd all assume I was saying it wasn't true because I was embarrassed. The sex part is plausible, and that makes the rest of it plausible too.

Tuesday, February 13
I finished my homework early and decided to do an hour

of phonebanking. As usual, my ratio was 97% voicemails to 3% humans, but one of the humans was a woman who said "Hello?" in a warm, quavery voice. When I told her why I was calling, she said, "How wonderful! My granddaughter ordered me one of those fabulous Planned Parenthood book bags—you know, the ones that list all the services—and it's my favorite library tote!" She sounded so kind and understanding. For a second I considered telling her about Reese and asking her what to do, but I got control of myself and stuck to my script. Still, I was thinking, *Maybe we'll start talking, she'll ask me about myself, we'll become friends, and THEN I can tell her!* But of course we only discussed dwindling access to health care for women, which is much more important than me and my "problems."

Wednesday, February 14

My Valentine's Day present to Grady was a heart-shaped box of chocolates, a handmade card, and a promise not to mention Reese or my hashtag for the entire day. He said, "Why would you say that? Talk about it all you want. It's a big deal!" He is my valentine for life, and it doesn't matter if we break up when we get to college. I'll always love him.

Thursday, February 15

Whenever I'm with Grady at school, even if I'm not

touching him, everyone around us leers and stares and whispers.

Friday, February 16

Reese posted a picture of herself kissing her own reflection and captioned it "menage a moi." So many likes. So many cheerleading comments. So many subtweets about what a disgusting slutbag I am. (I'm paraphrasing.) I hate going to school. The only thing that helps is pretending I'm a statue, like Noelle told me to do back in September. A statue with a stone brain that can't process what's happening to me. Thank God break starts tomorrow.

Saturday, February 17

Hannah thinks I'm being punished because I lied to my dad (punished by God, I guess) and that it'll be her turn next. I don't believe in God, but I get where she's coming from.

Sunday, February 18

Hannah has ruined my life.

She felt so guilty about getting away with lying and drinking that she confessed to her mom, who promptly called Noelle's mom and my dad. Dad doesn't yell, but he yelled "CHLOE!" from downstairs, and from the tone of his voice, I knew exactly what had happened.

He was irate. I'd lied to him *again*, I'd endangered myself, I couldn't be trusted, etc., etc.

"If you think I'm going to give up on you, you have another think coming. You're grounded again, for a month. I'm going to check on you every single night and morning to make sure you are where you're supposed to be, and I'm considering installing cameras in public areas of the house—"

"Oh yeah? Oh yeah?" I shouted. I wasn't even trying to be calm. I was screaming like a little kid. "Go ahead! Install cameras! I'm moving in with Mom!"

"Chloe, calm down."

"Don't TELL me to calm down!"

"You living with Veronica—that wouldn't work for either of you."

"This again! You think I don't know she's a mess? I know that! I don't care! At least she's not a dictator! At least she understands that I'm not 10 years old anymore!"

"I think we should both take a break and discuss this again once we've cooled off."

"Great! Whatever! I'm not changing my mind!"

Chloe: Dad grounded me for
a month

Mom: Not again! What was
your supposed crime this time?

Chloe: I jumped out the
window to get to a party
after he told me I couldn't go

And then stayed out all
night

Mom: Oh darling, nothing could
be more healthy at your age.

Chloe: Would I be grounded
at your house?

Mom: Of course not. I'm
philosophically opposed to grounding.
Read up on the Stanford Prison
Experiment. I would never turn
myself into a prison guard, or you into
my prisoner.

Chloe: I might need to move
in with you for a while

Maybe until college

Would that be ok?

Mom: *Darling, of course! This is*
what I've dreamed of!

Perfect. Wonderful.

Monday, February 19

Dad has seriously installed one camera in the front
entryway and another one, an all-weather model, on
the roof of the screen porch, overlooking the backyard.
He showed them to me and explained that they connect to his phone. "I didn't want to resort to a hidden
nanny cam," he said, like I was supposed to thank him
for being so open with me.

Tuesday, February 20

Dad and Miss Murphy fought about me. Or discussed
me, I guess.

"It seems extreme, Charlie," I heard Miss Murphy
say. I was sitting on my bed with the door open, and
they were in their bedroom with their door closed. They
seem to forget our house was built by colonial Ameri-
cans who knew nothing of soundproofing.

"I put them out in the open," Dad said. "It's not like
they're in her bedroom."

Miss Murphy didn't respond.

"I know I'm losing it a little," Dad said. He probably

sighed, although I couldn't make it out. "She's terrifying me. I never thought she'd act like this."

"She's a teenager."

"But she's not like other kids. I expect more of her."

Again Miss Murphy didn't say anything.

"What am I supposed to do?" Dad asked. He sounded angry. "Just let it happen? Let her do God knows what? Have you seen the stats on heroin deaths in this county over the past five years?"

"Charlie, you know she's not a heroin addict."

"Not *yet*."

"I can imagine how scary it is to know she might get hurt, but you can't keep her locked up until she graduates."

"I can't let her defy me like she's been doing."

There was a pause. "She's your kid," Miss Murphy said. "I don't want to interfere."

It's not that she said anything wrong. I am his kid. She's not my mother. But it feels like a superhero appeared on a rooftop and was about to fly down and rescue me but then changed her mind and flew home to do the crossword puzzle.

Wednesday, February 21

Mom: Let me know if and when you think you might like to move in. Fingers crossed you'll say SOON!

Chloe: Sorry to be a flake but
I'm not sure what's going on

Thursday, February 22

That was the last straw, I'm pretty sure.

Miss Murphy has spent the break reading, going to prenatal yoga, and looking at websites about baby names, baby furniture, baby clothes (gender-neutral, because they've decided not to find out what they're having), and baby-raising advice. I can tell she's trying not to talk about it too much in front of me, but Dad always brings it up at dinner, and then they get carried away and have a 40-minute discussion about, for example, whether cord-blood banking is a scam or a worthwhile and relatively low-cost gamble.

Tonight they got onto the topic of sleep training, and Miss Murphy brought up her college friends.

"Devorah and Ben still have Ezra in their room, and he's got to be five by now," she said. "But Jillian sleep-trained Claire at four months. She said it was two weeks of screaming, and then Claire caught on. Now she sleeps for 12 hours straight, apparently."

"Wow, two weeks of screaming," I said. "So you're not gonna go that route, right?"

"What's your concern, Chloe?" Dad said, staring at me.

"I mean, I have to get up really early in the morning.

I don't think it's fair to make me wake up all night."

Dad looked at Miss Murphy, then back at his plate. I saw him decide to say nothing and then change his mind. "It doesn't seem to have sunk in yet, Chloe, so let me spell it out for you," he said. "Our family has changed. Miss Murphy is part of it now, and soon a new sibling will be too. We'll all have to accommodate each other and be flexible. Do you understand?"

"Yeah," I muttered.

Now he was angry. "Do you understand?" he said again.

"Yeah."

"Try again, Chloe."

"Yes." My tone still wasn't perfect, I guess, because he said, "Again."

"Charlie," Miss Murphy said.

"Yes," I said.

"Again," he said.

I took a breath. "Yes."

"Good."

He can punish me, he can be disappointed in me, but for him to talk to me like he can't stand to be in the same room with me? For him to tell me the baby comes first, and if I don't like it, I can shut up about it? I'm not sticking around for that.

Friday, February 23

I'm packed. I'm going. I'm sitting by the window watching for Mom's car.

Dad's at work and Miss Murphy's at yoga. I got up early this morning after a bad night's sleep and started putting my things in bags. I'm taking only the things I like, which turns out to be almost nothing. A few pairs of jeans. A couple of tops and sweaters. My favorite books. Etc. It all fit into a rolling suitcase and a few zip-top bags. When I was ready, I called Mom. She started twittering with excitement as soon as I told her I was ready to move in. She said it's fine for Snickers to come too.

Dad's going to be furious, but this is for the best. He doesn't want me. Like he said, he has a new family. Mom doesn't want me either, even though she thinks she does. But if neither one of them is interested in being my parent, I'll choose the one who doesn't treat me like Rapunzel.

Saturday, February 24

Dad hit the roof. Mom told me she had to call him to tell him I was safe, and a few minutes after she did, he showed up at her door. They stayed on the balcony outside her apartment to talk. I was in the guest bedroom with the door open, and at first I couldn't hear anything they were saying, but then they raised their voices, and I got bits and pieces.

". . . her decision, Charlie. That's what I'm trying . . ."

". . . in her ear, spewing lies . . ."

". . . outrageous accusation . . ."

". . . not staying here . . . ludicrous."

I crept out of the bedroom and closer to the front door so I could hear better.

Mom said, "You're so used to being the quote unquote good parent, you can't conceive that she might actually want to live with me!"

"She's here because she's mad at me," Dad said, "which is fine and developmentally appropriate."

"Please don't lecture me on child development, Charlie."

"Even granting the premise that she wants to be here, which I'm not, what makes you think you're fit to take care of her?"

Mom laughed bitterly. "Besides 14 years on the job?"

"Not quite 14," Dad said.

"And now you throw Mexico in my face."

"Jesus Christ, Veronica. Mexico wasn't a little tiff we had that I'm raking up because I'm annoyed. You abandoned her! Do you think any judge would consider you a fit guardian?"

"I'm her *mother*, Charlie. Her *mother*. And don't you dare threaten me. I'm not a lawyer, as you love to remind me, but I am a storyteller. And the story I'd tell a judge is that Chloe fled an overbearing father and his live-in girlfriend after months of feeling like an unwanted guest in her own home."

Huh. I'd never said anything like that to her, but she'd understood my motivation anyway. Maybe her novel wasn't as terrible as I'd assumed.

Dad said, "Is that how Chloe explained it to you?"

"I'm not going to betray her confidence by confirming or denying."

"I'd like to talk to her."

"I'm sure she's heard you bellowing out here. If she wanted to talk to you, she would emerge."

"Just go get her, Veronica."

"I'm afraid I won't do that."

Silence. Snickers was by my side, staring at the door. He looked up at me to see what was going to happen next. I half hoped Dad would push past Mom and barge into the apartment, but he didn't, and after saying something I didn't catch, he left. Mom came in glowing with self-satisfaction and excitement, wanting to tell me exactly how the conversation had gone and then dissect it with me for hours. I got away as fast as I could and hid in the guest room—my bedroom—feeling sick. Had I really run away from home? Was I really going to sleep in this strange, half-empty place?

Sunday, February 25

Dad called me three times yesterday and another three

today, but I didn't answer. I couldn't. The most I could muster was a text telling him I'm fine and I'll call him soon.

I haven't slept a wink since I got here. I have the same feeling I got the time we visited Uncle Julian in New Orleans, like I'm twice as awake as normal and all my senses have been heightened. At home—at Dad's—I hardly even looked at my surroundings. Everything was so familiar, I didn't need to observe things consciously. Here nothing is familiar. The mattress is thin. There's no lamp on my bedside table, and the overhead light makes the room look bluish. The walls are bare. The window looks out on a very tall, very thin evergreen tree.

I've never been so grateful for my phone, or this little diary, or Snickers, who is currently sitting on the end of my bed, staring at the closet with a nervous expression. They are the three things that make me feel a little bit less alone.

Monday, February 26

I thought maybe people would forget about my supposed threesome attempt over the break, but no, nothing has changed. If anything, everyone seemed refreshed, like they'd spent the vacation resting up so they could come back and make fun of me with new energy. One of Reese's minions actually called out "Hey, Chloe Ho!" across the hall to me. Some kids looked shocked, but many laughed. I pretended I hadn't heard, when of course I had, which everyone knew, especially since I was blushing bright red. I thought maybe my parent problems would put my school problems in perspective, but it turns out school is still torture.

Tuesday, February 27

Miss Murphy pulled me into her classroom after first period. "Do you have a minute?" she said. "I'll give you a late pass for your next class."

"Don't you have kids coming?"

"Not for a while. This is my prep."

We sat next to each other at two student desks. Someone had written *Fuk this shit* on mine. Was the defacer a bad speller, or did s/he think leaving off the *c* would make the word less sweary, or more cool?

"I'm not going to lecture you," Miss Murphy said.

"OK."

"I guess I'm wondering if you went to your mom's to escape me." She said it with a little laugh, but I knew she wasn't joking.

"No," I said.

We sat there in silence for a moment.

"I don't think we realized what an impact it would have on you," she said. "Me moving into your house, I mean."

I traced "Fuk" with one finger. "Well, I don't think you're going anywhere now," I said. "Since the baby's coming and everything."

"That's true," she said. "I guess it's too late, but I wanted to apologize for intruding."

I looked over at her teacher's desk. She'd draped a cardigan over the back of her chair. She'd worn that cardigan the day she and Dad went apple picking. Also the night after she moved her mom into Woodcrest.

She said, "I know your father can be rigid, but . . ." She sighed. "I told you my dad moved out west when I was a kid, right? I used to dream about living with him. Whenever I visited, he bent over backward to be the cool parent. He never gave me a curfew, he thought it was hilarious when I came home drunk, that kind of thing. I begged my mom to let me move in with him and his new family, which I'm sure just about killed her. But when she refused, some buried part of me was relieved. My 16-year-old self wanted to live with the more permissive parent, but my ageless self knew it was a terrible idea. Hedonism is fun for a day or two, but it doesn't actually make you happy."

"It doesn't make me happy being grounded for months on end either."

She was trying to make eye contact, but I wouldn't look at her. "I understand how you feel," she said.

"I don't want to live with my mother," I said. "I don't want to live anywhere. I'm just counting down the days until college starts."

"Right. That makes sense."

Silence.

She said, "All I can say is that I know I've made it worse, the feeling of not wanting to live anywhere, and I'm sorry."

"That's OK," I said, because that's what you say when grown-ups apologize.

I was on my way out the door when she said, "I shouldn't get involved, but, Chloe, if you could call your father, it would mean a lot to him."

"I definitely will," I said, and I meant it at the time, but now it's almost midnight and somehow I still haven't done it.

Wednesday, February 28

Dad showed up in the parking lot of Mom's building right as I was locking up my bike. He must have left work early. The only other time I can remember him doing that was the day he came home to catch me hooking up with Grady.

"Hi, Dad," I called. It was hard to speak, because seeing him in person was such a surprise, and so sad.

"Is it all right that I drove over here unannounced?" he said.

"Sure," I said.

We sat on these uncomfortable wooden benches by the parking lot that no one ever uses. The air was damp and cold, but I was warm from my ride.

He was going to make a big effort to stay calm. I could tell that right away.

"How's it going so far?" he said. "Living with your mother?"

"It's fine."

He thumped one heel against the brown grass underfoot. "She can be a little harsh."

I laughed. "'A little harsh'! Yeah, tell me about it."

"I worry about you," he said.

"You don't have to," I said. "I'm not eight anymore. I'm not, like, scared of her."

"That may be true, but it would be irresponsible of me—"

"Dad, I'm not coming back." I took a breath. I would be calm, like he was being. Adults really respond to a nice, measured tone. "I'm not mad at you, and I'm sorry I snuck off like that without talking to you about it first. I just need a break. It's hard, living with you and Miss Murphy. I like her, but she was my English teacher, you know? And now she's your girlfriend, and she's pregnant. Which is great. I'm happy for you guys. But it's weird for me. I'm sure you can imagine."

He didn't respond, but he nodded.

I said, "I mean, I don't know if you could get a judge to, like, order me to go back to your house."

"Oh, probably I could," he said. The way he said it, I knew he wouldn't.

"Dad, I'll still visit you on the weekends. It's not like I moved to another state."

He didn't smile. "If you change your mind, tell me. Don't be embarrassed. And don't worry about the consequences. I can deal with Veronica."

"OK. Thanks."

He rested his elbows on his knees and stared down at the ground. "I should bring over all those banana chips we have. You're the only one who likes them."

That's when I knew this was really happening: he was going to let me stay with Mom. I felt sick. *Stop me,* I thought. *Don't let me do this. Insist that I come home with you this minute.*

But I didn't say it out loud, and he didn't read my mind. I watched him get in his car and drive off, and then I sat on the bench until I was freezing cold.

Thursday, March 1

Mom is so excited I'm here and trying so hard to make me feel at home, she's vibrating like a hummingbird. Tonight she made a quinoa salad and told me about her new job.

"*Two* new jobs, actually. Until the divorce comes through, I still have access to the shared accounts, but I won't take a penny more than I feel I'm owed. It's essential for women to be able to support themselves, Chloe. Don't feel you can depend on a man to prop you up. You never know what life will bring. Divorce, disability, death . . . You don't believe me now, but you will someday. Or maybe you'll never find out. I pray you don't."

"Yeah. So, what kind of work are you doing?" I said.

"That professorship didn't pan out. Apparently 20 years of writing workshops count for nothing. You need to publish work to qualify even for the interview stage. So, for the moment, I'm teaching an MCAT prep class in the morning and assisting at Greenworks Yoga in the afternoon. I'm seriously considering getting certified as a yoga instructor, too."

"That sounds interesting."

"I'm so glad you think so!"

While she told me about the classes she's been researching online and the "unprivileging of the mind over the body," I sat there half feeling sorry for her and half hating her for being so pitiful. I don't *want* to feel bad for her. She's my mother! She's supposed to be a lighthouse in the fog. Instead she's flailing around, breaking up with her boyfriend and being a test-prep tutor like she's 23 years old.

"Has it been lonely, being here by yourself after school?" she asked.

"I'm used to it," I said. "Dad and Miss Murphy worked until 6 or 7 too. Or *work*, I mean. Obviously they still do."

Mom gave me a fake smile. "How *are* your father and his friend?"

"They're good," I said.

"I assume she approves of all this grounding he's doing," Mom said.

"I'm not really sure." Parents! They think they're being so subtle. They might as well wear a poster board that says PLEASE TELL ME YOU LOVE ME BEST.

Friday, March 2
At least I'm not grounded here. And Grady and I can relax after school, knowing no one will burst in on us and have a meltdown. We were naked together for three hours in a double bed today! Living with Mom has its good points.

Saturday, March 3
I still can't get to sleep in this weird room with its weird evergreen-tree view, though.

Sunday, March 4
One thing about Mom is, she's not big on traditions. Dad loves them and has them for every holiday, and I'm realizing

now he also has them for days of the week. On Sundays we'd sleep in, eat a late breakfast, putter around, and do work/homework. Mom slept in today, but then she took some coffee to her room and stayed in there with the door shut for a long time, and now she's out somewhere. Snickers is getting sick of sitting on my lap, but if I don't have him to snuggle with, I'll expire from loneliness. I phonebanked for hours upon hours today, for the comfort of hearing human voices, even in the form of recorded greetings.

I'm sure I'll get used to living here. It'll take some time, that's all.

Monday, March 5

I saw Miss Murphy in the hall, and maybe her baby's had a growth spurt, or maybe I'm seeing her with more objectivity now that I'm not living with her, but wow, her bump has gotten big. I feel maybe 5% sad that I won't live with this little brother or sister and probably will be basically a stranger to him/her, and 95% embarrassed and enraged that my dad knocked up my English teacher and that she's walking around my high school all smiles, occasionally pressing a hand to her belly.

Tuesday, March 6

Mom hasn't gotten mad at me yet. Maybe she never will again. Maybe yoga has melted away her anger. I can't stop worrying that she will, though. I think it'll always be like that, even when I'm 50.

I don't want to be here, but I don't want to be at Dad's. And here I can see Grady, and no one's watching me come and go on a camera connected to his phone.

The best parts of the day happen when I forget where I am because I'm so engrossed in writing or goofing around on my phone or doing homework. The screen, the pages—they're like Lucy's wardrobe. I'm in my new bedroom; then something happens and I'm in another world, and snow is falling.

Wednesday, March 7

Mom had to stay late at the yoga studio, so I heated up a frozen burrito and ate by myself. Which is fine. Most kids do that kind of stuff all the time. It's unusual, the way Dad cooks dinner every night. I guess I got spoiled.

Thursday, March 8

I called Dad before school to ask him if this would be a good weekend for me to stay at his house.

"Oh, honey!" he said. "I would love that, but we have plans. Maybe we should cancel them."

"Don't worry about it," I said.

"Marian found a last-minute deal on a flight and

hotel package, and we're supposed to leave for Miami in a few hours. Just a long weekend. We can probably reschedule."

"Dad, come on," I said. Like he was really going to cancel a sexy beach trip to hang out with his surly teenage kid! It was annoying that he'd even pretended to consider it. "I'll see you around," I said.

"Next weekend for sure, right?" he said.

"Tell Miss Murphy I hope she doesn't get Zika," I said, and hung up on him.

Why do I have to do that? I lose my temper, say something horrible, and give up all the moral high ground. It's genetic: Mom does the same thing. Am I going to turn into her? God, in a few decades I'll probably be doing sun salutations and eating coconut oil by the tablespoon.

Friday, March 9

"Miami!" Mom said, pouring soy milk into her coffee so fast it slopped onto the counter. "Isn't that lovely for them."

"Did you see we're supposed to get five inches of snow on Sunday?" I said. "Where's the cereal?"

"I don't buy cereal anymore, sweet one. Why start the day with a carb explosion?"

I found a jar of natural peanut butter and a spoon.

Mom sat down at the table with her coffee. "I had

been having second thoughts about applying for the teacher training course, but now I can see lavish trips are fair game."

"What training course?"

"I'm sure I told you," she said. "Saint Thomas? The entire month of July? Vinyasa on the beach? I just hope I'm accepted."

"The whole month?" I said. "What will I do?"

"Oh, you'll be off at some camp, I have no doubt," she said, waving her fork. "Or why not consider getting a summer job?"

"I'll have a job," I said. "I work at the pool, remember? But I'll still need to eat dinner."

"You'll be 17 by then, darling," she said. "Presumably you'll be able to press start on the microwave. Besides, think of that contestant on the baking show— she was 17 and already making vol-au-vents like Julia Child!"

Her name is Martha and she didn't make vol-au-vents— that was Flora, from season three, not that I was going to mention that and give her the opportunity to tell me I'm petty and missing the point.

The actual point is that Mom's going to leave me on my own again. Has she seen me trying to operate an iron? It'll be a miracle if I don't burn the place down before she gets home. Not to mention I don't have a credit card, a driver's license, or a car. I guess I could move back in with Dad for the month. If he'll even let me.

Of course Mom is abandoning me. This is what she does. I knew that when I moved into this dump. It's not like I thought she'd changed. I knew she hadn't. I didn't come here to rebuild our relationship or anything. I came here because I had to get away from Dad. So I don't feel betrayed now. I really don't.

Saturday, March 10

That didn't take long.

I was sitting on my bed doing my homework. The headboard was cutting into my back, and I couldn't hold my textbook and my notebook on my lap at the same time. After an hour I went to find Mom, who was sitting on the couch, wearing her striped bathrobe and reading a book. I said, "Do you think I could have a desk for my room and maybe a lamp for it, and also a lamp beside my bed?" I admit, I could have phrased it a lot more politely.

Mom sat up fast. "You WILL speak to me with respect," she said.

"Sorry, Mom. I'm sorry. I'm sorry." My heart pounded. I knew I couldn't prevent what was coming, but I had to try.

"Do you know how much care I took with that room?" she said. "Hours to put together the bed with that little Allen wrench. And the new duvet, which you've never even mentioned. Here I am cooking dinner, rushing home from work, catering to your every whim, and your response is to demand more from me."

Anger rushed up from under my ribs. At least I can get mad at her. The day I can't, I'll know she's beaten me. "You've made dinner, like, three times since I got here. Congratulations. Do you know how long Dad's been cooking for me?"

She loomed over me, hissing, "I'm not your dad."

In the span of an instant I thought about saying nothing, and then decided I'd hate myself later if I didn't talk back to her. I faked a scoffing laugh. "Yeah, I noticed."

She got in my face and screamed, "YOU TAKE AND TAKE FROM ME LIKE A LEECH. I WILL NOT ALLOW MYSELF TO BE USED THIS WAY. YOU'RE AN ENTITLED FUCKING BRAT."

When she loses it like that, her pupils contract and her lips quiver. It feels dangerous to look away from her, but I forced myself to turn and walk to my room. Snickers had been sleeping, but he sat up to stare at me when I came in. I locked the door and lay down on the bed with my face next to his doggy face, smelling his venison jerky breath and looking at the tiny black dots on his nose like they were a secret code explaining how to find a new family.

Sunday, March 11

The worst part is the apology. Mom came into my room sobbing and actually kneeled by my bed. "I didn't mean it," she said. "I'm so, so sorry."

"It's fine, Mom," I said. She'll never shut up and leave if you don't say you forgive her, so you might as well do it fast.

"It's not," she said, still sobbing, but I could hear the relief in her voice.

I waited. Eventually she calmed down and sat by my feet. "I'm not excusing myself for losing my temper," she said. "But you can understand why I got angry, can't you? It's fine to ask for things you need, but to be asked in a tone like that . . ."

I didn't say anything. I looked out at the skinny evergreen. What if I were a giant and could rip it out of the earth with my bare hands and smash the condo building to bits with its trunk?

It's not like she hits me. Other people have it so much worse than I do. Some people are impoverished or persecuted or both *and* their mothers yell at them or hit them.

I don't know. I guess I am an entitled fucking brat.

"I'm not asking for an apology, of course," she said. "It's I who need to apologize. And I do, profusely."

I kept waiting. Finally, finally she left, but not before kissing my forehead.

Monday, March 12

"Are you OK?" Grady said after school. We were in bed, and I had my face pressed so far into his neck, I couldn't breathe very well. It felt great.

"I hate my mother," I said.

"Yeah?" he said, and waited.

"That's it," I said into his neck. "We're fighting. No big deal."

He nodded. I could tell he wanted to keep talking, but I didn't, so I went down on him, and that changed the subject effectively.

Tuesday, March 13

This is the part where Mom plays the role of a perfect mother. She brings home fresh muffins for my break-fast, leaves flowers on my dresser, reminisces about cute things I did when I was a toddler, surprises me with a new desk and two lamps. Everything she does means *Is it OK yet? Do you forgive me? Do you still love me?* I'm trying to be aloof, but it's hard not to give in to the bar-rage of affection. She can be charming when she wants to be. Also, the longer she keeps tenderly smoothing my hair away from my face and asking about my day, the less real Saturday seems. This hair-smoothing, how-was-your-day-asking mother is the kind of mother who would never scream at her daughter, so maybe she didn't really scream at me. Or maybe it was someone else, some other version of her.

She always tries to erase what she did, and it shouldn't work. It doesn't, because I never forget. But after a while it feels too awkward to keep making things unpleasant in our daily lives. She wears me down, and I don't have the strength to stay cold. Maybe this time will be different, and I'll ignore her until it's time to leave for college.

Wednesday, March 14

I went to Grady's after school. We sat around with Bear and his babysitter, drawing pictures with scented markers and assembling emergency-vehicle puzzles. When Mrs. Trevor came home, she said, "Chloe, I'm so glad to see you! You can stay for dinner, right?" I said yes, and I didn't text Mom to tell her I'd be late. When I finally made it to the condo, she didn't ask where I'd been. "There are leftover quesadillas in the fridge," she said cheerfully. "Should I heat some up for you?"

"I ate," I said without looking at her. That's the good thing about this stage: I can skip dinner and be rude to her with impunity. She's too repentant to get mad.

Thursday, March 15

Tris and I went to Hannah's to watch movies. No boyfriends allowed. We gave ourselves temporary tattoos

(Teenage Mutant Ninja Turtles, from Bear's babysitter) and ate Peeps and chocolate eggs.

"Is your mom gonna get mad that we're going through all the Easter candy?" I said.

"She gets extra for the whole month," Hannah said. "She'll hide different stuff for me to find on Easter morning."

"She still hides candy for you??" Tris said.

"I think it's nice," I said way too angrily. Tris and Hannah stared at me. "Sorry," I said.

"What's wrong?" Tris said.

"Nothing," I said.

I could talk to them about it. They would understand. Hannah's parents basically called her a prostitute for having a boyfriend freshman year, and Tris's dad is half a bigot. But it didn't even occur to me to be honest. I couldn't betray my mother like that.

"Is it the Reese situation?" Hannah said.

"Yes," I said, because it's that, too. "I'm so miserable."

They rubbed my arms and told me how awful she is and how terribly her life will turn out. "She's peaking now, right this second," Tris said. "It's all downhill from here."

"Cruelty is only rewarded in high school," Hannah said.

"At *best* she'll be a flight attendant wearing way too

much foundation," Tris said. "But I'm thinking more like nail technician with three ex-husbands."

I knew they were telling me the kinds of things their moms tell them. They'll be great parents someday.

Friday, March 16

People still stare at me in the halls, especially when I'm with Grady, but it's not quite as bad as it used to be. Maybe Reese has done her worst.

Saturday, March 17

I kind of wanted to lie around in my old bedroom wasting time on my phone while scratching Snickers behind the ears, but Dad and Miss Murphy had planned a day full of treats. First they took me out to brunch. Then all three of us got pedicures. Dad even read *US Weekly* while his feet soaked. He refused to get his toenails polished, however. For dinner, he grilled on the deck, even though he had to wear his winter parka to do it. We watched a movie together afterward. I was too self-conscious to enjoy the Junior Mints they'd picked up for me. How is that possible, when a few weeks ago I was lying on their/our couch wearing a T-shirt and no bra, licking my finger and pressing it into the Sour Patch Kids dust at the bottom of the package while watching *Real Housewives* and also scrolling through Instagram? Now I feel like a guest.

Dad said, "How's everything with your mother?" and I said, "Pretty good." That was that.

I asked Miss Murphy how she's feeling, and she said, "I'm having bad heartburn." And that was that.

Sunday, March 18

I was almost glad to see Mom after Dad dropped me off tonight. At dinner, I laughed at one of her jokes. So it's over. I caved. Now she can relax, knowing everything will go back to normal. I'm so weak. I hate myself.

Monday, March 19

Reese must have launched phase two today, because the whispers and glances and mean giggles were back in full force. Jacqueline came up to me in the hall looking excited and hustled me over to a corner.

"You should know everyone's talking about you," she whispered. "Reese said . . ." She trailed off.

"What?"

"She said she felt bad mentioning this before, but she's concerned for your health. She said she saw warts on your . . . you know."

"My . . ." Neither of us could say it. We nodded at each other to confirm that we were talking about my vagina.

"She said it's definitely HPV and you'll have to get the warts frozen off with dry ice. Is that true?"

I stared at her. "Of course it's not."

I walked around for the rest of the day loathing everyone. I don't know who's spreading lies about me and who's not, so I assume every single person I see is my enemy.

Tuesday, March 20

Mom was slamming things into the dishwasher this morning. I could tell she was mad, so I said, "Sorry. I was going to do that after I brushed my teeth."

She said, "You certainly get through a lot of drinking glasses!" Her voice was fake cheerful. It's too early in the cycle for her to freak out on me, but she's letting herself be mean already. Nothing has changed. What did I think, that yoga has magical healing powers?

At school, Harper came up to me after lunch. She looked excited and nervous. Reese and her friends were watching in the background, giggling to each other, so I knew it was going to be bad. "This is for you," Harper said. She handed me a bottle of extra-strength Tylenol. I should have slapped it onto the floor, but instead I took it.

"Thanks," I said. *Thanks.* I thanked her. That's the part that embarrasses me the most, thinking about it now.

"It's for your you-know-what," she said. Her voice quivered with, I guess, glee. "All that dry ice must hurt."

"Oh my *God*," Reese squealed, hiding her face in one of her friends' shoulders.

I said nothing. The Tylenol was still in my hand. Only a few people had overheard, but that was enough. The whole school would know in an hour. Maybe some kids would think, *Poor Chloe*, or, *They're so mean*, but no one would publicly side with me. My low status is contagious. No one would risk her own standing to speak up for me.

As they walked away, laughing together, a huge fury filled my stomach and poured out into my arms, legs, hands. Maybe Mom feels like that when she loses it. If so, I understand why she doesn't change. Rage feels really, really good.

Wednesday, March 21

I texted Noelle at 6 a.m.

Chloe: Is your mom home?

Noelle: No away for work

Chloe: Wanna skip school?

Noelle: Yeah sure

Come on over

I rode off on my bike at the usual time, so Mom wouldn't suspect anything, then went right to Noelle's house.

"What's wrong?" she said when she opened the door.

"Nothing. I didn't feel like showing up today."

"But you look awful."

"Thanks."

"Not like that. Your face. Whatever, your expression. Did Snickers die?"

"NO," I said, knocking on her doorframe.

"What, then? Here, come in."

She led me through the house to the kitchen and got a bottle of vodka out of the freezer.

"Vodka?" I said.

"Bloody Marys."

"You know how to make them?"

She held up her phone, which is in a white case decorated with the words "YEAH OK" in bold black letters. "The internet tells you how to do everything, in case you hadn't noticed."

I knew when I texted her that Noelle was going to be mildly bitchy, like she always is. That's why I wanted to see her.

She pulled a few items out of the fridge. "So spill it," she said. "Why are we ditching?"

"Give me a break, Noelle," I said.

She was opening the Worcestershire sauce and wouldn't look at me.

I said, "You're a bad friend, you know that?"

She laughed. She's impossible to offend. It's an enraging but also relaxing quality.

"Oh yeah?" she said.

"I've noticed you're never around when Reese has one of her little servants attack me. What a coincidence!"

She pushed my drink across the counter to me. I took a sip. It tasted spicy and salty. I could feel it racing through my bloodstream, lighting me up red along the way. No wonder grown-ups are so obsessed with brunch.

"Good, right?" she said. I didn't answer. I wasn't about to give her the satisfaction. She sighed. "Would you rather I stand there watching you get humiliated? Would that make you happy?"

"No!" I said. "I'd rather you stood up for me!"

She rolled her eyes. "Like that would make any difference."

"You could at least text me," I said, "and let me know she's planning something."

She stirred her drink with her finger. "Yeah. I could do that."

It didn't make me feel better that she'd conceded that much. It made me angrier. "That's not enough, Noelle."

"It was your suggestion!"

I looked into my glass. I could see flecks of horse-radish and pepper in the tomato juice. "She did this to you last year," I said. "Don't you remember how it felt?"

"I remember it sucked, but honestly, the details have faded. I'm over it. You'll get over this."

"Jesus, Noelle."

"What am I supposed to do, Chloe? I'm not cheering her on, or whatever. I'm still friends with you, even though Reese hates that I am. That's as much as I can offer."

"But have you said anything at all? 'Chloe's my friend, so please cut it out'?"

"You know that would only make things worse."

I took a big sip. "You're a good person. How you can stand being around her?"

She twirled the Tabasco bottle around by its little neck. "I never claimed to be a good person."

I gave her a shocked look. This is why I love her and why she scares me. Who admits, even to herself, that she doesn't care about being good?

"I told you that from, like, the first conversation we ever had," she said. "I know you remember."

It was the second conversation we ever had, but I took her point.

"I like the drama. I like being popular. Any popular kid who says she doesn't is lying. I want my life to be exciting. That's it."

She finished her drink, pulled my empty glass over, and started mixing two fresh Bloody Marys. She wasn't going to apologize, and she certainly wasn't going to step in and save me from Reese. All she could be was her terrible, interesting self.

"Do you still have your hair-cutting scissors?" I said.

"Shears, not scissors. Yeah, upstairs."

I headed up. I wasn't sure she would follow me, and I didn't care either way, but she did.

The shears were under Noelle's bathroom sink, in a clear plastic box that also held dyes and bottles of product with names like "toner" and "developer." I pulled them out of their case, gathered my hair in my left hand, yanked it above my head, and cut into it.

"Not like that!" Noelle shrieked. She was holding our drinks, but she put them down on the counter and tried to take the scissors from me. I wouldn't let her.

"Stop! Don't cut across!" she said. "You have to dip into the hair straight down, from above." She mimed to show me. I didn't say anything, but I copied her.

"Wow," she said when I'd finished. Most of my ponytail was lying on the floor, and I looked like . . . Well, I looked like I'd cut my own hair. "Will you let me fix it, or are you too out of control right now?"

"Go ahead," I said.

She guided my head under the sink, got my hair wet,

then flipped me upright and combed it out. She put a towel over my shoulders and stood behind me, snipping.

"Are you having a breakdown?" she said.

I looked at her in the mirror. I didn't feel like I was. I didn't even feel drunk. I felt calm.

"I want to dye it too," I said.

"What color?"

"What color says, 'Think whatever you want about me. I could give a rat's ass'?"

"Black?" she said.

"Too obvious." All the emo kids and all the goth kids and all the kids going through a tough time wear black clothes, nails, hair, everything. Black says, *I'm rebelling by fitting in with all these other people who also think they're rebelling.* Black is conformist.

"What's your favorite color?" Noelle asked.

I opened my mouth.

"And don't lie and say, like, orange," she said.

I had been about to lie, although I was going to say red. The real answer was embarrassing.

"Pale pink," I said. When I was little, my favorite Barbie had a pale-pink ball gown dotted with tiny flecks of gold. I must have studied that dress for hours, holding it up to my bedroom window to watch the sun light it, twirling Barbie by her feet to make it spin.

"Not bad, but kind of basic," Noelle said. "Millennial

pink is already over. And every celebrity has had pink hair at one point."

"Perfect," I said. Nothing could be more truly rebellious than not caring if you look basic. If you actually want to be cool, rave about your love of pumpkin spice lattes, wear UGGs, and learn all the words to pop songs. I tried to explain this to Noelle, and she said, "So you want to be ironically basic?"

"I guess so."

"You could never pull it off, but I'll give you the pink anyway. It'll look conventionally cool, which is probably the best you can hope for. No offense."

It took hours. Noelle opened the window, but the chemicals still gave me a headache. I didn't care. The bleach turned my hair dry on the spot. I didn't care. Noelle mixed up Manic Panic with conditioner, then painted it on my head with a big brush and worked it through my hair with her gloved fingers. I watched my reflection in the mirror like it was someone else's.

"We have to sit around for an hour to give it time to soak in," she said. "Want to come outside with me while I smoke a butt?"

"Sure," I said, but I didn't move.

"You're not freaking out about the color, are you?" she said.

"No."

"It'll fade in a few weeks," she said. "If you want to keep it up, we'll have to redo it. Try to take cold showers if you can, and don't wash your hair too much."

"OK." I was looking out the bathroom window at the bare black branches jiggling in the wind.

"Hey." She poked my foot with her foot. "Are you with me?"

"Yeah."

"Good. Let's go downstairs."

She stood there waiting for me. She'd skipped school because she knew I needed her. She'd spent a good part of the day cutting and dyeing my hair. She was delaying her cigarette and waiting patiently while I moped and gave her one-word answers. I was an outcast to most of my class, but she hadn't abandoned me, even though it was her best friend who'd cast me out, and she was endangering her social standing every time she saw me. I said, "You're not a bad friend. I'm sorry I said that."

Thursday, March 22

I went to school spoiling for a fight. My new hair looked like a wig, and it made me feel protected, like I was in disguise.

It started early. Reese's friend Lianna said "Nice makeover" in a laughing voice as she passed me before homeroom.

"THANKS!" I shouted, in a tone of crazed enthusiasm. She looked back at me with a surprised, almost scared look on her face. I gave her a huge fake smile, like the Joker. She hurried away.

Tegan Kinney, some sophomore I don't even know, posted a picture of the back of my head, captioned "Witness protection program lol." She hadn't tagged me, so by the unwritten laws that everyone follows, I was supposed to pretend I didn't know the photo existed, which is absurd, since you can't post a picture of anyone or anything without the entire school knowing about it and discussing it within minutes. I commented three times. "Lol," "Lol," "Lolololololol." She deleted the picture between second and third periods. I was with Noelle when I happened to see Tegan in the hall, walking along with two of her friends. "Hang on," I said to Noelle, and went right up to Tegan. "Hey," I said. "Did you want a better picture? I'll pose for you."

"That's OK," she said. She looked terrified.

"Take a picture," I said.

"I'm sorry if I—"

"Take a picture," I said.

"Do it," Noelle told Tegan. "You don't want to insult her, do you?"

"We'll take a selfie," I said, holding my hand out for Tegan's phone.

She gave it to me like she was forking over a loaded weapon. I leaned in until our shoulders were touching, gave the camera the finger with one hand, and pressed the white circle with the other.

"Enjoy," I said.

Noelle gave me an admiring look as we walked away. "You're in rare form," she said.

I glowed inside. "Rare form," yes. I felt like a big bloody boxer.

I couldn't concentrate at lunch. Tris and Hannah were asking me delicate, careful questions. They were concerned about me. Grady was too, although his concern was almost canceled out by his excitement about my new hair. He was looking at me like I was made of cotton candy and he was a kid at the fair. It was all a distraction. I wanted complete silence so I could focus on . . . something. I wasn't sure what. The warm fury in my stomach.

Ten minutes before lunch ended, Reese stood up from her table. Her squad followed. As she walked toward the exit, closer to me, I stared at her. *Say something,* I ordered her silently. *Come on. Say something.*

She didn't, but Harper did. She muttered, "Hooker hair," and her friends burst out laughing. Reese smacked her lightly and said, "Stop. You're so bad."

It was enraging, the way she pretended to be the

sweet one, the nice one, and every single person at MH propped up this lie. She said whatever venomous thing she wanted to, pretending she was only speaking up because she was so concerned/so hurt/so truthtelling, and then she unleashed her minions to do the enforcing while she sat on her throne calmly observing the chaos she'd caused. Maybe I snapped because I couldn't take her lying, or maybe I snapped because I was always going to snap at that moment, but whatever the reason, I swept my lunch onto the floor and climbed up on the table.

"Hey!" I screamed, and put my arms in the air in a cheerleader V. The cafeteria got quiet fast. Tris and Hannah and Grady looked up at me, worried. Noelle looked up at me with interest. I dropped my arms and smiled down at them like everything was fine, even though my heart was beating out of my chest. "Hi," I said, looking out at the hundreds of kids now staring at me. A few of them said hi back.

"I know it's a little weird that I'm yelling at you from a cafeteria table," I said. "But I have no choice." I looked at Reese. She was looking back at me with an incredulous smile. I WOULD make her stop smiling if I had to stand up here until the semester ended. "She's lying about me, and you might not believe me when I say that, because she's also telling the truth about me." People were quiet and attentive. They wanted to see what I'd say next. Even the lunch monitor was listening with a rapt expression. "I didn't invite her up to a bedroom at Noelle's house and time it perfectly so she'd catch me having sex with Grady. Honestly, I'm not good enough at having sex yet that I'd even be able to pull that off." Sex! I'd just said "sex" twice in front of a giant crowd of my classmates. And it wasn't that hard. Courage surged through me. "And I didn't ask her to have a threesome with us." As I said it out loud, it sounded so ridiculous that I laughed a little, and from the looks on people's faces, I could tell that the laugh was convincing. They were wondering if Reese was lying after all. "What really happened isn't that different from what she said, though. She did catch us having sex. I'm pretty sure she walked in on us on purpose. Not in a creepy way, or maybe in a creepy way. I think she still likes Grady, she wants him back, and she's mad that I lost my virginity to him and she didn't. Maybe that's why she's telling you all I have HPV, which I don't, because I got vaccinated. You should too, if you haven't yet. It's only two shots and it prevents cervical cancer." People were glancing at each other, exchanging shocked, excited looks. This was going to be so fun to text about later. I was giving everyone the gossip fodder of their lives.

"I know I'm the freak with pink hair and you think

you'll never be like me, but you could be tomorrow," I said. "She could do this to any one of us, and you know I'm right. If she comes after you, be brave. Don't let her lie about you. Don't let her make you feel ashamed of yourself. Stand on a table and tell the truth. That's all. Thank you."

Reese wasn't smiling anymore. She looked furious. I didn't care. Let her spread a million more rumors about me. I'd get back up on that table every day if I had to.

I was hoping no one would boo me or throw food at me, and no one did. And although it wasn't like a slow clap started in the front row and slowly spread and turned into a roaring ovation, a few kids actually did clap as I climbed down. A few more yelled, "Wooo!" And as Reese's minions formed a phalanx and escorted her away, someone called, "Bye-bye, Reese!" and maybe I'm imagining things, but it sounded like a bye-bye to her entire reign of terror.

Friday, March 23

My friends are freaking out. Tris keeps sending me quotes from my speech followed by the skull and cross-bones emoji. Noelle is suddenly all up in my biz. She's never texted me so frequently or politely before. Even Hannah seems proud of me, and she's not one to approve of dramatics. "You spoke truth to power," she said.

I thought Grady might be mad or embarrassed that

I told a cafeteria full of kids we're doing it, but I was forgetting that for guys it's simple: if you're having sex, congratulations; you're getting laid, and every other dude is happy for you and jealous of you. Even if you're boning someone who's supposedly not attractive, congratulations are still in order: once again, you're getting laid, and that's the most important thing. Guys don't get slut-shamed. Apparently freshmen have been following and friending Grady like crazy, and boys he's never met before are coming up to him in the hallway and asking questions. Some of the questions are sweet ("I like this girl. What should I do?"), some are nosy ("How long did she make you wait before, you know . . ."), and some are pervy and porny ("Have you gone in the back door yet? KNOW WHAT I MEAN?"). Actually, I would hate it if I were him, but so far he seems entertained, not annoyed.

Reese didn't even come to school today. She had her squad tell everyone she might have mono, and she even posted a picture of herself lying in bed looking wan, but I'm not sure people fell for it. Her core friends posted sympathetic comments, but she didn't get the usual hundred extra remarks from sycophants trying to butter her up.

Saturday, March 24
Sleepover at Hannah's, just the two of us. Her parents ordered pizza, and after we ate, we fled to her room.

"So what are you going to *do?*" she asked me as soon as she'd shut the door.

"Do about what?"

She paused. "I'm not sure. After the cafeteria, it seemed like something else was about to happen."

I knew exactly what she meant. But what am I supposed to do next? Usurp Reese?? How would I even go about it? What would I do if I managed to pull it off? These questions scare me. My mind skitters away whenever I think about them.

Sunday, March 25

Mom met Grady for the first time. It wasn't a big thing. I'd invited him over because she'd said she was going out with a friend from the studio, but her plans fell through, and I didn't want to bail on him for no real reason. A few minutes before he arrived, I said, "My boyfriend's coming over, if that's OK."

She put down her book and said, *"Boyfriend?"*

Urhhaggahhhh. If parents didn't make such a big deal about everything, kids would talk to them more. Don't they remember this from their own youth? Why do they gasp and make shocked faces?

"Tell me *more!*" she said. "Chloe, this is thrilling!" I saw something occur to her. "Is this the reason—no, no. I won't ask."

She looked at me hopefully, like I would say, "If you're referring to my UTI, yes, Grady's penis is the reason I got one."

When I didn't say anything, she went on. "What's his name? How long have you two been an item? What do his parents do?"

I was about to answer her when the doorbell rang. She leaped up.

I didn't think I cared about the meeting, but when I saw Grady standing in the doorway, partially obscured by her body, I realized I did care. Not what she thought of him, but what he thought of her.

We sat in the living room with her for maybe 20 minutes. She interviewed Grady, and he was relaxed and nice. She was on her best behavior, and aside from a few dramatic hand gestures and one reference to her chakras, she didn't say anything too humiliating. I was wondering if we'd sat there long enough that it wouldn't be rude to go to my room when she said, "So, Grady, what's Chloe like at school?"

"She's great," he said.

"But describe her as you would to a total stranger! What does everyone think of her?"

"*Mom,*" I said.

Grady looked at me. "I think people would say she's a theater kid."

"Not anymore," I said.

"No, still," he said. "And as of, like, a week ago, she's popular."

"Really!" my mother said. She didn't sound pleased.

Grady smiled. "She is if she wants to be."

"This is certainly a surprise," Mom said.

Sitting there with Grady made me see my mother in a slightly different light. I could imagine how someone who didn't know her—Grady—would find her interesting and appealing. "Were you ever popular in high school?" I asked her.

"Hardly," she said. "Shakespeare-obsessed non-athletes don't generally attract the adulation of their peers."

Mom was a theater geek, like I am. Like I used to be, I mean.

She said, "Grady, tell me: how did Chloe come by this popularity?" She looked like she was settling in for a long chat.

"Well," I said, standing up, "we've got a lot of homework to get to."

I didn't think she'd let us leave, but she gave us a knowing look and said "Have fun!" in a disgustingly suggestive tone of voice.

"We can't mess around," I said, as soon as we were in the room with my door closed. "She'd love it too much. She'd probably wait outside to say a bunch of sex-positive things."

"All right, but I wore the boxer briefs you like," Grady said.

"Don't tell me that!" I said.

We sat on my bed. Grady picked up my hand and kissed it.

"I don't know if I want to be popular," I said.

"Yeah, it might suck," Grady said.

It probably would suck. Or would it be amazing?

Monday, March 26

Reese is back. According to her Instagram, the mono turned out to be "just a horrible stomach flu. #blessed #yayforflu?" She's still ignoring me. Maybe I'm imagining things, but I think the ignoring has a different quality. She's less haughty ice queen, more Marie Antoinette pretending not to hear the peasants screaming for blood.

Also, Tegan showed up with her hair dyed pink! I did a double take when I saw her in the hall. She looked at me and gave me a shy smile. Was it a coincidence? It probably was, right?

Tuesday, March 27

Two more girls have dyed their hair pink.

A senior, this artist everyone thinks is so cool, including the cool kids, came up to me in the hall to introduce herself and ask if she can take my photo for a series she's working on.

Kids still whisper about me when I pass by, but it's different. No one's laughing.

Someone named NachoGirlfriend tweeted, "If you use #chloeho you're part of the problem and you missed the movement."

Ella Green replied, "Can we reclaim it tho? #chloehoforpresident."

It was sunny and warm for the first time this spring, and Noelle and I met up in the clearing to eat lunch. We had it to ourselves, aside from a few skater kids sitting on a log, smoking weed and whispering together.

"So what's it like to have fans?" Noelle said.

"The pink thing? Is that really because of me?"

"Oh my God, Chloe."

"Well, *I* don't know! I don't want to assume anything!"

"You're like a folk hero, dude."

Joy flooded my body. I wish I didn't care so much, or at all, about what other people think of me, but I care sooooooo much.

Wednesday, March 28

Noelle and I went back to the clearing, and it was packed. *Packed.* Kids were sitting on every free inch of grass and dirt.

"What's going on?" I whispered to Noelle.

"Take a wild guess," she said.

No one actually talked to me, but I could feel people watching me, and I'm almost positive this freshman whose name I don't know took a picture of me with her phone when she thought I wasn't looking.

This is really happening. People are studying me. They're copying the things I do. Suddenly I have power, and it's scary. I'm not sure what to do with it or if I even want it.

Thursday, March 29

Reese and the squad were sitting on the top step this morning, as usual. As Hannah and I walked up the stairs toward them to get to homeroom, someone called, "Hey, Han!" It was Zach, jogging up behind us. "Do you have a second?"

I thought she might say she was busy, but she said "Sure" in a calm voice, and went off with him after saying goodbye to me.

I looked at Reese, who was watching Hannah and Zach walk away. She sat there motionless and expressionless. *Hannah's in big trouble,* I thought, before remembering that Reese will think twice before she messes with any of my friends now.

Friday, March 30

That's it. I've decided. I'm seizing the throne.

Before lunch Jacqueline pulled me aside in front of

the main office and said, "Is Hannah OK?" Her voice was hushed.

Even though I didn't know the specifics, I instantly understood what was going on, and I saw what I was going to have to do. "I don't know what you're talking about," I said.

"She sent this super-long text to Zach begging him to take her back. Did you see them running off together before classes started? Right after that, he told her she has to stop stalking him."

"Jacqueline, that's not what happened."

She bristled. "Yes, it is. I've seen the text! Zach sent it to Reese because he wanted her advice about how to turn down Hannah."

I put my hands on her shoulders and looked into her eyes. "Jacqueline, I would bet my college tuition that Reese wrote that text herself and has been sending it around saying it's from Zach."

She didn't believe me, but I didn't care. In a few weeks no one will be interested in Reese's forged texts.

Saturday, March 31

I think Zach might like Hannah again. Oh, the irony! Apparently the real reason he wanted to talk to her on Thursday was to apologize for cheating on her with Reese and to see if she's still mad at him.

"We have to tell everyone the truth," I said to Hannah on FaceTime.

She shook her head. She was sitting on her bed, leaning against her flowered sham. "No one would listen. It doesn't matter anyway."

"No, it *does* matter. It *does*. It's evil, the way she lies. She lies about you, the nicest person in our school! And for what—because her ex-boyfriend talked to you in front of other people and she's jealous? She thinks she can control you and put words in your mouth like she's playing dolls with you. You're not a doll! You're a real human, with human dignity!"

Hannah smiled. "I might as well be a doll. She has all the power."

I brought the phone closer to my face. "I'm not going to let her do this to anyone else."

"You mean you're going to . . . What are you going to do?"

"You know." It seemed melodramatic, to put it into words, but we both understood: I'm going to lead a coup.

Sunday, April 1

I never should have waited this long. I hope I haven't lost all the momentum I got from my cafeteria speech. And now that I've decided on a course of action, how do I set out? What do I do exactly? I need help.

Monday, April 2

Another day of pink hair (three new dye jobs today alone!) and respectful hallway glances. I'm walking differently. Less hunched in on myself. I take up more space. I hold my head up.

Between classes Nadia came up to me. "Hi!" she said. "I don't know if you even remember me."

"Nadia, we worked together all summer. I remember you," I said.

"Oh good!" she said. "I just wanted to say the cafeteria thing was so cool. You're really brave. There's a girl like Reese in my class—"

"Hang on," I said. Across the hall I'd spotted Noelle and Reese. Noelle was standing with her head bent, listening to something Reese was saying in her ear.

"I don't want to be rude, but I have to go," I said to Nadia. I started to walk away, then turned back. "Listen: whoever your Reese is, she's not as scary as you think."

Nadia seemed awed. I crossed the hall and touched Noelle's arm. "Can I talk to you for a second?"

Reese looked at me directly for the first time since the cafeteria. "Noelle and I are busy," she said.

I looked back at her. Is she beautiful? I don't know what an objective observer would think. We've all agreed, as a class, that she looks like a movie star. It's a conclusion we reached together as kindergartners. This whole time we've probably been confusing strength and merci-lessness with beauty! And even supposing she is beauti-ful: Who cares? Why did we ever assume we should be governed by whoever is the most conventionally attrac-tive person in our class? What are we, a bunch of fashion magazine editors?

"*Are* you too busy, Noelle? Or can you come with me?" I said. Nadia was still watching from across the hall. A bunch of other kids were too.

Noelle looked back and forth between me and Reese with her eyes narrowed.

"I'll come," she said.

"Noelle," Reese said.

"We'll talk later," Noelle said.

"Bye," I said to Reese, and waved in her face.

As we turned the corner, Noelle said, "This had bet-ter be good."

When we got through the double doors that led to the underused staircase off the math wing, I stopped. "You have to choose between me and Reese," I said.

"What are you talking about?"

"It's not a good look for me," I said. "One of my clos-est friends is also close with Reese? It makes me seem weak."

She crossed her arms. "Why should I care how you seem?"

"I'm going to do it, Noelle." I didn't explain further, because I knew she'd understand what I meant.

She got closer to me. "You've been waffling for days now. You had a good moment, but you haven't done anything with it. You're like freaking Hamlet."

"I'm not waffling anymore," I said. "Come on. Do it with me. Help me. You said I'm a folk hero! Everyone's scared of Reese. Everyone loves me. Wouldn't you rather be on my side?"

She was studying my face. "You'll have to make them scared too. If you're going to do it right."

"No, I won't," I said. "I'll change the whole thing."

She rolled her eyes.

"She deserves to lose you anyway," I said. "Don't forget what she did to you last year."

She looked off to the right.

"Let me think about it," she said. "I'll tell you tomorrow."

"Fine," I said. "Meet me in the clearing before homeroom."

"Cloak and dagger," she said, but she wasn't making fun of me. She was respectful. I liked it.

Tuesday, April 3

She was waiting for me when I got there. The air was cool and the sun felt thin. When she saw me, she put out her cigarette on the bottom of her shoe.

"I choose you," she said. "But I have some conditions."

"Let's hear them," I said.

"You have to let me redo your wardrobe. You look—I won't say it. I have to help you."

"Fine."

"You have to keep up with your hair."

"My hair doesn't matter!"

"Trust me when I say it matters. If you don't understand that, I'm not doing this."

"Ugh, fine."

"And you have to consolidate your group. What's it going to be—me, Tris, Elliott, Grady?"

I nodded. "And Hannah," I said.

"She's so religious," Noelle said.

"Hannah's nonnegotiable," I said.

"All right." She looked into the distance, thinking. "Elliott's cute. Grady obviously has status because he's gone out with Reese and you. Hannah at least got that good haircut last year." She looked back at me. "You have to get everyone together as a group more. None of this hanging out in pairs, or whatever you do. It doesn't work like that."

"OK."

"And you have to do something to show everyone it's you now, not Reese. Tomorrow. No more procrastinating."

My stomach dropped, but I didn't want to disappoint her. "All right."

"I'm sure I haven't thought of everything, and even if I have, other stuff will come up. When it does, you have to listen to my advice. I'm way better at this than you are. You have raw talent, but you don't know what you're doing."

"God, Noelle. Fine."

She put out her hand, and we shook on it. She smiled for the first time since I'd arrived. "Reese is going to have kittens," she said.

Wednesday, April 4

As soon as I woke up this morning, I knew what to do. I got ready as fast as I could and texted my friends, "Meet me on the top step ASAP." I arrived half an hour before school started. Grady came soon after, then the rest of them.

"We're sitting here?" Hannah said.

"We are," I said. Noelle gave me a small nod of approval. More and more kids were arriving, and we were getting lots of fascinated looks. It didn't take a sociologist to understand what I was trying to do. Everyone who saw us got it.

We talked about nothing and laughed in a way I hope came across as genuine and not nervous. No one mentioned the thing we were all clearly waiting for.

When Reese arrived and saw us, she immediately got out her phone, like she'd heard a notification.

When Harper showed up a minute later, Reese whispered something to her, and then they both headed up the stairs. My heart was pounding. It was a few minutes before homeroom, and kids were streaming toward the open doors all around us. Even the ones who weren't staring at us were aware of what was going on. What would Reese do? Would she physically drag me off of her seat? Would she say something cruel? I tried to look amused and calm, in the hopes of tricking myself into actually feeling amused and calm.

"Hey, guys! *Such* a pretty morning, right?" Reese cooed. She didn't even slow down.

"Gorge," I said, deadpan.

This is so much easier than I thought it would be.

Thursday, April 5

Back to the clearing with Noelle before school. It was too early for anyone else to be there, and the trees seemed to lean in close, listening to us conspire.

"How good was the steps thing?" I said.

"Really good," she said. "I'm proud. I don't think she'll try to reclaim her spot today, but let's hurry up and get there just in case."

I wanted to revel in my victory more, but she was rushing on to her next agenda item: getting the squad together at my mom's condo after school tomorrow.

I told her if she said "squad" again, I was calling the whole thing off. "We couldn't be whiter," I said. "Stop appropriating."

"But—"

"'Squad' is so dated anyway," I said. That one got her.

"What, then?"

"Nothing! These people are my friends. They don't need a group name."

She was Googling. "What about 'crew'? The crew. That's not bad. Hang on, let me read you the synonyms."

"I'm not doing it like Reese did," I said. "Do you know how much the rest of the school hates the squad and its stupid name?"

"That's the point!" Noelle said, but maybe she saw on my face that I wouldn't change my mind, because she said, "Fine. No group name for now. We'll come back to that one."

"No, we won't," I said.

"How's tomorrow for the hangout?" she said. "Where's your phone? You have to text everyone."

Is this what Noelle did with Reese? She's like a puppeteer!

After I'd sent the message, we headed to school. On our way, we bumped into Jacqueline.

"Hey, Jacqueline," I said. "By the way, I talked to Hannah about the Zach thing. He was actually apologizing to her for something that happened a while back. I'm sure you remember."

"Can I tell people?" she asked, with her eyes wide.

"It's not a secret or anything," I said, meaning, *Yes. Shout it from the rooftops.*

"We gotta go," Noelle said.

We rushed to the entrance. The top step was empty.

Friday, April 6

Noelle ran our hangout like it was a meeting. She let everyone prowl around my mom's condo for a while—only Grady had been there before—and then went into the living room, clapped her hands, and said, "Guys. Guys!" Everyone came in and sat down.

"You probably heard I broke up with Reese," she said. "Because Chloe's the new Reese."

Everyone looked at me. I tried to appear self-deprecating, even though inside I felt like Caligula.

"First thing," said Noelle. "I spoke to Mr. Grayson, and he's agreed to move our lockers so we're all together."

"*What?*" Hannah looked shocked. If there's one thing she hates so much she doesn't even want to believe it exists, it's favoritism. I could tell she was appalled that the vice principal would grant Noelle's request just because Noelle's beautiful and popular.

"We're all going to move up by Chloe," Noelle said.

"It will give us more time to talk and hang out between classes."

"But what about the kids whose lockers we're taking over?" Elliott said.

"Second item," Noelle said. "Let's start thinking about prom. Limo rental, hashtag, date for Hannah."

"Hannah should go with Zach!" Tris said. "Reese would expire!"

"I don't think so," Hannah said.

Noelle gave Tris an approving nod. "Third item. We need to make a statement. What would you all think about dying your hair pink for Monday?"

"No, Noelle," I said. "You can't ask them to do that."

"Why not?" Elliott sounded excited. "We should!"

"I can't," Hannah said. "My mom would be so upset."

"I'm in kind of a live-and-let-live situation with my dad," Tris said. "Pink hair would send him into a coma."

"Why pink?" Hannah said. "I mean, I know it's . . ." She gestured to my hair. "But isn't it Reese's color? It reminds me of girly girls. Mean girls."

"It's ironic," I said. "It's, like, making fun of pink being girly."

Hannah looked skeptical.

"She overthinks it," Noelle said, brushing off my color explications. "And if you associate pink with meanness, that's a good thing."

"No, it's not," I said.

"We could do something else pink," Elliott said. "Even if it's not our hair."

"Pink Vans!" Tris said.

"Not bad," Noelle said, "if the shade works. Anything magenta-ish is obviously a nonstarter." She was already on her phone. "Actually, these are perfect." She flipped the screen out to show us. "Tell me your sizes and you can pay me back."

Elliott said, "'On Wednesdays we wear pink.'"

Noelle gasped, which I'm not sure I've ever heard her do before. "YES! Elliott, you're a genius. Pink Van Wednesdays."

Well, it's happening. I'm turning into Regina George. (Not really. I'll never get mean. I can do this and still be myself.)

Saturday, April 7

Noelle slept over last night. We stayed up late, so I assumed we'd sleep in, but I woke at 8 a.m. to find Noelle standing in front of my open closet with her hands on her hips.

"All of this has to go," she said. "What's your dad's credit card number?"

I groaned and put my pillow over my face. Noelle came to the bed and shook my shoulder.

"I don't know," I said through the pillow.

"You don't *know*? How do you buy stuff?"

"He gives me some money in September to get clothes for the year."

"Do you have any cash left over?"

"Not really. I have a little saved from my summer job."

Noelle sighed. "We'll have to go thrifting. Which is fine, actually. Get up! Let's eat and leave."

"Noelle?" I said.

"Yeah?" She'd walked over to my dresser and was looking into a drawer with horror, like it was full of ancient tuna salad.

"Why are you doing all this for me?"

She shrugged. "It's a challenge. I want to see if I can pull it off." She took a pale-blue sweater from my drawer and waved it at me. "Which I can't do if you're dressed in stuff like this." I was half insulted, half excited to see what she'd pick out for me.

Sunday, April 8

Noelle spent most of my money on black jeans and two pairs of black leather booties, one with perforations, the other with straps and gold buckles. At the thrift store she drove us to after we went to the mall, she bought clothes for a dollar a pound: about 30 tops, mostly gray or black or white, mostly oversized. Some old band T-shirts. Some boxy button-downs.

"We're doing generic cool girl," she said. "It's a good contrast with Reese, since she goes for feminine and sexy. Avoid bright colors and anything tight, except on your legs. No more sneakers except on Wednesdays, OK? And this is your new backpack." She showed me a beat-up black leather bag. "That green nylon thing with your initials on it you can toss."

"I'm not tossing it! My dad gave me that!"

"Keep it for your camping trips, or whatever. Next weekend we're touching up your color, and I want to give you heavier bangs. Also, you need to start wearing eyeliner more. It's fine if it's messy. I'll show you at my house."

It's very restful, being bossed around.

When I got back to my mom's, I washed everything, then tried it on. I looked so good, I started panicking about Noelle. What would I do if she left me and went back to Reese? I need her! To reassure myself, I texted her a bunch of selfies, and she texted back the fire emoji, which calmed me down.

Monday, April 9

I felt self-conscious showing up at school today. It's always potentially catastrophic to debut a new look, which is why people do it in September, when everyone else is doing it too. But I didn't get any weird looks, and a bunch of different girls said, "I like your outfit."

Tuesday, April 10

Noelle passed out handwritten notes from Mr. Grayson excusing us all from homeroom so we could move into our new lockers first thing this morning. Grayson doesn't have a crush on her, does he? I can't understand why else he'd bend over backward to give her what she wants.

Everyone was talking loudly and laughing as they put their stuff away. Noelle took tons of pictures. "One for Insta, one for Snapchat . . . ," she said as she clicked.

"Take a picture of Tristan's *huge* locker mirror," Elliott said.

"Excuse me for wanting to see my entire face at once," Tris said.

A few teachers poked their heads out to see what we were doing, but no one told us to be quiet. Instead, they smiled at us indulgently. I think somehow they know that we've come to power. Even when it's working in my favor, it's disappointing and gross the way teachers respect our hierarchies.

Zach stopped by to say hi to Hannah between classes.

I took a picture of them smiling at each other and posted it with the musical notes emoji (for Zach), the haloed smiley (for Hannah), and a green heart (since I feel green is the most neutral, least romantic color among the heart options). Hannah gave me her blessing before I hit share, of course.

"Jacqueline said no one believes Reese anymore," I said. "About the stalking thing."

"Thank you for fixing that," she said.

"What's going on with you and Zach, anyway?" I asked. The hallways were emptying out, but neither of us had to walk far to get to our next class.

"Nothing," she said. "Really."

"Have you forgiven him for cheating on you?"

She thought. "I guess so."

"Hannah! No!"

She shifted her books in her arms. "Forgiveness isn't the same thing as masochism. I would never get back together with him."

"Do you think he wants to?"

"I think maybe." She smiled a little. "This might be terrible, but it feels good, seeing him so guilty and apologetic."

"That couldn't be less terrible," I said. "Enjoy it, Han!" I hope she does. I hope she revels in that guilt like it's a bubble bath.

Wednesday, April 11

We missed homeroom again because it took so long to get a perfect shot of our feet in their Vans. We thought the grass would be a good background, but it looked patchy and sad, so we moved to the sidewalk, which looked boring. Finally we settled on the wooden floor of the gazebo. Then we had to figure out how to choreograph the shot. I thought it would be fine if we all stuck one foot in; Noelle said that had been done to death. Next there was a lot of debate about the filter.

"We're really late," Hannah said at one point.

"Yeah," everyone else said vaguely. I couldn't imagine what homeroom announcement might be more important than figuring out the correct hashtags.

Thursday, April 12

I decided we needed a more prominent spot in the cafeteria. Reese and her friends sit all the way at the back, so we need to sit all the way in the front. Yes, the front has traditionally been the nerdiest section of the cafeteria, but that only made it more appealing. If you can take a dork zone and make it cool, you have real moves. So at the beginning of the lunch period, I marched up to the AP kids' table and said hi.

"Hi," they all said back, looking up at me.

"Is there any way I could borrow your table? I hate to

ask, but it's . . ." I'd planned to keep talking, but I didn't need to. They were all standing and packing up their lunches. One of them said, "Of course!" Another said, "No big deal!" Was I imagining that they looked slightly scared?

My friends and I sat down. The entire cafeteria was watching us carefully, even the people who were pretending not to.

Noelle tried to start a conversation, but I couldn't focus.

"Was that mean?" I said. "That was mean, right? I'm regretting it already."

"Well . . . ," Hannah started.

"No," said Noelle. "Look—the AP kids are right there." She gestured toward a table in the middle of the room that they were sharing with some marching band members. It didn't look like there was enough room for everyone. Some people seemed to be sitting two to a chair.

"They look squashed," I said.

"They're fine," Noelle said firmly.

Eventually we managed to discuss normal stuff (a meme, a show, who'd slept the least the night before), but it was as if we were all acting in a play together, reciting lines someone else had written for us.

Friday, April 13

I was planning to leave the AP kids alone and revert to our old spot, but when we got to the cafeteria, the front table was empty. One day of us sitting there, and the whole school has ceded the territory. I felt guilty, and to drown out my own guilt, I started laughing and talking loudly. My friends got loud with me. I sat on Grady's lap. Elliott sat on Tristan's lap. Noelle yelled "Mark! Mark!" across the room until Mark got up from Reese's table and came over to ours. "Sit with us," she said, and he shrugged and said, "Sure."

"What do you think of him?" Noelle asked as we threw out our trash after we'd finished eating.

"Cute but boring," I said. "Why?"

"We might need to pull one or two more people into our group," she said.

"Not him," I said.

I thought she might make me explain myself, but she only nodded and said, "It's your decision."

"Why do we need anyone else?" I said. "We're fine like we are. Just the six of us."

"The Six!" she said. "That's our name."

I rolled my eyes, but just because I knew she expected me to. As soon as she said the words, I knew she'd struck gold. The Six. It sounds so good.

Saturday, April 14

I snuck Tristan over for a sleepover without telling Noelle.

"Don't mention you were here," I told him, once

we'd eaten dinner and were hanging out in my room.

"How come?"

"Noelle thinks we should only get together in a big group. All six of us."

"But you're in charge, not her," he said.

"Kind of," I said. "I think it's more like she's Machiavelli, and I'm the random generic prince."

Tris shook his head. "You were the one standing on the table. That's all anyone cares about. You don't even need her."

"Do you not like her?"

"I think she's impressive. But I'm scared of her too."

"Same," I said. "Same."

We looked at the skinny evergreen in silence for a minute.

"I can't believe we're popular," Tris said. I felt a rush of relief. We were going to talk about it! It was fun, sitting at the cafeteria table like careless celebrities, pretending we were so used to the attention that we didn't even notice it anymore, but it was also an exhausting charade.

"I can't *believe* we're popular," I said. "Are we, really?"

"Yes!" Tris said. "Do you know how many kids say hi to me in the hall now?"

"I've started hugging people," I said. "It's so Reese-y. Like I'll hug Nadia because I can tell she worships me and I feel bad for her. Or, no, that's not true. I do it because hugging her makes me look nice. 'Look at the popular junior hugging that unknown freshman.'"

Tris laughed. "That's extremely Reese-y."

"I can do this without turning into a monster, though, right?"

"Totally," Tris said.

Normally we talk about our boyfriends for at least an hour when we're alone, but today we hardly mentioned them. There's no time for romance when you're establishing a new government.

Sunday, April 15

The six of us piled into Noelle's mom's car and drove to the botanic garden near the city. It was Noelle's idea. She wanted to post pictures of us sitting under cherry trees. It felt half fake, kissing Grady knowing she was snapping away on her phone, but still, there I was with my beautiful boyfriend, standing in the sunlight, listening to the blossoms brushing against each other in the breeze. If I really concentrated, I could stop thinking about how many likes we were going to get and focus on the feeling of Grady's mouth on my mouth.

Monday, April 16

Dad called. I almost hit decline when I saw his name on my phone, but at the last minute I swiped right. We said hi-how-are-you stuff for a few minutes, and then he said, "Marian and I missed you this weekend."

"Sorry to skip again," I said. "I've had tons of homework."

"You can do homework over here. We'll give you space."

"OK."

"So can we count on you for next weekend?"

"Sure," I said, because I wanted to get off the phone.

After we hung up, I spent a few minutes regretting what I'd said and thinking of ways to weasel out of the visit. Then I clicked on #thesix to see if any new results would surface. Then I tried #the6. Then I forgot about the weekend. I'm so busy thinking about my new position, I have no space for my parents. It's like they've become holograms of themselves. I can see them, I can hear them, but they don't seem real.

Tuesday, April 17

Mom swept into the kitchen wearing a silky robe and flip-flops with thin black straps. "Good morning," she said, pausing to kiss the back of my neck. The back of my NECK! Who does she think she is, Grady?

"Morning," I said, trying not to flinch away from her.

"You've been so busy recently, sweetheart," she said. "Always on your phone . . . always with your friends . . ."

"Mm-hm."

"Keeping up with your schoolwork, too, I hope."

"I have a 3.89," I said.

"Fantastic!"

I'd made my screen dark when she came into the kitchen, since she considers clicking while talking the height of disrespectfulness. Now that she'd gone quiet, I wondered if I could wake up my phone without enraging her.

She stopped with one hand on the refrigerator door handle, turning back to look at me. "How's the quest for popularity going?" she said with a laugh.

"Good," I said. "I did it."

Her peppy mood vanished. "You *did* it?" She sounded surprised and disgusted, like she'd just found a year-old lemon in the crisper.

"Yes," I said. "I won."

She frowned. "You know, Chloe, popularity in high school isn't exactly a predictor of future success," she said. "The idol of my class is living with his mother, and if his online presence is any indication, he still spends most weekends drinking beer with his cronies."

I muttered something like, "Yep, thanks," and scuttled to my room.

A few months ago I was exactly like my mother was in high school: an unknown theater nerd resentful of the popular kids who barely knew I existed. Now I'm the person who could have squashed my mother like a bug.

And she's *jealous* of me. My own mother is jealous that I'm popular and she wasn't. It feels awful, and good.

Wednesday, April 18

Noelle, Tris, Elliott, Grady, and I were walking through the hall when Reese and two squaddies turned the corner and headed toward us. We didn't flinch, of course, and neither did they. It got quiet, though. Reese was eating a protein bar, and as she approached, I looked at it, wrinkled my nose in disgust, and loudly said, "Ew." I saw her face get pink, and then she was gone.

As soon as we turned the corner ourselves, Tris said, "Chloe!"

"What?" I said, but of course I knew. I felt terrible.

"Yeah, what, Tristan?" Noelle said. "Those bars are disgusting. Chloe was only being honest."

Grady didn't say anything or even look anything, but I could tell from his blank face that he was disappointed in me.

I feel ashamed, but why should I? She deserves it and more. She's the one who spread lies about me. I'm not going to apologize for taking a tiny bit of revenge. It's silly that I'm lying awake, worrying about what Grady thinks.

Thursday, April 19

"Hellooooo! I'm taking my clothes off now!" We were in

my bedroom, and I was on my phone. Grady waved his hand between me and my screen.

"One sec," I said. The pink Vans pic from yesterday was still getting likes, and I couldn't stop checking. It had been my idea to lie on our backs and lift our feet into the air, where they photographed well against the blue sky. I am a social media savant.

I knew I should put my phone down and look at Grady, and I did, after I quickly reread all of yesterday's comments and all the new ones from today. When I looked up, Grady was naked except for his undies, and he looked annoyed.

"Sorry," I said.

"You're addicted," he said.

"Like you're not!"

"I'm not as bad as you!"

"Did you see that Hazel Field liked it? She's the Reese of the senior class. Or the me, I guess."

Grady groaned. "Can we please not talk about Six stuff for 10 minutes?"

"Fine," I said.

We were both so grumpy that I thought we might not have sex, but after a few seconds passed in silence, I started kissing him, and he kissed me back, and it was OK again.

Friday, April 20

Harper is one of Reese's top lieutenants, so when she

came up to me, I assumed she was going to deliver a threatening message. Instead she said, "That picture of you and Grady was so cute. The TBT one? Where you're wearing those big heart-shaped glasses?"

I stared at her. She'd called me a hooker. She'd handed me a bottle of Tylenol for my nonexistent wart-removal pain. Did she think I'd forgotten?

"We've never really hung out," she said. "Maybe we could sometime."

I wanted to say something honest to her, but I was scared. I've spent 14 years trying to get people like her to like me. I don't have any practice being real. How to do it? I told myself I *wasn't* myself, exactly; I was a girl with pink hair who didn't care what anyone thought of her. What would that pink-haired girl say? My heart sped up, but I got the right words out: "Are you serious?"

She looked taken aback. "I didn't mean to—"

Now that I'd said one bravely rude thing, it was easier to say the next. "You're Reese's friend. Not mine."

"I'm sorry," she said, but I was already walking away.

I don't care if she was just following orders. I'll never forgive her, and now that I'm popular, I don't have to.

Saturday, April 21

The worst part about going to Dad's is Snickers. Every time we arrive, he thinks we've moved back for good.

You can see the relief flood over him as soon as he gets in the door.

The second-worst part is acting like a distant acquaintance of my own father's.

Today was low-key, at least. We hung around the house, went for a walk, then had dinner. Dad asked me about school. Miss Murphy asked me about my friends. Then it was my turn, and I asked Miss Murphy about the baby.

"I can feel it moving now," she said.

"What does it feel like?" I said.

"It's hard to describe. Like a tiny pain. The echo of a tiny pain."

I tried to avoid looking at her belly. It's not huge, but it's there. A stranger would know she's pregnant. It doesn't make sense, but the bigger she gets, the more I feel like I'm permanently stuck at Mom's. The baby's arrival is getting closer and closer, and pushing me farther and farther away from my old life.

"Do you think it's a boy or a girl?" I said, to be polite.

She smiled. "I've dreamed that it's a girl, but I've also dreamed it's a kitten I accidentally left locked in a tool-shed with no milk while I flew to Florida, so I'm not buying pink rompers yet."

Usually there's nothing more boring than hearing about other people's dreams, but this one interested me.

"So, in the dream, did you fly back from Florida?"

She shook her head. "No. It was a terrible nightmare, actually. I realized on the plane that the cat was going to die and that I couldn't get back in time to save it. Then my alarm went off. I still worry about that cat occasionally."

Dad said, "The really strange thing is, we saw a tail and two triangular ears during the last ultrasound."

"Hardy har," Miss Murphy said.

They're so cute together. It should make me feel happy, not depressed and slightly disgusted. Poor Mom.

Sunday, April 22

It's impossible to relax here, because I keep wondering if I'm in the way and they're wishing I'd go back to my mother's already. Like this morning, I went downstairs (fully showered and dressed, because it now feels weird to show up in the kitchen in my jammies) and interrupted a conversation. They were speaking in low voices, so I couldn't make out the words, but I could tell it was about something serious because of their postures and the look on Miss Murphy's face.

"Oh, sorry," I said when I realized I was interrupting them.

"No, it's fine," Miss Murphy said.

"Come on in," Dad said. He turned to pull the clean

coffeepot out of the drying rack, like he wasn't going to say anything more. Miss Murphy looked at him, then me, and said, "We were talking about your uncle Julian."

"Oh," I said. "Is he OK?"

"Yes," Dad said. Then he caught Miss Murphy's eye and said, "He's been better, actually."

"What's wrong?" I said.

Dad sighed. "He lost his job. He has a complicated explanation about a rival co-worker and a manager who's intimidated by him, but I assume he was fired because he's drinking again and he's been showing up to work drunk or hungover."

"How do you know?" I said. "Does he sound slurry on the phone?"

"He sounds like he's making a huge effort not to slur his words," Dad said.

Since I don't have a sibling (YET), I can't know what it would be like to worry about a younger brother, but I'm sure it would be terrible. Dad looked sick.

Monday, April 23

I feel bad for Mom when I see Miss Murphy and Dad laughing together. I feel bad for Dad when Mom asks how my weekend was and I say, "Eh, not great." I feel guilty whenever I snap and call Grady to say something like, "I can't stand my parents," or text Noelle, "Did your dad ever kiss Tara's earlobe right in front of you?" plus the emoji barfing a puddle of green. There aren't many minutes in the day when I don't feel terrible about my parents.

Tuesday, April 24

Everything about school is easier when you're popular. Take lunch, for example. When you're not popular, you have to get through lunch as unobtrusively as possible. The worst mistake would be drawing attention to yourself. If you bring smelly leftovers, laugh loudly, or get caught staring, you could be labeled WEIRD, which is the first step on the road to total social ruin. When you're popular, you can roar with laughter, chase your friends around the table, and scream at each other for stealing food. You can burp! Whatever you do is interesting because you're doing it. The kids at the other tables soak it all up like their eyes are tiny cameras.

Wednesday, April 25

Everyone's looking a lot sharper. Elliott got new glasses. Hannah had her lob cleaned up. I haven't worn a single item from my former wardrobe since Noelle took me shopping. Tris never needed help, but even he's intensified his look with some extra-preppy items (penny loafers complete with actual pennies, a beaded belt, an aggressively plain canvas tote). I've been trying not to ask intrusive questions—no one likes to be interrogated about what they're wearing—but today when I saw Elliott by the bike rack, the sunlight was actually sparkling off the corner of his frames, and I couldn't resist.

"I love your new glasses," I said.

He touched them. "Thanks!"

"Did Noelle pick them out, by any chance?"

He nodded, looking embarrassed. "I asked her for help. I felt like . . . I don't know. I want to look good in all the pictures. That sounds so dumb."

"No! I do too. I want to look HOT. Hot, cool, pretty. All of it."

He said, "I really like your new clothes."

"Noelle chose everything. That's why I thought . . . anyway, thank you."

We smiled at each other. Elliott's so nice. He deserves everything that's happening to us, unlike me.

Thursday, April 26

We were all at our lockers, and Noelle was calling down to Tristan, "No, let's go to my house. My mom's leaving for a work trip, remember? I had an amazing idea: we should bust out the Ouija board. Wouldn't that be hilarious?" Nadia was passing by, and she looked at us quickly, only for a second, but there was so much longing and anxiety in her tiny little glance that I felt bad—I felt truly terrible—that I'm now part of the group that screams about plans in the halls and makes everyone else feel left out. But that's the weak part of me talking. The same part that makes me forgive Mom every time she screams at me. I have to crush that part. It's not wrong to have a group of friends. It's not wrong to like each other, make plans, be loud. If other people are jealous, that's their problem.

Friday, April 27

I've been avoiding hanging out with Hannah alone, partly because I'm scared to defy Noelle, partly because I'm worried that Hannah will want to lecture me about how snotty we're being and tell me we have to stop. I miss her, though, and when she whispered, "Want to come over after school?" I whispered "Yes!" right away. The fact that we were whispering proves that Noelle is really in charge, not me, and we all know it.

We took the bus, since Hannah lives too far away to walk.

"How are you?" I said, once we'd found seats. "Tell me for real. How's school? How's guy stuff?"

"I'm stressed about my grades, obviously. Getting ready to apply to schools. All of that."

"Right. Of course. Junior year."

"Junior year."

We nodded. Teachers had been warning us for years about how hellacious junior year would be, and they were right.

"Guy stuff . . . ," she said, and stopped.

"What?"

"Say, theoretically, Zach and I got back together."

I'd been slumped down with my knees resting on the seat in front of me, but I straightened up when I heard this.

"What are you telling me?" I said.

"Do you think it's a bad idea?"

We were shoulder to shoulder. I could smell her herbal shampoo. Every part of her was so familiar to me. Her hand with the clean nails she never bites. Her legs on the seat, in the unripped, unfaded jeans she wears. What if Zach hurt her again? Zach, with his sexy man-bun and his artfully curated social media presence—he's so unworthy of her.

"Maybe," I said.

"I think he's changed," she said. "He's apologized a hundred times for what he did. He even wrote a song about how sorry he is."

Sappy, obvious, self-centered, I thought. "That's sweet," I said.

"I'm not saying I've decided," she said.

"You're mulling it over," I said.

"Right."

We stared out the window for the rest of the ride. The spring leaves looked so healthy and hopeful, like little freshmen.

Saturday, April 28

How am I going to fake politeness when Hannah brings Zach around? I'll never forgive him for cheating on her. And what if he does it again? I'll lose my mind. I'll go full Reese on him.

Sunday, April 29

Six hangout at Mom's condo. Mom was levitating with happiness. She made us nachos and said, "I'm SURE you won't touch the Coronas in the fridge," then winked at us. "Limes are in the crisper," she called as she went to her bedroom.

"Why are you always complaining about your mother?" Noelle whispered.

"Trust me, she's awful," I said.

Monday, April 30

Text from Noelle in the middle of chemistry.

Noelle: Major news

*Get a hall pass and meet me by
the North Wing stairs*

When I saw her, I said, "I almost got detention for looking at my phone in class."

"But you didn't," she said, not very patiently. "Listen, I saw Felix Nicholson this morning."

"Oh yeah?" I said. Felix is a shoo-in for the Most Class Spirit superlative. He's the head of about 16 committees.

"He told me something," Noelle said. "Teachers aren't picking prom king and queen this year. Students are voting on it."

"Why did they change the rules?"

"Something about making our school more democratic in the name of giving us all an appreciation for democracy in general. But that's not the point."

"What's the point?"

She looked at me like *hello!* "You're running for junior prom queen."

"But I couldn't run. It's not like it's a student council position."

"Oh my God, you're so naive," she said.

She's the only person left who has the nerve to insult me to my face. It's annoying, actually. Doesn't she realize who I am?

Tuesday, May 1

Six meeting at lunch. "Junior prom is just over a month from today," Noelle said. "And it's on a boat."

"It *is?*" Tris said.

"Felix said so."

Everyone looked convinced. If Felix said so, it was on a boat.

"But this is the interesting thing," Noelle said, and told them about the prom king and queen change. We were in the cafeteria, leaning toward the center of the table, murmuring with our heads close together. I could feel everyone around us wondering what we were talking about.

"The prom committee is announcing the rule change tomorrow," Noelle said. "The way it works is, at least six people have to nominate a candidate by next Thursday. The juniors vote on the nominees the week before prom. It's a paper ballot. So Tris, Hannah, and I will nominate Chloe, and I'll round up three more votes. Now, obviously, Grady can't run as prom king, since he's not a junior, so I suggest we go with Tris."

"Oh!" Tris said, sitting up straight. "Really?"

Hannah said, "What about Reese? She'll run too, right?"

"I'm sure," Noelle said. "She'll force Harper and Lianna and those guys to nominate her. And it's not like she's going to sit back and let Chloe win out of the goodness of her heart."

We all nodded soberly except for Grady, who was scraping hummus out of a little container with a baby carrot.

"I have to tell you guys something," Hannah said. "I got back together with Zach."

Everyone shrieked or gasped.

"No!" Tris said.

"But didn't he—what about Reese?" Elliott said.

Noelle was looking thrilled. "This is perfect. Have you already discussed prom?"

"Yes, actually," said Hannah. "I told him how devastated I was when he invited me to his junior prom last year and then wound up going with Reese, and he asked if he could make it up to me this year. Don't you think that's nice, that he doesn't mind going to our prom, even though he's a senior?"

"Oh, *Hannah!*" I said. "No! I think he's lucky you're letting him come with you."

"I agree with Chloe," Noelle said. "Stop feeling grateful."

Maybe if Hannah listens to Noelle and takes her advice, she and Zach will be OK this time around.

Wednesday, May 2

> Chloe: *I'm worried about*
> *Hannah*

I don't trust Zach

Grady: Yeah he's trouble

Chloe: He'd better make
prom the most magical night
of her life

Grady: I hope not

You don't want to hit your
lifetime magic high at prom

Better to wait till you're like 35

Chloe: Are you talking
about me?

Grady: ?

Chloe: I get the sense you
think prom queen is lame

Grady: I mean kinda

Don't you?

Chloe: Yeah

I don't CARE about it

It could be fun though?

Good profile pic

Me in a tiara

Grady: I guess

Chloe: Don't rain on my
parade

Grady: I guess it would be
cool if you won

But I'll love you either way

Chloe: So you don't think
I'll definitely win?

Grady: CHLOE

Chloe: What??????

Thursday, May 3

We were heading outside after school, yelling to each other and bouncing off the lockers. Hannah was showing Elliott something on her phone, and I maneuvered myself so that I was next to Zach, then tugged on his arm until he slowed down.

"What's up?" he said, smiling at me.

"Hang on a sec." I slowed down and let the others get ahead of us.

"What's going on?" he asked. "Is everything OK?"

"Fine!" I said. "I was just thinking we never really talk."

"True."

At that moment Nadia passed by going in the opposite direction and called, "Hi, Chloe!"

"Hey!" I said.

"You have a lot of fans these days," Zach said.

He probably expected me to say something modest, but instead I said, "Last year I was too unimportant for you to say hi to in the halls, and now look at us! I'm the one deigning to talk to you!"

"Ha!" he said uncertainly.

"So, listen, how's it going with you and Hannah?"

"Great. But I'm sure she's told you all about it. I know how you girls love to gossip."

The September version of me would have giggled.

The May version of me said, "I don't need to gossip, Zach. I have spies everywhere."

He looked at me to see if I was joking or not. I didn't smile. (I also didn't tell him I was mostly thinking of Jacqueline. "Spies" sounds more sinister than "spy.")

"Wow, OK," he said, and laughed nervously.

"You really hurt Hannah last year," I said. "I would hate to see anything like that happen again."

"No, I know, I—"

"It would *really upset* me," I said, turning to stare into his eyes.

"I understand," he said.

I've never been so glad I overthrew Reese. I'm using my powers for good! I'm protecting Hannah!

Friday, May 4

It occurred to me that a nice person would nominate her best girlfriends for prom queen, and that also, I really don't want to nominate Noelle and Hannah, because I want to win.

I want to win.

I wouldn't tell even Grady that. It's a relief to write it down here.

I felt guilty enough that I asked Noelle if I should nominate her and Hannah, and she almost rolled her eyes out of her head. "Do you listen to anything I say?

Don't make my life harder than it needs to be." Her annoyance was comforting. She's always giving me permission to be selfish.

Saturday, May 5

It's 68 degrees and the sun is shining. My mom wasn't home last night, and Grady and I figured out this new thing where I kind of plank over him while he—it's too X-rated to even write down, but it was so good, thinking about it now is giving me the shivers. I'm young! My skin is soft, my hair is shiny, and sometimes I'm so full of energy, I have to dance wildly in my room for a while so I don't explode. And because of all of this I CANNOT STAND being around Dad and Miss Murphy right now. They're so *slow* and *sleepy*. They come into the kitchen yawning, releasing terrible grown-up morning breath into the air. They grab their lower backs and wince. They hunch over their laptops and say, "Open the link I just sent you— pretty sweet undercrib storage drawer." It all makes me want to scream!!!!!!!!! I would rather feel angry and upset at Mom's than cooped up and bored at Dad's.

Sunday, May 6

I took Snickers out for a two-hour walk this morning so I could escape the house and also talk to Grady on the phone. When I got back, I was tired and a little sweaty, and Dad and Miss Murphy were sitting at the island drinking coffee.

"You got up early," Dad said.

"Yep." I walked to the sink to refill Snickers's water bowl.

"When you were little, you woke up at 5:30 a.m. on the dot. This was every day for three, four years," Dad said. I turned back and saw that he was looking at me affectionately.

I know there's something wrong with me, because I didn't think, *Oh, how sweet*; I thought, *I'm not a baby anymore. I'm 16 and I'm getting laid constantly, so take your affectionate look and shove it in your undercrib storage drawer.*

Monday, May 7

Of course, when I got back to Mom's, the sink was full of dirty dishes, the recycling bin reeked of red wine, there was no food in the fridge, and Mom was out and hadn't left me a note or texted me. It did make me feel almost scared for a second, but then I told myself it's better this way. I don't need parents. I need to be left alone.

Tuesday, May 8

Lianna came up to me in the hall and said, "I love your boots. I've been meaning to tell you that."

"Thanks," I said.

"Where did you get them?"

"I don't even remember," I said, because I didn't want her rushing out and buying a pair. They're *my* signature boots.

She pressed her notebook against her chest. "I don't know if you knew that Noelle and I are, like, really tight? Or used to be. We were best friends in junior high."

"Oh yeah?"

"I miss her," she said.

"She's the best," I said. What did she want from me? She used to be friends with Noelle. Now I am. Maybe if Lianna hadn't decided to serve a tyrant, she wouldn't be in this position, but she had, and I didn't feel obligated to help her.

"I actually have to meet Noelle now, so . . ."

"Oh, OK. Talk to you soon!" Lianna called as I walked away.

Wednesday, May 9

Noelle told me Lianna wants to come to prom with us. "It would look good," she said. "A defector coming over to our side."

I wrinkled my nose. "She's so annoying, though." *And she said "nice makeover" to me in the hall to humiliate me after I dyed my hair pink*, I thought, but did not say out loud, because I wasn't sure Noelle would consider that a good enough reason for me to resent Lianna for life.

Noelle raised her eyebrows. "She was a million times more popular than you in September."

"It's May now," I said.

We were sitting at the same picnic table where Reese had tried to find out if I was still a virgin. I'd been scared and freezing then. Now I was confident, and the sun was making my skin warm.

"Lianna's not coming to prom," I said. "I don't like the way she kisses up to me. It's gross."

Noelle laughed.

"What?" I said.

"Nothing. You sound like Reese."

I waved my hand in the air, pushing the smoke from Noelle's cigarette out of my face. "No, I don't. I'm not excluding Lianna to make her feel bad. I don't like her, that's all."

Noelle looked away and didn't respond.

I'm *nothing* like Reese. It's my right to choose my friends! I don't have to pull in someone who used to be awful to me and only wants to hang out now because I'm a star.

Thursday, May 10
I officially got nominated for junior prom queen today.

So did Reese and so did Izzy, the music theater geek/ clarinet player. Junior prom king nominees are Tristan, Griffin Gonzalez, and Mark Philips. They read the list during homeroom, and everyone in my class clapped and whooped when they heard my name. I smiled and tried to look surprised.

Friday, May 11

The musical's opening tonight; I'm going tomorrow. I wish I could skip it—it'll be three hours of stewing in the dark, feeling jealous of the people onstage and sorry for myself—but I could never do something so rude and selfish to Hannah and Tris.

Saturday, May 12

Went to the show tonight. For the first 15 minutes I couldn't stop wondering if everyone around me was staring at me and feeling sorry for me or even whisper- ing about me (*That's Chloe Snow. She got the lead as a freshman, but I guess it was a fluke. She didn't even try out this year*), but holding Grady's hand helped, and after a while I got absorbed in the show and stopped obsess- ing about myself. And Tris! Oh my God, Tris. He's my best friend, but sometimes I think I don't know him at all. How does he transform into other people like that? It's like he's not even inside himself, like the character he's playing has sucked out his soul and is using his body as a shell. As Gomez Addams, he was dignified, soulful, in love with his wife. At moments when he was upset, he did this thing where he briefly closed his eyes and turned his head to the right. I've never once seen him make that gesture in real life. Everyone else was fine—Elliott was adorable as the dead caveman, and Hannah was good as a nonspeaking ancestor—but it was Tris's show. I could barely get to him afterward to give him the flowers I'd brought, he was so mobbed by fans.

I didn't talk to Miss Murphy. She was mobbed too, and I don't think she noticed me.

Dad was there, of course, and he and Grady and I talked awkwardly for a few minutes while he waited for Miss Murphy. He offered us a ride back to Mom's, but I said we had our bikes. After that it seemed like there was nothing to do but leave, even though I would have enjoyed hanging around for a while.

When we got outside, the air was soft and the night seemed especially quiet after the noise of everyone yelling and congratulating each other in the auditorium.

Grady put his arm around me and said, "You good?"

I said yes even though my heart was hurting like a sprained ankle.

"If you want to try out again next year, I'll do it with you," he said.

"Maybe," I said. I can't think about it too much—the fun I would have had with everyone, the inside jokes and Tris hangtimes I missed, the fact that the cast has four more shows to look forward to. Planning to try out next year would mean admitting that I made a terrible mistake not trying out this year.

Sunday, May 13

For Mother's Day, I gave Mom a generic card and made chicken salad for dinner. A pretty lame effort, but she seemed happy with it. While we ate, she talked for 45 minutes about Isla, this adorable and brilliant girl in the test-prep class she teaches. Apparently Isla and she really connect, and Isla stays after class to confide in her about her cheating boyfriend and her difficult parents. "Her mother sounds like a real piece of work," Mom said, shaking her head. I rarely think about the drawbacks of being an only child, but in that moment I was dying for a sibling, someone to catch my eye across the table and make a tiny face that meant OMG, *she has zero self-awareness.*

After the Isla soliloquy wrapped up, Mom said "What's new with you?" in an uninterested tone, as if there couldn't possibly be anything notable going on in my life. I hadn't planned to tell her, but that was before she rhapsodized about some girl my age who she's known for a few weeks but already loves more than me, and I found myself saying, "I got nominated for junior prom queen."

"You *did?*"

I nodded.

She poured herself more white wine. "Have you ever heard of a movie called *Carrie?*"

"Of course. What, you think someone's going to pour pig's blood on me?"

"I'm just trying to understand how this happened."

I laughed angrily. "Is it so hard to believe that people at my school like me?"

"I was well liked, Chloe, but I was never nominated for prom queen."

That's probably because I'm a million times more popular than you were, I thought, but did not say.

"Of course, you may not win," Mom said, like she was comforting herself.

Now I have to win. I have to see the look of sour shock on my mother's face when I come home wearing a sash and carrying a bouquet of roses.

Monday, May 14

I was sitting in the kitchen doing homework when Mom got back from work. Right away, as she put her bag down, she said, "I was thinking about *Carrie* today." It was actually tempting to stay there and let her provoke me into a froth of anger, pride, and defensiveness, but I'd promised myself I'd do two hours of phonebanking, so I said, "I have to call Hannah to discuss a group project," and went to my room. I would never tell her about volunteering for Planned Parenthood. She'd be way too enthusiastic about it, and then she'd find a way to take credit for the whole thing. ("I'm so glad I insisted that you see Dr. Stauffer! I knew meeting a proper OB would change your worldview.")

Tuesday, May 15

Six lunch in the clearing, because Noelle wanted to strategize and she thought we'd have more privacy there. It turned out to be crowded, so we sat on the ground behind some trees, which will probably make sitting on the ground behind some trees the new cool thing to do.

"I've been giving this a lot of thought, and I think we need to campaign without campaigning," Noelle said. "That could backfire."

"It would look desperate?" Elliott said.

"Exactly. I think our angle is, a vote for Chloe is a vote against Reese."

I swallowed a bite of turkey sandwich and said, "What about, vote for Chloe because she's a nice person?"

No one looked at each other, but there was a certain quiver in the air. I could feel myself getting angry. "What's wrong with that?" I said.

Noelle sounded soothing. "People want to get revenge on Reese. They've hated her since kindergarten."

Hannah said, "'Hate' is a strong word."

Elliott elbowed Grady in the ribs and said, "This guy didn't hate her last year!"

They were all driving me nuts. "Do whatever you think will work, Noelle," I said. "You know best." I was trying to sound biting, but I don't think she noticed.

"Good," she said. "Chloe, don't even mention prom queen out loud outside of the Six. Act like you forgot you were nominated. The rest of you, don't make a big deal about it. If you can work it into conversation naturally, say something like, 'I heard Reese thinks she's a shoo-in,' or 'I wonder if Reese will have a temper tantrum right there on the dance floor if she loses.'"

I thought for sure Hannah would object, but she was nodding along with Tris and Elliott. Grady was the only one who seemed uncomfortable, but even he didn't say anything.

Wednesday, May 16

It was 80 degrees today, which would be exciting and fun if it didn't foreshadow the implosion of our species.

Bear's babysitter had a dental appointment, so Grady and I watched Bear. We set up the sprinkler in the backyard, and we all ran through it, even though Bear was the only one wearing a bathing suit. First we did standard runs, then we jumped, and then we jumped while pretending to brush our teeth or eat corn on the cob. Bear was laughing and screaming with happiness. I thought, if I can get through high school, college, a terrible first job, and some less-terrible subsequent jobs, this will be my reward: I'll get to run through the sprinkler with my own kid, and I'll love him even more than I love Bear, because he'll be mine.

After a while Grady and I sat on lawn chairs and watched while Bear kept running.

"Am I a nice person?" I asked Grady.

He paused for much longer than I thought was reasonable. "No one's nice all the time," he said.

I'd been fine a second before, but instantly I could feel tears behind my eyes. "You don't think I'm *nice*?"

Another pause. "You've been a little different the past few weeks. But this is a weird time."

I stood up. "This isn't a time. This is how it is now."

He didn't say anything. Bear slipped on the wet grass, landed hard on his leg, got up laughing, and kept running, getting ready for his next leap.

Thursday, May 17

I feel almost shy around Tris after seeing him in the show—that's how good he was. Maybe he sensed that I'm hanging back, because he invited himself over after school. It was a beautiful day, and obviously my mom doesn't have any private outdoor space, so we sat on the wooden benches by the parking lot. I told him again how incredible his performance was, and he waved me off.

"It's not like I'm mining coal," he said. "It's easy for me, and I love it."

"That doesn't make it less amazing," I said.

We watched a guy in his 30s pull up in an Infiniti, disconnect his phone from its dashboard holder, and start texting.

"Are you happy in general?" I asked Tris. "Is everything good with you and Elliott?"

"Yeah. The Six stuff has been weird. Elliott and I are definitely the most famous gay kids in school now. People watch us. I can feel myself watching us too. Do you know what I mean? Like, I'm walking down the hall with him, but I'm also thinking about how we look walking down the hall together."

"I know exactly what you mean."

"I can't tell if it's good or bad."

"Grady thinks it's bad."

"Oh yeah?"

"I don't know. He seems frustrated with the Six stuff, or with me."

Tris picked at a splinter on the bench. "'The Six' used to sound ridiculous to me, and now it sounds normal."

"I told Noelle we'd never have a group name," I said. "Now look at us."

Tris made a sound that I couldn't interpret: he was either disgusted, proud, disbelieving, or rueful. Or maybe I'm just listing all the things I'm feeling myself.

Friday, May 18

Reasons it's great to be popular and I should stop fretting and enjoy it:

1. It irritates my mother.
2. By association, my power has brought my friends to power (including Grady, although he doesn't seem to appreciate it at this moment).
3. The entire class has been freed from Reese's tyranny.
4. I've finally stopped longing to be liked by girls who couldn't stand me and were casually cruel to me IRL and on the internet.
5. I'm getting revenge on the people who tormented me. Well, not *revenge*. That

sounds bad. It's more like I'm serving them justice.

6. I'm protecting Hannah from heartbreak.

Reasons it's horrible and soul-crushing to be popular:

1. I'm not going to make this list. Being popular is wonderful. Writing about all my little doubts and worries will only make them seem bigger, when what I should be doing is ignoring them until they shrivel up and die. End of diary entry.

Saturday, May 19

Noelle and I went to the mall to shop for prom dresses in the palette we'd picked out after hours of deliberation in our Six group text: pink (for me), black (for Noelle), and white (for Hannah). Classic black tuxes for the guys.

Right away, Noelle found a black dress that looked like a trash bag on the rack and expensive and directional on her. It goes all the way up to her neck but ends right below her butt.

I didn't even bother picking out things to try on, since I knew Noelle would hate whatever I selected. After she'd found her dress, she hunted for me. It's quite something, watching her sort through options. She whisks hangers along the racks at a high speed, looking disgusted the whole time. When she sees something she thinks she might like, she yanks it out and frowns at it, then either slams it back or tosses it to me to try. I never would have chosen any of the dresses she picked for me, and they all looked so good on. In the end Noelle told me to buy a floor-length pink taffeta skirt, and a silky pink crop top that shows a good chunk of my torso.

"You have to promise not to slouch," she said, narrowing her eyes at me in the dressing room mirror.

"I promise," I said. I wasn't really listening to her. I was imagining the tiara sparkling in my hair.

"I got you a little present," she said. "It's something I found on Etsy."

She was holding her hand out to me in a fist. When I walked over, she turned her hand palm-up and opened it to reveal a pin.

"What does it say?" I picked it up. It was a pink heart, and on it, in black letters, was printed BOO, YOU WHORE.

"*Mean Girls!*" I said. "Oh my God, it's perfect."

"It's a little on the nose," Noelle said, "but I couldn't resist."

"No, it's brilliant," I said. "It's reappropriating Reese's slut-shaming!"

"You get it," Noelle said.

After I paid for the skirt and top, we drove to the

thrift store, and Noelle picked out armloads of summer clothes for me from the dollar-a-pound bins. I tried to tell her how grateful I was, but she didn't want to hear it. "Just promise me you won't wear those sandals you lived in last summer," she said. "That's all the thanks I need."

Sunday, May 20
At the last minute Grady and I decided to go to the final matinee. I brought giant bouquets for my friends, which was a little awkward, since I had to hold them on my lap through the whole show. The house was packed. Am I wrong to think that attending the musical has become cooler because Six members are in it?

Monday, May 21
Tris, Hannah, and Elliott look exhausted and depressed. That's one upside of not being in the show: no post-run blues.

Tuesday, May 22
Great Scott, that was the best birthday of my life!!! Is that what it's been like for Reese since kindergarten?! Being popular is amazing!! When I arrived at school, you couldn't even see my locker, it was so thickly covered in pink balloons and pink streamers. It felt like every single person in the school, including most seniors, wished

me a happy birthday. Nadia made me a card. Annoying Lianna baked me chocolate chip cookies. My friends brought a big pink cake to lunch, and most people in the cafeteria sang to me. I didn't understand what I was missing all those years when I was a nobody.

Wednesday, May 23

Mom took me out for a birthday dinner, drank too much, told me the story of my birth (36-hour labor, C-section, breastfeeding problems), cried, and said I was worth every moment of pain I've ever caused her.

Thursday, May 24

Senior Costume Contest! That'll be us next year—me, Noelle, Grady, Tris, Elliott, Hannah—showing up half in the bag, dressed as Disney villains or Minions, dominating the hashtag, winning the top prize in a romp. I can't wait.

Friday, May 25

Dad called and left a voicemail. "Hi, Chloe. Just wondering what time you want to come over tomorrow. Marian's been craving steak, so I'm planning to grill. Hope you can join us for dinner. Give me a ring." I texted him back. "Hi so sorry but I can't make it this weekend. Sooo much homework. Bummed to miss steak." Lies, lies, lies.

I texted Mom to tell her I'd invited my friends over after school, and she texted back, "Make it a sleepover. I don't want anyone driving drunk." When I got home, she was waiting there with a case of beer. "I remember how this works," she said. "If you don't have beer, you'll resort to shots. You understand I'm not trying to be a cool mom, right? I'm facing facts and keeping you safe." She was attempting to sound serious, but I could tell she was delighted with herself.

Saturday, May 26

When I pictured high school, I assumed I'd live with my parents in our old house. I thought Dad would drag me out of bed to help with yard work, review my report cards with me, let me go to parties only after making me sign a contract that I'd respect curfew and stay away from alcohol. Never in a million years did I picture living in a condo with my negligent mother, sleeping with my drunk friends and boyfriend in a pile on the floor.

Sunday, May 27

I know I shouldn't drink. I don't even want to. I'll never forget those MRIs they showed us in health class. These scientists found some sober kids and some drinkers, and they made them all take a memory test, scanning their brains while they did it. The non-drinkers had all this pulsing healthy pink activity. The drinkers had empty white blobs with black squiggles, plus one tiny pink chip. So I do understand how bad alcohol is for my body. The problem is that drinking is so fun! It makes me feel happy and relaxed and like I can say anything to anyone. When I'm about to do it, some quiet dark part of me says, *Don't forget the MRIs,* but then the brittle sequiny part of me shrieks, *Who cares about the stupid MRIs! Don't miss your youth! It's one beer! Relax!*

Monday, May 28

Is this how Uncle Julian felt when he was my age? I don't want to turn into him. I have to keep myself under control.

Tuesday, May 29

Intense lunchtime discussion about our non-campaigning campaign. Reese has been handing out key chains and stress balls and cellophane bags of Reese's Pieces, all printed with the words VOTE REESE RILEY FOR PROM QUEEN!

"Shouldn't we do *something?*" Tris said. "Maybe personalized pencils?"

"No," Noelle said. "We have to stay the course. The more money Reese spends, the more desperate she looks."

"Maybe Tris could run his own campaign," Elliott suggested. "He could do pencils even if Chloe doesn't." We all looked at him, appalled, and he blushed and dropped it.

Hannah and I got a few minutes alone together after lunch, and I asked her about Zach.

"Did he rent his tux? Is he acting excited about going, or just tolerant? Will he appreciate how beautiful you look in your dress?"

"Please don't worry," she said. "I'm fine. He's good to me. He's doing all the right things, OK?"

I said OK, but I'm not sure I believe her.

Wednesday, May 30

On my way to fill up my water bottle during fifth period, I ran into Nadia in the hallway. From the way she said hi, I could tell she wanted to talk to me, so I paused and smiled at her.

"I just wanted to say good luck," she said shyly. "It's so cool that you might be prom queen. Are you excited?"

I smiled. "I can't imagine I'll actually win, so not really." I hadn't prepared this answer, but it sounded good as I said it.

"I bet you will win," Nadia said. "I would vote for you if I were in your class."

"Thanks, Nadia," I said. I gave her a hug before I left, which was extra nice of me, since there wasn't even anyone around to witness my niceness.

Thursday, May 31

I asked Noelle how the campaign's going, and she said, "Hard to tell. There's a lot of excitement about voting against Reese, so that's promising."

"Why do you say it's hard to tell, then?"

"It's a three-way race, which is dangerous. You and Reese might split votes."

"Me and *Reese*? Wouldn't it be me and Izzy splitting votes? The two nice girls?"

Noelle looked at me and raised her eyebrows. "I guess that's possible."

Friday, June 1

At Dad's, hiding in my room. Snickers is sitting on my old bed looking anxious. At this point he understands that we don't live here, and I think he'd rather not come at all than hang out for two days and then leave. Or maybe I'm projecting.

I asked Dad if I could have my friends over tomorrow night, and he said, "Oh. Sure. I was looking forward to spending some time alone with you and Marian, but I don't want you to feel you have to put your life on hold while you're here." After that of course I had to text everyone and say the hangout's canceled.

Saturday, June 2

Things I've learned about Miss Murphy's pregnancy this weekend:

1. It's turned the inside of her belly button purple.
2. She has heartburn so bad she can't sleep at night unless she's sitting up.
3. It's making her break out (that one I'd already noticed).
4. The tip of her nose is always itchy.
5. She can't stop Googling cord death.
6. Her tailbone hurts, and the only thing that helps is sitting on her exercise ball.
7. She's not going to hire a doula because her best friend from college did and said it was like paying someone $2,000 to stare at her while she had contractions.

A few different times Miss Murphy said things like, "I'm so sorry, Chloe. This must be incredibly boring." But I said, "No, no, it's interesting." That wouldn't be a lie if I were in my 30s and also pregnant. Unfortunately,

I'm 17 years old, and hearing about Miss Murphy's heartburn makes me want to run away screaming.

Sunday, June 3

There isn't a worse point in the month than the moment I step into Mom's condo after a weekend at Dad's house. I've left this place that's beautiful but doesn't feel right, and I've stepped into this place that's objectively depressing and also doesn't feel right. When I go to the pink bathroom to wash my hands, I look at my reflection in the mirror and think, *You don't belong anywhere.* I run to my bedroom, but even FaceTiming Grady or pressing my eyes into Snickers's fur doesn't really help.

Whining in my diary helps a little. I have to get through a few more hours of this weekend, most of which I'll spend asleep, and then I'll be back at school, where people like me and want to be around me.

Monday, June 4

Now that the show's over and Tris and Elliott and Hannah aren't busy with rehearsals and performances, there's nothing preventing the Six from texting and talking about prom details whenever we're awake.

> Noelle: *We need to finalize the limo*

Grady: I was thinking we
should rent a fire truck

Noelle: Very funny now do we
want black or white?

Tris: Either is fine but we need
to discuss flowers

                      Chloe: I'm not wearing a
                      corsage, I refuse

Noelle: Fine by me

Hannah: Zach is getting
me one

Tris: Good because I'm wearing
a boutonniere!

Elliott: Same

Grady: What's a boutonniere?

Tris: I'll pick one up for you so
you me and Elliott match

Is that OK Chloe?

Chloe: Yep

*Noelle: Hannah have your shoes
arrived? Text pics*

*Hannah: They came, but none
of them fit.*

*Noelle: !!!!!!!! Send me links to
new options ASAP*

Etc., etc., etc. I'm enjoying it, but it's stressing me out, too. I didn't realize my first prom-going experience would be so visible. Not to sound conceited, but the fact is that everyone's going to be staring at us all night long. We have to do it right.

Tuesday, June 5

Tris and I were late to class because we were talking about how long we should allot for pre-prom photos, and when we finally agreed we had to get going, we loudly continued our conversation while walking backward in opposite directions. Mr. Hicks popped his head out of his classroom and said, "No loitering after the bell, and that applies to future prom queens!" Then he winked at me. Does he have inside info?? Even if he does, there are three days of voting left before the final tally, so he can't know for sure. Anyway, he was probably messing with me.

Wednesday, June 6

I trust Noelle. I'm sure she's right that I shouldn't mention my nomination to anyone. Probably it would look vain or insecure. But I couldn't resist posting a picture of my shoes and nail polish and pin. It took me about two hours, seriously, to find the right background (a piece of expensive wrapping paper I found in a bin in Mom's closet), realize that I needed to take the picture outside to get the best light, position and reposition all the objects, and pick a filter. Grady refused to help me, which annoyed me even though I understand why moving a bottle of nail polish seven eighths of an inch might not be as interesting to him as it is to me. After I posted the pic, the likes came instantly. The pin got the most love, but people commented on all of it, even the rainbows on the wrapping paper. I don't want to jinx anything, but there were even a handful of #promqueen hashtags in the comments.

Thursday, June 7

Reese came up to me for the first time since the cafeteria incident. When I saw her heading my way, I was instinctively terrified for a second, and then I remembered she can't hurt me anymore. Also, she looked nervous.

"Can I talk to you for a second?" she said in a breathy voice.

"Go ahead," I said.

"I just wanted to say I hope we can let bygones be bygones. I'm totally rooting for you on Saturday."

"Oh yeah?" I said, and smiled at her. "Did you vote for me? Because I didn't vote for you." It's still scary, saying stuff like that, but when you force yourself to do it, you feel exhilarated.

She flinched a little. "Whatever happens, it's an honor that we were both nominated."

She's so cheesy. I said, "You didn't happen to see my post yesterday, did you?"

I could see her deciding how to respond. Then she said, "I think I did. I love your shoes!"

"Do you love my pin?"

"Yes?" she said, like she wasn't sure what the right answer was.

"I thought you would," I said, "since you like accusing people of being whores."

My heart was racing as I turned and walked away.

Here's how I know I've beaten her: she called out to me, but instead of saying something to defend herself

("I don't do that") or attack me ("It's not my fault you're a whore"), what she said was, "Good luck this weekend!"

Friday, June 8

Grady seemed quiet when he came over after school. We didn't talk much, just took off our clothes and had sex right away in my bed. When we were done, he lay there staring at the ceiling. I put my arm across his chest and said, "Sorry I've been kind of preoccupied recently. It'll be better after prom is over." He turned and smiled at me for what felt like the first time that day. "I can't wait for summer," he said.

"Me neither," I said, which wasn't actually true. The thing I can't wait for is happening tomorrow night.

I'm pretty sure you can shed your high school life like a snakeskin the instant you graduate. Probably by the time you're 30 no one can tell what you were like at age 17 or where you fell in the pecking order. Even if they could tell, they wouldn't care. But I bet even 30-year-olds feel a twinge of interest if they find out you were prom queen. Prom queen! It'll be like wearing an invisible crown for the rest of my life. Even if I struggle to find a good job, or my dad gets so wrapped up in his new family he forgets about me, or my mother vanishes again, I'll know that at one point people loved me.

Saturday, June 9

We're almost ready! I'm sneaking a diary entry while Noelle's outside smoking. She came over at noon so we could get dressed together. Mom made us mimosas, which are delicious. They're what fairies would drink, if fairies were real. I only had one, even though my mother kept offering me more, because I want to remember every minute of tonight. She stayed out of our way while we prepped. Noelle got my hair wet and blew it out. Same for herself. I'd assumed we'd get our hair done at a salon, but Noelle said getting an updo in the suburbs is liking paying someone to make you look middle-aged. After our hair was done, she did our makeup. She spent 45 minutes on my eyes alone.

My mom's going to drive us over to Noelle's house in a few minutes. Grady and Tris and Hannah and Zach and Elliott are meeting us there with their parents so we can take pictures. Dad and Miss Murphy are coming too. The sun's shining, and I'm about to stand on the grass with my arms around my friends, smiling and pretending to be embarrassed by all the attention. My skirt is so comfortable, and when I walk, it swirls around my ankles. My top is so skimpy it's shocking. When I blink, my fake eyelashes are like WHOOSH, WHOOSH. I'm about to put my pin on my waistband. I feel like I could rule a planet. I know I'm going to win win win win win win win.

Sunday, June 10

I lost. Maybe there's a lot to say about it, and maybe that's all there is to say. I lost.

Monday, June 11

Tris was right: pre-prom is the best part. When it's happening, it feels like a prologue you have to get through before the real event begins, and it is that, but it's also the part when nothing's gone wrong yet and you have an adoring audience of parents and you know they're thinking, *It seems like yesterday she was a baby,* and, *I can't believe how tall and handsome he is,* and for a second you can see yourself through their eyes and appreciate yourself as a young person full of promise rather than the tormented basket case you feel like on the inside.

Grady looked so beautiful. My heart jumped up when I saw him coming across the backyard toward me, smiling in his tuxedo. He never looks sheepish. He always looks confident. How can you resist someone like that, especially when he also has deep-set eyes and a full mouth and a sharp jaw? When he got to me, he took both my hands, leaned in close, and whispered, "You look amazing." He kissed my earlobe and snuck a tiny bite onto the end of the kiss. I wanted to say, "Grady, I haven't been paying enough attention to you, and I'm sorry," but I was too shy, so I tried to beam the thought out to him silently.

The parents took millions of pictures on their phones. Mom and Dad and Miss Murphy chatted pleasantly for a minute and then avoided each other. We kids ate some of the food Noelle's mom had put out, but not too much, because we were so nervous. And then the limo (standard, black) arrived, and we took a million more pictures in front of it, and then it was time to go.

Felix Nicholson will probably grow up to produce the Academy Awards. He pulled off prom on a boat like it was his hundredth time doing it. We boarded, we ate dinner at long tables inside, we took pictures in the photo booth, we stood outside on the deck looking at the lit-up buildings and taking more pictures of ourselves, we went back inside to find the tables had been cleared away and the dancing had started. Felix moved us around like chess pieces, and it didn't even feel like he was doing anything. When he came to tell me prom king and queen would be announced in 20 minutes and I should meet him and the other nominees by the DJ booth in 15, I commented on the lack of nautical theming. "I thought for sure there'd be anchors everywhere," I said. "Or waves."

He looked offended. "I loathe themes," he said.

I admit my first thought was *How dare you speak to me like that?* It didn't occur to me that he knew I'd lost and he didn't feel he had to be polite to me.

Noelle and I went to the bathroom so she could touch up my makeup and smooth out my flyaways.

"You're doing a good job standing up straight," she said. "Keep it up."

"I have shrimp in my teeth!" I said, looking in the mirror.

"Here." She handed me a tiny plastic wishbone strung with floss.

Two girls came in, saw us, said, "Sorry!" and turned around and left. Noelle and I rolled our eyes at each other. How quickly you forget that non-popular people are terrified, not ridiculous.

"Feeling good?" Noelle said when we were alone again.

"Feeling great," I said. "Feeling calm."

We smiled at each other. "Whatever happens, keep it together," she said.

I nodded. I thought she was telling me not to scream or over-emote when Felix read out my name. I *thought* I understood that I might not win, but I didn't really. I was only telling myself I didn't know the outcome. In my heart I was convinced I had it in the bag.

When the nominees were assembled, the lights went dim, aside from a spotlight shining on us, and the music stopped. Felix cleared his throat, then brought the microphone to his mouth and said, "As head of the prom committee, I'd like to thank you all for joining us tonight!" The crowd cheered as if we'd all accomplished something by showing up for a dance. Reese was on my left, wearing a turquoise dress with triangular cutouts. I could feel her presence like a bonfire pouring heat onto my skin. Izzy was on my right, in a flowered gown with an empire waist and a bow that tied in the back. She was no threat. She might as well have been a centerpiece. On the other side of Felix were Tris, Mark, and Griffin. Right at the front of the crowd stood the other four of the Six, looking at me with excited smiles, or maybe nervous smiles.

Felix was making a speech about the values of our class, which apparently the nominees are meant to embody. Tolerance. Generosity. Open-mindedness. I let myself raise one eyebrow, just a millimeter. Who was Felix kidding? Reese is about as tolerant and open-minded as a honey badger.

"I'm pleased to announce the runners-up for prom king. Mark Philips." The crowd clapped and wooed. "Griffin Gonzalez." As the cheers continued, I realized who had won. "And now I'd like to introduce your prom king, Tristan Flynn." Shouts of approval from the crowd. Tris ran over to Elliott and kissed him before coming back to Felix and accepting the crown, which the prom committee must have shelled out some real cash for: it looked heavy, it was trimmed with what appeared to be white fur, and in the center was a cushiony part made of maroon velvet. Tris didn't get a sash, I'm guessing because Felix considers sashes tacky.

I was still smiling at Tris when Felix said, "And now, your prom queen runners-up. Reese Riley. Chloe Snow." I don't remember hearing him say Izzy's name, although he must have. But I remember her grabbing my hand and looking at me with real shock on her face and then turning to Felix and bowing her head so he could put the glittering tiara on her hair, which he did carefully, making sure he didn't mess with her updo.

Tris gave me an apologetic look as Felix said, "Tristan, if you'd lead Isabelle to the dance floor?" Off they went to dance to "I'm Yours." The first verse lasted an eternity. I could feel everyone staring at me. I kept a serene smile pinned to my lips. I was so close to crying, but I knew I couldn't, so I knew I wouldn't.

I glanced at Reese, who was smiling too. I understand now why she covers up her real self in public. You have to. It's not even covering up—it's holding on to your dignity.

We stood there smiling and smiling until the DJ invited everyone to join the royal couple on the dance floor. Even before Noelle gave me a firm nod, like *Start dancing immediately*, I was walking to Grady.

When he put his arms around me, I thought I really might start crying, from the relief of him, but then I spotted the back of Reese's head over his shoulder and I got it together. Hannah was dancing with Zach and giving me sympathetic looks whenever she caught my eye. Zach hadn't left her side all night, and more than once I'd seen him lifting her hand to his lips. At least I'd done one good thing with my popularity.

"You got robbed," Grady said.

"Better Izzy than Reese," I said.

"Good point." He pulled back to look me in the eye and said, "You know this is all bullshit, right? It doesn't matter. It's dumb high school nonsense."

"I know," I said, and at the time I thought I should agree with him, but now I think, why is it bullshit? Why is it wrong to care about your life, whatever kind of life it is? If your high school years don't matter, why does your first job, or your wedding, or your pregnancy, or anything? It all matters or none of it does.

Tuesday, June 12

Mom was waiting up for us when we got to the condo for our after-prom party. "Should I open the champagne?" she said as soon as we came in.

"Sure," I said. "But for Tris, not for me. I lost."

Everyone rushed to talk about the photo booth, the

dinner, and whatever else they could think of to make me feel less self-conscious. Mom listened to all of it and asked a lot of fascinated questions. She also snuck glances at me, and the glances were smug, like *I knew you wouldn't win,* or maybe more like *This will knock that chip off your shoulder, you popular bitch.*

Wednesday, June 13

Everything seems normal at school. We wore our pink Vans. We sat at our table. Nadia clung to me when I hugged her. It's not like it all turned into pumpkins and rags at the stroke of midnight on Saturday. We've still got something.

Thursday, June 14

OK, we've still got something, but it's not the *same* something. At lunch Tris and Elliott talked quietly together, Noelle played on her phone, and Hannah and Grady looked at their food while they ate. We've lost some of our fizz. We had a goal, we were moving upward in a straight line toward glory, and now we've leveled off.

Friday, June 15

Reese laughed in the hall. I haven't heard her laugh since before the cafeteria incident. I realize how ridiculous I sound, but I'm worried. I don't want her laughing.

As a class, we've already endured OVER A DECADE of Reese's rule. That's longer than two-term presidents serve! Maybe I'm paranoid, but I think she could be mounting a comeback campaign, and even if it only exists as a figment of my imagination, I'm going to squash it. She had her turn, and it's my turn now. If someone like Izzy were up for taking the throne, I'd cede it to her, but Izzy is back to toting her clarinet around in a carrying case with a cartoon unicorn on it and wearing giant promotional T-shirts tucked into khakis. Which is great! I'm not criticizing her. But she's not the kind of person who's going to keep us safe from Reese. I alone can do it.

Saturday, June 16

As I was getting ready to leave for Dad's, Mom called, "Hang on!" from her bedroom. Then she came out wearing a white bathing suit with long tassels hanging from the neckline to the crotch. "What do you think?" she said. "For Saint Thomas!"

"Oh," I said. "Right."

She walked to the mirror by the front door and turned around to check out her butt. "You didn't forget about the training course, did you? What's your plan for next month? Did you find a camp?"

I felt a surge of anger and looked at her cellulite with satisfaction, enjoying being disgusted by her. She must know it doesn't work like that. Kids don't research camps, choose the one best suited to them, email the director, fill out the application, put down a deposit, pick up the bug repellant and sunscreen, figure out how long the drive's going to take, and send care packages to themselves.

"I'll stay with Dad, I guess," I said.

She made a face. "You'll have to arrange that with him yourself. We're not exactly on speaking terms right now."

"Fine," I said quickly, hoping to cut her off before she started complaining about him in more detail.

"All I can say is thank God you're old enough to have your own relationship with him without my involvement, because I can't bear even to discuss scheduling with that man. The inflexibility! The self-righteousness!"

She went on like this for a few minutes while I tried to tune out and think of something happy, like Snickers running on the beach and barking at the waves.

"You'll have the keys, of course, if you need a mental health break from your father." She headed back to her bedroom, calling, "But no parties!" Like I've ever thrown a party before, and like I ever would.

Sunday, June 17

I couldn't pay attention at the Father's Day brunch Miss Murphy made for Dad, because as soon as she brought out the French toast casserole, it came to me: PARTY. Party of the century. Rager that will make me an MH legend for generations to come. July Fourth–themed bash that kids will skip their vacations to attend. Triumph that will make everyone forget junior prom even happened. I'll make sure Izzy comes, and I'll treat her like a princess so that everyone can see I'm the cool banger-thrower who's already forgotten about prom, not some basic nobody sweating over a tiara. The squad will show up, even if they tell themselves they're coming to make fun of it, and when Reese arrives, I WON'T LET HER IN. Let's see how long her comeback campaign lasts after that.

And another thing: I'm not telling Dad about Mom's trip. I refuse to stay with him. I'll be fine on my own. I'll go to his house a few times, like I normally do. I'll ride my bike over there, and if he comes to pick me up, he'll wait for me in the condo parking lot, like he always does. He hasn't once come up to say hi to Mom, so he won't figure out that something's wrong. And he and I text to arrange these visits, so it's not like he'll get in touch with her and figure out she's not there. It'll be a cinch to get away with this. Actually, it's sad to think about how easy it'll be.

Monday, June 18
Six huddle by the lockers. "Party at my house on July 6th,"

I said. "Tell everyone cool, and start with the seniors. Red-white-and-blue attire is mandatory."

"Whoa," said Noelle. "I like it. But isn't it a little early to start telling people? You know how word spreads. The entire school will find out in an hour."

"It's not too early," I said. Everyone looked at each other and shrugged. My word is law. It does feel wrong to have this much sway, but it's also so convenient!

Tuesday, June 19

At least a dozen people have come up to me to ask about the party or tell me they're excited for it. Even Lianna dared to mention it, but I pretended not to know what she was talking about.

This was our last day. We're not juniors anymore. We're rising seniors, and next year I'm going to rule with an iron fist (in a nice way, of course).

Wednesday, June 20

Grady and I had our first full shift at the pool today. It was hot, dry, sunny. Shining blue sky. I spent the morning in the concession stand selling Popsicles and chips and blowing kisses to Grady whenever I could catch his eye. I assumed he'd come over during the first adult swim, but he disappeared into the lifeguard shack, so I went to find him.

"Hey!" I said. "Listen to my idea. I have a little money saved up. I was planning to spend it on groceries for July, but I was thinking, if I eat ramen for lunch and dinner, I could buy party supplies with the rest. Not alcohol, because I don't have an ID, and people will bring their own anyway. But sparklers. And I saw these American flag sunglasses online—you couldn't *not* Instagram yourself in them. Maybe we could get a hashtag trending! I was thinking #4thon6th. Do you think that works? Grady?"

He was holding the water testing kit, staring at it like he'd never seen it before.

"Grady, hello? Are you listening to me?"

He didn't say anything for a second. "Chloe . . ."

"Yeah?"

"No, nothing."

"Tell me," I said.

"Adult swim's almost over. Really, it's nothing."

He said he had to pick up Bear as soon as he finished at work, and now he's not responding to my texts. What's his problem?

Thursday, June 21

I can't believe what just happened.

I got it out of him at work, first thing. I didn't want to wait to talk to him, so I pulled the grate down over the concession stand window and taped up a sign saying, *Technical difficulties. Back in five minutes,* then went and sat next to him on his lifeguard chair. Thank God Reese hadn't arrived yet.

As soon as I'd climbed up, I said, "What was yesterday all about?"

"Chloe, you're gonna get in trouble if Mrs. Franco finds out the stand's not open."

"I don't care. Why are you being shady?"

He narrowed his eyes at the water. There was no one swimming yet. We'd only been open for 10 minutes, and it was a warm morning, but not hot. He glanced at me. "I don't think I can make it to the party."

"What??"

"My mom wants to go away that weekend."

"So tell her you can't."

"I don't want to lie."

"It's not a lie! You have a preexisting commitment. You can't miss the party! Do you realize how many Six pictures we'll take?"

He shook his head. "The Six stuff—honestly, Chloe, I can't stand it. I'm so sick of it."

"What are you talking about?"

"I don't care about being popular. I've been telling you that for months."

I stared at him. "You don't like it when people are

nice to you and interested in you? Because that's all being popular is." Not true, of course, but he was being so difficult, he was basically forcing me to contradict everything he said.

"Do you really believe that? You don't even—never mind."

"Grady, you can't start saying something rude and then say 'never mind.'"

"I'm not trying to be rude."

"What don't I even? Tell me."

A kid wearing a Puddle Jumper walked down the stairs into the pool. His mother followed behind, saying, "Careful!"

Grady said, "You're like a different person now. All you think about is Six stuff. Last summer we talked about everything. My art classes. Bear. New York. Even the dumb things—do you remember that day it was freezing but it wasn't raining, so we couldn't close the pool, and we tried to remember the plot of every single Harry Potter book without looking at our phones? We never talk for real anymore. All you're interested in is hashtags and your personal brand, or whatever."

"That's not true," I said. Was it true? I pushed the thought out of my mind.

"Do you realize you never invited me to prom? Not like I wanted some big thing, but you didn't even ask me the question. You just assumed I'd go with you. You're taking me for granted."

"Grady." I put my hand on his lower back and wriggled my fingers underneath the waistband of his bathing suit. He caught my wrist and set my hand back on my thigh.

"And whenever you think I'm upset, you try to distract me with sex."

"Are you saying you don't like having sex?"

He shook his head without taking his eyes off the kid in the pool. "I'm trying to tell you how I feel. Don't pretend you don't understand. That's what my stepfather does—he twists my words around."

So now I was like his evil stepfather? "OK, yeah, I talk about different stuff now. A lot has changed this year."

The front gate opened, and Reese walked in, wearing her aviator sunglasses and a straw hat. She waved at us and headed across the pool to the deep end, where the second lifeguard chair is positioned.

Grady said, "I don't want to be with Reese."

"Uh, good, because you're with me."

He shook his head. "You might as well be her."

"I can't believe you'd say that to me, Grady. She's my archenemy."

"This is what's freaking me out," Grady said. "You don't even see it."

I climbed off the chair and glared up at him. "I'm nothing like her. Nothing." Then I stormed over to the concession stand, ripped my sign off the grate, and started working.

Friday, June 22

You've got to be kidding me. Grady freaking dumped me.

I went to the pool intending to charm him out of his bad mood. I left Nadia in charge of the concession stand, then went over and apologized for cutting our conversation short yesterday. I told him how hot he looked in his red trunks. I asked him if he wanted to mess around in the lifeguard shack during adult swim. He was polite but not enthusiastic. Finally, after I said, "All we need is some make-up sex," he said, "Chloe, no. I want to talk to you, not ignore it."

"Talk to me about what?"

"All the stuff that's bugging me."

We were standing by the shallow end. It was 2 p.m., and the pool was packed.

I said, "I know I've been distracted, or whatever. I promise I'll change. OK?"

"OK what?"

"Are we done talking?"

He looked at me like he didn't even like me, much less love me. "No! I can't even pay attention to you right now—look at all the kids swimming. This doesn't count as talking."

I crossed my arms over my ribs. "I don't want to have some thing where we're analyzing our relationship constantly. We're not in our 40s and dating after a divorce. This is supposed to be fun."

"You really think that's what I'm asking you for? We've never even discussed our relationship."

"We've never needed to! That's what's so great about it!"

He shook his head while gazing at the pool.

"All you do is shake your head at me," I said. "I feel like you can't stand me anymore."

"Chloe, seriously, let's talk about this later."

"No, you know what? Let's not. I don't want to, and you can't make me."

"You sound like Bear. Are you four?"

"That's really nice," I said sarcastically.

"If you're so uncomfortable being honest with me you can't even have a real conversation for 10 minutes, I can't do this, Chloe."

"What are you saying?"

No one was paying attention to us, which made it seem impossible that we were breaking up. The littlest kids were in their mothers' arms. The big kids were cannonballing off the diving board. The nannies were looking at their phones. Even Reese seemed more interested in the game of Marco Polo going on by the five-foot mark than she was in us. If Grady was dumping me, shouldn't a cloud eclipse the sun? Shouldn't everyone at least notice what was unfolding?

He said, "I don't want to be with you if you're going to be like this."

I sneered to cover up the fact that tears were rushing to my eyes. "Fine by me," I said.

Are those the last words I'll ever speak to him? What just happened?

Saturday, June 23

I'm at Dad's. I haven't texted Grady. He hasn't texted me. I look at my phone every two seconds. Dad and Miss Murphy can tell something's wrong, but I've said I don't want to talk about it, and they're not pushing me.

I'm not going to be the one to apologize. Most guys would kill to be Grady. He's a sophomore dating the most popular junior in our school. Not only that, but he lucked into a girl who would rather bone than analyze. If anyone should be apologizing, it's him. I'm sure he will. Maybe he'll need a few days to come to his senses, and that's fine. I can wait.

Sunday, June 24

I worked the morning shift. Quentin and Jeff were

lifeguarding, so I didn't have to face Reese or Grady. When I got back to Dad's, he was standing in the kitchen holding his phone. He had a worried look on his face.

"Everything all right?" I said.

"Probably," he said. "I've been having trouble getting in touch with Julian. I'm sure he's fine, though."

It's weird to think that everyone cares about their lives just as much as you care about yours. Dad might occasionally wonder how I'm doing, but then he goes right back to thinking about Julian or the baby or a case, or whatever's on his mind. Meanwhile, Uncle Julian's thinking about his boss or his new girlfriend; Tristan's thinking about Elliott; Hannah's thinking about Zach and his latest melancholy song, or most likely, youth group; and on and on and on. My problems seem huge to me, but that's only because they're mine.

Monday, June 25

Grady didn't ignore me at the pool, but he didn't rush over to apologize, either. We said hello when we arrived. After that we didn't even make eye contact. I pulled my baseball cap low over my eyes and focused on making change and smiling at whoever came to buy food. In terms of providing excellent customer service, I've never had a better day at work.

Tuesday, June 26

Mom's so excited about Saint Thomas, she's singing in the shower and dancing while she does the dishes. Tonight she took a bite of the bulgur bowl she'd made, smacked her lips, and said, "If I do say so myself, that is delectable." I'd planned not to tell her about Grady— it's none of her business—but "delectable" was the final straw. I had to pull her out of Veronicaville for two seconds, by any means necessary.

"By the way, Grady broke up with me," I said.

She made a concerned face but kept eating. "Oh, my darling," she said. Her mouth was half full, and a tiny speck of feta was stuck to her lower lip. "How horrible. Do you want to talk about it?"

"I don't know," I said, flipping my fork tines-down and then back up.

A few moments ticked by. I kept messing with my fork while I waited for her to ask me more questions. When had it happened? How was I feeling about it? Did I think there was any chance we'd get back together?

She looked thoughtful. "It's the strangest thing," she said. "I got a text saying my sarong was delivered, but I haven't seen a package. Did you bring one in, by any chance?"

I told myself I'd eat every bite of my dinner and make pleasant conversation so she wouldn't even realize how much I despise her. But without my permission, my body decided to stand up and walk away from the table.

"You *said* you didn't want to talk about it!" my mother called. "Forgive me for trying to respect your wishes!"

When I got to my room, I punched my pillow a few dozen times. It didn't help.

Wednesday, June 27

During our shift change, Nadia said she'd heard about me and Grady and asked if I'm OK. Reese was sitting on the lifeguard chair by the deep end, pretending not to listen to our conversation.

"Honestly, I'm fine," I said, and then looked around like I wanted to make sure no one could hear us. "I think looking forward to the party helps." I tried to create the illusion of whispering while still speaking loudly enough that Reese would be sure to overhear me. "Friday the sixth. Late July Fourth celebration at my mom's. You can come, but bring your own beer."

Nadia looked nervous and thrilled. "I heard about this. Am I really invited?"

"Show up around 9. Don't tell too many people. It's kind of an exclusive thing."

Nadia nodded with wide eyes. Poor kid. She doesn't even realize I'm using her to lure Reese into my trap. But that's her problem. I can't be held responsible for every underclassman's naïveté.

Thursday, June 28

I wore a minuscule bikini to work and spent my breaks diving into the pool and climbing slowly out of it, going up the ladder Grady and I used to make out on last summer. Wiggled my butt around. Absentmindedly trailed a hand over my wet stomach. Ran my fingers through my hair. No dice. Grady sat with his arms folded and his expression stiff, refusing to look in my direction.

Friday, June 29

Reese bought a package of Skittles from me and said, "Rumor has it you're throwing a party."

"People love to talk," I said pleasantly.

She stared at me, saying nothing, counting on me to crack as the silence stretched out and got more and more awkward. I put on my sunglasses and smiled at her. I could say nothing with the best of them.

Eventually she gave up and left. It's almost a pleasure to think back to last summer, when I was terrified of her. What scared me, exactly?

Saturday, June 30

I was being a brat. Maybe it was my fault.

Last night after dinner Mom started packing for her trip. Within a few minutes she was sighing, yanking drawers out and then shoving them shut, and swearing under her breath. If there's one thing that makes her furious, it's doing a chore while someone else (me, Dad) sits around looking idle. I know this, and yet I was lying on the couch texting with Noelle, trying to figure out how many kids could realistically sleep over at the condo on Friday.

Mom went to the hall closet and tried to pull something off the high shelf. A bunch of bags and umbrellas fell on her and she shrieked in annoyance. Then she looked over at me and said, "Has it occurred to you that I could use some help?"

I was waiting to see what Noelle would text next, so I said, "One sec," which I knew would infuriate her—and if I knew, why did I say it?

She rushed over to me. "You have no regard for anyone but yourself," she hissed. "You act like a princess. You're popular at school, and you think that actually means something, don't you? Well, let me enlighten you. It doesn't mean shit. YOU don't mean shit." Now she was yelling. "YOU'RE NOBODY. YOU'RE NOTHING."

Then she grabbed my phone out of my hands and winged it at me. If I hadn't ducked, it would have hit me in the face. But I did duck, and it smashed into the wall and fell behind the couch. I knelt down immediately and fished it out. The screen was cracked down the middle.

I thought she might apologize, but no, she was standing there still puffed up, breathing hard, glaring at me.

I stood and headed to my bedroom.

"Don't you dare slam that door," she called after me.

I slammed it so hard, I shook the wall.

In my room, I examined my face in the full-length mirror on my closet door. Did I look like nobody? Maybe I did.

An hour ago she knocked on the door. "Chloe, I'm so sorry," she said. I was lying on my bed staring at the ceiling. It's hideous: one of those white ones that looks like it's been painted in cottage cheese. I didn't speak or move. She sobbed outside my door for a while, then gave up.

Sunday, July 1

I didn't want to leave my room this morning, but I had to pee. Mom was waiting outside the bathroom door. "My darling," she said when I came out, opening her arms like she wanted to hug me.

I pushed past her and went to the kitchen. She followed me.

"You know I would never hurt you," she said, and started crying again.

I feel *bad* for her. That's what I really can't stand.

"Yep," I said. I hadn't looked her in the eye yet.

"I'm going to cancel the trip," she said. "We need to work through this."

I didn't reply. I didn't want to play pretend with her. OBVIOUSLY she wasn't going to cancel the trip.

"Unless you'd rather not be around me right now," she said. I glanced her way and saw tears dripping from her chin. Jesus Christ. "Which I utterly understand," she said.

"Do whatever," I said.

Snickers came with me to the bathroom while I took a shower. I stayed in there for ages. When I finally finished and got dressed, Mom was standing by the front door with her suitcase, wearing harem pants, Birkenstocks, and a fedora.

"It's good that I'm going," she said. "I need to be far away so that I can dig deep. I will never lose my temper like that again. Never. I promise you that."

That old, familiar line. "Bon voyage," I said. Noelle would have been proud of me. I wasn't even close to letting my mask slip.

I could tell she was going to lunge toward me for another hug, so I turned and walked back to my room before she could make a move. She called "I love you" in a disgustingly quavering voice, and then I heard the door close and lock.

Monday, July 2

This isn't what I thought it would be. I imagined my month alone as nonstop, gross fun: peeing with the bathroom door open, listening to my most offensive music at top volume, having sex with Grady in every corner of the condo, walking around naked, ordering junky groceries Mom would never buy (Cheetos, fruit snacks, ice cream that's mostly cut-up candy bars). I haven't done any of those things. I went to work. I read a little while I scratched Snickers's neck. I ate a PB&J for dinner. I'm feeling somber and sorry for myself.

Tuesday, July 3

It's scary, being here alone. Not that I want my mother around. But the rooms are so quiet I can hear my ears ringing. Every time someone walks by the front door, my heart seizes up and I freeze until I'm sure the sound I heard is a neighbor heading down the stairs, not a murderer lurking outside waiting to pounce on me.

Going to work this morning was a relief. I texted Mrs. Franco and offered to do a double, but she said she was covered for the day. I wrote back saying I'll take as many extra shifts as she can give me for the rest of the month, and she sent me back the thumbs-up emoji.

Hannah was busy with a youth group meeting. Tris and Elliott were going to Elliott's house for dinner, but I begged them to come over for a little while in the afternoon, and they took pity on me and said yes.

"Thank God you're here," I said when they arrived. I was trying to sound amusingly over the top, but it must not have worked, because Tris didn't smile.

"Come stay with me for the month," he said.

"No, no," I said. Of course I'm dying to stay with him, but his mother would feel sorry for me, and I couldn't handle that.

"Then go to your dad's house," Tris said. "I can't believe he's letting you stay here alone anyway."

"He doesn't know my mom's gone. He'd freak."

"So tell him!"

"Maybe I will," I said.

We hung out for a while, and then off they went to dinner, heading to a happy house where a mother would call them "honey" or "sweetie" and offer them seconds, and probably dessert.

Wednesday, July 4

Dad's annual BBQ. He called to ask if I wanted a ride over, and I said, "No, thanks. You must be busy getting ready. I can ride my bike."

"That would be great, if you're sure."

I took my time getting off the phone. I was expecting him to hear it in my voice, that I'm alone in the condo, that Mom's run off again, but of course he didn't. He's not a mind reader.

When I arrived, I snuck around to the back instead of going inside to say hello. My friends came early, and we got food and spread out a blanket in a quiet corner of the yard.

"I think we're set for Friday," Noelle said. "I got the sparklers. You ordered the sunglasses, right? Oh, be sure to clean out the fridge to make room for booze."

"Good one," I said, and made a note on my phone.

"You were right, by the way," Noelle said. "Telling everyone early was smart. It built buzz. I heard some college kids might even come."

"Will it be too many people?" Elliott said. "What if they destroy the apartment?" He's so nice.

Noelle waved her plastic fork to dismiss his worries. "I'm good at kicking people out."

"Zach's out of town the whole week," Hannah said, "so he can't come, which is too bad, because he'd be a big help."

I nodded, not really listening.

"Is it upsetting to hear me talk about Zach?" Hannah asked. "Sorry! I was forgetting about—I was forgetting."

Grady. She meant Grady, who hadn't texted me or called me or even talked to me at work beyond saying hi and bye. I remembered Noelle's advice and pinched some skin on my palm.

"Glad you could make it, Chloe." It was my father, who'd appeared beside our blanket wearing an apron that read KING OF THE GRILL. I hadn't technically said hi to him, but here I was eating his excellent potato salad. I scrambled to my feet and gave him a hug. My friends called up, "Hi, Mr. Snow" and "Thanks for having us."

"Marian would like to say hello, if you have a moment?" Dad said to me. I don't think he used to be this polite, but I can't say for sure. I followed him over to the hydrangea bushes, where Miss Murphy was standing in a circle of people, saying, "Nothing but flip-flops. I can't reach my feet, but even if I could, they're way too swollen to cram into regular shoes." When she saw me, she put an arm around me and said, "And here's the big sister!" She turned slightly away from the group to show people we were going to talk to each other.

"Should you be standing?" I said. I'd looked down at her feet when she mentioned them, and they were shocking: like two loaves of bread someone had painted Havaianas onto.

"Probably not," she said, and bit into a hot dog. "I don't think I should be eating this either, but what the hell."

I wasn't sure what to say. I defaulted to "How are you feeling?" which seemed safe.

"Happy! I love being pregnant. It's so interesting. I

wish it would go on forever. Which it probably will. I saw my OB yesterday, and she said nothing's happening. No dilation, no effacement, nothing. She's going to induce me on July 24 if I don't go into labor on my own before then, so stick around, OK?"

"OK."

How strange to think that on July 25 I'll be a big sister, and there'll be a baby living in my dad's house. I can't imagine it. Will I have to change the baby's diapers when I go over there? Will it, like, barf on me? Will I be interested in it, or will it seem unrelated to me?

Thursday, July 5

I went up to Grady at work and said, "You're still invited tomorrow night, you know." He was sitting next to Reese on the lifeguard chair, so it was really outrageously rude that I didn't speak to her, look at her, or acknowledge her in any way.

"Uh, thanks," he said.

I watched him and Reese openly for the rest of the afternoon. It didn't look like they were flirting, but whatever. Flirt. Get back together. Screw on Grady's striped towel. I can take all of it.

I can't wait to destroy Reese in front of everyone tomorrow night. I've never cared less. I hope the condo is overrun with everyone from my school and dozens of kids from other towns and cities and colleges. Neighbors calling the police? That's nothing. I hope there are so many kids the condo building collapses.

Friday, July 6

The party's starting in a few hours. I was feeling nervous, so I went and looked in my mother's closet to remind myself of her and how much I hate her and how satisfying it will be if all her new stuff gets ruined. Noelle's on her way over. Let's do this, Snow.

Saturday, July 7

I can't possibly write about everything that happened in one entry. And I can't possibly write about anything at all now, since I've hardly slept in 36 hours. Goodbye.

Sunday, July 8

The party started at 9 p.m. and for half an hour, maybe 40 minutes, it seemed like no one was going to show up but the Six (Five) and a few sophomores I sort of recognized who were perched on the edge of my mom's couch, whispering to each other. I was panicking. For one thing, Noelle had talked me into wearing nothing but white cowboy boots, an American flag bikini top, and cutoffs so tight you could see the outline of my bike lock key through the left pocket. I felt exposed and ridiculous. More importantly, where was everyone? It would be impossible to publicly humiliate Reese if there wasn't a public.

Then, like they'd pulled up in a bus, a huge group of seniors poured in. Then half our class. Then some guys with actual beards—alums, I guess. Noelle stood by the door. "I'll yell to you as soon as I see Reese," she said. "Go have fun."

And oh, I had fun. Somehow I'd implemented my plan: this WAS better than prom. It was the best party I'd ever seen in real life. The lights were off. The music was on. Everyone had observed my dress code. There were red shorts, white halter tops, blue button-downs. There was a star-covered jumpsuit. Some people were wearing sparkly pom-poms sprouting out of headbands. One guy had on a giant Uncle Sam hat. The near-costumes gave people an easy topic of conversation. "I like your Captain America shirt!" "Stars and stripes leggings—so cute!" It was like I'd accidentally provided an icebreaker. More kids arrived, and more, and more. A serious and disgusting dance zone developed in the kitchen—it looked like actual intercourse was going to take place through people's shorts.

I drank a beer and wanted to keep going, but I couldn't make it two steps toward the kitchen without someone stopping me for a high five or a hug. A college kid I've never seen in my life shook my hand and said, "This is epic, madam." A senior named Isaac kissed my bare stomach after asking my permission. Every girl I saw complimented me on my bikini top, which I didn't take too seriously—sometimes giving compliments is a way of covering up your shock—but by this point I was happy to be shocking everyone. When Izzy arrived, wearing blue soccer shorts and a red T-shirt, I made a huge fuss over her and insisted we pose for a series of selfies. Nadia threw herself on me, probably to show the two friends she'd brought how close we were, and presented me with a tiara covered in red, white, and blue plastic gemstones. When I put it on, people cheered.

Around 11 p.m., I made it to my room to check on Snickers and found Hannah hiding in there with Tris and Elliott. "What are you guys doing?" I asked.

"Just taking a break," Elliott said.

I leaned down and spotted Snickers under my bed, looking wary but not terrified.

"Break time is over," I said, clapping my hands together. They stood up immediately and followed me back to the living room. I was heading toward the kitchen when Nadia said, "Chloe, Noelle's trying to find you."

I shouldered through the crowd like a defensive lineman, looking back to make sure my friends were right with me. I knew why Noelle wanted me. Reese had to be at the door. My heart boomed. My life might be in tatters and my soul might be a lump of coal, but I'd seized power, and I was going to hold on to it.

When I got to the door, Reese was saying "This is so ridiculous" to Noelle, who was smiling like the Mona Lisa. Reese was wearing white shorts and a sheer American flag tank top that revealed her blue bralette. She had one measly squaddie by her side: Harper, who was pressed against the railing behind her like someone had backed her up at knifepoint.

"What's going on?" I asked Noelle, adjusting my tiara.

"She wants to come in," Noelle said, gesturing at Reese. I'd imagined the scene wrong: there was no crowd. Everyone was too busy having the time of their lives inside to pay attention to new people arriving. But it was better this way. The party sounded like a tornado behind me. Reese was physically straining toward it.

"Sorry, we're at capacity," I said.

At that moment five strangers carrying a keg arrived at the top of the stairs, lifted their chins in greeting, and pushed past me into the condo.

"Looks like you can squeeze in a few more," said Reese.

"Yeah, I can, but you're not coming in. Leave," I said. Noelle giggled. I could feel Tris, Elliott, and Hannah stiffening in surprise behind me.

Then Reese started crying. Tears filled her eyes and her mouth got jagged. "You're mean," she said. "You're so mean."

All the air went out of me. I felt like I was watching the Wicked Witch melt into a puddle. The evil one, suddenly revealed to be vulnerable, even pitiable. And of course, Reese isn't evil, and she's not a witch or a dictator. She's a high school kid. Yeah, flawed, selfish, sometimes awful. She's not perfect; fine. Neither am I. That doesn't mean either of us deserves abuse.

Seeing her cry, I realized I'd done something truly cruel—I'd told another girl to leave, I'd humiliated her—and I'd done it in cold blood. I'd planned it for weeks. I'd said this terrible thing and *I hadn't even felt nervous while I was saying it.* I'd had so much practice being icy, I was getting used to it. I was turning into a statue, like Noelle said I should. What kind of stone-hearted monster tells someone to leave without her pulse speeding up? I didn't want to be a statue! Was it too late? Could I turn back into myself, or the myself that I used to be before I intentionally trashed all the goodness that was in me?

I turned around to look at my friends. They looked at me, scared. SCARED. Of me!

When I turned back, Reese was running down the stairs, trailed by Harper.

"Reese!" I called, and started to follow her.

Noelle stopped me. "Where do you think you're going?" she said.

"To apologize," I said.

"Don't weaken," she said. "You just did it. Now stick with it. Enjoy it! Go have a drink."

Reese was getting away. I tried to push past Noelle, but she stood in my path.

"I don't want to be like this, Noelle," I said.

"This is only the beginning," she said.

"What are you talking about?" It felt urgent to have it out with her, even if it meant I couldn't apologize to Reese. "Stop blocking the door. I won't leave. Tell me what you mean."

Without discussing it, the five of us stepped out of the doorway and onto the balcony that runs along the length of the building. It was hot and dark outside.

Noelle glanced at my tiara and said, "Why do you think you lost prom queen?"

"Because Izzy won."

"Yes, because you and Reese split votes, exactly like I told you you would. And why is that? Because you're both mean girls." She raised her right palm. "Some people voted for this mean girl." She raised her left palm. "Some people voted for this one."

It made me feel sick, listening to her. My phone

rang. I reached into my back pocket and declined the call without looking.

Noelle was staring at me intently. "Saying 'ew' to Reese in the hall, excluding people from our conversations, flaunting our plans, deciding you hate Lianna for no reason, doing Pink Vans Wednesdays—you know what all of that was, right? Listen, I'm not criticizing you. I'm proud of you! You won! But you did it like every other popular person in history has done it. You got mean! I just want you to face the facts, because you have to keep it up now. You have to get *meaner*. You know how Reese kicked people out of the squad every so often and then brought them back in? You have to do that." I looked at Hannah and Tristan and Elliott. They looked back at me like they'd been sentenced to execution. My phone buzzed. I ignored it. Noelle kept going. "You have to start rumors. You have to ostracize random people in our grade and get everyone to hate them. You have to make everyone so scared you'll turn on them next that they fawn all over you. You have to be like a reality-TV producer—make drama out of nothing. Create conflict. No one will ever challenge you if you put on a good enough show."

She didn't look demented. She looked as calm as she always does. She is the scariest person I think I've ever met. But who am I to judge—I've been scaring everyone around me, including my best friends, who now wouldn't look me in the eye. Noelle was right. Making Reese leave? That was only more of what I'd been dishing out since the cafeteria incident. I'd displaced the AP kids! I'd refused to let Tris campaign for prom king! A thousand horrible memories washed over me. Just minutes ago I'd casually ordered my friends back to the party like some kind of despot. I'd been treating them like shit for months, and now here they were, waiting to see what I'd say in response to all the truth Noelle had told me. Tris and Elliott were holding hands. Hannah was holding her own two hands tightly. And Grady. Grady wasn't there, because I'd been such an idiot. He'd tried—in a gentle, sensitive way!—to tell me I'd turned into a demon, and I'd disappeared on him because I couldn't face the facts. Instead of listening to him, I'd chosen to marinate in my own delusion like a big sick steak. I'd pretended what I was doing wasn't that bad. I'd told myself Reese deserved everything she got. I made believe I'd only wanted to protect Hannah. All lies.

My phone buzzed again. "I think I have to go," I said.

Noelle narrowed her eyes. "You said you're not leaving, and you're not," she said. "I made red, white, and blue Jell-O shots, and you're handing them out at midnight."

"Listen, Noelle, you're right: I got mean. And you didn't force me to do it. I did it all by myself. I'm sure it'll take me months to go back to normal, or maybe I never will. But I have to try."

She scoffed. "What, do you think you're being noble or something? You can't change the system by stepping down. If it's not you at the top, it'll be someone else just as bad or worse. It could be Reese again."

"You're right," I said. Maybe it was my calm tone that made her angry.

"Do you understand how much work I've put into you?" she said. "And all of you," she said, turning to Hannah, Tris, and Elliott. "You would be invisible with-out me." She looked at me again. "You promised me this would not happen. You said you'd take my advice."

I pulled off my tiara. "I'm abdicating."

It's not like I'm the queen of England. I do realize that. I'm nobody, as my mom likes to remind me. We weren't royals discussing regime change on some vast estate; we were a bunch of kids in an unimportant sub-urb sweating on a concrete balcony. Still, what I'd said meant something to me, and maybe it did to the others, too, because I heard at least one quiet gasp.

I handed the tiara to Noelle. "Why don't you stop being a professional second banana and promote yourself? If you weren't so scared of failing, you could take over this school and probably this entire state in about a month."

She squeezed the fake platinum. "What if I decide to do it and crush you and all your little friends?"

I shrugged. "I don't think you will, but if that's what you feel, go for it. Tris, will you take care of Snickers for a few hours?"

He nodded. I headed toward the stairs.

"But the condo!" Hannah called. "People will trash it!"

"Call the police if it gets scary," I said, starting to jog. "I have to leave. I have to find Grady."

When I got to the bottom of the stairs, I turned and looked up to wave. Tris and Elliott and Hannah waved back at me. Noelle was already inside.

Monday, July 9

As I walked to the bike rack, I pulled my phone out of my pocket. I was positive the missed call and texts were from Grady. They had to be, when I'd been thinking about him so hard, when I'd had this revelation. He must have sensed me through the ether somehow. But it wasn't Grady trying to get in touch with me. It was Miss Murphy.

Have you heard from your dad?

Call me when you get this

Immediately I wondered if my dad was dead. And still, for more than a second, I considered turning my phone off and pretending I'd never seen the messages. All I wanted was to ride over to Grady's house as fast as I could and beg him to forgive me. Then I pulled myself together and called Miss Murphy. That's when the really wild part started.

Tuesday, July 10

She picked up right away. "Is Dad OK?" I said. She didn't respond. All I could hear was a whooshing noise, like she'd left her phone out in a windstorm.

"Hello?" I said.

"Hang on," she said in a tight, odd tone. It sounded like she was barely forcing air over her vocal cords.

"What's happening?" I said. Now I was picturing Dad lying murdered in the living room and Miss Murphy upstairs being slowly strangled by intruders (who were for some reason allowing her to answer her phone). I waited and waited and finally she said, in her normal voice, "I think I'm in labor."

"Oh my God. Where's Dad?"

"In New Orleans. I can't get in touch with him."

"Why is he in New Orleans?? Wait, who cares. Call 911!"

"Labor is not an emergency. Or so all the books claim."

"What does your doctor say?"

"I talked to her a while ago, and she said to come in when the contractions get closer together."

"Hang on. I'll be there as soon as I can."

"Stay where you are. Oh God. Here comes another one. No, no, no, no!" I wedged my phone between my ear and shoulder and listened to her panting and squealing while I unlocked my bike. Then I paused to think for what felt like half an hour but was probably only a few seconds. Was there any way to get my hands on a car quickly? I could run upstairs and try to find someone sober. Fat chance, and even if there was one person who wasn't drinking and had her own car, it would take me precious minutes to track her down. Should I call someone's mom to come get me? No, that would take forever. Even the thought of wasting 30 seconds explaining what was going on to a confused mother was agonizing. Could I somehow STEAL a car? Ridiculous. The baby would arrive by the time I'd YouTubed my way into understanding hot-wiring. What if I called one of Miss Murphy's friends and asked her to meet me at the house? I wasn't positive Miss Murphy had any good friends in our town, and even if she did, what was I going to do, ask her to scroll through her phone and share a contact with me via text? Maybe there was a sensible course of action to take, but I couldn't think of one. I threw my leg over my bike. But wait, I wasn't wearing a helmet. Instead, I was wearing a bikini top, cutoffs, and cowboy boots. Oh well! There was no time to worry about my embarrassing outfit.

"I'm hanging up," I said into the phone. "See you in a few minutes." Miss Murphy was still wheezing and saying "No" sporadically when I ended the call.

The streets were empty and still. There was no breeze. I rode as hard as I could. Five minutes in, I was covered in sweat. My feet kept slipping off the pedals because of my stupid cowboy boots, but I figured out a way to keep them on by pushing with the middle of my foot, not the toe. I wanted to be back at Dad's house so urgently, it felt like I could transport myself there instantly by wishing to do it, and so why in the world was I still on this bike, panting along in the dark?

When I arrived and went inside, the house was dark and quiet. "Miss Murphy?" I called. Had she gone to the hospital after all? My heart lifted. Maybe I was off the hook! Then I heard a noise, a moan, coming from upstairs. I started running, and even as I ran, I thought, *I can't do this, I don't know how to do this, I don't want to be here.* It was like a reverse horror movie: I was breaking into a house, but I was the scared one who didn't want to find what I was looking for. There were no lights on upstairs. I decided to check in Dad's room first. The door was ajar. I pushed it open and fumbled to turn on the lamp on the bedside table, and there she was.

She was wearing a T-shirt and undies and sitting next to the bed on her green exercise ball, leaning forward with her arms up on the mattress and her forehead resting on her crossed wrists. She was holding her breath and then letting it out while she said, "No, no, no!"

I was so scared, seeing her there, hearing the fear in her voice. I decided I had to find a handy adult who would know what to do. I was trying to think of someone who lived close by and wouldn't mind getting out of bed to come help me when suddenly Miss Murphy lifted her head and turned to look at me.

"Hi, Chloe," she said. It was frightening, how normal her voice was. How could that be, when she'd sounded like a dying animal two seconds earlier?

"Did the labor stop?" I said.

"No. You get breaks between the contractions."

"OK. OK, OK, OK. I think you need to get dressed. Stand up and I'll help you."

"I can't," she said. "I might start to contract again."

I wasn't sure what would be so bad about that. I decided to be brisk and cheerful, like Bear's babysitter is with him. "Well, then you'll contract again. Come on!" I kind of hauled her up by her armpits and tried to get her into sweatpants, but she said God no, she was so hot, so

I found a pair of soft shorts. Her prediction was correct: she had a contraction mid-change, with one leg in the shorts and one leg out. I waited while she shrieked and said "no, no, no." Then I got her other leg in. I grabbed a random shirt out of her drawer and threw it on over my bikini top. When I turned around, she was back on the exercise ball. I said, "Miss Murphy, it's time to go to the hospital now."

"I can't," she said.

"Well, you're not going to have the baby here!"

"I just can't," she said. "I can't move. I can't walk downstairs."

"I'll help you," I said.

"No," she said, and I wavered. What was I going to do, physically force her to leave the house? Maybe she was right—maybe this wasn't actually labor, or she was days away from giving birth and the doctors would laugh at us if we went to the hospital.

I could tell from the look on her face that another contraction was starting. I kneeled down next to her and held my hands out. She ignored the left one but squeezed the right one like she was trying to crack my bones. "You've got it," I said. "Good job. You've got it, you've got it. You're doing it." I couldn't tell if I was helping, but I kept babbling. She started panting. "Keep breathing. In through your nose, out through your mouth." That one I got from a movie, I think, and to my shock, it seemed to do something. She stopped panting and started breathing more evenly. "You're more than halfway done with this one," I said, now just making stuff up. "You're on the downhill. You're coasting. You've got it."

After it ended, she opened her eyes and looked at me, waiting to see what I'd say next. There was no adult around, and I couldn't figure out how to break eye contact with her for long enough to call one. My choices were to get her to the hospital, call 911 (but she'd said this wasn't an emergency—what if the EMTs came and refused to put her in the ambulance?), or deliver a baby alone in a dark house and hope no one died. *Make a decision and stick to it,* I told myself.

"We're going to walk downstairs now," I said. "Come on."

I thought I might have to drag her, but she got up and walked with me. She had a contraction in the hall and another one, a bad one, on the stairs. She hung on to the handrail to wait it out. In the kitchen I pulled a reusable shopping bag out of the drawer and threw in her wallet and keys. Then I had to run back upstairs for her phone. I took the steps two and three at a time. It was worse being out of Miss Murphy's sight. For one thing, I was worried about her. For another thing, it gave me time to think about how scared I was.

Her phone started ringing right as I reached it. Dad. I swiped right.

"I'm so sorry—" he said, and I cut him off.

"It's me. Miss Murphy's in labor. Where's she delivering?"

"Wait, what? Hang on—"

I could have screamed. I wanted to extract the address from him instantly, without having to listen to a single extra word come out of his mouth. He seemed irrelevant and not completely real. Miss Murphy was the real one. She was downstairs, wracked with pain. I couldn't sit around chatting with a disembodied voice while she waited for me.

"Dad, she's OK. I can't talk. Please, please tell me the name of her hospital."

He told me, and I said, "Thanks. Meet us there when you can," and hung up on him. He called again instantly. I silenced the phone and put it in my back pocket.

I leaped down the stairs and ran to the kitchen, where Miss Murphy was having a contraction, leaning over the island, saying "no, no, no." I called encouraging things to her while I looked for her shoes. "You've got it. Keep breathing," etc. The contraction ended, and she said, "I like the island. I'm going to stay near the island for a while."

"I'm sorry," I said, and bent down to guide her giant feet into her flip-flops. "We're leaving now. Quick, before another one comes."

But it's not like you can stop them from coming. Getting her down the two steps to the garage took about 15 minutes. There was nowhere she could lean, and nothing she could grab, so she hugged me, dragging me forward. I held her up, staggering a little, while she screamed into my neck. We got into the Jeep, and I buckled her in. I decided now would be a good time to call her doctor, which I did while squeezing Miss Murphy's hand as she contracted. The doctor sounded calm. She asked me how far apart the contractions were and how long they were lasting. I said I wasn't sure. "You haven't been tracking them?" she said. I wanted to scream, "I'M A KID!" but instead I said, "I think every five minutes." She said, "She should labor at home until they're three minutes apart and have been for an hour." I glanced at Miss Murphy. She looked like Snickers does when he knows he's about to get a shot. "Three minutes apart," I said. "That's what I meant to say. We're driving in now." I hung up and typed the hospital address into my phone.

Miss Murphy said, "Chloe . . . ," and I thought for sure she was going to say, "You're a terrible driver. I don't trust you to do this." But instead she said, "You know that stuff you were saying about coasting earlier? That helped."

So as we drove, every time she had a contraction, I talked about coasting. When one started, I'd say, "You're on your bike. You're riding up a really steep hill. It's hard. It hurts. But you're doing it. You're still going. Keep working! Work! Work! Breathe! You're almost at the top of the hill!" When I thought she was about halfway done, I'd say, "You're through the worst part. Now you're coasting. You're going downhill. Your legs still hurt, but it's better. You did it. Keep going. Keep breathing." I felt like a SoulCycle instructor shouting out motivational slogans, and it was embarrassing, but who cared? It was helping Miss Murphy.

I was driving with my left hand so my right hand was free for her to mash to a pulp. I was braking and accelerating while wearing cowboy boots. I was going 80 miles an hour on Route 2. I was in the city, trying to follow street signs that announced an exit two feet before the exit appeared. I was parking across the street from the hospital entrance in a spot I was pretty sure was illegal. I was petrified the entire time, but what choice did I have? I had to do it, so I did it.

I thought that as soon as I got Miss Murphy into the hospital, someone would rush over to us with a wheelchair, tell me to sit down in the lobby, and whisk her away. What actually happened was I yelled, "She's in labor!" and a bored security guard called, "Take the elevator to the fourth floor," and pointed back over his shoulder. We had to make it the entire way ourselves! It's not like walking through a lobby, getting on an elevator, and following signs to the labor and delivery unit would normally be challenging, but when you're dragging a huge shrieking woman with you and pausing every four minutes for her to have an agonizing contraction, you might as well be scaling Mount Everest. As we inched along, I looked ahead for anything she could lean on when the next contraction came. We found a gurney in a hallway—that was good. But mostly she had to hang on to me.

Even when we got to labor and delivery, no one seemed that interested in us, especially once they heard this was Miss Murphy's first baby. I checked her in while she leaned over the nurses' station counter and screamed. Wasn't anyone going to help me? Were they really going to chat with each other about traffic on the Sagamore Bridge when a clueless teenager was squinting at an insurance card and trying to figure out which one was the group number and which one was the ID number, all the while feeling terrible for filling out paperwork while this poor woman suffered beside her? Yes, they really *were* going to chat with each other about the Sagamore, and then they were going to tsk-tsk about the opioid epidemic on the Cape. *Talk about drug deaths later!* I wanted to yell. *Miss Murphy is dying right before your eyes!* But I kept quiet and focused on the forms.

Nothing was like I thought it would be. I didn't see a single doctor around. We didn't get a room right away. No one said, "Where's the father?" or "Who drove her here?" or "Exactly who do you think you are, young lady?" We were sent to a place called triage, which turned out to be a rectangular room filled with moaning pregnant women on beds separated by flimsy curtains. A nurse came in and asked Miss Murphy a bunch of questions, which she couldn't answer because she was contracting. As soon as her contraction stopped, she asked when she could get an epidural. The nurse said "The first step is to get the fetal monitor on" in an irritated way and then said she'd be right back. Ten minutes went by.

"I hate this bed," Miss Murphy said during a break. "I can't lie here for one second longer." She was actually trying to get up when another contraction started. They seemed to be coming closer and closer together. I was an expert at this point—I knew how her breathing would change, how her head would dip down, how the second half was different from the first half. So when she started grunting, I noticed.

"What are you doing?" I said. Naturally, she didn't answer. It was dumb of me to have asked her a question.

By this time I'd figured out that she couldn't carry on a conversation while she was contracting. Besides, I didn't have to ask. I knew exactly what she was doing. I ran out of triage and back to the nurses' station.

"Excuse me," I said to the nearest nurse. "My stepmother is pushing."

That got their attention. Two nurses ran back with me. A doctor appeared out of nowhere. They helped Miss Murphy onto a gurney and wheeled her into a room fast, then transferred her to her new bed. No one told me I couldn't come, so I stayed right with her, letting her squeeze my hand, which was actually bruised by this point.

"This is your daughter?" the doctor asked Miss Murphy. Miss Murphy looked at me, and I said, "More or less." The doctor smiled at me. She was young, maybe Miss Murphy's age, with locks pulled into a bun and a diamond on a thin gold chain sitting between her collarbones.

"Chloe," I said, pointing to myself.

"Dr. Darbonne. Chloe, you're in charge of Mom's left foot," she said. "You hold her heel and let her push against you, OK? Like Nurse Green is doing on the right."

Miss Murphy looked up at Dr. Darbonne and said, "The epidural?" and Dr. Darbonne said, "We missed the window, but you're almost there."

Then Miss Murphy looked at me and said, "He's not going to get here in time."

I considered saying something optimistic, but then I just said, "I know."

Another contraction came. Nurse Green said, "Breathe in for the count of five. One, two, three, four, five. Now exhale and push! More, more, more, more, more, more, more, more, more, more!"

It took about an hour. After 30 minutes, the top of the head appeared and I screamed, "I SEE HAIR!" and everyone laughed except Miss Murphy, who burst into tears.

"You can reach down and touch it, Mom," Dr. Darbonne said, and she did.

I was seeing Miss Murphy's entire nether region, I was seeing a human head emerge from her vagina, I was seeing blood and something whitish, but none of it grossed me out even a little bit. I was electrified with the shock of it. Women make new people inside themselves and then push those new people into the world! I'd always known it, but now I KNEW it, and I couldn't believe the magic of it. Guys pulled off the biggest con in human history when they made God a man. Of course God isn't a man! If God exists at all, she's a woman. Miss Murphy was a god and so was every other woman who'd had a baby.

The head retracted a little bit and then came back out, retracted and came out more, and then Nurse Green said, "Let's do it on this one, Mom. Big breath," and she DID do it—the whole head came out! It kept coming and coming, and I couldn't believe how big it was, and it had a FACE, a tiny reddish-purple face, with a perfect smooth nose and an outraged expression, like *where the HELL am I?* and a long lick of dark hair, and then THE REST OF IT CAME OUT, and it had an entire BODY, also reddish purple, with LONG LEGS and LONG ARMS and PERFECT TINY TOES AND FINGERS!

Dr. Darbonne did not seem as shocked as I was to see a miniature human emerge into the air. She gave the baby a little twist, pulled it out like a cork, and said, "Is big sister calling the gender?" Miss Murphy nodded, and for a second I wasn't sure what I was supposed to do, but then I pulled myself together and looked between its legs and saw A TINY VAGINA! I said, "It's a girl!" Then I burst into tears myself, because I have a sister. A miniature sister who's already shocked by the flawed world she has to live in. I thought of her whole life. All the terrible things that could happen to her. Someone excluding her, someone calling her a slut, someone hitting her. And the wonderful things too. Someday she'd kiss a boy, or a girl! She'd have sex for the first time! She'd dream about college! Maybe she'd be a mathematician or a senator or a human rights lawyer! Maybe she'd push out her own baby! Now she was on a table under some kind of heat lamp, screaming bloody murder, and I thought, *Scream, scream. You're right to scream. It's the worst and most glorious world you can imagine, and you have to get in its face every day and scream, "I'M ME. I DEMAND JUSTICE. I WILL NOT BE QUIET!"*

Wednesday, July 11

I didn't even mention the following amazing facts I learned:

1. The umbilical cord isn't like a piece of cooked rotini, which is what I was imagining. It's thick and tough. I should know, because I cut through one with scissors on Beatrice's birthday. (Her name is Beatrice, BTW.)
2. The placenta is amazing! It's the size of a small throw pillow, and it's dark red and I totally get why people want to eat it. It seems like a shame to throw out something so juicy. I picked up the tray it was resting on, showed it to Miss Murphy, and said, "You grew this!" and she said, "No wonder I was so exhausted all the time."

3. Babies (at least wonder babies like Beatrice) know how to breastfeed somehow, even though they were born two seconds ago and are trying to adjust to the fact that they're no longer swimming in warm amniotic fluid but are instead shivering in slightly gross-smelling hospital air.

4. If your vagina tears open while you're pushing out your baby, the doctor will numb it and then sew it up with a needle and thread, smiling and chatting like it's no big deal to stitch your private parts like a quilt.

5. After you see a baby being born, you feel like you have your life permanently in perspective and will never again refresh your Instagram, watch a GIF, or agonize over filters. I'm not sure yet whether this feeling lasts.

Thursday, July 12

Dad didn't make it until 2 p.m. on Saturday. He arrived out of breath, looking terrible, worse than me and Miss Murphy, which is really saying something, because she'd just had a baby, I hadn't showered or slept in what felt like a week and was still wearing a bikini top that had come to feel like a permanent part of my body, and we'd been up all night. Beatrice was born at 2:04 a.m., Miss Murphy fell asleep at 4 a.m., I dozed off in a chair for a while, and then the hospital seemed to switch back on at 6 a.m., and none of us slept after that. I'd seen Miss Murphy's boobs nonstop since the sun came up. I hadn't thought to bring her a button-down shirt, and to breast-feed she had to struggle out of her hospital gown, so after a while she left it off. She told me the milk doesn't come in for a while and asked me if I thought Beatrice was starving. I said, "Definitely not. Look at her, she's barely cried at all." I tried to sound confident even though I had no idea what I was talking about. Other things I'd done: Taken the elevator to buy muffins and coffee for us using Miss Murphy's credit card. Refilled her pink plastic water jug in the nurses' kitchen. Talked to her about the birth in great detail, over and over again. Texted Tris to tell him what had happened and ask him to take care of Snickers until I got back. Called Mrs. Franco to tell her why I'd have to miss work for the day (she was so excited and told me to take my time and come back whenever). Stared through the clear sides of Beatrice's bassinet, try-ing to permanently imprint the memory of her sleeping face in my mind. Sat with Beatrice in the green plastic hospital chair after she woke up, looking into her eyes and saying, "I'm your sister. I love you, baby," and trying not to drip tears on her cheeks. Watched her looking at me and listening to me. Her eyes are blue. Miss Murphy says they might change color, but I know they won't.

When Dad came in, haggard and gray and already in tears even before he saw Beatrice, I mostly felt furious. How dare he miss the birth, and how dare he pick up Beatrice when he hadn't even seen her emerging into the world, and how dare he hug Miss Murphy and sob, "I'm so sorry. I'll never forgive myself"? He had no idea what had happened, and it didn't matter how carefully we explained it. He'd never understand.

Miss Murphy wasn't mad at him, though. She asked him right away if Julian was OK, and Dad said his burns were only minor and he'd gone to rehab willingly enough. "We'll see if it sticks this time," Dad said. Then he said, "I could kill him for making me miss this," and I thought, *No one MADE you miss it*, and pointedly didn't ask him what was going on with Uncle Julian, even though it was obviously a good story. I didn't want to give him the idea that whatever he'd been doing in New Orleans was worthy of a moment's attention compared to the ongoing mind-blowing miracle of my little sister's existence.

Then Beatrice started crying, and Miss Murphy looked around him at me and said, "Chloe, which one did I stop on last time?" and I said, "Left, because I remember the sun was shining on her hair." I could tell

Dad was lost, and it gave me mean satisfaction that Miss Murphy was talking to me over his head, like we were the two adults in the room. Then she said, "Charlie, Chloe saved my life last night, and I'm not exaggerating," and he said, "Tell me all about it," and she did.

Friday, July 13

At 4 p.m., Miss Murphy's dad arrived (thick gray hair, tan face, tough-looking). Dad and I talked to him for a while and then went to pick up food for everyone. Miss Murphy wanted sushi, so we left the hospital to find some. As soon as we got out the front doors, I saw the Jeep, which had two orange envelopes tucked under one of the windshield wipers.

"Aha," said Dad, when I pointed out the tickets. "I guess we should move the car, huh?" That was it. No hard time about what I'd been thinking, parking illegally. He hadn't even blinked when Miss Murphy told him I drove her in, even though of course he knows I flunked my test and shouldn't be trusted to drive anyone anywhere. Seeing Miss Murphy through labor and getting her to the hospital had given me protected status, at least for a few hours. I decided to take advantage of it.

We crossed the street and got in the Jeep. "Uh, Dad," I said as he started it up. "I had a party at Mom's last night."

"OK."

"With alcohol and probably weed and stuff, although I didn't get stoned or anything."

"OK."

"I'm not sure what happened after I left. Maybe something bad."

"Your mother must have seen the evidence by this time. Haven't you heard from her?"

"That's the other thing. She's in Saint Thomas for the month."

"*What?* She left you on your own?"

"It seemed simpler not to tell you."

As a line of defense, this made no sense, but he didn't point that out.

"She's unbelievable," he muttered, which for him is like calling my mother a war criminal.

The sun was shining gold. Outside the Jeep, people walked around wearing shorts and holding hands as if everything was normal and Miss Murphy hadn't had a baby a few hours ago.

"I was thinking," I said. "If you can stop grounding me, maybe I could move back in for the month. Or maybe I could even move back for real. Miss Murphy might need help with Beatrice."

He didn't say anything.

"Only if you want me to," I said.

"I would love for you to come home," he said. "I never wanted you to leave." He wasn't crying, but I could tell he was struggling not to. It didn't seem like the right moment to extract a promise that he'll quit imprisoning me in my bedroom. I kind of wanted to tell him how I feel—that I still hate him for being so disgusted with me, but I love him and I've missed him—but instead I said, "Snickers will be relieved," and then pointed out a good parking spot.

When visiting hours ended, Dad drove me to the condo. On the way I asked him what had happened in New Orleans. At first he said "family emergency" in a vague voice. Normally I would have badgered him for details, but I was too exhausted to follow up and sat there in silence. Eventually, without me doing anything at all, he told me the story. He'd gone down there after getting a call from a hospital administrator who said Uncle Julian had been admitted with second-degree burns. Miss Murphy insisted Dad travel to help him, which hadn't even crossed Dad's mind. At first he refused, but she said she was positive she wouldn't go into labor for weeks—Dr. Darbonne had basically told her she'd have to be induced—and he couldn't ignore his only brother in his hour of need. So he went, and it turned out Julian had fallen asleep with a lit cigarette in his hand and set fire to his couch. Dad was with Julian's doctor when

Miss Murphy was trying to get in touch with him. The next morning he checked Julian into rehab and got on a plane.

"It's good that he's in rehab," I said.

Dad shrugged. "Not for the first time," he said.

"Alcoholism is a disease!" I said. They've been drilling that into us in health class since about fifth grade.

"I know, I know," he said. "I remind myself of that, but it's hard to stay patient with him. At least he went without a fight this time. We'll see how it goes."

This was the most honest Dad had ever been with me about Uncle Julian, and I wanted to hear more, but I was struggling to keep my eyes open. It was Saturday night, and I hadn't really slept since Friday morning. Was it possible that the party had taken place only the day before? It seemed like a week had gone by.

We arrived. The building looked normal. It wasn't a burned-out husk, which was what I'd half expected. The door to Mom's unit was unlocked, since I'd left with the only spare set of keys. Dad pushed it open and I followed him in, already wincing. But it was fine! Empty. Quiet. The TV was still sitting on the console. No Snickers, but I knew he was with Tristan. I walked from room to room, looking for damage. Nothing! The bathroom was sparkling. There were no cans or bottles anywhere. The beds were made, and when I pulled back the covers, I didn't see any suspicious stains. The sheets even smelled like laundry detergent. I found one purple blotch on the couch, but that was it.

> Chloe: Did you clean the condo?????

Hannah: We couldn't leave it like it was.

> Chloe: How bad was it?

Elliott: A bunch of people threw up

Tristan: Also there were empties, broken glass, cigarette butts, stains on the couch, etc.

> Chloe: Oh my god

> I'm so sorry

> Thank you guys so much

They texted back "sure" and "no problem." Were they mad at me? Probably. I'd been terrorizing them for months now. I had to apologize in person. I texted again, very politely, inviting them to come over once Miss Murphy was back home. They all said yes.

The plan was for Dad to pick up Snickers at Tristan's house while I showered and changed. Then Dad would come to get me and drive me to his house, where we'd spend the night before heading back to see Miss Murphy as soon as visiting hours started on Sunday the eighth. I wanted to call Grady as soon as Dad left, and that was still my intention when I sat down on my bed to pull off my cowboy boots. The next thing I knew, it was noon the next day and I was waking up still wearing my damn American flag bikini top.

Saturday, July 14

If you want the best physical experience of your life (aside from sex, obviously), try showering after 36 hours of wearing the same clothes, panic-sweating, and gutting it out in a hospital that smells like the inside of bodies. I felt like a new person after sleeping and getting clean. I had a text from Dad: "You're not answering the door. Assuming you conked out. I'm bringing Marian home in a few hours. See you at the house tonight?" I texted back the thumbs-up, got dressed as fast as I could, and rode my bike to Grady's house. I'd imagined falling to my knees to beg for forgiveness as soon as he opened the door, so it was anticlimactic to get there, ring the bell, wait and wait, and finally accept the fact that no one was home.

He was probably at work. I biked to the pool slowly. Yes, I was desperate to see him and talk to him, but I hadn't imagined doing it in front of an audience.

It hadn't occurred to me that Reese might be on the schedule, but she was the first person I saw once I opened the gate. She was standing at the water fountain refilling her purple Nalgene bottle. She glanced up, probably wondering who was coming in. When she saw it was me, her expression shut down like she'd pulled a shade over it. I went right up to her.

"Reese," I said. She looked back at her bottle, watching the water approach the top. I kept talking anyway. "I'm so sorry about the party. I was awful. I have no excuse. And I'm sorry about all the other horrible things I did this year."

She took her thumb off the fountain button and turned to look at me. "Don't even worry about it!" she said brightly. "So not a big deal. I was double-booked for Friday night anyway."

I studied her. Was she still scared of me? "I don't want to be popular anymore," I said. "You can have it back. Or Noelle. Whoever. Anyone but me."

Her eyes widened. "Um, OK," she said, laughing.

Her tone of voice said, *You're being a weirdo*. We weren't supposed to talk openly like this. A little lighter of courage sparked inside me. I'd stepped down, but things were still different than they used to be, and she couldn't change that.

"I hope you won't spread any more rumors about me," I said. "Or about anyone at school. I might have to come out of retirement if that happens."

"I would never do that," she said, frowning. Believing your own lies: that's the key. As soon as you let the truth about yourself creep into your mind, the whole thing crumbles.

"I'm glad to hear it," I said, and walked away from her.

Grady wasn't there. I kept looking back and forth between the two lifeguard chairs, like he was going to appear on one of them.

"Where's Grady?" I asked Quentin, who was observing the shallow end.

"Canada, I think?" he said. "He quit."

"Quit what?"

"Lifeguarding."

"WHAT?"

Quentin raised his eyebrows like I was being hysterical. "Calm down," he said. "It's not like he died. His mom wanted to visit her sister, and he decided to spend the rest of the summer up there. Or something like that. I don't know. Text him. He'll tell you."

Sunday, July 15
I did text him.

> *Chloe: Grady I'm so sorry about everything*
>
> *You were right*
>
> *I was wrong*

No response. After an hour of waiting, I texted Elliott, who confirmed that Grady really is in Canada and will be until the beginning of August. Elliott wasn't sure whether or not Grady could use his phone, so I have to keep wondering whether he isn't seeing my messages or is seeing them and ignoring them because he hates me.

Monday, July 16
I'm so far behind in these entries, but there's a lot to cover. It's taking me hours to get through it all, and my hand keeps cramping. If I ever try to reread this when I'm a grown-up, I'm sure my grown-up self will be so confused. Sorry, future self.

I'm only up to July 8, a Sunday. Miss Murphy got home at 6 p.m. I was waiting at the house, and I had water boiling. As soon as I heard the car, I started the pasta. I'd already made a salad. Dad walked in the door first, carrying Beatrice in a gray car seat. I couldn't believe the sight of her little pink face in there. A tiny baby, only one day old! Carried through the air like it was no big deal! She should have had a parade of worshippers bowing before her all the way home. She was like a being from another planet.

When she saw me, Miss Murphy started crying. "You made dinner," she choked out.

"It's just rotini!" I said.

"I'm a mess," she said, wiping her eyes. "I've been sobbing since I woke up this morning."

We hugged for approximately 20 minutes. It turns out watching your dad's girlfriend give birth is a great shortcut to a good relationship. Maybe it won't last, but right now I feel closer to her than anyone else I've ever met.

Tuesday, July 17

On Monday, I saw my friends in the morning, before we had to go to work. It had only been three days since the party, but it felt like several years had passed. I was petrified. Were they going to kick me out of their group? Maybe they'd gotten together and agreed that they couldn't forgive me, and they were coming over to break the bad news in person.

They didn't seem angry when they arrived. Maybe a little stiff, though. Then Miss Murphy came downstairs with Beatrice, which bought me some time, because everyone gathered around to admire her. Tris was the only one who would pick her up. Elliott and Hannah were too scared, even though Miss Murphy told them not to worry. When Beatrice started crying, I took everyone out on the deck so Miss Murphy could breastfeed in peace.

"She's so tiny," Tris said. "She's smaller than a cat."

"She's a cutie," I said, playing it cool. I could never say what I really think: that she's the most miraculous baby ever created, that there's never been a more beautiful, more perfect newborn.

We talked about the birth, and then, to stall, I coaxed them into telling me about the rest of the party: who'd messed around with whom (at least 12 hookups and one major cheating scandal), how many kids had slept over (40, they estimated, although they weren't sure), and why none of the neighbors had called the cops (away for long weekends, maybe?).

When we'd exhausted party gossip, a silence fell, and I started panicking. Was this it? Were they about to drop the hammer? Then Hannah said, "Did you mean it, what you said to Noelle? About abdicating?"

My heart sped up. "Yes," I said. "Is that OK?"

They all nodded. "It's a relief," Elliott said.

"I mean, you guys can still be popular, or whatever," I said.

"Chloe, you know that's not true," Tris said. Not meanly, but matter-of-factly.

"Are you mad?" I asked him.

He shook his head tightly. Of course he was mad.

"I'm sorry, you guys," I said. "I'm sorry I got so mean, and I'm sorry I was in denial about it."

No one would make eye contact with me.

"And I'm sorry if I scared you," I said.

"You did scare me," Tris said. "I thought if I contradicted you or did anything wrong, you'd boot me out."

"No, never," I said.

"But you heard Noelle," he said. "That's part of it."

"I'm mad about prom," Hannah said suddenly. "I didn't want to wear that white dress. I looked like a bride."

"I thought you liked it!" I said. "You should have said something!"

"I couldn't," Hannah said. "You would have freaked out."

My skin was burning. It was painful to listen to this. "I probably would have," I admitted.

"You turned into a different person," Tris said. "And now, what, you're just back to normal?"

"I'm trying to be," I said.

"We weren't perfect either," Elliott said. "We all went along with it."

Hannah nodded. "One day when I saw Reese in the hall, I kind of wrinkled my nose like she smelled bad."

Tris said, "I saw this freshman guy wearing cargo shorts and I said, 'Cargo shorts—really?' to Elliott. In a loud voice, too. The kid looked so shocked."

"Well, when you said that, I laughed," Elliott said. "I did so many mean things."

"It's all my fault," I said. "The fish rots from the head."

No one spoke for a while. Then Tris said, "I am going to miss our Instagram shoots," and we all laughed.

The air was clear and the sun was shining on the green leaves, making them look like wedges of lime. My friends were with me, and it seemed like they were still my friends. I didn't deserve any of it. I'd been so awful, and I couldn't go back in time and change it. All I could do was try to be better from now on.

Wednesday, July 18

The next day, while Beatrice and Miss Murphy were sleeping, Dad drove me to Mom's and helped me pack up my stuff. When we were done, he stood looking around the condo.

"Are we good?" I said. Snickers was pacing back and forth in front of the door, wondering when we could leave.

Dad didn't seem to hear me. "I remember your birth so clearly," he said. "In some ways it seems like it happened yesterday. I can't believe you're 17."

Parents must experience time differently than kids do, because to me those 17 years have taken an eternity to go by. I can remember single boring summer days from my childhood that felt decades long.

Dad was staring at Mom's couch. "I never anticipated this moment, that's for sure." He didn't elaborate, but I could guess what he meant: no one gets married expecting to one day stand in his first wife's condo, helping his kid move out and hoping he makes it home before his new baby wakes up. He turned to me. "How was it, living with Veronica?"

"Fine," I said automatically.

"Yeah?" He gave me an intent look.

"Yeah." We've never talked for real about what she's like. Maybe he wanted to start, but I didn't.

Thursday, July 19

And now I'm all caught up on the most eventful week of my life.

Since Beatrice was born, the days have passed quickly.

I've texted Grady a few more times, but I haven't heard back from him. It makes my heart ache to think about it, so I try not to, and I'm so busy, I usually succeed. I work a lot. When I'm not at the pool, I'm with Miss Murphy. She's still crying all the time, she said mostly because Beatrice is changing at the speed of light and she's tortured by her inability to stop time.

"But she's going to *talk* someday!" I said. "It'll be so exciting!"

"That's a much healthier attitude," Miss Murphy said.

I looked around online and read that in the few weeks after they give birth, women go through a bigger hormonal shift than teenagers do over the course of six years. Miss Murphy seemed impressed when I told her that.

She needs water every time she starts breastfeeding, so I get her that, and bring her the Boppy, and bounce Beatrice around so Miss Murphy can shower, eat a sandwich, or just take a break. I'm positive Bea knows who I am. She stares right into my eyes like she's seeing something fascinating in my pupils, and sometimes she concentrates really hard and then makes a tiny warbling sound when I'm singing to her.

I'm not congratulating myself for being helpful. Helping is actually selfish in a way, because it makes me feel useful and like I'm making up for my months of bad behavior. "A penance," Hannah said when I told her. I guess so, but a happy penance.

Friday, July 20

A bunch of people have come to meet the baby—teachers, one of Dad's co-workers, some of Miss Murphy's college friends. With the women who don't have kids, Miss Murphy sums up the birth in a sentence or two: "It was really fast for a first labor" or "Everything went smoothly, all things considered." With the women who have kids, she takes 45 minutes and tells them every single detail. I like the parts about me best, obviously. I wasn't in denial, exactly. I understood I was in labor. But you know how contractions are—I couldn't imagine standing up, much less walking downstairs. I thought, 'I'll just have the baby alone on this birthing ball.' That truly seemed like the best plan. Thank God Chloe raced over and dragged me to the hospital. Actually dragged me. I don't think her back has recovered yet, has it, Chlo?" At this point everyone asks how I did it, how I got her out the door, and Miss Murphy says, "It was like she channeled the mother she'll be in 20 years. You know, upbeat but firm." She always mentions that I don't have my license yet. (People love that detail.) She always repeats my biking visualization word for word and says, "I couldn't have done it without that imaginary bike ride."

I admit I love hearing the praise. Still, I feel like a fraud. I'm not a saint. I'm not even a reasonably good person. Once, after Miss Murphy's college friend Jillian left, I said, "I know you think I was brave, but I wasn't. I was terrified the whole time." She said, "Of course you were! That's what being brave *is*! It's doing the hard thing even when you're scared. If any human exists who doesn't feel fear, that human has never had to be brave."

Saturday, July 21

There's a thing at Thalia Rosen's tonight. Tris, Elliott, and Hannah will be there, and they told me I have to come, at least for a while. A few minutes ago I went downstairs and told Dad I'm going to a party at 9 p.m. He said, "A party? At whose house? Will the parents be there?"

"Thalia's," I said. "And no. They're out of town. That's why she's having people over."

He looked at me. I didn't break eye contact. In the living room, Beatrice started screaming, and Miss Murphy said something to her in a low, sweet voice.

Finally Dad said, "I'll expect you back by midnight."

Victory!

Sunday, July 22

Maybe it's because it's summer and people aren't constantly reminded of the pecking order, or because Noelle or Reese spread the word, or because my pink hair is fading, or because I was wearing a generic top and unremarkable shorts and the sandals Noelle tried to ban, or maybe it's because I'm imagining things that aren't there, but I think I've lost some currency. No one was rude to me last night, and many people went out of their way to congratulate me on Beatrice or tell me how much fun they had at my party. But there was no hush when I came into the room. No one darted nervous glances at me while whispering to a friend. I was just one more high school kid sitting on a couch nursing a beer. It mostly felt great, blending into the background. I don't want to admit it, but for a few seconds here and there, I felt sad, like I'd lost something valuable.

Monday, July 23

Noelle came to visit Reese at the pool. They sat on the lifeguard chair together talking, laughing, admiring each other's manicures, and whispering with their heads together and then gasping or giggling at the outrageous thing the other person had said. I assumed Noelle would leave without acknowledging me, but after a few hours she walked over to the concession stand, opened the door, and came in without being invited.

"How many times have you and Grady done it in here?" she asked, looking around.

"Only, like, twice," I said. "It's pretty cramped. Those days are over, anyway. He's finished with me."

"Yeah?" She sat on the stool next to me and I told her about Canada and the unanswered texts. I thought she might say, "He probably doesn't have phone service up there," but she didn't.

We looked out at the turquoise rectangle of the pool.

"Back together with Reese, huh?" I asked her.

"I'm sure you saw that one coming," she said. I could tell she wanted a cigarette. Suddenly I missed her so much. Her poise, her coolness, her wryness, her strength. None of my other friends are like her.

"Do you hate me?" I said.

She didn't roll her eyes or pretend it was a dumb question. "You disappointed me," she said.

"Have you decided what to do?" I said.

She glanced at me, then across the pool at Reese. "I'm going to give her the summer, and then I'm going to take her down," she said.

A thrill ran over me. She'd listened to my advice! It was so flattering. Also, I couldn't wait to watch her conquer our class. "Have you picked your squad members?"

"Working on it," she said. "None of you guys, though."

Ridiculously, I was hurt, even though I never dreamed she'd ask me and wouldn't have said yes even if she had.

"I didn't mean what I said at the party," I said. "I don't want you to crush us."

She tapped an index finger on the counter. "You're not worth the effort," she said. "No offense."

"None taken, you jerk."

She laughed at that. At least I could still make her laugh. "You've already crushed yourselves," she said. "That's all I mean."

A kid in swim trunks printed with dinosaurs came over and bought a Chipwich and a Coke. When he'd run off with his treats and napkins, I said, "I do appreciate it. Everything you did for me."

She smiled a little. "Don't let yourself off the hook. You did it too."

When she stood up, I didn't want to let her go. Worse than that, I had the urge to say something wildly corny, like *I'll always love you* or *Maybe we can be friends again when we're grown-ups*. But I refrained, and in the end it was her who leaned in and bonked her forehead gently against mine. Then she walked away without looking back.

It would be easy to pretend to myself that Noelle was the true ruler and I was merely her pawn—a decoy masquerading as a queen, like in that one Star Wars plot Grady's told me about six times. But Noelle's right. No one forced me to do the things I did. She made the plans, but I executed them.

Tuesday, July 24

Zach broke up with Hannah, goddammit.

"It's all right," she said when she called to tell me. "It's for the best."

"I hate him," I said.

"No, no."

"Yes, yes! Wait." A horrible thought had occurred to me. "Please don't tell me he's getting back together with Reese."

"Not that I know of. But I do think . . . Well . . ."

"Tell me."

"I think he started liking me again because I was popular, and now that I'm not—"

"Oh, Hannah!" My mind was racing. Could I regain power somehow, so that Zach would fall back in love with her? Would that be the right thing to do, for the sake of her happiness?

"I knew what was happening," she said. "Or I was pretty sure I did. And I went along with it. I even enjoyed it. It was exciting, knowing that people were interested in us."

"How could he be so shallow?"

"I'd be a hypocrite if I blamed him. He's in a band— I loved that about him. Does that make me shallow? It's not a sin to be attracted by someone's social status."

"You sound so calm and wise," I said.

Then she did start crying a little. "I don't feel calm or wise," she said.

I started crying too. "This is all my fault," I said.

"I was in the Six of my own volition," she said. "You didn't make me do anything."

Hannah, my dearest Hannah. I hope next year brings her a sweet guy who sees her for the gem she is and would never dream of cheating on her or breaking up with her.

Wednesday, July 25

Mostly I feel deep regret and shame about the way I behaved this year. But sometimes I'm glad it happened the way it did. Today I was waiting to order at Dunkin' Donuts and some middle-aged dude wearing teal shorts and a pink Oxford shirt was shouting into his phone ("I'm gonna be late, dude. There's a massive line here and it's not moving") and edging closer and closer to me until his elbow actually brushed my back, like if he only crowded me enough I'd dematerialize and he'd be able to order his coffee two minutes earlier. I turned around and smiled at him. "Hang on," he said into his phone, and returned my smile, because I am, I've realized this year, a cute teenager, and he was probably hoping I was about to start flirting with him. I kept smiling and said, "Could you take, like, three steps back? You're in my personal space." He retreated immediately. I NEVER would have had the balls to say something like that before this year. Unfortunately, or fortunately, I've now had a lot of practice saying awful things out loud, and at the very least, that teaches you that the world doesn't end because you say something less than sweet.

I think when you're a girl, you have to be a little mean if you want to survive. Or no, not mean: tough. Gritty. Brave. I'm going to teach Beatrice about that when she's old enough.

Thursday, July 26

I'm still phonebanking. I haven't missed a week since I started. Miss Murphy saw me making calls in front of my laptop today and asked what I was doing, and I told her.

"Good for you," she said. "It must be scary, calling up strangers."

"It was at first," I said. "I'm used to it now, though." And I am, I realized as I said it.

"Does anyone actually answer?" she said.

"Hardly ever," I said. "But it doesn't bother me." That's true too. Phonebanking still feels frustrating and futile sometimes, but now I understand I'd have that same feeling if I were volunteering for the ACLU or Swing Left or any other organization. At some point

I figured out that most kids don't get to see clear evidence that their hard work has changed society. Most *adults* don't. But you can't use the lack of evidence as an excuse to give up. If there's a chance that the thing you're doing might make a difference, you have to keep doing that thing. And sometimes someone picks up the phone and promises to call her rep, and you feel a burst of joy. You feel a calmer sort of joy after you're done, too, because you know you could have fallen down the endless rabbit hole of the internet for two hours, but instead you did something good.

Friday, July 27

When Dad's at work and I'm off, I sit around for hours and hours with Miss Murphy. All we do is stare at Beatrice while she sleeps, freak out with excitement and coo at her when she wakes up, and then try to help her when she starts crying. Usually she's upset about something that's easy to fix (she needs a blanket, a new diaper, something to eat, a bouncing walk around the house, etc.). If we try all that stuff and she's still sad, the only thing that works is to sit in the glider with her and basically bore her to sleep by talking nonstop. It doesn't matter what you're saying—this morning I told her about all the guys I've had crushes on, starting in kindergarten. The key is to never stop talking.

Miss Murphy and I talk all the time too, sometimes about Beatrice (the way she moves her hands through the air like a tiny conductor! The incredible softness of her skin! The little red blotches on the back of her skull, which are called a stork bite!), and sometimes about dumb stuff (TV, Instagram), and sometimes about real stuff. Miss Murphy told me she's still bleeding a tiny bit, but at least she's wearing normal pads now and not the pillow-size ones they give you at the hospital. She told me she feels guilty that breastfeeding is so easy for her, when friends of hers have struggled with it. She told me she's irrationally angry with her mother for being too sick to help her. I've confided in her, too. I told her Grady dumped me. I told her I'm afraid I'll turn out like Uncle Julian. Today I told her I was the most popular girl in my class for a few months and that I hate myself for the things I did.

"Try to practice self-compassion," she said. "No one's at her best in high school."

"You're just saying that because I drove you to the hospital so you have to love me," I said.

"Speaking of which," she said. "You need to get your license."

"I know, I know," I said.

"What if there's an emergency and you have to take Beatrice somewhere?"

I'd never thought of that, but as soon as she brought it up, I was on fire to go out and get some driving practice in.

We both looked at Beatrice, who was asleep but making a vigorous sucking motion with her tiny lips. I would happily throw myself out of a moving car for her. The least I can do is master parallel parking.

Saturday, July 28

Dad took me out in the Jeep after he got back from work. It's not like chauffeuring Miss Murphy to the hospital magically turned me into an excellent driver, but I do feel more optimistic that eventually, if I keep practicing, I'll improve. If I can make it to the city one-handed, in a stone-cold panic, I can pass a road test someday.

"Let's get on Route 2," Dad said.

"OK, but I think Beatrice will wake up soon, so we shouldn't go very far," I said.

I didn't look at him, but I could sense him smiling, which annoyed me. "I haven't, like, transformed," I said. "I'm still a bad kid."

"Come on," he said. "You're not."

"Yes, I am, and that's normal," I said, getting on the on-ramp. "You treated me like a criminal this winter."

He waited while I looked over my left shoulder and then accelerated onto the highway.

"I do think I was too punitive," he said. "I apologize."

Hearing him admit guilt only made me madder. "You never should have let me move out," I said.

"If I'd stopped you, you would have interpreted it as more authoritarianism," he said.

"So?" I said. "You'd rather expose me to Mom than deal with me being bitchy?"

After a pause, he said, "You're right."

He should have left her years ago. She's the scary one, but he's the one who didn't protect me from her.

Sunday, July 29

Mom's coming back in a few days. She's going to throw a fit when she sees my empty room. Maybe I'll have Dad talk to her, so I can avoid the drama.

Monday, July 30

I asked Dad, and immediately he said he'd be happy to explain the situation to her. I should feel relieved, but I just feel cowardly.

Tuesday, July 31

It's like Miss Murphy said: I don't have to feel confident. I can be scared as long as I do the hard thing anyway. So that's what I'll do. I'll go over there and tell her to her face that I don't want to live with her anymore.

I have the strength. I watched a baby being born. I was a mean girl. I'm sure Mom will scream and cry and probably fall to her knees and beg me to stay, but I can handle all of it.

Wednesday, August 1

I figured out roughly what time Mom would arrive home after picking up her checked baggage and finding her car in long-term parking, and I arrived at the condo 10 minutes before I thought she might get there. I wound up waiting for half an hour. I tried to distract myself with my phone, but I was too nervous to get sucked into it. Finally I heard footsteps coming up the stairs, and then the front door opened.

"Darling!" she said. She dropped her bags and rushed over to give me a hug. Then she stepped back and said, "You are a sight for sore eyes! Are you hungry? Let's order food."

"I can't stay," I said. "I just came over to tell you something. While you were gone, I moved back in with Dad."

She was still holding my shoulders. She looked all over my face. Forehead, eyes, mouth. I couldn't tell what she was thinking.

"Oh, Chloe," she sighed, and let go of me. "That's probably for the best."

She's going to apologize, I thought. *She's going to say*

she's so sorry for screaming at me all these years.

She dipped her head and smiled. "I met someone in Saint Thomas," she said, looking back up at me. "Spencer, a fellow yogi. A genius, really—he made a fortune founding and selling four start-ups, and now he's embarking on a new journey of self-discovery. Not that he's gone soft. In fact, he's found this fabulous divorce lawyer for me. She's moving ahead quickly, and I'm all for it. On to the next chapter!"

"Moving ahead, meaning you're really going to get divorced?"

"As soon as possible. I don't want to jinx anything"—here she reached out and knocked on the small table by the entrance—"but I think it's serious between Spencer and me. We've discussed moving in together."

"Good thing I won't be around to get in your way," I said. I hated myself for sounding sarcastic, the fallback tone of every wounded teenager in history.

"I so enjoyed our time together," she said, touching my cheek.

I ducked away from her hand. *Say something,* I told myself. *Now is your chance. Tell her.* It was almost impossible. To understand how you're feeling, to think of the words to explain it, to find the nerve to say the words— you have to do it all so fast, and it's so difficult.

"I didn't," I said. "I didn't enjoy it."

That was all I could manage. What I said sounded bratty and petty, not.searing. But it was the best I could do, and it was something. I walked out the door before she could speak again.

Thursday, August 2

I keep wondering why I didn't say more. I keep thinking, *If I'd said THIS, she would have admitted the truth.* But I don't think it works like that. I think even if I'd talked for an hour, she wouldn't have let herself hear me. She might have been a loser in high school, but now she's got it down like the meanest mean girl: believe your own lies and they aren't lies at all.

Friday, August 3

I guess I've been quiet, or weird, or something, because Miss Murphy keeps asking me if everything's OK. Theoretically I could tell her about Mom, but I've never talked to anyone about it. Not Tris, not Hannah, not even Dad, really, except in an abstract way. I don't think I could find the words. They're not inside me. It would be like trying to make a castle out of dry sand.

Saturday, August 4

Thank God for Tris and Elliott and Hannah. It still feels like we're getting away with something, hanging out without Noelle around. Tonight we went to a stupid superhero movie and then sat on the benches outside the theater and ripped it to shreds. Well, Tris and Elliott and I did. Hannah tried to find nice things to say about it, because she likes to be charitable even to cynical corporate cash grabs.

"I can't wait until Grady sees it," Elliott said. "He'll hate it so much."

Tris gave him the tiniest leg prod, but I saw it.

"No, it's fine," I said. "I'm not going to burst into tears every time I hear Grady's name, or something."

"That's great," Elliott said. "And don't feel like you have to say yes, but do you think you guys would mind hanging out? Not the two of you alone, I mean, but in a big group? Because now that he's back, I wanted to—"

"Grady's back from Canada?" I said.

"Um, yeah," Elliott said. "He got in last night."

I was going to attempt a cheerful remark, but then I gave up and leaned forward to rest my elbows on my knees and stare down at the pavement.

"He's probably waiting for you to text him!" Hannah said.

"Elliott?" I said. "Is Grady waiting for me to text him?"

Elliott looked at Tris like he wished he could clear

his response with him. "Maybe," he said. "But if he is, he hasn't mentioned it."

I turned to Hannah and motioned toward Elliott like, *There you have it.*

Sunday, August 5

It seems safe to assume that Grady isn't pining away for me, or even wondering how I'm doing. And that's fine. All I want to do is apologize to him. I'm not even hoping he'll take me back. My expectations are realistic.

I mean, they're not, and obviously I'm dying of love and will probably die for real if he doesn't want to get back together, but I don't WANT to feel that way.

Monday, August 6

Texted Grady after editing and reediting for about 20 minutes. This is what I finally sent.

> *Chloe: Hi! I heard you were in Canada. Welcome back! Would you be able to talk before work tomorrow? Meet at the pool at 9?*

He texted back seconds later.

Grady: Sure see you there

No punctuation and an unclear tone. Is he angry? Uninterested? Wary? I want to text back and get him to clarify his feelings somehow, but I don't know how I'd do that.

Nine a.m. That'll give us an hour. If he shoots me down in the first five minutes, I'll swim laps or hide in the concession stand or something until opening time.

God, I'm nervous.

Tuesday, August 7

I arrived at 8:50 so I'd have time to pull myself together. He got there at 9:02. When I saw him walk through the entrance, I couldn't even look at him, I was so shy and worried and overwhelmed by the physical fact of him. His tan, his sticking-up hair, his familiar watch and swim trunks and rubber band bracelets, his good posture.

He headed toward the concession stand, and I came out to meet him. We intersected by the deep end.

"Hi," I said.

"Hi."

I'd practiced a speech, but I couldn't remember any of my lines. I felt stunned, being alone with him after all these weeks.

"I heard Miss Murphy had the baby," he said. "Congratulations." He sounded polite but not warm.

"Thanks," I said. "Beatrice. That's her name."

He nodded. "Beatrice. Pretty."

It seemed impossible to switch from this half-fake, civilized conversation to the part where I talked with total honesty, but I had to do it anyway. I took a breath. "Grady, I'm so sorry. You were right about everything. We *did* stop talking for real. I *did* ignore you. I *was* obsessed with my brand. I *did* turn into Reese. Everything you said was true."

He was watching me carefully, squinting the way he does when he's really listening.

"Why did it happen?" he said.

I looked at the water. A drowned bee was floating near a filter.

"I don't know," I said. "I haven't thought about that. I guess . . . I got meaner, and then a little meaner, and by the end I was doing things that would have shocked me last year, and they seemed normal."

"But that doesn't explain why."

It felt like he was digging into my soul with a spoon. I didn't want him to dig—I didn't know what was in there myself.

"I wanted to be popular," I said. "I don't think it's more complicated than that."

He sat down at the edge of the pool, putting his feet in the water. I sat down next to him, not too close.

"I thought we were going to talk," he said. He sounded disappointed.

"We are!" I said. "We are." I didn't want to talk. Not one bit. The tantrum I'd thrown on the day we broke up—I still felt like that. Let's end this painful conversation and have sex! But it wasn't an option. I could see that from the way he was sitting there expectantly. He wouldn't take me back if I didn't start telling him real stuff now, and keep doing it forever.

"I'm trying to think," I said. "My parents—my parents getting divorced. I felt like, um, like no one wanted me." How humiliating, to sound so pathetic and so self-pitying. Grady didn't say anything. There was nothing to do but keep dragging the words out of myself. I hated it; I had to force myself to do it. It felt like staying underwater when you're dying for a breath. "And my mom. She's mean to me. Like, really mean. I hate it, obviously. But the thing I hate most is that I always forgive her. It makes me feel spineless. When I got popular . . . I don't know . . ."

"Go on," Grady said.

Back underwater. I would do it for him. "I was awful. I was SO awful! And that was a relief. It's easier to feel cruel and strong than scared and weak."

Grady nodded.

"I'm not making excuses," I said. "I know other kids have it way worse. Maybe my mother has nothing to do with this year. I don't know why I do the things I do."

He put his hand over mine and squeezed it tightly. What did that mean? Maybe just that he felt sorry for me.

"My stepdad calls me a useless piece of shit," Grady said.

"My mom calls me an ungrateful fucking brat!" I said, like we'd discovered we both love the same obscure candy.

"Is every name she's called you burned in your brain?" he asked.

"Yes! When I'm trying to fall asleep at night, I hear her voice in my head telling me I'm nothing."

"You're *not* nothing."

"Neither are you."

Grady was looking at me intently. "You know they were like us when they were kids, right? Their parents treated them like this."

"Yeah, probably."

"Yeah, and they thought the way you did. They got mean because they didn't want to feel weak, and look what they turned into."

I gripped the side of the pool hard. "I'm not popular anymore. I fired myself. I refuse to turn into my mother."

He was still holding my hand. "They call us names because they're disappointed with their own lives and they're scared we'll be happy and successful."

"You will be. You'll be a famous artist."

He laughed. "No, I won't. I love painting, but it's a hobby. I don't have the talent to get big. I'm going into finance. I want to make so much money I can take a helicopter from Manhattan to visit my mom. I'll land it right on that asshole's archery range."

"Finance?" I said, shocked.

"What about you? What are you doing after school?"

I was embarrassed to realize I'd never thought about it, not for real. Freshman year, I wanted to be an actress, but that was never a plan; it was a fantasy. "I'm not sure," I said.

"Like you said, college isn't that far away," he said. "Don't let your mother trick you into aiming low."

"Oh, man," I said. "I missed talking to you."

"Don't start crying," he said. "You're going to make me cry too."

"I'm so sorry," I said.

"I'm sorry I ran away to Canada."

"Do you still love me?" I said.

"So much. Do you still love me?"

"So much," I said, and then we were kissing, thank God, thank God, thank you, God.

Wednesday, August 8

We didn't talk about our parents again yesterday, and we didn't today, either. Instead we had crazy fast sex in the concession stand (I wish I could tell Noelle!), during which we knocked over both stools *and* the jar of lollipops, and then we stayed after closing and had sex a million more times on the grass, and didn't get caught, and lay on Grady's striped towel staring into each other's eyes and then kissing and staring some more.

I know my mother is more than awful, and I know I don't understand her or what she's done to me or how she's messed up my life. I don't want to understand yet. Even writing these words makes me feel sick. There's a wardrobe in my mind, the door is mostly shut, and on the other side is a vast land full of witches. I could open the door and go poking around in there, and maybe someday I will, but not yet.

Thursday, August 9

Beatrice wouldn't stop crying tonight. I shoosh-shooshed her. Dad walked her all around the house, in the carrier and out of it. Miss Murphy breastfed her every 20 minutes for two hours. No dice. "She needs someone to talk to her," Miss Murphy said. She sounded exhausted.

"I'll do it," I said. I took her up to her room and sat in the glider. "It's OK, baby," I said. She screamed. "I know!" I said. "I know, I know, I know, I know. You're so right. It's a hard life. And I can't lie to you: Things will go wrong. You'll make mistakes. People you love will hurt you. You'll hurt yourself, and disappoint yourself too." She was still sobbing. "But it's OK, it's OK, it's OK, it's OK. You won't shatter. You're a little lump of steel. Yes, you are, baby. You can go into the fire, and the world can smash you with a hammer, and it'll feel terrible, but it'll shape you into your adult Beatrice self." She was a little quieter now. "You don't need me or anyone else to tell you about it. You'll figure it out, baby. You'll turn into a strong woman all on your own." I could feel her falling asleep, getting heavier in my arms. I was late to meet Grady, and I knew I had to leave soon, but for a few more minutes I held my little sister, listening to her breathe, looking at her glowing skin, smelling her sweet, pure scent. She's a sister, she's a daughter, she's a granddaughter, she's a niece, and maybe someday she'll be a wife, but she's more than any of those things. She's herself. She's a person. She exists.

Acknowledgments

Jesseca Salky, you do everything for me. Thank you for your energy, kindness, and patience. Carrie Hannigan, I'll never forget that conference call with the terrible connection and all the nice things you said. Liesa Abrams, you are right about everything, always. Thank you for improving my work and saving me from myself over and over again.

Melissa Albert, I hope one day I can be half the writer you are. Emily Winter, you work so hard and you're so funny and you inspire me. Lauren Passell, thank you for boosting my morale and my books. Susanne Grabowski, I can't wait to see that draft and then brag to the rest of the world that I got to read it when it was still a Microsoft Word doc. Suzi Pacaut, thank you for writing hilarious and observant letters to me for almost thirty years. You're a much better friend than Chloe. Also funnier.

The team at Simon Pulse—Mara Anastas, Chriscynethia Floyd, Katherine Devendorf, Sara Berko, Caitlin Sweeny, Alissa Nigro, Christina Pecorale, Karen Lahey, Heather Palisi, Mike Rosamilia—you are the heart-shaped glasses of my dreams. Thank you for your unending support, expertise, and optimism. Erica Stahler, please never leave me. I do not care to imagine what my books would be like without you.

Adrienne Verrilli, thank you for your seal of approval. Alexis Sattler, I appreciate your excellent suggestions. Ambika Panday, thank you for your help and your friendship—and get in here, Ariel Berson, Sarah Krohn, and Emily White. Group hug in the acknowledgments, seventh-floor Sulzberger! Greg Chaput, I stole your nurse-and-doctor joke, but at least I'm confessing to it here. Milan Popelka, I still think of the advice and help you gave me five years ago, and I'm very grateful.

Anita Lannom, Patricia Chastain, David Chastain, Carl Chastain, and Laura Emmons, thank you for everything.

Jared Hunter, I love you more than Chloe loves Grady. Wesley, Malcolm, and Fiona: I adore you.

To everyone who's written to me on Instagram and Twitter: I'm so glad you like this series. Thank you for reading it.